Airwaves

PROMISES
A ROMANCE

Airwaves

SHERRIE LORD

Chariot Victor Publishing
A Division of Cook Communications

Chariot Victor Publishing
Cook Communications, Colorado Springs, Colorado 80918
Cook Communications, Paris, Ontario
Kingsway Communications, Eastbourne, England

AIRWAVES

Editor: LoraBeth Norton
Designer: Bill Gray
Cover Illustration: Matthew Archambault

1 2 3 4 5 6 7 8 9 10 Printing/Year 01 00 99 98

**Published in association with the literary agency of Alive
Communications, Inc., 1465 Kelly Johnson Blvd., Suite 320, Colorado
Springs, Colorado 80920.**

All Scripture references are from the *New King James Version* of the Bible. ©
1979, 1980, 1982, Thomas Nelson, Inc., Publishers. Used by permission.

                    Library of Congress Cataloging-in-Publication Data

Lord, Sherrie.
        Airwaves/by Sherrie Lord.
                p.cm.--(Promises)
        ISBN 1-56476-706-X
        I. Title. II. Series.
    PS3562.0728A47 1998   98-5409
    813'.54--dc21   CIP

Thank yous

A lady once asked me if my husband was a writer, too. You think I'm crazy? Besides, that kind of patience is more rare than talent. So thank you, Harry. You're the second greatest gift God ever gave me.

Long-distance hugs to my new friends and professional support—my agent, Kathy Yanni, and the legion of gentle experts at ChariotVictor Publishing, including Julie Smith, Greg Clouse, LoraBeth Norton, Bill Gray, Cynde Pettit, and some friendly sales reps who didn't eat a new author alive when they had the chance.

Hugs and kisses to my volunteer support—imaginative screwball, Barbara Campbell; best bud and *Airwaves'* first fruits, Deb Edgerton; fabulous plotter, Jonnie Landis; prayer partner, Debbie Samson; and a few dozen prayer recruits.

Massive quantities of gratitude to those who put up with a pesky perfectionist—Scott Benson, who revealed more about masculine thinking than he probably should have; Curt and Teri Hein, who taught Colin how to dance; Russ Novak (not his real name), who taught him how to program a radio station; the Marvelous Marv Hepworth, who taught him how to engineer one; and the gang at KUPI-99, where there used to be gas pumps in the parking lot.

My sons, Mike and Erik, who slipped into the office to give me spontaneous hugs. My father, Will Snyder, who always said, "You should be writing." Mother and Fred, who showed me never to go back to what you've already conquered. Grammie, who bought me figure skates and told everyone I was a writer; still have the ice skates—without a scuff on them—but as for writing . . .

To Michael W. Smith, whose music loved me home to still waters. To all who stop long enough to ask an artist how they're getting along with their obsession. And to my Daddy, the Carpenter from Nazareth, Who gave me the greatest gift—Himself.

One

*H*e was stunning. Flawless. Absolutely traffic-stopping gorgeous.

"Hello, Emily," he said—as if a sculptor's perfection should speak and smile like warm flesh. He held out his hand. "I'm Colin Michaels."

Inwardly Emily Erickson jumped, which must have been what jarred the heat loose to crawl up her neck.

"Hi," she replied, smiling as she pushed forward her hand, and not sounding a bit like a candidate for an FM studio. "Thanks for seeing me today."

"My pleasure. Sorry I'm late; I got tied up in production." He claimed the other chair on the interrogatee side of general manager Sterling Barclay's desk.

"We just got settled ourselves," Sterling assured him.

Colin nodded, then turned back to Emily. "How was the drive?"

"Beautiful, thanks."

It was only 180 miles from Coeur d'Alene, Idaho to Missoula, Montana, but it was light years between the patched-together studio of KBTS, K-93, and Diamond Country KDMD. She'd been awake into the early morning polishing her résumé, after Sterling had phoned to request it. Two days later her stomach still effervesced in disbelief—Diamond Country's general manager liked the way she sounded.

She studied the portion of the station she'd heard first. Sterling Barclay was as tall as he sounded over the phone, and he sat in his executive chair as if it were a throne, forearms resting on leather and palms curled over the wood accents. His cheeks were jowly and his black hair was threaded with silver, but his liquid brown eyes danced with a youthful mischief that said it was no imposition to attend to station business on a Saturday morning. He'd be here anyway, and besides, he was already sold—he'd invited her here. It was Colin Michaels, the station's PD—program director—she had to convince.

She turned to the younger man who supervised the broadcast, as opposed to the sales, side of the station, and who at the moment held her future in his hands. He sat in the chair beside hers, one ankle set on the opposite knee, elbow on the desk, fingers braced in an arch over his coffee mug. The mug didn't carry the Diamond Country logo, but only orange and gold block letters on a beige background, and for another station, KMLA. And the left hand arched over it wore no wedding ring—she definitely looked—but its owner sure was beautiful to look at.

Emily let her gaze lift from the dimples so prominently pressed into his cheeks to follow the strands of hair that were luxurious in both their thickness and color, so brown it was almost black. Parted off center, it lifted a little before it swept back in shorter wisps over his ears, then fell in lush volume, length, and gentle curl over his collar. He didn't tug creases into his blue-and-white Oxford, but neither did the shirt hang shapeless. He apparently didn't spend all his time at the station; it took more than standing at a microphone to produce bulk like that.

Only his eyes moved as he looked from the cup to Sterling, then to Emily. Their intensity, in mood as well as hue—navy blue and rimmed with dark lashes—threatened to puddle her blood, but this was a job interview, so she sat a little straighter for the sparring ahead, and prayed.

Make it okay. Daddy's wrong. I can handle this. I'll show him. I'll show You. I'll show everyone.

"Your résumé is a little thready," Colin said, his voice all-radio, all-professional, with a tone that promised perfect diction, inflection, and levels. "But your presence is strong—that is, your delivery is good, you're creative, and your voice carries well."

How does he know all that?

"I've heard your show," Colin added, as if he'd heard her thoughts.

Emily looked to Sterling, who explained, "I took the liberty of taping portions of it when I was in Coeur d'Alene. It's so much more like the real you than a spec tape you record yourself."

"You have nice pipes." This from Colin. "Good female voices—ones that have the depth to carry over a dusty speaker in the back of a muffler shop—are rare. But are you teachable?"

"How intelligent would I be if I said no?" Emily replied.

For a second Colin merely stared. Then he gave a full-dimpled chuckle. "Not very."

"Could you clarify what you mean by teachable?"

His stare shifted to his mug, and he narrowed his eyes, considering. "You have the personality for it, but it's obvious Kyle hasn't worked with you."

"You know Kyle?" she asked, referring to Kyle Larkin, her general manager at K-93.

Colin nodded. "Oh, sure."

This bedroom community called radio knew no geographic barriers such as Lookout Pass on the Idaho-Montana border.

"I worked with Kyle in a little AM station in Green River, Wyoming," Sterling added.

Of course. Sterling Barclay had the voice, knew how to say words. He wore his graying hair as if it should come from a bottle, filled a green golf shirt as if it were tailored, and spoke with a command that said he was accustomed to being listened to.

While Kyle Larkin had also elevated himself to general manager, he was still at a not-quite station. He drove a blue AMC Pacer that looked as if he'd rescued it from a car crusher, scuffed about on the hems of his trousers, and admitted he had a face for radio. He didn't golf. Whatever it took to go further than where he was, Kyle didn't have it.

Aloud Emily said, "You worked with Kyle? When was this?"

Sterling rocked back in his chair. "Must have been the sixties. You weren't even born—but you don't have to respond to that. I'm not asking your age, you understand."

Emily laughed. The distinguished exterior and that dignified name carried no warning. It was the glint in his eyes that gave him away; Sterling's sense of mischief would find like company around a cowpoke campfire.

"I'm twenty-one, you didn't ask, and I'm not accusing you of discrimination," she replied.

To which Sterling smiled. "Good. Just wanted to make sure we understood each other." Then he looked to Colin as if to say he was finished with the detour.

Emily's thoughts raced. *Don't make me go back, begging for a job I just quit. Please give this to me. . . . I can do all things through Christ Who strengthens me. . . . Whatever things you ask in prayer, believing, you will receive.*

Colin plunged right in. "You rattle around, Emily. You aren't consistent, but I can fix that, if you're willing to listen and work on it."

Hey, if it's up to me, bring on the W-4 form, insurance application, and key to the front door.

Aloud she said, "Tell me more" and crossed her legs—and tipped her coffee! It spilled. Hot!

Emily stifled most of her squeal before righting the mug. She pulled her jeans away from her flesh and looked to see if Colin and Sterling had noticed—as if they wouldn't.

"Are you all right?" they asked in unison.

"Yes." No. The cup was dripping on the floor. Where to set it? Sterling's desk? Not there. Let it drip on the carpet? Not that, either. Then Colin's large palm thrust out to catch the drip.

"No, it's all right," he said when she started to move the cup away.

Their eyes met; his held kindness.

"Why don't you go to the ladies' room? I'll take care of this," he said, reaching for the cup as she breathed her thanks and leaped to her feet. As she reached the door, he added, "Turn right and follow the hall to the back of the building."

Her leg burned, though not nearly as much as her cheeks. She pressed a wet paper towel to her leg to ease the scalding, but there was no fix for the jeans that had been sky blue and so tidy below her rich green sweater. Now they were sky blue with a brown spot resembling a map of Brazil above the right knee.

When she didn't dare be gone any longer, she treaded the carpeted hallway, soaking in the lonely calm of a Saturday morning radio station; no lights, empty chairs, silent phones. The stereo speakers that seemed to be hidden throughout the station sounded forth with a classy Diamond Country jingle—K-93's were tacky, nothing like this—to one hard hit on a snare drum, followed by a flurry of guitars, drums, and a melodious lead line that could be the best rock on radio if it weren't for the twangy slide of select notes.

At the doorway, Emily paused to draw a breath, compose her features, and smooth her sweater over her hips.

"Are you okay?" Colin asked, glancing at her leg.

"Yes. Thank you." She reclaimed her seat. "I'm sorry."

"Don't apologize," Sterling told her. "We're just glad you're all right."

Her mug was on the desk, a white square of paper towel folded beneath it, and two packets of sugar beside it. The mug was full to the brim.

"We thought we'd give you another chance," Colin said. "It's obvious you take cream, but I wasn't sure about the sugar."

Laughter—from relief as much as mirth—burst from her.

"Think you can handle it?" Colin asked.

"I think so," she replied with grave solemnity.

Colin returned to his relaxed position. "Good. Now, how's your production?"

Back to business, and if it were going to fall apart, this was where it would happen. She wouldn't lie. Not for a job. Not for anything. She was at least that good a Christian. She lifted her chin and looked him in the eye. "Virtually nonexistent."

His left eyebrow twitched. "Define that."

"Three." It was humiliating; three lousy commercials.

"Did you mix them?"

"No. Kyle ran the recording equipment."

Colin sipped his coffee. "At least I won't have to break

you of any bad habits." The anxiety must have shown on her face, for he shook his head in dismissal. "Don't worry about it. You probably lost the work to the receptionist, because she was handy and already on the clock."

He didn't like it, that was plain in the sigh that hovered in his voice. The frustration made him grow more human than the picture of perfection he made, catching the sunlight that spilled over her shoulder as if he were waiting for the portrait artist to arrive.

"What shift do you have in mind for me?"

"Weekdays, six to eleven, with some production thrown in," Colin replied.

"The same shift I had at K-93," Emily said, to which he nodded. He seemed to know all, yet her resume wasn't anywhere in sight. "I put the station to bed," she continued.

"And attended classes the next day," Colin added, proving the thread of her thoughts. "Will you attend the university?" he asked, referring to Missoula's campus.

She held the urge to wince, to run, to fold in on herself. No more demands, no more responsibility, no more life-defying sameness. It was time to have a rent payment of her own, to add her name to the phone book, to accept a date without checking the plans already made for her—though *he'd* never see it. *He* hadn't even realized how serious she was until she began dropping makeup, shampoo, and earrings into a box, and carrying hangers of clothes to the car. The haste hadn't been part of the plan—not without some farewell—but he'd pushed it.

Darn it, Daddy.

One hundred and eighty degrees, and one hundred and eighty miles from all that came before, that's what she'd have now—except church. That could stay, even if she did dirty the pew she occupied.

Emily said only, "No, I'm afraid I couldn't betray North

Idaho College by attending one of its rivals."

The men laughed—and laughing, Colin revealed his only flaw: his right front tooth rocked on its side and overlapped its partner. It should have been an imperfection, except it was slight and . . . *cute.*

Colin's laughter rolled to a stop. "Good. That's the third time you've laughed, and it's consistently pleasant."

Heat flushed through her. Her *laugh?*

"Do you know country music?" he continued.

"No."

His eyes fell closed for a second. "Are you always so frank?"

Truthful?

"Yes."

That eyebrow twitched again, while Sterling chuckled behind his steepled fingers, as if she were not only his discovery but his creation.

Colin's dimples peeked from his cheeks. "Okay," he said slowly. "Do you like it?"

"Country music? I don't know. I haven't really listened."

"Think you could learn?"

From the lobby, the tune was catchy, the harmony rich, and the beat undergirding it, strong. It was just so . . . twangy.

It was also freedom.

"Watch me," she told him.

Navy eyes studied her, then Colin gave Sterling a minuscule nod, while the ruler over all this grinned a little wider.

Colin shifted in his chair. "Actually, Emily, the format is the least of your worries. I'm going to work you pretty hard. The songs are shorter in country than they are in a Top 40 format, and the intros are ghastly quick. It will move fast, and we carry double the commercial load of K-93." He paused. "Did you know this is a part-time position?"

Anything—everything—he'd spoken before, danced compared to the impact of the words that had just fallen from his mouth. These had the power to take it all—the apartment, the food, the *release*—before she'd even fingered it.

"How many hours is it?" she asked.

"Thirty a week. No benefits. Still interested?"

She stared at the corner of Sterling's desk, mentally multiplying numbers. The hourly rate Sterling had mentioned was better than minimum wage, more than what K-93 had paid, but not by much. What a lie, those care-free career-girl images portrayed in sit-coms and magazine ads. Should have squirreled more money away. Her attention drifted to the mug, whose logo matched the sign towering over the parking lot—KDMD in mirror-silver on a navy background, with a cowboy hat hanging off the left stand of the K.

She turned to Colin, head-on. "I need more money than that." Before he could shame her into silence, she explained. "I know you're going to have to spend time with me. You already said that, but I'm going to be working just as hard. Probably harder. How about you give me a raise . . . later . . . when I'm where you want me to be?"

Colin set his elbow on the desk and his cheek on his fingers, while she held her breath. "You mean, like a probation period?" he asked.

Praise God, he hadn't said no.

"Yes. A probation period."

It was a moment before he nodded. "We could do that. Let's say . . . three months, then we'll renegotiate. How's that?"

She'd come to win a full-time job, but her clothes were already in the car.

"Fine," she said. "I'll take it."

hy don't you sit down, Emily?" Colin said as he stepped behind his desk.

She'd followed him in silence from Sterling's office, though she slowed as they passed the FM studio. Her eyes *should* bug out, he thought with satisfaction. The Diamond had some of the finest broadcast and recording equipment in the region. At least, unlike K-93's, it was from this century.

Now she claimed one of the two guest chairs in front of his desk, while he dropped into his own seat and swiveled to turn down the music from the control box on the bookshelves behind him. He glanced at the wall clock. "Excuse me a minute," he said, lifting the telephone receiver to his ear and punching a button to autodial a number.

The connection rang once. A second time. A third. He hung up. Vicky had a cell phone; she'd have answered by now, and it wasn't like her to be late. Maybe if he called Channel Six—

Someone tapped on the open door, then Vicky leaned into the room in that drapey, blood-red dress she

wore when she wanted to look sensational. No one
expected her to dress up for the videotaping of a station
promotional spot, especially not on the weekend, but it
was an image thing—an authority thing.

"Oh, I'm sorry," she said, eyeing Emily, though her
voice held a note that said any female who stepped into
the station had better go through her.

"That's okay," Colin said. "Emily, this is Vicky Millian,
the station's sales manager. Vicky . . . Emily Erickson, a
friend of mine."

He watched Emily's reaction to his introduction. She
stayed composed. Good. It was necessary for damage
control. If he hadn't offered some explanation for her
presence, Vicky would have come right out and asked.

"Nice to meet you, Vicky," Emily said.

"Hello," Vicky replied, giving her a smile that didn't
quite meet her brown eyes. If Emily had been a prospec-
tive client, she would have slid into the room, hand
extended. As it was, she turned away as if she'd just
dropped a few linty coins from her pocket into the little
pot, and could go about her shopping. "Are you still
planning to shoot today?" she asked Colin.

The "Boot Scoot for Granny" promotion was a station
invention that partnered KDMD with a local dance hall
to raise money for wheelchairs, walkers, and hearing aids
for the elderly poor. They were scheduled to tape the TV
commercial for it today.

"I was going to ask you the same thing," Colin
replied.

Halloween was only four weeks away, and he had a
live remote broadcast at Heirloom Furniture—Vicky's
client—next weekend.

Vicky leaned against the door frame and swung one
of her feet back and forth on a black high heel. Pretty

ankles, pretty hands, pretty skin, each part female, until they were added together. Then the bones were too sharp, the fingers too long, and the flesh too white to be alive. Her black hair said it all: short, hasty, and just a little too harsh to be . . . *feminine.*

"Bob and the crew are supposed to be here at one," Vicky said.

An hour and forty-five minutes from now.

"You have all the props?" Colin asked.

"Of course, but do you know how hard it is to find Halloween gift wrap—or even orange bows? You owe me big time for this one."

Right. She owed him a string of favors, and she knew it.

"The limo needs washed," she said, leaping into a safer topic.

"I'll take care of it," he told her, since she didn't even have an ignition key.

"What are you wearing?"

He nodded toward the wall behind the door. She peeked around it and, with a throaty "ooh," lifted the hangers from their hook, holding the black jeans in one hand and the red-and-gray western shirt in the other. A black belt and oval, sterling silver buckle dangled against the jeans. His black boots stood on the floor.

"You have sensational taste, Colin," Vicky said with a seductive smile. "You're going to look delicious."

She was as transparent as she always was—once one tuned to her frequency.

"Forget it, Vicky. I'm not wearing that cowboy hat," he said. A country station could be western without it.

Her smile turned knowing. "Yes, you will, because you'll do anything for this station," she said, returning the clothes to the hook. "Those aren't veins threaded through those muscles, Colin, it's microphone cable. Nice meeting you," she said to Emily, then to him, "I'll see you at one, and don't worry about anything except the bottom few inches of your hair."

Colin chuckled—the tricky minx. She swept from the room and closed the door behind her.

He leaned on folded arms and watched Miss Emily Erickson swivel back to his desk. Pretty smile. Prettier eyes. Green, like the truest emerald, with chestnut hair that fell in gentle layers a little past her shoulders—not the usual corky curls, but touchable. This one wasn't afraid to be different, to wear what looked good on her. She wasn't beautiful, but she was attractive and . . . *fresh.* The kind of girl Bryan would have dated.

Colin lifted his brows and widened his eyes. "Salespeople," he said, as if he spoke of goblins.

She laughed. She should do it more often.

"You think fast on your feet," he told her.

Good thing. Her chosen career demanded it.

"What do you mean?" she asked.

He tilted his chin toward the door. "When I introduced you as my friend instead of as the newest member of the air staff, you walked right along with it. You see, the gentleman you're replacing doesn't know he worked his final shift last night. That has to be our little secret until I talk to him."

Just faintly, the dance in her eyes tripped.

"Don't feel guilty about it," he told her. "It has to be that way. An announcer with a pink slip and an open mike might get tempted to vent his anger on the air. It can turn ugly."

Colin's explanation didn't do much to sweeten the line of Emily's lips. In fact, she could have been flattered, thinking she was good enough to edge someone else out, but she just nodded. Maybe she knew more than she intimated, that her most attractive feature was her gender. She had potential, true, but mostly the station needed a female on the broadcast side to make the Equal Employment Opportunity people happy.

"I'm sorry for him, but glad for me," she said. With a heavy dose of sincerity, her green gaze attached itself to him. "Thanks. I'll work hard."

If she only knew.

She sighed. "Well, you can say what you want about rednecks and twang. The clothes are colorful."

"That they are," he replied.

And her comment sounded more like the warm and bubbly woman Sterling had captured on tape. He'd have to talk to Sterling about going a little easier on his interviewees. This one was wearing her coffee.

"Are you hungry?" Colin asked. "I haven't eaten since early this morning."

The implied invitation seemed to stumble between transmission and reception. Ol' Kyle had never even offered her a handful of M&Ms from the candy dispenser.

"Come on," he said, deciding for her. "I'll take you to breakfast." He cast a meaningful glance at her pants. "But we are going out in public. You want to borrow some jeans?"

Emily stared at the menu far too long to be choosing breakfast; she was choosing carefully, economically— except the dollar breakfasts were at the drive-through down the street.

"This will go on the KDMD account," Colin told Carol, the waitress, when she arrived.

The woman's eyebrows twitched in puzzlement, but the information wasn't for her benefit, though it didn't seem to alter Emily's choice either. She still ordered one of the cheapest things on the menu—pigs in a blanket. Vicky would have selected steak and eggs, then starved herself through dinner to preserve her perpetual diet.

Emily poured cream into her coffee and stirred it slowly. "The station is nice," she said. "The building that houses K-93 used to be an A & W."

"Radio stations locate in the oddest places," Colin said. "KDMD used to be a service station."

"It was?"

"They did a nice job on the remodel—except for the service island. They tried to disguise it as a flower garden and added that wagon wheel, but it's just ugly. They should have torn it out."

"I'd take it if it had gas pumps in it," she said. "At K-93, you can still smell french fries."

He laughed. "I've worked in worse."

"What could be worse?"

Colin stretched his arm along the back of the booth. "KIMA, near Tulsa, was this little daylight only, gerbil-in-a-treadmill AM in a trailer not much bigger than a family camper—except the records were stored where the bathroom used to be."

"So it didn't have a bathroom?"

"Nothing even close."

"Aren't there laws about that?"

"Oh, sure, but they hadn't found KIMA. You had to put on the longest song you could find—and we were still using 45 rpm's, you understand—then race to the gas station next door. And if you had any . . . intestinal distress, shall we say? Forget it. Dead air."

She laughed, and her mouth relaxed into a happy smile. She smoothed the napkin in her lap. "Tulsa, Oklahoma—that's where you're from?"

"Near there," he said, "though I spent most of my early air time on an FM station in Escondido."

"California. Did this place have a bathroom?"

"It did." He laughed, then took a sip of coffee, watching Emily watch the Saturday breakfast crowd at Cottage House Pancakes, her elbow on the table and her chin in her hand. The crystalline green of her eyes caught the light from the window.

"They know who you are, don't they?" she asked suddenly.

"Who?"

She scanned the room, indicating with her gaze. "Everybody. They watched you come in. Do you record many commercials for TV?"

He looked around. Everyone seemed absorbed in breakfast or conversation. "A few. I cut all the spots for Will Walker BMW, but they don't air that often." He shrugged. "It's the car. People always react to the limo."

She had, pulling in eyefuls of the interior after she'd slid into the passenger side of the front seat, swiveling to stare through the chauffeur-opening into the back.

"Didn't your date rent a limo for the junior prom?" Colin asked.

Her answer was a moment in coming. "I didn't go. I had other obligations."

Less-happy diversions, judging by her shallow smile. "You can borrow it any time you want," he said.

"Really?"

"Just ask Sterling."

"Gee, Dad, can I borrow the car?"

"Something like that." Then Carol arrived with their food. "How do you feel about taking a pseudonym?" he asked when they were alone again.

Emily was giving her pigs the rise-and-shine, separating them from their blanket. "A different name? For my show?"

He seasoned his Denver omelet. "I'd recommend it. This isn't L.A., but Missoula has its share of weirdos. It's just wise."

She lifted her fork to fill it, except her hand settled back to the table. "Gosh, I wouldn't know what name to pick."

Gosh? Cute.

"Think about it," he said. "I can help you brainstorm on Monday if you haven't come up with anything."

"That would be great." She cast him a playful glance. "So, can a California boy learn to like country music?"

"No learning about it. Remember, I'm originally from Oklahoma. Besides, country music is dancing music."

She looked up from buttering her pancakes. "Really?" Her soft lips smiled. "That sounds fun."

Not only that, it sounded like a good way to teach the emerald-eyed, soft-lipped, missed-her-junior-prom Emily Erickson to appreciate it.

"It is," he said, letting it go for now. The opportunity would present itself.

For a moment they ate in silence.

Emily broke it. "You don't know of any vacant apartments for a modest budget, do you?"

"No, but I can probably help." Colin wiped his mouth and laid his napkin on the table. "There's a newsstand in the foyer. I'll get a paper." He gave her no time to protest and was back just as quick. She was already thanking him when he set the Saturday edition of *The Missoulian* beside her plate. "After we wash the limo, you can make calls from the station," he said. "You might want to look for something in my neighborhood. It's in an older part of town, near the university. Lots of oak trees. I think you'd like it."

Three

*T*he Communion plate progressed from hand to hand down Emily's row. She glanced over her shoulder. There were probably a hundred people in the sanctuary, and she'd have to pass most of them to get to the door.

But let a man examine himself, and so let him eat of the bread and drink of the cup. . . . For he who eats and drinks in an unworthy manner eats and drinks judgment to himself, not discerning the Lord's body.

So she'd heard many times before—when it meant less.

She stared at her knees. Let the stacked pages of her Bible flick down the pads of her fingers, over and over.

Sin, unforgiven? *Unforgivable.*

To her left, the wide lip of the tray shot a shard of reflected light to her eyes, prompting her to lean across the two empty chairs for the representation of Jesus' body, broken for her. The piano played softly, a pencil tinkled to the floor and rolled across the hardwood, a child whined in boredom, and she stared into the elements. So real.

Unleavened—no sin.
Whole wheat—complete.
Uneven chunks—broken.
Sin, unforgiven? *Judgment.*
Emily passed the tray, untouched, to the woman on her right.

Someone's hands poised over the keyboard at KDMD's traffic computer, called up the program log for the next day's broadcast, scrolled through a list of available ads, selected several, and sprinkled them into the day's commercial load between 6:00 A.M. and 6:00 P.M. The total number added to the electronic log of spots—commercials—to be broadcast in that twelve hours, was twelve. The total number passing through the station's billing department was zero.

The phone rang, the receptionist answered it. A dot matrix printer zipped at the computer station on the far side of the lobby. A plump woman with graying hair strolled toward the studios, a bulk of papers in hand. Another phone rang in what appeared to be a sales office; the man inside answered it. The air smelled of perfume and fresh coffee, and the stereo speakers played what was on the air—some female artist. It was fenced bedlam.

It was also wonderfully, if a little frantically, alive.

The receptionist, identified by the sign on her desk as Marilyn Dawes, sent Emily a glance that said she'd be with her in a moment, except it promised to be longer than that when the phone rang again. When Marilyn answered it, adding a third person to those begging her attention, Emily peered down the front hall to rescue herself. No Colin. She stepped back for a view into Sterling's office. No Sterling either, which eased her breathing but clenched her stomach. The awful discovery was only postponed: she, who'd been hired to talk, had lost her voice.

She turned to Marilyn, who was rocking her pen impatiently between her fingers, tapping it against a long bronze thumbnail.

"Can you fax me a flyer or something that has all the information?" Marilyn asked.

The answer threatened to get lengthy. Emily occupied herself, looking around. With the weekday in motion, the twin nylon velvet love seats to the left as one entered the front door were an oasis of serenity. They sat at right angles to each other, with a glass coffee table and dusty dried floral arrangement between. A small computer station, where the printer toiled—possibly for traffic—sat beyond them, probably printing tomorrow's program log. In the studio window above it, the man at the microphone was a different announcer from the one who'd been on the air Saturday morning.

Marilyn's desk stood to the right, with cupboards and a busy countertop behind her. At the entrance to her work space, the Mr. Coffee carafe, only half full, sat on a narrow printer table that had been pressed into service as a beverage station. Sterling's office, on the other side of the wall, was apparently the first of several along the perimeter of the building. Another block of rooms, three wide and two deep, sat in the center, with a wide hall tracing a rectangle between the offices on the outside and those on the inside. Two of the three rooms in front opened on the lobby. Offices for sales staff, no doubt.

Every office light was on; no recession here. Daddy should see this place. He'd change his opinion about radio stations and country music. By golly, there wasn't a pickup truck, beer, or cheating heart in sight. Emily shook her head. Forget it. No sense in even talking to him. He wouldn't change his mind.

"I'm sorry, we don't normally take public service announcements over the phone," Marilyn was saying into the mouthpiece pinched against her shoulder, "but I might have time, if you'll wait a minute. I have another call on hold."

Though Marilyn's voice sounded pleasant enough, the tightness around her mouth implied she might have rolled her eyes if she knew Emily could be pulled into the conspiracy. "Okay, I'll be right back," she said, put the caller on hold, and spoke over the mouthpiece. "Are you Emily?"

Emily nodded automatically.

"Colin just left, but he said for you to fill out your paperwork until he gets back," Marilyn told her. "Go see Betty—last room on the right." She waggled her fingers toward the right leg of that rectangle of hallway. Then, as if she'd just checked Emily off her list of things to do, she released a caller from orbit and said, "Hi, Burt. Thanks for waiting. It's a little nuts around here."

Emily headed down the hall, passed Sterling's office, and stepped into the room in the corner. Judging by the nameplate on her desk, Betty and the plump woman with the graying hair were one and the same. Emily cleared her throat and asked anyway.

"You must be Emily," the woman said, her smile warm, her voice gentle. She was tidy, if not exactly stylish, in her blue slacks and white blouse with blue piping.

Emily nodded, prompting the woman to rise behind a desk laden with stacks of forms and envelopes. A line of file cabinets marched away from her, except their tops weren't adorned with plants. They were crowded with stuffed animals. Not ordinary bears and dogs in fur coats; these wore clothes.

"Why don't you sit here," Betty said, indicating the chair in front of her desk.

"Do you mind if I get some coffee first?" Emily asked. This afternoon, without fail, she'd buy a coffee maker.

"Not at all," Betty said, waving toward the door and obviously taking no notice of Emily's croaky voice. "You go ahead, I'll get the papers together."

Emily didn't hesitate. When she returned to the corner office, Betty had cleared a space in the front few inches of her desk, though she filled it again with paperwork as soon as Emily took off her coat and sat down.

"I know you already have the job, but we need an application anyway," Betty said as she lifted a leashed pair of half-glasses from her ample bosom to her nose. "That's so we have a little background on you. Sterling likes to know who has a key to the front door."

Fine with Emily, considering she'd be working in a deserted building until eleven-fifteen every night. She gave Betty a grin and started on the form, last name first, first name last, middle initial.

"Are you from Missoula?" Betty asked as she resumed folding the forms—billing, it looked like. She stuffed them inside KDMD envelopes and dropped them into a coffee creamer box at the end of her desk.

Emily shook her head. "Coeur d'Alene."

Here it comes.

Sure enough, Betty's brown eyes widened. "Oh, my. Has Colin heard you talk yet today?"

Emily shook her head grimly.

"Does your throat hurt?"

"A little."

"Well, maybe it will get better before tonight." Betty pulled open a drawer and plopped a bag of lemon-flavored cough drops on the desk. "Here, these will help," she said, then, "Do you mind if I pray for you?"

Pray for her?

"No. Not at all," Emily whispered.

To which Betty smiled. "Good. I will. And I like Coeur d'Alene, by the way. It's such a pretty little place, nestled against the lake, like it is."

Emily grinned.

"Are your folks there?"

"My father is," Emily whispered, but it was half an answer.

Betty asked for the rest of it, saying, "Is your mother here in Missoula, then?"

Emily shook her head. "She died last April."

Six months ago. Behind her. Time to move on.

But Betty wasn't so cooperative. Her face scrunched into puckers of compassion. "You poor dear. She can't have been very old, and you're barely grown yourself. Was it an accident?"

"Diabetes."

Betty's mouth formed an O. "Works slow, that one does. Myself, I lost my husband a year ago May. I'd have never made it this far without Jesus."

Emily stopped writing and looked up. "You're a Christian?"

A familiar voice sounded in the lobby.

Betty disregarded it, smiling as if she'd just recognized Emily in a crowd. "Why, yes. Are you?"

Emily's own heart lifted. This was more than coincidence. God was in this move and job, after all. "We were members of the Lakeside Christian Church," she said.

Now that familiar voice was giving Marilyn a departure and heading this way. Betty and Emily looked up when its owner stepped into the doorway, and he was a shock all over again. No man should be that handsome. At the least, he should have been striding into a television station or modeling agency, not a business that showcased voices, even if the one broadcasting his was top in the market.

"You didn't change your mind and go back to K-93 over the weekend," he said.

Emily shook her head. If anyone was going to change his mind about her working in Diamond Country, it was going to be him. Dark clouds built in her stomach.

He held up a Burger King sack and his mug of coffee. "Are you about finished? I brought breakfast."

Emily looked from the forms to Betty.

"Go on," the woman said. "Just get that back to me by tomorrow or the next day."

"She will. I promise," Colin said.

Betty peered over her half-glasses at him. "Uh-huh, and who's going to keep you in line?"

"That's enough out of you," he scolded with a wink. To Emily he said, "Double-check the deductions on your pay stubs. She's been embezzling for years."

He led Emily past the reception desk and love seats and into the front leg of the rectangular hall. She paused at the studio window.

Diamond Country . . . Diamond One-O-One, FM.

She smiled. It was only a station jingle pouring from the speakers, but it sounded important, planned, and expensive. The song that followed it plunged into a driving beat that begged everyone within hearing distance to abandon whatever they were doing for a dance in the lobby. Emily nodded her head in time. The announcer standing at the control board grinned.

"This is the FM studio," Colin said beside her, close enough for her to smell the leather of his sheepskin coat. He nodded toward the man at the microphone. "That's Starvin' Marvin Sturdevant—Marvin Matthews, to his audience. I don't suppose an explanation is necessary."

Probably not. The man towered like the Washington Monument over the board, but Emily owned shoes that weighed more. She bit back a laugh.

"He's a radio fool," Colin continued. "Another one of those who's been in the business since the Pony Express was big news."

The man wore a baggy beige T-shirt with a Far Side cartoon on the front and looked as if he hadn't combed his salt-and-pepper hair since yesterday, though his walrus mustache ended at two sharp points.

"I'd introduce you, but Mrs. Starvin' is insanely jealous," Colin was saying. "At this very moment, she has us in her scope from the RV lot across the street. Give her cause, and she'll drive that Winnebago right through the window. At the least, she'll crush your little car."

Which he'd obviously made note of when it was parked in the lot on Saturday.

"This is the AM studio," he continued, passing to the first outside room in the left leg of the hall. No one stood at the control board, but its red and green "off" and "on" buttons shone like Christmas in the dark, and the sound level meter beside the digital clock lit and lost little lights in its row, with the rise and fall of the Motel 6 ad playing quietly. This broadcast ran automatically, originating from a satellite feed somewhere far from Montana.

"This is the transmitter room," he said of the next

room in line. "You can hang your FCC license there." He pointed to a corkboard on the wall. Then he crossed the hall to the two rooms on the left end of the center block, stepped into the closest one, and turned on the light. "These are the production rooms."

Emily steered for the control board in the center of the U-shaped counter. Unlike the console in the on-air studios, this was set low enough for sitting; a castered chair was rolled up to it. What she hadn't been tall enough to see through the FM window was that the wedge of wood that was the "board" contained ten "pots"—short for potentiometer, the volume control segment. Each pot had those green and red buttons, a long vertical slide-control for volume, and paper labels, neatly typed but peeling, dirty, or both. Digital displays at the top of the console told the time of day down to the second and waited to show sound levels or count up seconds of recording. A stand-mike, telephone, computer screen, and keyboard sat on the left counter. Some unknown component sat on the right.

"That's the digital efx processor," Colin told her, stepping up beside her. "Speak into the mike, and I can adjust the pitch so you sound like a chipmunk or give you an echo that puts you in a bigger room. It's a fun little toy."

He reached around her to a group of master control buttons to the right of the last pot. When he pressed one of them, the on-air broadcast leaped through the speakers suspended from the ceiling. "All the studios, production and on-air, are identical and connected," he said, almost in her ear. "Once you learn one board, you know them all, and we can record or broadcast to any of the four rooms from any of the other three." He grinned down at her. "We can also listen in, so be careful what you say around an open mike."

Eavesdropping? She raised her eyebrows.

"Oh, yes, it can be most entertaining," he said. "You never know what you're going to hear. Gripes about station policy, recounts of weekend entertainments, flirtations—all kinds of things. Consider yourself warned." He turned. "Come on, I'm hungry."

The moment was only seconds away, and he wasn't going to be happy. She'd groan if it wouldn't call attention to her problem.

He led her back to his office in the corner between the FM and AM studios, allowing her to step into the room before him, where his cologne—musky, inviting, expensive—lingered faintly in the air. The curtains to the left of his desk were closed.

If the items on the oak bookshelves behind his desk described Colin Michaels, he was music, in the several rows of CDs. He was sentiment, in the racquetball trophies and the stuffed bear in cowboy boots and Diamond Country cowboy hat. And he was business, in the stack of cassette tapes, the CDs, and the set of headphones on the top shelf. One of the cassettes was probably her show, and the CDs were, no doubt, the one-song promotional cuts record companies sent, hoping he'd propel them to the top of the charts by giving them plenty of airplay.

His desk was L-shaped, with the computer table at his right hand, the monitor facing away from the window. Three stacks of papers graced the desk, one of them mail, another newspapers and tabloids, and the last *Radio & Records* and *Billboard* magazines, identifiable by the size and polish of their paper. The room's only photos were the promotional posters of country artists on the three windowless walls. Some of them were autographed.

Emily claimed one of the guest chairs, let him have

her parka to hang beside his coat, and cleared her throat. "I have something to tell you," she croaked.

Colin was opening the curtains. Now he swiveled. "Does it have anything to do with the voice you used to say that?"

Four

C olin yanked on the curtain pull, giving the room a shot of natural light and a view of the parking lot.

"What did you do to yourself? Is it a cold, or were you cheerleading a tournament all weekend?" he asked, walking around behind her to the entrance of his work station, humor in his eyes.

Emily tried to clear her throat. "It's a cold."

"Oh, good," he said, taking his seat. "Be sure to cozy up to the microphone so all the air staff can share your good fortune. Are you too sick to work?"

Emily shook her head. She'd be at that board if she had to prop herself up to it. "It doesn't hurt that bad. Mostly I'm hoarse."

"You are that," Colin replied. "At least it doesn't fade in and out. You sound bad steadily." He shook his head as he dug into the Burger King bag. "What a debut, Emily. Don't you know, you can get the plague and wheel an IV bottle around with you. You can break every bone in your body, and we'll stuff you in a wheelchair. But you don't break your voice." He handed her a wrapped breakfast sandwich. "Drink lots of water—not pop, not coffee, just water—whisper, and take a nap this afternoon. When you're tired, it will always show in your voice. Take care of your pipes, and they'll take care of you."

"I will," she whispered, and motioned with the sausage-and-egg sandwich. "Thanks. You didn't have to do this."

"You're welcome, and sure I did. I couldn't very well eat in front of you." He paused. "Did you find an apartment, or have you been sleeping in your car?"

Oh yes, yes, yes. It wasn't a palace, but she had a new mailbox, and a new key on her ring. The glee of that thought was enough to make her throw her hands in the air and dance. Instead, she spread a napkin on her lap and whispered, "An old two-story. I got the top floor."

"Where?" Colin unwrapped one of his sandwiches and took a bite.

"University." The area he'd suggested. "Down from the frat houses."

"Good. Have you thought any more about a pseudo-nym?"

She nodded.

"What did you come up with?"

Emily shook her head and shrugged.

Colin's laugh was spontaneous, as if she'd caught him by surprise. "All right," he said slowly. "Time to brainstorm. What's your middle name?"

"Elizabeth."

"Pretty, but no good for our purpose."

She raised her brows in question.

"No good for a last name. Lots of announcers use their middle names—Starvin' Marvin Matthews is Marvin Matthew Sturdevant, and John Vaughn is John Vaughn Brown. But it rarely works for women, as you so clearly illustrate."

She studied her boss and whispered, "So that makes

your name Nicholas Michael . . . ?"

"Kavanaugh, lass," he replied, wrapping his tongue around an Irish brogue. "And how would you be knowin' that Colin be a wee title for Nicholas? Most people don't be connectin' the two, you understand."

"A character in literature class, I think," she said.

"Emily Elizabeth Erickson. You're all Es. Any sisters or brothers?"

She held up one finger. "Sister."

"What's her name?"

"Erin."

"And your father is Edward and your mother Elaine."

"No. Gordon and Margaret."

"That's a relief." He popped the last of his sandwich into his mouth, stuffed the wadded wrapper into the sack, and began unfolding a second. "We aren't any closer to finding a name for you." He took another bite and chewed thoughtfully. "Emily East? That would keep you in the 'E' vein of things."

She wrinkled her nose.

"Okay, how about Emily North? Emily West? Emily North-by-Northwest?"

She laughed.

"Don't like any of those?" He frowned, the picture of serious concentration. "How about Emily Spud?"

"No Idaho jokes," she warned.

His dimples dipped in and out of his cheeks, though he conceded with a nod. "Emily Barrett?"

She made her own suggestion. "Emily Sims."

It was his turn to disagree. "I'd avoid that many Ss."

"Emily Sassafras?"

He glared a reprimand before he took a bite of sandwich and studied her face, his navy eyes grazing thoughtfully.

On Saturday morning, she had watched him from his office while he taped that station promo, she on the phone, calling about apartments. He'd worn those cowboy clothes as if he belonged in them, because he looked good in red-and-gray shirts whose yokes emphasized the breadth of shoulders already wide, and black boots that added height to what was already tall. He'd played up the drama of his concession with corner-of-the-eye glances at Vicky, but he'd worn the cowboy hat after all. It—

"Colin?" someone called through the intercom speaker of his phone.

"Yes?"

Yes. Not yeah. Not sloppy.

"Is Emily in there?" It was Marilyn, at the front desk. "I have a call for her."

Emily's gaze shot to meet Colin's. His brows lifted in silent question.

It had to be Daddy. Emily's breakfast balled in her stomach—as if it were past curfew and she was in deep trouble. His voice would suck her back into rooms that still remembered closed curtains, silence hollowed by the metallic tick of the grandfather clock in the entry, and Mother's television upstairs. There was neither sunshine light enough nor entertainment bright enough to rewrite what lingered. He, Daddy, owned it all. Still wanted to share it with her, as if it were preferable to sleeping under a hedge beside the on-ramp to the freeway.

Emily fought the urge to run the other way, nodding that she'd take the call. Her shoulders found a new, lower level when she heard the voice on the other end of the line.

"What's the matter with your voice?" Gordon Erickson asked, his own laden with alarm. "Are you sick?"

"Just a cold," Emily replied, with a heart full of hope

that he wouldn't drag her into a worried-parent thing.

Daddy didn't hear her heart. "Have you been to a doctor?"

"No. I'll be fine."

"I could give you my credit card number—"

"I'll be fine," she said more firmly.

Colin ate the last of his sandwich and dropped the napkin and wrapper in the sack.

"So, I guess you got the job," Daddy said in a tone of resignation.

"Yes," Emily replied, daring him to begrudge her this.

"Did you find an apartment?"

"Of course," she said, though the tone was too harsh, so she added, "Do you want the address?" She could give him that much.

"Please," he said. She waited while he fetched a pen and paper, then gave him the information. Colin sorted through his mail.

"Have you ordered a phone?" Daddy wanted to know next.

"No. It may be a while," Emily replied.

A long while, since this job wasn't even in the career category, yet.

"Mmm," he said.

He'd really get hyper about her part-time status—no insurance—but only if he found out about it on his own. She wasn't telling.

Now Colin was slicing through an envelope with a letter opener he'd pulled from the center drawer. If he was curious about her call, he hid it well.

"If you need to reach me, you can call here," she told her father. "Just leave a message."

"What about the weekends?"

"Call my landlady, I guess—if it's an emergency. I don't

have the phone number with me. I'll mail it to you."

"When are you on the air?"

"Nights. Six to eleven."

"Do you like the station?" he asked. "I mean, is it better than K-93?"

"No comparison." *They even have a limousine,* she might have said. *And I found a good church,* but she glanced at Colin and didn't volunteer that either.

"Good," Daddy replied, then lapsed into silence, which got heavier. "Emily, I—"

"I've got to go," she said. What he had to say, she knew well enough to recite back to him. "I'll write as soon as I get settled."

She waited. He was silent. He finally sighed; he wouldn't push it.

"Okay," Daddy said. "Call if you need anything. Anything at all. Okay?"

"Sure. Thanks."

She was the first to say good-bye and the first to hang up. Too bad she couldn't cut off the feelings as easily. They hung on. Gnawed. Ate her a bite at a time.

Colin pushed aside his stack of mail and fingered the letter opener, his gaze steady enough to make a study of her. She leafed through the half of the conversation he'd heard, trying to recall what clues he might have picked up. Not many, though probably enough to figure out it had been her father on the line—or at least someone who asked caring questions.

Oh, so what? It wasn't juvenile. Everybody had a father.

"That was my father," she said.

Colin nodded.

"He's not too happy about my . . . relocation," she added.

Colin returned the letter opener to its drawer. "Of

course. You're his little girl, but he'll get used to the idea."
He paused. "I have your new name, by the way."

"You do?"

"How about Emily Brooks?"

"Emily Brooks?"

"Brooks. No reason. Just Brooks."

Hi, I'm Emily Brooks . . .

"I like it," she said.

"You're sure? That quick?" he asked.

She smiled. Nodded.

"Good. If I have time, I'll make you a liner this after-noon so you can start your show with a proper introduc-tion."

A liner. No one at K-93 boasted one of those glitzy pre-recorded introductions letting the radio audience know whom they were listening to. No one at K-93 could stir up the motivation or pride to bother. Nicholas Michael Kavanaugh, Diamond Country's PD and star announcer, had a steady measure of both.

He also had a hefty list of format guidelines.

"This is the way I want you to run your show," he said, setting his folded arms on the desk and nodding toward the instructions he'd handed her.

Emily scanned the list that was printed on letterhead and bound in a silver-on-navy sales presentation folder. It was very formal, but fairly simple. He wanted no more than five commercial breaks—stopsets—per hour, leading with the national spots—motel chains, soft drinks, automo-biles—followed by the sixty- and thirty-second spots, in that order. In addition, she was to play a station ID—*KDMD, Missoula*—at the top of the hour, to pacify the FCC; KDMD's were prerecorded, rather than spoken live as K-93's had been. Weather breaks were always at the quarter hour and recited over a twenty-second "music bed" of instrumental music. The first song in any group, whether at the top of the hour, after a stopset, or after a weather report, was to be a toe-tapper, and either a male vocalist or a male group. Never a female, and never was she to play two females back-to-back.

"If you have any questions, I'll be here most of the afternoon, or you can call me at home tonight," Colin said.

That got Emily's attention. He seemed so much an extension of the station—and the station so much an extension of him—it had to be an invasion to connect with him in the place where they were separate.

"If you think it's important enough to call me at home, I'll trust that it is," he continued, answering her thoughts. "I usually snooze on the couch for an hour or two after work, so I'm generally up until ten or so."

"What time do you get up in the morning to be on the air at six, if you don't mind me asking?"

"About four, four-fifteen."

Four o'clock. Did anything even have a heartbeat at that hour?

"You get used to it," he said, breaking into a full-dimpled grin. "Anyway, don't hesitate to call if you need to. As for your show, be polished, be tight, don't ramble. In fact, don't open the mike unless you have something to say. But have fun. This is supposed to be kickin' country. If you're having fun, you'll sound fun—and smile, like you do. Your warmth is probably your greatest attraction."

How did he know she actually smiled while she was talking?

Colin's navy eyes twinkled with knowing. "I could hear it in your voice—on the tape Sterling recorded."

Emily's cheeks warmed. He was dangerously adept at reading her.

"Now, how comfortable do you feel about flying solo

tonight?" he asked. "How quickly can you catch on to the board?"

"I think I can learn it pretty fast," she said. "It can't be that hard, even if it is vastly different from the one at K-93." Whose little piece of machinery was nothing more than a sheet of pot metal with toggle switches and huge rotary volume dials.

"Let's do this," he said. "I'll turn you loose to practice in one of the production rooms. You can watch Starvin' Marvin run his show for a while, then I'll stay with you in the studio for your first hour or so this evening. You should have it by then."

She would have choked, had there been anything in her mouth. The board was one thing. The board with him watching her operate it was another. Just thinking about it made her stomach tumble like a clothes dryer.

"Think I'll make you nervous?" Colin asked, teasing in his eyes.

The stink. He probably had a sister—a little sister—he tormented endlessly.

Emily lifted her chin in playful defiance. "Not a chance."

His eyes narrowed, and the dimples poked his cheeks. "You said you never lie."

"Why do the buttons on the drive-up ATM have Braille on them?" John Vaughn's voice asked.

Emily stopped midstride in the twilight lobby.

"I mean, I could be rigid in my thinking," he said, "but this is a drive-up automated teller machine we're talking about."

Emily chuckled, watching John Vaughn through the lobby window, hearing him in every corner of the station. He dropped his did-you-ever-think-about wit into the airwaves as if it were his mission not only to see every Missoulian home from work, but arriving with conversation for the dinner table.

"And I wonder why anyone would ever go into a business as labor-intensive as raising boneless chickens," he said. "They have to be turned every hour, you know."

Now Emily laughed out loud as she headed for the FM studio and her first shift. As she passed the hall window and got a closer look, she mentally shook her head. John looked as though he belonged on a rock format, not country. The first clues were his blond ponytail and surgical green shirt.

"You're fifteen minutes early," he said as she stepped into the room. He flashed her a smile. "A little anxious?"

She nodded and might have actually spoken, except there was no way he was going to hear her over the music. Push it another decibel or two, and it would not only rattle the speakers but the chain they were suspended by. She hung her purse and coat on a hook behind the door.

"I'm John Vaughn, by the way," he continued. "You must be Emily Brooks."

She nodded again and shook his hand over the U-shaped counter, the center of which faced the hall window. The outside window, curtains drawn, was at his back, with the lobby window on the right, and a long wooden case of music CDs under it. A large block of the left counter was a different color where turntables had once sat. Two cheap bookcases on the wall behind the door held everything from KDMD mugs to carts—old commercials on eight-track tape cartridges—to a dusty ukulele.

John tilted his head. "You're really quiet. You plan on

talking tonight, or did Sterling hire you to do a phantom-DJ thing or something?"

"I have a bit of a cold," she said, rather hoarsely, and pointed to her throat. She'd have done it sooner if she'd known it would prompt him to lower the studio monitor volume to a level below the pain threshold.

His sky-blue eyes, set in fine and narrow features, widened. "Wow. What a drag, your first night and all." He leaned away dramatically. "What kind of disease is this?"

"Just a cold."

"Yeah, and we'll all get it now."

She gave him an apologetic grin.

John grinned back as if it had never truly mattered. "Oh well, that's the breaks." He glanced at the clock, checked the playlist—the computer-generated list of songs to be played that hour—and turned around to select a CD, filed by number, from the rack.

It was Emily's turn to widen her eyes. His hair, his golden blond hair, fell all the way to his waist, and that was a long way, considering his height. Not as tall as Colin, not even close to Starvin' Marvin, but he knew there was a top on the refrigerator, and he had more hair than the rest of the air staff put together.

"Do you like country music?" Emily asked. He didn't look as if he should.

John Vaughn shrugged. "It pays the rent." He slid a CD—case and all—into the broadcast machines designed to play them that way, and punched up the proper song. "How about you?"

"I don't know. I've never really listened to it."

He nodded, lifted the headphones from where he'd hung them on the microphone, and set them on his head. Then he pressed the mike button, cutting the studio speakers that would squeal with feedback were they facing an equally open microphone, and set his lips an inch from the black foam cover.

"Diamond Country, Diamond One-O-One . . . on a miserable Monday—any Monday is miserable. . . . The good news is, it's evening," he said in a wonderfully solid voice, the fingers of his right hand tapping an irregular tempo on the counter. Every announcer had an open-mike habit; this was John's. "We almost have this one licked, folks," he continued, "and dessert's coming up when Emily Brooks steps in at six o'clock. You won't want to miss it."

Five

*C*olin let Emily read the weather report unschooled, to see what she'd do with it. Few got it right; Emily joined their ranks.

"Give the *when* or *where* before you give the *what*," Colin told her after she closed the mike. "If you say, 'It'll be thirty degrees tomorrow night,' your listeners turn to the people next to them and say, 'How cold did she say it'd get?' They were listening for 'tomorrow night' and missed the temperature that came before it. If you alert them that the information they want is coming up by mentioning it first—'Tomorrow night, expect a low of thirty degrees'— they're satisfied. They can't say why it's easy to hear, but they'll know when it's not."

Emily nodded. She was giving him solid and steady attention, though she didn't smile much as she received his instruction. She seemed to be dealing with a case of the jitters—her introductions were few and a little awkward, though she actually did a pretty fair job, considering she didn't know the music.

Little thing that she was, she looked even shorter against the stand-up board, well above her waist. And slender, though soft—not starved—in her pink T-shirt, green sweatshirt jacket, and blue jeans.

She probably had a boyfriend back at North Idaho College. Colin looked to her fingers. One ring, a high school class ring. If there was a relationship, it didn't warrant a marking of territory.

Those green eyes were wasted on the microphone. They looked like gems, with all their facets of different hues, and her lashes fanned above them each time she stared up at the computer monitor. Now they fell on her cheek as she glanced down. Lightly, daintily, her hands moved over the buttons and slides of the board, her fingers small and the nails pretty; at least they were hers, and a believable length. No polish, either. Just fleshy pink. All of her appeared tender and sort of . . . brand new.

Bryan's kind of woman.

Her boyfriend, if she had one, was probably studying architecture or nuclear physics or something. Some guy who could discuss that Nicholas—aka Colin—character from her literature class. Some guy with a future, and a past not buried under a rock.

Emily set her headset over her ears, picked up her pen—she never got far from it; her own open-mike habit was holding that pen—and poised her mouth at the microphone, watching the clock at the top of the board add seconds to the elapsed time of the song. Colin donned his own earphones and closed his eyes.

At a good moment in the fade of the music, she spoke: "Diamond Country, Diamond One-O-One, and the latest from Alabama."

Straight and simple, but not what had prompted Sterling to call her in the middle of her show. Her voice was less than what it could be, but even hoarse and nervous, Miss Emily Elizabeth Erickson had an edge of professionalism, a honed sense of timing, and a smile in her smooth inflections.

"We'll take a look at the weather . . . coming up," she added as a wrap-up.

Let her limber up, aim her a little, and her audience would adore her.

Colin opened his eyes as she slid the earphones down to hang, at ready, around her neck, and Starvin' Marvin told the world about the fine dining at Madalaine's. She set her attention on selecting the next song on the playlist from the rack of CDs and cued it up in the number one machine. Colin set his headset on the counter.

"You make me nervous when you watch me so hard," Emily whispered suddenly, though she appeared engrossed in the playlist.

She didn't look nervous. Rather, she looked as if she were doing something as careless as shelving books. She might not appear so detached if she knew he was watching more than her studio skills.

He shifted on his stool, setting folded arms on the counter. "You're doing fine."

"I don't feel fine," she said, and shot him a glance from the corner of her eye. "But watch me do the weather. Somebody showed me how."

He grinned, set his headset, and watched more casually, while she put on her own earphones and poised her hand over the button that would start the twenty-second "weather bed." She pressed the button, the singsong introduction of Diamond Country weather began, and she fed the weather report to her audience perfectly, giving subtle signals about every piece of information she was about to supply. As the music bed closed with a station jingle, she cast him a hesitant glance; not so confident after all.

"That was good. You catch on quickly."

She smiled her thanks, and all was going well—until after the next break, when she announced Marty Stuart and got Holly Dunn, whom she'd already played. When she tried to start another song—something her audience hadn't heard in the last three-and-a-half minutes—she was rewarded with nothing at all; there was no CD in the machine whose button she pushed.

She was all green-eyed panic now.

"Relax, Emily," Colin told her calmly. "Find Marty."

Her glance was almost too quick to be called one.

"Check your playlist," he said quietly.

Her greedy stare dropped to the list of songs to be played that hour, while silence—the dreaded dead air—dripped loudly from the speakers suspended in the front corners of the studio.

"What's the cut number?" he asked.

"Twenty-two," she croaked.

"Find the machine cued to twenty-two."

Her attention, with furrowed brows, snapped to the stack of players at her left, scanned the red digital numbers, and obviously found what she was seeking, for she all but drove the board through the counter in her haste to press the button that started Marty Stuart into a guitar-licking agony of heartbreak and woe.

The crisis over, Emily groaned, plopped her arms on the counter, and dropped her head on top. "That was awful." She shook her head, as if to shake the memory away. "Oh, and in front of you. Just shoot me."

He chuckled. "I've already slaved over a hot turntable once today."

Her head popped up, cheeks blazing. "Does that mean no?"

"I'm afraid so." He shrugged. "It's radio, Emily. The mistakes get a bigger showcase here than in other jobs, so give yourself ways to cover them. Think ten minutes ahead. Defensive driving, if you will. Load all your machines in the order you intend to play them, then if one fails or you make a mistake, you have a fallback."

She nodded sadly and began systematically doing it, but she was way too hard on herself.

"Your show began again this moment," he reminded her. "Everyone who just tuned in is a whole new audience."

She nodded, though the agreement didn't reach any interior space that could receive it. A perfectionist, this one. He could show her more, but it was her first night. Let her get some time behind her, get more relaxed. As it was, she had all the CD players ready to fire, and the blaze in her cheeks had cooled.

Colin stifled a yawn. This particular Monday had begun at 4:00 A.M. and included thirty minutes of show prep, four hours on the air, one with Emily in his office, two in production, forty-five minutes polishing the Halloween promotion with Vicky, another forty-five minutes gathering gags and stories for tomorrow's show, an hour generally tending to business, and another walking Emily through her first show. That was eleven hours of work; Sterling didn't pay him enough.

"Well, Emily, you look like you've got it. I'm just in the way at this point." Colin gathered up his headset and slid from the stool.

Not only that, she was only one more song away from back-timing into the news. Her concentration was already rattled; she'd need what she had left to end the last song at the top of hour, cleanly and timed to the second.

"Any questions before I go?" he asked.

She shook her head. Her gaze lingered and warmed. "Thanks," she said, as if she meant it. "And thanks for the liner. You did a sensational job."

"You're welcome," he said, fighting the urge to smile. Sensational? It was only a liner he hadn't even spent much time on. So, not only did Emily look better at that board than anyone ever had, but she was agreeable to work with . . . and teachable and intelligent and eager, proving that slow-in-the-head Kyle Larkin hadn't known what he'd had. She wasn't ready for a hundred-thousand-person market, but she could get there with some experience—if she didn't get tired first. Maybe that was the problem; Larkin already had.

"Come in Thursday morning and we'll talk about how things are going," Colin said, steering for the door. "You should be more yourself by then."

When he walked past the hall window, she was stacking the CDs she'd need for the next hour. She gave him a parting glance and a little grin.

Green eyes, soft mouth . . . and fresh, she was, framed that way.

A forestry student, maybe. Or perhaps Emily's College Joe was some geology type who was not only book-smart but rock-rugged, too. And he, whoever he was, no doubt knew exactly what he had.

It's radio.

Easy for him to say. Colin hadn't been the one disgracing himself in front of his boss and hundreds—maybe thousands—of listeners.

The humiliation, hot and cold at once, drenched Emily all over again. She'd dive under the counter if it would do any good, make everyone forget, or let her back up and try again.

Help me with this, please, God. Just this.

She watched the time-lapse clock at the top of the control board. The last song would run out at three minutes and fifty seconds away from the top of the hour, so she'd selected a song that was three minutes and thirty-eight seconds long, and talked for seven seconds before she started it. It ended with a five-second space for the five-second station identification. Colin would never have to talk to her about her back-timing.

The phone rang. Emily automatically looked at the clock. It had every possibility of being someone from the station, someone who knew not to call when she was about to open the mike, or already talking. Too soon to be Colin though, unless he had a cell phone.

She picked up the receiver but stumbled when she couldn't remember where she worked. Then no one had told her about the long button on the inside of the handset, which had to be held down in order to activate the phone's microphone—to avoid feedback when broadcasting telephone conversations.

"KDMD," she finally croaked.

"Hi," the male voice on the other end said in that distinctive inflection that clued her this was not a song request and not a need for weather information. It was one of *those* calls.

Six

*Y*ou're new," the caller said.

"Yes," Emily replied, selecting her liner from the list on the computer screen and double-checking that the first song was cued up. The other three machines were just as ready.

"You're good, except you sound like you have a cold," the man said, chuckling as if they'd had lunch last week.

"I feel pretty good," she said. "I just sound bad."

Seven-o-two, forty-five; fifteen seconds left in the three-minute newscast, and the news announcer was winding up her last story.

"No, not bad. Just a little hoarse," the man said, while the network newscaster recited her outcue, "This is Anita Burkhalder . . . Radio Network news."

Emily pressed the button that started her liner—*Diamond Country . . . Diamond One-O-One . . . and Emily Brooks.*

"Are you a student, or do you do this full-time?" the caller asked as she bridged to a bass-drum, bass-guitar-hopping song. She was safe for a few minutes, the length of three songs, before the first stopset of commercials.

She smiled to herself. Full-time? Not a good topic right now. "This is it," she said, adding, "I don't mean to sound unsociable, but I need to save my voice. Is there something you want to hear?"

"Oh, I'm sorry."

"That's okay. I just need to take it easy."

"I understand. How about some Hank Williams, Jr.?" the man asked.

"Anything in particular?"

"Anything you like will be fine."

That meant three-and-a-half minutes of dead air, but Emily said, "You got it," adding, "And, thanks for calling."

The pickup truck slowed as it approached the lighted navy sign with the fancy silver letters. The driver down-shifted, backing the V8 to a throaty rumble as he peered across the lanes of oncoming traffic. The parking lot was empty, save for one car. The driver looked to the line of windows marching to the left of the front door . . . then he was too far. He wheeled into the Gas-N-Go, turned around, and approached from the other direction. . . . All the windows were dark except the middle of the three, where light seeped around the edges of the closed curtains. Had to be the FM studio.

He sped up, turned around at Lewis Auto Parts, and pulled into the parking lot, watching the window for signs of curiosity. There were none.

The first three chords of a Hank Williams, Jr., tune thumped from the truck's speakers.

"Just for you . . . from Diamond Country, Diamond One-O-One," she said.

The driver smiled to himself. She hadn't forgotten—*just for him*—and if the music sounded good, she sounded better.

The pickup truck eased up behind the car. Idaho plates, "K" county, with a North Idaho College sticker in the window. She was young, though surely not one of those who sped over Lookout Pass and into the valley to trade saliva with the frat boys at the University of Montana. Not her.

He pulled an old parking ticket from the glove box, rooted around for a nub of pencil, and looked more closely at the license plate.

"Hello?" Emily said, hastily adding, "KDMD."

The man on the other end laughed. "You forgot where you were for a minute there."

And she didn't need him to remind her.

"Hi, Daddy," she said, stifling the urge to sigh in his ear. She'd talked to him only this morning. She was still fine, her apartment was fine, her throat was fine, her job was fine, *everything* was fine.

She checked the playlist for the song's length. Less than fifteen seconds remaining; the story in the ballad was winding down.

"You sound good," Gordon Erickson said as brightly as if there'd never been a disagreement between them.

"You're in town?" Emily asked, watching the clock, hand poised over the green button for pot number six, which would start CD player number three.

"Almost around the corner," he replied.

Her heart sank. He'd want to get together after she got off the air, while she'd want nothing of his graphic reminder. If he was alone and lonely, it wasn't her fault . . . much.

When the tune had five seconds left, she started the next one.

"You're a natural at this," he told her. "I hope they know what they've got."

"Yours is a biased opinion," Emily said flatly. "Are you at a motel, or on your way somewhere else?"

"Headed for Butte, and I've already stayed longer than I should have, but I wanted to hear your first night. Maybe I'll get back through later in the week."

"Okay," she said. She'd deal with that when it came. "Thanks for calling."

"You're welcome," Daddy said, sounding as if he meant it and more. "Hey, I like this music. Can you play me some Johnny Cash?"

"Johnny Cash? He's old."

"He's still good, and any country station worth its salt has some Johnny Cash lying around."

"Okay. I'll look."

She did, but never did find any. It haunted her all night.

Someone's hand rested on the steering wheel, while the other cupped the gearshift knob, sliding it back and forth in neutral. Surely she wouldn't be much longer, unless she was having trouble putting the station on the bird—switching to the satellite that broadcast a generic feed from Dallas after six on Sundays, and after eleven every other day. Stupid budgets; no times, no temperatures, and no local road or weather info, because it was too expensive to stand a breathing announcer at the mike twenty-four hours *a day. It wasn't right. It didn't serve the listening public. But stations all over the country were going to it.*

There. She finally emerged from the building, though she'd left the light on in the FM studio. That was okay. Better to make the station look inhabited—encourage the illusion of a live broadcast, and discourage vandalism. Now she pulled the door closed and turned the key in the lock, giving the handle a final tug to be sure it was secure before she strode to her car. A few seconds later she backed into the glare of her own red and white lights and sped onto the nearly deserted street, leaving the late-night visitor to work on tomorrow's log without having to make excuses for the late-night presence. No sense in even raising questions.

Colin slid the pin to the next weight, increasing the setting to one he'd been trying to reach, straddled the bench, lay back on it, gripped the handle overhead . . . and closed his eyes.

Now, Emily. Now.

Sure enough, she spoke over the fade of the song, saying, "Diamond Country, Diamond One-O-One . . . with Trisha Yearwood." Then she launched into a live public service announcement about the fifteenth annual Mexican dinner at St. Anthony Catholic Church.

He'd have to hit that next Tuesday night. The food was authentic and abundant, and it was a good cause. . . . And, man, Emily had a great voice. It poured like a sailor's dream from the speakers in the spare bedroom he'd converted to a weight room, telling him about that fundraiser—and just as he'd taught her, piquing interest, then providing details. When she closed the mike and started an ad for Dave Newell Dodge, Chrysler, Plymouth, and Jeep,

Colin began the first set of five bench presses.

Her croaky throat had been nerves, more than anything, since this was Wednesday night, she sounded as if there'd never been a problem, and no one else had gotten sick. Her only trouble now was, she was still too tense and too forward. He'd talk to her about that when she came in tomorrow.

He gritted his teeth. Fresh perspiration popped out on his forehead and chest as he strained to lift the bar.

Four.

He repositioned his grip, cleansed his lungs with several quick breaths, inhaled, and focused every muscle—even the ones not actively involved—in pushing that bar up one more time. His muscles trembled, burned, had little left, but he got his arms to full extension.

Five.

His breath escaped in a rush, his arms collapsing to dangle beside him as he closed his eyes and pulled in oxygen. Time to close the bedroom door and open the window. The burn felt good, but maybe it was too soon for this weight.

Maybe it was time to find out if Emily had a boyfriend. With two breakfasts behind them, she was used to the idea of eating with him. She'd nudge into lunch or dinner pretty easy by now—if she didn't have someone. Shoot, even if she had a steady date on the other side of Lookout Pass . . . out of sight, out of mind, as they said.

He reached for the bar for his next set of five.

Maybe a girl like Emily would go out with a guy like the elder of the Kavanaugh brothers. Since she hadn't met Bryan, had no choice between the two, she just might.

"KDMD," Emily said into the phone.

"Hi."

Voices, she knew, caught the little nuances of timbre, tone, and resonance those outside of radio seemed to miss. It was the man who'd phoned Monday night, the one who'd wanted to hear Hank Williams, Jr., though they both knew that wasn't really why he'd called.

"Hi," Emily replied.

"You sound better tonight," he said, sliding into conversation as if they were friends. Fans were that way, as if she should know them as well as they knew her. "They should pay you double what they pay everyone else."

"Don't I wish."

"It's true," he continued. "I'd rather listen to you than any of your colleagues."

"Well . . . thanks," she said. "Were you in the mood for some Hank Williams, Jr.?"

"Always." He paused. "Are you busy?"

She should be working toward her degree in counseling; she'd done enough of it. Who else but a DJ would answer the phone and listen—without charge and anonymously—at nine-eleven at night?

"I have a few minutes," she told him, dragging the stool around to her side of the counter.

***

"How's it going?" Colin asked the next day. He rocked back in his chair, which was swiveled off center, his right arm stretching across the desk, his finger hooking his mug. Today's attire included a navy turtleneck; his eyes might have been cut from the same cloth.

"Pretty good," Emily replied, relaxing herself. "I love

your machinery. K-93 never had anything like what's in that studio."

"It's your machinery too, now." Colin grinned. "Sterling's bullied the owner a little to put us ahead of anyone else in the market." Suddenly his eyes fell closed, and the line of his lips leveled. "Excuse me," he said, picking up the handset of the telephone and pressing buttons. Their gazes met over the desk while he waited, then whoever he was calling obviously answered. "Okay, Marv," he said into the mouthpiece. "You win." Colin broke into a smile over the reply. "Thank you," he said politely and casually hung up the phone.

Emily's confusion must have shown, for Colin sat back in his chair and explained, "Starvin' Marvin and John Vaughn have a running contest to see who's the best at playing consecutive songs in the same key."

Her gaze leaped to the volume control box on the shelf behind him. "The same key? Two songs in a row?" It was absurd—and hilarious.

"They used to see how many they could play," Colin continued. "When I jumped on them for that, they switched to working from random songs. At any time during a shift, one of them will challenge the other to match the song that's playing."

"Starvin' Marvin did it?" she asked, ready to laugh.

"He always does. The man has an ear, but Vaughn keeps testing him."

Suddenly a door flew open and a bark of laughter erupted in the hall.

"Liar," Marv said, so calmly. "You said he was busy."

The accused—John—tried to offer a defense, though it was garbled in laughter. He stumbled from the FM studio and collapsed against the door jamb. "Sorry, Marv. I thought he wouldn't notice," he said over his shoulder, and his remorse was profound; he dissolved into another belly laugh.

"You did it on purpose," Starvin' Marvin replied, stepping beside him. "Half the fun for you is getting me into trouble. And you're supposed to be at breakfast," he told Colin, with a pointed stare.

"I'd make him buy me a trophy," Colin told Marv.

"Good idea," Marv said, casting a speculative gaze on John. "Open your wallet, Vaughn."

"A word of advice, John," Colin added. "Buy something you like. You might end up wearing it."

Emily laughed. Marv most heartily agreed.

"You'd have to catch me first," John told Marv.

Whose reply was a calm declaration, "I'm out of music." He spun and disappeared into the studio.

John Vaughn turned back to the office. "Sorry, Colin," he said, though one could count his teeth in his smile.

Colin just nodded—*Sure you are.*

"Hi, Emily," John said with a mischievous glance, then he waved and departed, shoulders shaking.

Behind it all, Starvin' Marvin's voice sounded in the speakers, sedate and unhurried, as if he'd been standing at the mike the whole time.

It was surprising that Marv could meet the challenge. It was astounding that Colin had caught the whole game while he'd been talking to her. And it was fun to be privy to what the rest of Missoula couldn't even guess at.

"Do you ever do stuff like that?" Emily asked Colin.

The expression in his eyes turned secretive. "Maybe. The difference is, I let the audience in on the jokes so they can have fun with them too."

That's what put him behind that desk, rather than in front of it.

He stepped around the desk to close his door—revealing a toy basketball hoop hanging on the back.

Emily smiled to herself and shifted in her seat. "So, how am I doing? I assume you've been listening."

He sat again and grinned. "Of course." He paused for a sip of coffee, his eyes narrowing, as seemed his habit when he was about to address something serious. "Let's start with the positive," he began. "Your timing is exact. That is, you have that sixth sense for flowing from the outro of one song to the intro of the next, and your back-timing stands without fault."

Except a "but" hung on the air.

"But you might want to tease your audience, earlier," he continued. "Every time you open the mike, tell them what's coming up. You know, Alan Jackson, Garth Brooks, the news, whatever. Give them a reason to stay tuned—it's more important than anything behind you—but do your tease before the stopsets. Come out of the commercials with a jingle, not more talk. Step out of the way, because less is more."

Emily nodded. "Okay."

Colin stared. There was more—and more important.

"Go ahead and say it," she said finally. "I can take it."

He almost grinned. His gaze held for a moment. "You run a tight show, but it's almost too tight."

Too tight. No such thing. She was tempted to scowl. "What do you mean?"

"Loosen up. Relax. Have fun," he said. "You're announcing, and you're capable of more."

"Announcing?"

"Announcing. Giving information. Relating facts, not conversing. Where's that warmth that caught Sterling's attention?" He studied her for a moment before his expression softened. "They're only people, Em."

"They're country western people," she replied. "I don't

know how to relate to them. I mean, I can't get an image of who they are. The guy in the muffler shop?"

His dimples winked. "Sure, and the insurance salesman, and the bank teller, and the city councilman. The Tupperware lady. Well, why not?" he added when she laughed. Then, as if he'd landed on a new thought, his eyes narrowed again. "You need to have fun with it. Want to learn how?"

"Sure."

"There's a bar in town with a good dance floor and the tunes we're looking for. How about I pick you up Saturday night and teach you how to two-step?"

Seven

*H*e should blow a whistle, she thought, yell "Fire in the hole," or something before he sparked explosions like that, though the invitation was as bittersweet as it was unexpected.

"I don't drink," Emily said. She could stand holy and blameless in that much.

Her admission seemed no threat to Colin's balance. "Okay. How about Boots? It's a dance club in East Missoula, and there's nothing stronger there than the caffeine in the Coke—unless one counts Monica, the owner. She's a bit of a . . . challenge."

Emily smiled, gathering courage as well as well-placed words. "This is . . . business . . . right? I mean—"

"Is this a date?" Colin finished for her.

"Right. Is this a date?"

Heat swept into her cheeks as his navy gaze stepped right into her eyes. "Do you want it to be?"

Emily's stomach practiced somersaults. "I don't date coworkers," she managed to say gently. "Especially not my boss."

"That's sound policy," Colin replied, matter-of-fact. "I

wouldn't have dated Larkin either. Not only is he married, he's profoundly ugly."

If he meant to break her composure, he won; she burst into laughter.

"Come on," he continued. "You'll gain a whole new appreciation for the music and your audience. And don't eat beforehand. Monica serves up a Dutch oven dinner that's a lot warmer than her heart."

Now it wasn't just dancing, but dinner too.

He held up both hands, palms out. "I'll wear my head-set the whole time. I promise."

"I'll put the time on my timecard—"

"Colin?" This from the telephone intercom speaker.

He turned toward it. "Yes?"

"You have a visitor," Marilyn said from her reception desk, sounding as if Colin had far too many of them.

"I'll be right out," he replied, as if he didn't, then to Emily, "That does it for today. Tease your audience, and have fun doing it—oh, and watch your furs, gonnas, and walls."

"My furs, gonnas, and walls?"

He smiled. "Enunciate, Emily; that's 'for,' 'going to,' and 'while'."

She nodded sheepishly. "Got it."

"We'll talk next Tuesday," Colin continued. "In the meantime, I'll come by to pick you up about . . . say, eight, Saturday night?"

"Eight is fine, but I'll meet you there, boss," she replied.

He just grinned.

It was probably unwise. Was definitely dancing the line,

but she was actually making plans, without hesitation, and without waiting to see if Daddy would be home to care for Mother. That, in itself, was worth eating beans and weenies for the rest of Emily's part-timer days.

"I wouldn't go out there if I were you," Marilyn said from where she stood at the window behind her desk.

Emily was putting on her parka. Her hands slowed in straightening her collar. "What?"

Marilyn crossed her arms over her brown sweater and nodded toward the parking lot. "Colin and his visitor," she said. "He keeps trying to get her to go somewhere—his car, her car, anywhere—but she won't have any part of it. This one's going to let the whole world know he's a cold-hearted snake. The way he uses that name of his, you'd think he was a movie star."

Then the phone rang, dragging Marilyn into a lazy, hip-rocking stroll toward it, and Emily looked beyond the glass air lock to the scene playing at the rear bumper of a car parked on the other side of John Vaughn's Firebird. The woman was blond, dressed in a spangled denim jacket, and each line of her profile sketched anger—the stiff set of her back, the jut of her chin, her rapid speech and waving arms. She said something, obviously a question, for Colin shook his head. He had his fingers in the front pockets of his jeans, his shoulders hunched against the cold that made little clouds of his breath, but he appeared no more tense than if they were discussing receptionists who voiced commercials. Not his favorite thing, but nothing to raise *his* voice over.

"Has he asked you out yet?" Marilyn inquired as she hung up the phone and filed a pink telephone message in the carousel on her desk, peach fingernails flashing. She didn't wait for Emily to answer, adding, "He will. No one is off limits—although I think he draws the line at married women. He believes that makes him honorable."

"Must be talking about Colin," Vicky Millian said as she strode into the lobby from the hall. "Indoctrinating our new sister-in-the-trenches, Marilyn?"

"He's at it again," Marilyn offered as explanation.

Vicky stopped, her full skirt—red, of course—swishing around her shapely legs as she leaned to peer out the window. "Ooh, a blond this time. And cute. Nice to know there are some constants in this world." She aimed for the reception desk, papers in hand.

"He's cruel," Marilyn said.

"What's-her-name knows the rules," Vicky replied. She glanced at Emily, including her, and added, "You go to Barney's to get picked up, you're going to get picked up. No promises. No contracts. When it's over, at least have the dignity to let it die gracefully." She shrugged. "He has a nice car, a niiiice body, and he pays for everything. Who's using who?"

Emily flashed her a grin—what was she supposed to say?—before Vicky turned back to Marilyn, offered her the papers, and began explaining what she wanted her to do with them. In the parking lot, the blond woman folded her arms over her chest and looked away, giving Colin a profile. She wiped her fingers across her cheeks.

Time to get out of here. Heart falling, Emily wheeled the opposite direction. Something always ruined it. She'd been set to go dancing, to go out and have fun, and here was Marilyn, telling her every reason she shouldn't go, and what's-her-name in the parking lot, showing her.

"Hi, Emily," Betty said, peering over her half-glasses when Emily landed at her door. She smiled. "What brings you in today?"

Emily leaned against the door jamb and hiked her purse higher on her shoulder. "Colin's training me."

"I thought you already sounded pretty good. He'll have you ready for Nashville before he's done."

The warmth in Betty's eyes drew Emily into the guest chair. "How long have you known him?" she asked, setting her purse on her lap.

That made Betty pause over a stack of envelopes and checks. "Ever since he pulled into the lot in that old car, with all his worldly possessions stuffed in the back," she said, then chuckled. "He nearly knocked Sterling over with his confidence, though I think it was more desperation than anything, being on the verge of hunger as he was. Sterling liked him instantly. Colin's willing to work as hard as it takes, and he's so creative."

"He is, isn't he?" Emily agreed.

A secret sparked in Betty's eyes. "Have you heard him sing yet?"

"He sings?"

"My goodness, he breaks hearts with that voice."

"It is velvet, isn't it?" Emily said, then checked her enthusiasm with a lengthy pause. "Betty, can I ask you something?"

"Sure," the woman replied, though she kept right on slicing into envelopes.

"Is it true . . . what I hear about him?"

Betty stopped. Looked up from the letter opener that was suddenly interesting. "I wouldn't know for sure, but I think so."

Disappointment released the breath Emily had been holding.

"It's true, the women parade through this place like we're selling ten-cent burgers," Betty continued, "but I just keep praying for him. I think he's lonely."

"Lonely? Colin?"

Absurd.

"There's a heart in there," Betty said softly, "but you have to tiptoe to get close. He has it walled in pretty tight."

Emily looked in the phone book. Barney's was a bar—probably the one with the good dance floor and the tunes Colin was looking for.

From the studio window, Emily watched the season's first snow fall in cupcake dollops that leveled the cracks in the parking lot, slowed the cars on Broadway, and reflected a glow that knew no shadow, yet was nearly bright enough to read by. The snow would melt—too early—and Daddy would be on the road. He always ate up the pavement to get home Friday night. All the Caterpillar dealerships in his region were open Saturdays but never expected to see him after Friday afternoon, not with his wife as sick as she was—or had been. The wife wasn't sick anymore, but his schedule hadn't changed.

Emily returned to the FM board. From Billy Ray Cyrus to The Judds, the energetic to the calm; it was good. She scanned the console, computer monitor, and rack of CDs—dozens of them.

Mother would be proud. She'd always devoured every detail about K-93 and the work Emily did there. It was activity and people and privy to the core of anything important happening in Coeur d'Alene. It was life, the way it rolled along before Margaret Erickson's progress through it reversed. At forty-five, her regression was premature, skipping the part about losing her figure and teeth and hearing, and speeding straight to the umbilical cord; hers was connected to a dialysis machine.

Emily shook her head, as if she could lose the memories or go back and make them right. She scanned the studio for a distraction.

As if volunteering, the phone rang.

"How was your week?" Gordon Erickson asked, after the preliminaries.

"Pretty hectic," Emily admitted, "but I'm getting the hang of it."

"Good. Good." He paused as if he were gathering his courage. "You want to come home for the weekend? I'll cover you for the gas."

Interpretation: I'm lonely, and surely you have nothing more important to do than what you've always done—orbit life, be a spectator, lose yourself . . . take care of me.

The Judds were fading with a flash.

"Just a sec," Emily said and set down the phone.

She set her headphones, grabbed her pen, and watched the clock. Colin would be listening. She glanced at the CD players. Number three was cued up to some Travis Tritt tune.

She poised her mouth at the mike, pressed the green button, and smiled. "Diamond Country, Diamond One-O-One, plays the hits . . . including Billy Ray Cyrus and The Judds . . . and there's more where that came from."

Too tight. Too much an announcement.

She pushed the button for CD number three and tried again. "Stay with us,"—*right over the top of Travis*. The song started cold—no introductory music.

"We're Diamond One-O-One," she finished weakly and got out of there.

And wanted to die. No excuse for that, when the length of the intros—:00—was one of the columns on the playlist.

She hadn't checked, and Colin had heard it all.

She hung her headset on the mike and picked up the phone. "I'm back."

"How about tomorrow?" Daddy asked again.

"Sorry. I have plans," she replied, snatching up the local PSAs—public service announcements—Marilyn typed onto recipe cards.

Daddy paused for the tiniest second, as if he were genuinely surprised. "Already?"

Emily's hesitation lasted only a second. "Actually, I'm going out with the PD. He's going to show me how to dance, kind of give me an appreciation for this music," she said, sorting through the cards.

Sure enough, Daddy jumped on it. "The program director? Emily—"

"It's not a date. We're just going to—"

"A bar?"

"Not a bar. A dance club. We're not even going in the same car."

And it was really none of his business.

Honor thy father and thy mother.

She was. She hadn't been disrespectful. Besides, wasn't there something, somewhere in that Bible about parents letting their kids live their own lives?

She put the card about the station Halloween promotion at the back of the stack. A good cause, to be sure, but it was still a celebration with demonic roots. Not on her show.

Maybe God would notice and weigh that in the balance.

"I'm not trying to run your life," Daddy continued. "I simply believe this is a dangerous area. You'll drown before you even realize the water is rising."

"I appreciate your concern, but I can handle it."

It was his turn to sigh. "Just be careful. Maybe you can come home next weekend or something."

"Maybe." That is, if the rest of the world slid into the ocean and there was nowhere else to stand. She dropped the PSAs back on their copy easel; should be planning the next minutes of her show. "Listen, I have to go."

Daddy let her, though she shot the phone angry glances. He'd do them both a favor if he lost the number. She was—

The phone rang again.

Emily yanked the receiver from its cradle. "KDMD."

"Whoa. Easy, darlin'. I didn't do it. I promise," the voice on the other end said.

It was her Hank Williams, Jr., fan. His name, she had learned, was Brad, and he called about this time every night.

"I'm sorry," Emily breathed. "Did I sound abrupt?"

"You could say that," he replied. "What's up? The job, or home?"

"Home, but it's nothing I want to talk about. Sorry."

"That's okay. Just remember, I'm here."

"Here" being, literally, his job as a roving security guard for businesses that hired extra protection.

"Thanks," Emily said as she listened to the first few seconds of the next song, in cue—so it played only in the studio—just to see whether it started lively or slow. The intro was pure kickin' country, sounding like a good blend with the song currently playing, but it had to be. It was the only thing she had ready.

"I don't know how you listen to two things at once like that," Brad told her, obviously hearing all this through the phone. "You're something else."

The pickup truck waited among the motor homes until the Rabbit entered Broadway from the parking lot across the street, then it pulled in at a safe distance behind it. All the way, it followed . . . down Higgins Avenue . . . and finally to a two-story house behind the line of oak trees on University. The Rabbit parked at the curb. The truck drove by, as if this were part of its course.

Someone's hands leafed through the log—the hard copy, the one the announcers signed—searched, and found the later hours. A dainty signature, it was. Smooth and hard to mimic.

Eight

Colin was easy to find. He might have stood at the far end of the dance floor, but he appeared to be the center of it; he had a view of everything, and everyone had a view of him—fortunate audience, for his shoulders were much too broad in a western shirt with a contrasting yoke, his legs were much too thick in tapered jeans, and he was much too tall in cowboy boots. The man was much too good looking and much too confident—fingers casually tucked in his front pockets—as he conversed with a woman who could only be Monica, Boots' owner.

He spotted Emily about the time she found him, and raised his chin in greeting. She swam against the crowd, and all eyes followed her progress, once it was clear where she was aiming. Radio did that. Propelled its workers past the hopeful crowds, put them through the doors, behind the barricades, inside the dressing rooms, in the parades. Gave them tickets, passes, and privileges, although the perks at K-93, like the pay, had been feeble. So far, all Emily had been offered of Diamond Country was its limousine, except it seemed more somehow. Perhaps because it wasn't a consolation prize.

"Monica, this is Emily Brooks . . . evenings at the Diamond," Colin said when she joined them. "Emily, this is Monica Pierce."

Emily extended a hand to Monica, whose grip was one of those limp, cupped-palm greetings that said she feared the contact. Emily took back her dissatisfied hand and scanned the club. A short rail fence ran the perimeter of the hardwood dance floor, and a boardwalk of rough wood planks traced the outside of that. Picnic tables supplied the seating, and bridles and tack decorated the walls, highlighted by colored spotlights. The music hadn't begun yet, but the place was already crowded with people talking and laughing quietly as if they were waiting for the next act to begin. It was infectious. Emily's stomach fluttered in anticipation.

"This looks fun," she told Monica.

"Thank you," the woman replied through a tight smile. "You'll have to come earlier next Saturday. You missed the dance lesson."

And that was unforgivable.

"I'll do that," Emily promised, though Colin sent her a secret glance that said it wouldn't be necessary.

"Well, I have to get upstairs," Monica said to Colin. "Why don't you be my guests for dinner?"

"Thank you," he replied easily, as if the pursing of Monica's lips didn't imply she never gave away a strip of cellophane tape without weighing the trade.

When he offered his dimples, Monica gobbled them up as if they were enough. Another hollow smile, then she climbed a flight of stairs into a loft overlooking the dance floor.

"Is that the announcer?" Emily asked of the man at a long counter at the edge of the railing above.

Colin followed her gaze with his own. "That's him. He

does a pretty fair job, but he'll embarrass himself trying to sound like a real DJ once he knows we're here—and Monica will surely tell him." He turned to her. "Did you pay to get in?"

"Yes. Didn't you?"

"Never do. You should have asked her to reimburse you. She would have done it."

Emily's mouth fell open. "That's tacky."

A deep chuckle rolled from his throat. "Don't let that stop you. This is radio; everything's a trade." He motioned to the far side of the room. "Come on. They're serving."

Moments later, Colin and Emily sat at the picnic table Colin had already reserved by the dance floor. Unrolling a plastic fork, knife, and spoon from a paper napkin, Emily stared over the fence at a couple in the back corner. Nodding their heads in unison and watching the placement of their feet, they walked through dance steps. They held hands, but rather than face each other, they faced the same direction, the woman to the side and a little in front of her partner.

"What are they dancing?" Emily asked.

He watched for only a second before replying, "Looks like the Cotton-eyed Joe."

"Are all the dance titles that colorful?"

"That one comes from the song by the same name," he replied, picking up a chicken thigh. "That's a dance to work up to. We'll see in a few minutes how soon we can attempt it."

"Oh, I see. Our success depends on how good a dancer I am?"

"Mostly it depends on how well you follow," he said with a wry grin.

Emily stared at her plate . . . *Should pray* . . . and shot a hallowed pause skyward before sampling the chunky potatoes cooked with onions, peppers, and cheese.

"Mmm. This is good," she said, and it wasn't just because it was more than a can of soup or a chicken pot-pie.

Colin's only immediate reply was a nod. "It's a hassle, cooking for one, isn't it?" he said after a moment, as if he'd been peeking into her kitchen.

"Any tiny recipes you'd care to share?"

He scooped up some green beans. "I don't even try. If I cook at all, I make something big enough to feed off of for a few days—meat loaf, lasagna, that sort of thing."

There was a vision—Colin with his long and nimble fingers in a bowlful of raw hamburger, bread crumbs, and diced onions.

Emily tried not to, but laughed anyway. "Are you a good cook?"

"What makes you think I wouldn't—couldn't—be? Because I'm a man? Shame on you."

"It just surprises me, that's all. My father doesn't cook."

"Mine did, and I obviously haven't starved myself yet." He paused. "That's right, you don't have any brothers. Just Erin."

"How did you remember that?"

He shrugged. "Where does she live?"

"Moscow."

"Idaho?"

She nodded. It should have been the other way around, with Erin returning to Coeur d'Alene after she graduated. Should have been Emily's turn to move to Moscow, and the University of Idaho, rather than another year at North Idaho College. Surely there were as many jobs for a newly degreed anthropologist in Coeur d'Alene as in Moscow. Should have been Erin's turn to take care of Mother, and Emily's for a life.

Emily gazed across the table at Colin, who was now engrossed in stripping a drumstick of its tender meat. He looked ready for another promotional shoot. Closer now, his shirt took on colors—pink with a blue yoke—and showed pearly snaps on the front and generous cuffs. His rich brown hair was just tidy enough to look sharp and just unruly enough to look inviting, his shave appeared fresh, and he smelled like a Manhattan tycoon.

He'd worked a live broadcast—a remote—at Heirloom Furniture midday. She'd almost driven by to watch him meet the public he attracted to the store, except she couldn't afford any excuse for being there—even on six-months-no-interest. But she was with him now. No curfew. No leaving a number where she could be reached. No dread of a tomorrow that could make her frantic to pack all she could into tonight.

Colin, so confident, so socially literate, wouldn't understand that. He'd probably grown up . . . free.

"What does your father do for a living?" she asked.

"He's a geologist for Standard Oil," he replied without a glance. "How about yours?"

"A dealer rep for Caterpillar."

That stopped the chicken in midair. "Really? I could enjoy that."

"Why?"

The dimples that had been absent played in his cheeks. "I've always had an attraction to machinery—and the heavier and more powerful, the better. Peddling dump trucks and earth movers would be fun."

"Ooh, you played with Tonka Toys." Imagine that little scene.

Colin's left eyebrow shot up. "That's far enough, Emily."

She burst into laughter, just as a drumbeat shot

through the air like a bolt of lightning, followed by a thunder of guitar chords and a steady bass note. Like dogs summoned by the clattering of food in their dishes, couples rose from their tables and strode to the dance floor.

Emily watched them over the railing as they paraded past to the happy beat. Anticipation thrummed through her. It had to be magic to be able to dance like that. She glanced at Colin. He probably knew that magic, while she'd make a fool of herself. Hadn't danced four times, her whole life.

She watched again. If the dancers came in all heights, breadths, and ages, they had one thing in common—they were colorful. For the men, jeans and boots for sure, hat optional, and shirts with stripes, decorative embroidery, or stunning two-tones, like Colin's. For the women, the costume could be anything from jeans and crisp T-shirts to long skirts—or short skirts, bare legs, and boots. A young woman swung by, twirling as she passed, and the wind provided a view of ruffled panties, like the ones baby girls wear to church.

Emily watched the woman round the floor. Her own ensemble was dreadfully understated. She'd come as close as she could with jeans, a blue long-sleeved shirt, and ankle boots, but everyone around her looked ready for a western wear fashion show.

"I didn't dress for this," she told Colin. When he looked up, she shrugged. "My ruffled underthings are at the cleaners."

He smiled. "You look fine."

Emily rolled her eyes. "Why is it men think 'fine' is a compliment?"

"This one doesn't," he replied, never taking his gaze from the chicken—until the moment it lifted and impaled her to the bench. "Would you have argued if I'd said you look pretty tonight?"

No. Well, probably. I'd want to believe it. Never mind, this is business.

"Why didn't you wear your cowboy hat?" she asked her potatoes.

Colin's knowing glance said he'd noticed the lane change, though he said only, "I'm not crazy about hats." He motioned to her plate with his empty chicken bone. "Are you finished? We're here to dance, not jabber."

"That sounds pretty comical coming from someone who talks for a living."

Colin added the bone to the pile in his plate. "You'll learn to talk on Tuesday. Tonight, you learn to dance." The expression in his eyes was already two-stepping.

"I'm still hungry."

"That's refreshing. You must be the only woman in Missoula not obsessed about her weight. You can have seconds in a while. They're free anyway."

"We didn't pay for the firsts."

"All the more reason. Come on, no more excuses, Emily."

"I'm not making excuses. I'm just not a dancer. Maybe I should observe for a while."

"I'll teach you turns first, so you can see everything in a sweep." He plucked her plate from the table and spun away with his own, carrying them to the garbage. In mere seconds he was back, stopping on her side of the table and holding out his hand . . . open . . . palm up . . . waiting. She looked from it to his face, at dimples playing and navy eyes smiling dangerously into hers.

Oh my.

What had sounded simple and distant in his office looked very familiar in reality, but Emily gathered a breath and set her hand in his.

Nine

"Okay, start with your right foot and move in four steps," Colin said. He held Emily in the ballroom position, with one of her fine-boned hands in his, the other was a light touch on his shoulder, and his own rode a most feminine waist. "Slow . . . slow . . . fast, fast," he counted, then "Right . . . left . . . right, left. Right . . . left . . . right, left. Okay?"

She nodded, though there was doubt in her eyes.

"Let's try it," he said, and gently led her back.

Not so gently, she stumbled, but she laughed about it. "I'm sorry."

"That's all right. Don't stop," he said, and kept right on leading.

She stumbled twice more.

"Right . . . left . . . right, left. Right . . . left . . . right, left," he said again.

It helped. She began to slide into each step as if she knew it was coming.

"You're doing great," he told her.

Too soon; she missed the next step, and scolded him for it. "Be quiet. I can't talk and count at the same time."

"You don't need to count," he told her. "Just do it. Your feet know the beat." To prove it, he pulled her toward him, guiding them in the other direction.

That got him another scolding. "Warn me next time."

"You did fine. Just follow me." He shook the hand resting in his. "Stiffen this noodle-arm. Give me something to lead," he said and showed her; a push turned her clockwise, a pull, counterclockwise.

She put tension in the arm, but it must have been uproariously funny, for she nearly collapsed in laughter. "I can't tense my arm and stay relaxed everywhere else."

He laughed himself, when he pushed on her hand and pulled on her waist, starting her in a clockwise turn, except she wound up . . . wound up.

"Okay. Let's try again," he said, leading her slowly through another.

This one worked. After a jerky spin, she landed where she began.

"What did you do for fun at North Idaho College?" he asked, dancing them into the next song.

Probably not dances, though she was catching on well enough.

She shrugged. "Movies, plays, games, that sort of thing."

That sounded right. Group activities. "Do you play volleyball?" he asked, on a hunch.

She brightened. "Yes. Not often, but I enjoy it when I do."

And laughs the whole time, no doubt, in tidy shorts and a chestnut ponytail that bobs on its own curl when she leaps for a ball she's too short to reach. No off-color jokes screened on Miss Emily's T-shirt, and no beer in the cooler between the lawn chairs. This was a nice girl, the kind Bryan dated.

"Did you have a boyfriend to go to all those plays and movies with?" he asked, watching her eyes for what she wouldn't say.

Her eyebrows arched smartly. "Isn't that a little personal for a business engagement?"

"Just making conversation."

For a moment she didn't answer. "No," she said finally. "My mother was ill, and my father traveled. It was difficult for me to get away."

The words were simple, her expression amiable, but she could shrug with every beat of the music—there'd been no prom, little dancing, less volleyball, and it mattered.

"So this is my audience?" Emily asked suddenly.

Colin glanced over her head. "Yes, ma'am. These are the folks on the other end of the signal."

"Tell me about them."

"The psychographics?"

"I guess," she replied, obviously unfamiliar with the term.

"They're all ages, both genders, and blue-collar mostly," he said, "although there's a hefty share that's white-collar or professional. Some are real cowboys. They're the ones in the worn boots and crumpled hats. The others wish they were—or think they wish they were. It's hard work that doesn't give a whit for weather or time of day."

"You sound like you know that by experience."

"My grandfather was a rancher," he replied.

"In Oklahoma?"

"In Oklahoma," he said, taken back to pink-and-gold dawns, the sizzle of bacon, and the pungent smell of fresh hay. Gimpa and Gram could be dead, and he wouldn't even know it. Should call—but couldn't. "They're not hicks, Emily. They're down-home America. Simple folk—

who like songs with lyrics they can understand."

She stared up through large eyes he knew were green, even if the light was dim.

He shrugged. "You know, conservative, traditional. They'd vote for Truman if he were alive to run. They get in tiffs with their families, and forgive it all when one of them needs help. They have old camp trailers in their backyards, and the weeds are growing tall, but they won't sell because they won't give up on the hope there'll be time to get away and torch marshmallows over an open fire one day."

Still, she stared. Listened so intently.

He shifted his attention to an obscure spot above her head. "There's a town the other side of Great Falls—Fort Benton. . . . There was this dog, Shep, whose owner died, and the man's body was shipped on the train, but the family, back east, must not have known about the dog. He got left behind. And Shep must have seen the casket get loaded, knew his master was inside, because he met every train after that. He just stayed there, waiting for his companion to come back to him. Train workers and townspeople tried to take Shep home, but he wouldn't go. So they kept him fed, and he burrowed himself a lying-down place under the platform. Every day he met each arrival, with his eyes bright and his tail wagging . . . until the last person got off, and none of them was his master. Then he'd go back to his hole until the next train whistle blew. For five and a half years, he did that. Just waited, and got older. Until one time when an oncoming train seemed to catch him by surprise. It was like he didn't hear it coming. He looked up suddenly. Tried to get out of the way . . . and fell. It was winter you see, and the narrow rails were slippery. The whole town came to his funeral, and the people erected a monument to him. What kind of people do that, Emily? What kind of people do that for a dog?"

The pretty eyes of a faithful friend . . . the weatherworn faces of working folk . . . faded. The room zoomed into focus, the music took on clarity, and heat climbed Colin's neck. He risked a glance at Emily—who did he think he was? John Wayne? Except those green eyes weren't laughing at his foolishness. They were moist.

"It's depressing music," she said softly.

"Sometimes it's hilarious," he replied. "Sometimes it's just some old boy singing about how much he loves that woman, even though she drives him crazy."

The pickup truck slowed as it rumbled along the line of cars parked in the gravel lot. Near the end, it stopped suddenly, though its driver didn't bother to check the old parking ticket in his billfold. The Volkswagen was unmistakable with those 'K' county, Idaho, plates. . . .

None of the women in Boots acted so bold as to walk up and say hi, but they looked. All night long, they stared, put their heads together, talked all at once to share their bit, and looked again, while Colin behaved as casually as if the dance club were in a town large enough to get lost in. Except it wasn't. Marilyn, the station receptionist, knew. Vicky, its sales manager, knew. Shoot, even Betty knew. So it made no sense that Emily was letting him follow her out the door, letting him take her to pie in his car.

No. It wasn't a date. It was a business relationship . . . easy—and so free—to say yes.

✦

"Colin!"

He spun around. Monica stood in the doorway, her denim skirt swishing around her. She waved a sheet of yellow paper at him. "Here," she said, "these are the things I want to talk about in my next commercial."

Though Emily had turned from her progress toward the parking lot, Colin resisted the urge to pull her by the hand into the circle with Monica. Better to avoid fanning the rumors they'd no doubt already started. Rather, he scanned the list. Far too many items for one thirty-second spot. Vicky would have to talk Monica into a sixty, or two thirty-second spots on a rotating schedule. He gave Monica a smile and folded the paper into his coat pocket. "Thanks. I'll give this to Vicky."

Monica held the door open with her bottom, her arms folded tightly against the cold that wouldn't have bothered a warm-blooded creature. "Tell her to call me Tuesday. I'm closed Mondays."

It was a sure bet Vicky already knew that, since she'd been Monica's sales exec for three years, but Colin nodded anyway. "I'll do it. Thanks for everything. You deserve to do well."

That was no stretch of the truth. Even if she served nothing to wet a man's throat, she ran the best dance floor in town. Trouble was, she knew it.

"You're welcome. Come again. And come for lessons next time, Emily," she called, leaning to see around Colin.

"I will," Emily replied.

Monica flashed a plastic smile and stepped back into the lobby. Colin turned toward the parking lot—

That guy, the one who'd been strolling along the line

of tables from one end to the other all night. Monica hadn't said anything about hiring a bouncer, but the man sure held up that spot of wall in the pool of light beside the door as if he were being paid to keep the peace—except he wasn't watching the people fingering into the parking lot. He was eyeing Emily.

As if he sensed Colin's stare, the man's attention slid to him, though only for a second before he not only looked away, but turned away, giving Colin his back.

Let Emily bristle; Colin set his hand, boldly and possessively, at the small of her back and led her into the dim lot. She stepped between a pair of trucks. Colin glanced back. The man was still there, watching them over his shoulder.

Simply, like a quiet snow that begins one unnoticed and unassuming flake at a time . . . Gently, like the silent splendor of a sunrise that materializes one glorious pink and gold after another . . . Out of nothing, it happened. With the air at Cottage House Pancakes laden with the smells of coffee, french fries, and smoky perfume. With the sounds of stirring spoons clattering to rest, disjointed bits of conversation, and laughter. Over a piece of apple pie à la mode, Colin started a slow and glorious ascent.

No eyes had ever looked greener, no skin softer, no smile more radiant. No voice sounded more alluring. No one had ever been more sweet, had more integrity, been more intelligent, than Emily was at that moment, entertaining an audience of one, fork held loosely over a wedge of banana cream pie, while his own vanilla ice cream melted into a puddle around the flakiest crust in town.

She laughed, animating that intriguing mouth, green

eyes glittering, and bent her head to cut a bite. The light overhead poured gold highlights into the bangs that swept off her forehead, touched the fan of her lashes, slid down her cute nose, and looked to seep into the translucent skin of her hand. Colin turned to his own pie in stunned silence. Simple and complex, beyond reasoning, and with no definitive moment of beginning . . . falling in love was that way.

And he was in a world of hurt.

The pickup truck followed at a respectable distance, trailing the BMW more discreetly than the BMW followed the Rabbit. The woman at Boots had called the guy Colin. Had to be Colin Michaels, and all of Missoula knew about him—in his fancy coat and fancy car.

She better not be going to his fancy house. . . .

From East Missoula over the Clark Fork River, the truck followed them, hanging back so its headlights blended with others. When the pair turned onto University, brake lights blazing, the truck drove by and wheeled around the next block and beyond to approach from the other direction. The porch light on the two-story was just going out as he got there, and that DJ's BMW was driving away, apparently leaving Emily Brooks and her Rabbit behind. The truck wheeled around in the street and followed, but he lost the fancy car on Brooks.

"Thanks, George," Colin said as the bartender at Barney's set a tumbler of Maker's Mark on the bar napkin.

The "well-mannered" Kentucky bourbon flowed past Colin's teeth and over his tongue, smoother than any drink had a right to be, even for the price. He huffed to himself. Only a select few in this town even knew it existed, much less had an appreciation for it. Fewer were willing to pay for it. Fewer than that could afford to. But Colin had the best, the best he could afford of anything important—though Emily wouldn't be impressed. Didn't even drink. She did drive, however, and wasn't the least impressed with his car.

"Nice," she'd said.

Nice? One didn't describe a product of the Bavarian Motor Works as *nice*.

"German engineering at its finest," he'd said.

To which Miss Emily Elizabeth Erickson smiled over the console across her gray leather seat at him and said, "I know. I have a German car."

She had a Volkswagen.

Colin set his forearms on the padded edge of the bar and stared into the amber and ice in his glass. She wasn't impressed with anything. Not his car, not—

"Hi, handsome," a female voice crooned.

He swiveled his head to the source of the heat pressing against his arm. "Hi, Chastity," he replied, turning back to his drink.

Chastity. Who'd come up with that champion idea? If they'd named her Betsy Ross, would she have been a flag maker?

She dragged her fingernail down the line of skin in front of his ear. "What a coincidence," she said. "You're looking kind of lonely, and I'm kind of thirsty. How about you buy me a drink, and we can . . . talk about it?"

"Sorry," he said to her reflection in the mirror behind the bar. "I'm not much in the mood for company, but George will fix you a drink." He gave George a nod.

Chastity's excessively made-up eyes narrowed viciously in features too hard for a man to ever connect with mothering his child. The wrist draped over his shoulder slid off. "Well, forget it," she spat. "I don't need you for anything."

He watched the reflection of her indignant retreat. He and George exchanged a glance.

"She must be losing her touch," George said. "It's getting pretty late to be looking for somebody to buy breakfast."

Colin shook his head. "Happens to the best of us."

A wise man, George, for he let that slide, though he gave Colin a speculative glance.

That's another thing Miss Emily wouldn't be exceedingly impressed with—the Chastitys crowding his past. Not she, who wept over dogs who chose to die at their sentinel places rather than disappoint their masters—or deny their own eager hearts. Such fidelity. She wouldn't understand anything less, so it would be better if she learned nothing of him. She would, though—unless he scuttled her off to Fairbanks. And he'd never find a job—or Maker's Mark—in Fairbanks.

He drained the glass and slid it toward George. Like one of Pavlov's dogs, the bartender responded automatically, drizzling more gold inside.

The younger of the Kavanaugh brothers, not the elder, that's whose arm Emily should ride. She wasn't one of the girls from Barney's, to be taken home for a few hours' entertainment on a Saturday night. He should leave her alone, for Nicholas Kavanaugh had no future, and Colin Michaels had no past.

The pickup truck made itself part of the line pulling into the parking lot, except it slid past the driveway after the blue Rabbit rocked through it. Valley Bible Church; important enough to call her from bed on a Sunday morning. Not important to him. He'd been following her.

There was no Communion that Sunday, though Emily had been prepared in case there was. She sat in the back of the church, where she belonged.

Ten

*H*i, Marilyn," Emily said as she shook another cold drizzle from her hair and coat.

The receptionist grinned and nodded, pen in hand, while she gave the station address to the caller on the phone pinched against her shoulder. The other line was already ringing. Apparently, Tuesdays weren't any less busy than Mondays.

Emily peeked from the lobby into Sterling's office, and he waved her inside.

"What are you doing here?" he wanted to know. The tone was gruff, the smile warm. His gray suit and pink tie were crisp.

"More training with Colin," she told him, taking off her coat in the doorway. "Maybe even production today."

"Don't let him drive you crazy," he said.

"Why is that?"

"Let's just say you have my permission to hit him, but not in the mouth."

"Is that a polite way of saying he can be hard to get along with?" Emily asked.

"He has his idea of how things should sound," Sterling

said on a fresh grin, then plunged into another topic. "I hear the cowboys like you."

"Really?"

"That's what I hear," he said and nodded. "Just keep doing what you've been doing."

It was a polite dismissal, unless she had something further to discuss.

"Thanks, Sterling. I will," she said and gave him a wave, though she didn't head for the production room just yet.

Betty was straightening the floral skirt over the lap of a stuffed pink elephant on the furthest file cabinet. She—Betty, not the elephant—wore lilac pants and a multipastel blouse with a lilac bow at the collar.

"Hi," Emily said.

Betty swiveled, and a smile bloomed beneath the half-glasses perched on her nose. All but the edges of her rose lipstick had worn off. "That's no coincidence. I was just thinking about you," she said.

"What were you thinking?" Emily asked, claiming the guest chair.

"I was wondering how you were getting along," Betty replied, turning back for a final smoothing of the skirt before she plopped into her chair, which clacked and squeaked as she sat. "I meant to invite you to church."

"Oh, thanks. I went to Valley Bible on Sunday."

Betty propped her elbows on the desk and picked up her coffee cup, holding it in both hands; kisses of lipstick were stacked on the rim. "Did you like it?"

Emily nodded. "It's a lot like back home."

"Good," Betty said. "Just know you're welcome at the First Baptist, if you want to look for something else."

"Thanks," Emily said again. She stared at the edge of the desk and fiddled with the sleeve of her coat, rolling the outer shell between finger and thumb. "Colin took me dancing Saturday night," she said finally.

"He did? Where?"

"Boots."

Betty grinned politely. Let her mug settle to the desk. "I don't mean to pry, but is this going somewhere, Emily?"

"No. Never," Emily said. "I've already told him I won't date a coworker, much less my boss. Besides, I don't think he's a Christian."

Betty released a gentle breath. "When I said he was lonely, I didn't mean . . . well, I'd hate to think you thought—"

"I know what you meant."

"I wanted you to look a little deeper, that's all."

"I know. I'm too smart to get involved," Emily told her.

A moment later, she strolled across the lobby and waved through the window at Starvin' Marvin who, like an emaciated turtle, gave a phlegmatic lift of his chin in reply. He still hadn't combed his hair. John Vaughn was in the first production room, headset around his neck as he shuffled through a selection of CDs scattered on every flat surface around him. This morning his surgical scrubs were blue, rather than green, and his blond hair fell in braided ropes to his elbows. His greeting came in the form of a wide smile and a lift of his whiskery chin; he'd either forgotten to shave or was building a goatee.

Colin's office door was ajar and the light on, but he was down the hall in the second production room, his headset looping over his ears and a piece of copy in his right hand. His arm reached to the board, hand poised over the mike button, while his head bobbed and swung as he poured energy into the commercial he read into the microphone suspended before his mouth. Saturday's western shirt had been replaced by one of red flannel.

He must have seen her from the corner of his eye, for

he waved her inside once he'd finished.

"Hi," she said as she closed the door behind her, cutting off the phones and Starvin' Marvin's show. The room smelled of warm electronics and warmer cologne.

"Good morning," Colin said, sliding the headset to his neck. He nodded toward the chair on her side of the counter. "Have a seat while I finish this."

Emily set her purse on the floor and draped her coat over the chair, while Colin rolled the computer mouse around on its pad, his eyes following the movement on the monitor. A double-click, and the spot he'd just recorded leaped from the speakers overhead—and he was magic in the velvet he poured from his throat. He could go national with that voice and talent. When the spot ended, she told him so.

It broke him into a boyish smile—that crooked front tooth, so cute. "I've had offers. I like it here." He paused. "Are you looking for more than this?"

"More than KDMD?" It was an odd question, especially coming from her boss.

He nodded. "More than Missoula, Montana."

Even the question thrilled her. She had the choice. Could move anywhere that piqued her interest, satisfied her whim. If Portland, Oregon, phoned tomorrow, there were no responsibilities keeping her suitcase in the closet. Somehow, that was enough. For now.

She grinned. "Shoot, I can't even do production yet. It will be a while before I have to decide about going somewhere else."

He nodded, absorbing her answer, seeming to be satisfied with it, while his eyes grazed her face.

"Are you afraid I'm going to give notice next week?" she asked.

"After I've spent all this time training you? Yes."

She folded her arms on the counter. "Well, don't worry about it. As much as I dream about going somewhere else, I'll probably live my whole life within two hundred miles of Coeur d'Alene."

Because family was family, and that few hours' distance made them more comfortable to live with.

"Your folks?" he asked.

"My father," she corrected. "My mother died last April."

The pleasant expression slid from his face. "You said she'd been ill. I didn't know she'd died. No wonder they depended on you so much. I'm sorry."

It was her turn to shrug. She'd survived—though she'd had little choice. "Thanks," she said simply.

The gaze he gave her was steady and gentle. It held . . . and held, stirring flutters in her stomach.

She shifted under the attention. "I had fun Saturday night. Thanks for the dance lessons."

"My pleasure. You're a quick study," he said finally, except he wasn't himself. Either this was the norm for Colin in production, or he'd had a difficult morning.

"You're a good teacher," she said.

"You ready to put that to another test?" he asked, sounding more natural.

"Production?"

"Production," he said, handing her a sheet of copy from a stack beside the keyboard. "I'll engineer, show you the equipment today. You can take it tomorrow." He motioned toward the microphone and headset at her elbow. "Let's get a sound level," he said, donning his own headphones and turning on both microphones.

Emily slid the mike closer. "Test, one, two, three," she said, her voice coming through the headphones, since the "on" button cut the studio speakers. "Test, one, two, three. Mary had a little lamb, its fleece was white as snow."

"Hokey smoke, Bullwinkle, you never said anything about sheep," Colin said in a Rocky-J-Squirrel voice.

Emily chuckled.

Colin sent her a mischievous sideways glance. "Uh, gee, Rocky," he said, now sounding like Bullwinkle, "give it a read-through, and we'll hear how you sound."

Emily laughed again, remembered her pen, then pulled her mouth into a semblance of gravity, saying, "Don't be left out in the cold this winter. . . ."

"Pretty good," Colin said, "but let's make it better. Don't suck your air. Pull it in. Drop the back of your tongue and open your throat, otherwise you gasp. You hear?" he asked, then demonstrated, sounding like a decrepit set of bellows. "Okay, open the mike, take your breath, hold it, then jump into the spot with lots of energy—and no gasp. Ready to try again?"

She nodded. He closed his mike and waited.

Emily drew a deep breath, paused, then launched into the spot, "Don't be left out in the cold this winter. Not when Phil's Tire and Auto is having a preseason sale on snow tires, batteries, and everything you'll need to get started and keep going through the grizzliest blizzards and deepest cold. Have Phil's check your antifreeze, free of charge, or get a tune-up, for 10 percent off. . . ."

She read without a stumble, except the spot stretched into thirty-four seconds. The announcers on FM wouldn't care if the ad ran long, but the automated system on the AM side wouldn't know it was playing the next commercial over the four-too-many seconds of this one.

Not to worry. Colin had the answer, and a red pen, striking through the phrases "not when" and "through the grizzliest blizzards and deepest cold."

"Can you do that?" she asked, watching in horror.

"I'll quit cutting copy when the sales staff learn to

count," he said and handed it back. "Try it now."

She did, and finished the ad with a second to spare.

"Now that you have the pace, read it once more, just a little more relaxed," Colin told her. "This will be the final take."

It wasn't, but it was close.

"Very good," he told her with the final playback. It was the voice of Barney Fife that added, "You sound just like one of them Hollywood si-reens, Thelma Lou." Then he was Colin Michaels saying, "Let's add some sound effects."

He pulled a CD from a row shelved under the counter and dropped it into a machine. He pressed buttons, and a vicious winter wind whined from the speakers. This he added to the spot, then exchanged the CD for another—and an Indy 500 car buzzed like an insect through the room. Emily gave him an uncertain stare.

"No?" he asked. "Okay, how about this?" he said, just before horses' hooves clip-clopped.

Emily laughed. "A car, Colin. This needs to be a car."

"Oh, I see," he said, peering at the index on the CD case. He punched up another cut—of an ocean liner's blaring horn.

"Cruise ships don't need tires," she informed him.

"No, but Phil can keep those batteries charged."

She laughed. "What about parking?"

He shrugged. "Just make an appointment. It's a long street."

She laughed again, while he finally selected the cut of a car engine that just wouldn't turn over—to which he added a cheering crowd.

"That's the gang at Phil's," he said. "Business has been kind of slow."

He was impossible. Then he was an artist, layering in Phil's trademark music bed until the spot told a story; a piece of everyday art for everyday airwaves.

Colin was also a wit; he had her record tags—the final mention of the business name and address—for two commercials he'd written and recorded. One, for Dave Newell Dodge, Chrysler, Plymouth, and Jeep, was scripted as if the new pickup truck were for the dog who would ride in the bed. The other, an ad for This-Is-the-Life Hot Tub and Spa, had a cowboy—Colin in yet another voice—explaining that though his hot tub made a good sheep-dip tank in spring, a no-freeze watering trough in winter, and a great place to soak weary bones in the summer, the cows needed to learn to wipe their hooves before they got in.

She had a delightful laugh, and it was fairly easy to make her share it.

She also had the best of female voices, adding the perfect touch in her tags—"Make a new season deal on last year's models at This-Is-the-Life Hot Tub and Spa, on Russell, in Missoula," and "See the new line of Dodge trucks at Dave Newell Dodge, Chrysler, Plymouth, and Jeep, on Brooks, in Missoula." And didn't she look fine in white button-down sweaters?

"That wasn't so bad," Emily said as she placed her headset aside and pushed the mike out of the way.

Colin cast her a questioning glance as he gathered up copy.

That soft mouth grinned. "I'd been led to believe you're a little . . . difficult to get along with in here."

Sterling. Would have to talk to him about besmirching his reputation to someone he was trying to impress.

Colin shook his head. "Just do it my way—perfect."

She smiled.

"I haven't eaten. How about lunch?" he asked, then held his breath while he tapped the sheets of copy even.

"I'm sorry. I'm busy," she said, sliding her arms into her parka.

Already?

"Someone you already knew?" he asked so calmly.

She shook her head, rippling the fall of pretty hair layering around her face. "Well, not a date. More of a meeting. We got to know each other on the phone."

A groupie? She was going to lunch with some guy who'd flirted with her over the phone? Colin resisted the urge to groan—and it would be interesting to know exactly what the guy had said to make himself so irresistible.

"We may wind up going to the same church," Emily added as if it made any difference.

"Oh? Which one?" Colin asked, gathering a peek into her real life. It could be handy to know, should he ever want to find her on a Sunday.

"Valley Bible," she replied as she bent for her purse. "I've only been for two Sundays, but I like it. Do you go to church?"

He could lie, and say yes. He could lie, and say he hadn't had the chance to find a good one. He could lie, and say he'd been a faithful attendee in Oklahoma. Except she stared back with those emerald eyes, with the trust it took to meet a stranger for lunch.

"Not really," he said, gathering the copy and his headset in one hand, his coffee in the other.

"Oh. Well . . . that's too bad," she said, sounding as if it truly were. "Perhaps you've never found the right place. You might like this one."

"Maybe so," he said, but didn't really mean it. Her little nod said she knew it.

Later, and from the shadow beside the window, Colin watched, shoulder against the wall, while Emily scurried through the rain to her car.

She was going to lunch with a groupie.

She already had her key in the lock but swiveled her head when John Vaughn called to her on his way to the door. Over the top of the car, she gave him the gift of her smile, pretty hands canopying her eyes. John said something, but what she replied must have been as funny, for it was John who lifted his chin and laughed—amazing that he could be so entertained by such ladylike chatter.

A rare woman, she.

And totally beyond reach. Every time Colin talked to her, she threw up another obstacle. First he'd been her boss, and she didn't date coworkers. Then she was committed to her family and to her God, and he had neither.

She called a farewell to John and was still smiling as she slid into her seat, buckled the belt—so cautious, so *right*—started the engine, and drove out of the lot, turn signal and all. Colin watched until her car disappeared behind the furniture store next door. Then he watched the hole in the air where Emily had been.

He should trump up some excuse to fire her—lie, since he obviously wasn't so scrupled as she—and send her back to K-93. He narrowed his gaze. Maybe she needed such saving. Perhaps they were right. Perhaps it hadn't been an accident at all, but rather an unconscious retaliation, the bad Kavanaugh boy being bad to the ultimate by eliminating the good Kavanaugh boy. Though he hadn't blamed Bryan for being Bryan—with his turn signals, Bible highlighted in three colors, and dates who invited him into the house to meet their mamas and daddies. It was Nicholas, and it was no accident. That's what so many thought, though no one said.

Colin spun away from the window and stepped around to his desk. Stared at the copy in the middle of it.

Don't be left out in the cold this winter. . . .

It was a stupid commercial, as clichéd and predictable as every other spot that began with that same tired line, except Emily had read it as if they were her own words, her own anxious admonition to a best friend.

A thousand times today he'd nearly given himself away, stared until he tumbled inside her eyes, melted into a stuttering wreck . . . because she was sweet and fresh and so unlike the girls who'd sneaked down their drives to the Camaro waiting just out of sight, headlights off. So unlike the girls at Barney's.

He should fire her. Get her away from that groupie. Get her out of here.

Except she was the selfless one.

Eleven

*Y*ou were a sheriff? Where was this?" Emily asked over her cheeseburger.

The man across the table was good looking. Though he'd sounded stocky and dark on the phone, he turned out to be about six feet tall, with short blond hair, green eyes, and a close-cropped blond beard with precision edges.

"Pocatello," Brad replied to her question. "We had our hands full, I'll tell you that. Right on the border, and all those college kids with their pockets full of Daddy's money. It's the hub for drug traffic between Utah and Idaho."

All the college kids Emily knew scrambled for their cut of the pizza bill and were too frantic trying to stay up on economics and philosophy to spend much time stoned, but she only nodded and asked the obvious question. "Why aren't you on Missoula's police force?"

"I was for a while," he said, dabbing a fry in a puddle of catsup. "The politics got bad, because I had so much more experience with narcotics than anyone else."

"So they fired you because you knew more than them?"

"More than they," Brad corrected without pause, then,

"No, I quit. The pressure is bad enough without fighting it on the inside too."

"That's too bad," Emily said. "So now you're a roving security guard?" It seemed a waste.

"I think of myself as preventing the crime before it starts," he replied. "Just trying to keep some kid from ruining his life and breaking his mother's heart."

That was a rare view—a misguided young man with his wrists in cuffs and shards of broken window at his feet.

"You should be working with teen groups," she told him.

"I did. In Pocatello."

"Really?"

"It was no big deal. Just until some of the parents got involved." He mopped up the last of the catsup with the last french fry, wiped his mouth, and carefully folded his napkin beside his plate. He set his elbows on the table, balled one fist inside the other, and stared for a long moment. "I'm glad we finally met, Emily," he said. "I just want you to know, I'm here for you. I'll be your friend."

Colin stared across the carpet at Emily, who stood in the doorway of his office in jeans and hiking boots—almost athletic—and a silvery pink sweater that was just fuzzy enough to be downy—absolutely alluring. She didn't look as if she'd been out with another guy yesterday. Didn't look as if she would intentionally drive a man to yanking on weights half the night, while she smiled that voice into the stereo speakers suspended from the ceiling of the weight room. Perspiration had pasted Colin's tank top, shorts, and hair to his skin but had done nothing to cool his frustration. Even if he could work past her obstacles, he still had his own—no family . . . and Bryan.

Emily said hi to Roger Warren, one of the sales execs, as he passed behind her, then turned back. "You sure you're ready for this?" she asked.

If she hadn't already slain him with those green eyes, her smile was bewitching. She was kidding, of course. He'd been waiting all day, all night, and another all-day, but he said only, "Let's do it."

She sat at the control board in the production room while he stood behind her, walking her through the computer screens in the software that recorded faultlessly smooth commercials without splicing tape or a razor blade to cut it. If she nodded her head, the concept was there, understood and locked in.

"How do I find it again?" she asked.

"What?"

"The commercial. The spot I just recorded."

"Oh, like this," he said and leaned over her, setting his hand over hers on the mouse.

Baby powder. Not "Erotic Evening," "Whips & Chains," or some such sequined scent that overstated the statement. Rather, Emily smelled powdery, so soft and delicate that Colin inhaled deeply to get more.

"Go back up here to the menu," he said, rolling the mouse under her hand, under his, until the pointer pulled down a list of options. "Your spot, had you recorded one, would be in this list."

She nodded, moving the head of hair he was tempted to experience with his cheek.

"I think I've got it," she said, looked up and smiling with delight.

Mere inches. Breaths actually, the distance between them. There were flecks of blue in her eyes, embedded there in the tiny bands of a dozen greens, the prize for whoever was lucky enough to get close. He stole an instant to check his bearings—lips, chin, hairline, back to that mouth, up again to her eyes—and fell in. Her stare seemed to focus, to see things that had gone unnoticed. Then her smile fell, and slightly, almost imperceptibly, her eyes widened.

Yes, Emily. Yes . . . see me.

He'd spooked her. She nearly jumped in her haste to turn back to the monitor, stiffening and pulling her hand from under his as if he'd scorched her.

"I think you're ready," Colin said, straightening, his voice seeming to bounce off the foam walls in the startled silence. "Why don't you try one on your own while I stand by?"

Emily nodded almost frantically. He was on his way around the counter to his chair when she jerked to her feet. "I'm going to get more coffee," she said. "I'll be back in a minute." Then she fled—and she'd have a whale of a counter-shaped bruise on her thigh where she banged it on the way out.

Colin shoved his fingers into the pockets of his jeans and leaned against the hall window. Wrong, wrong, wrong. Too much, too fast. She wasn't one of the girls from Barney's. She was gentler than that. His gaze darted about the room. She'd left her coffee cup behind, and she'd die before she'd come back for it.

"I forgot my mug," she said suddenly from the doorway, then shot him a smile as she strode into the work station and seized the cup as if it had been trying to escape. "If you ever see one of these things with a buzzer that goes off after five minutes of undisturbed sleep, buy it. I'll pay you back. I always forget where I leave them." Her grin trembled, giving away the thin veneer of her bravado.

She'd been gone about three seconds when he chuckled to himself. Nix the regret. She had enough pluck to ensure her survival; he was the one in peril.

Later, Colin waited until Emily had settled herself in the chair before he claimed his own seat; that was old-fashioned Southern manners. Putting her on the other side of his desk, a symbol of his authority? That was strategy; he wanted information.

She gave him a guileless stare.

He turned down the volume on Starvin' Marvin. "I think you're ready to be added to the production schedule. What do you think?"

Emily nodded, matter-of-fact. "If I get lost, I can always ask for help."

True enough. And if her God had any grace, she'd ask him before she asked anyone else. He smiled. She smiled back.

Pretty.

"Okay. I'll let the sales staff know you're available. In fact, I'll encourage them to keep you in mind for spots that would be complimented by a female voice." Colin paused. "Your show is improving, except you're still a little tight, and still a little loose. That doesn't make any sense right now, but we'll get to that next week."

She nodded.

Only twenty-seven-and-a-half hours on the air and two-and-a-half in production each week; she had to be nearly starving. Even though her Rabbit was old enough to be paid for, there was still insurance to buy, and repairs. It took some of those to keep old iron rolling. He couldn't do anything to fix the budget, give her more hours—if he had that kind of money, he'd have a partner on his own show, rather than a newsman who doubled as sidekick—but maybe she'd call him if she needed a belt replaced or a battery charged or something. He'd have to work the offer into a conversation.

She recrossed her legs, looking relaxed and easy in his company.

He sat back, himself. "How are you getting along with Missoula?"

Her expression brightened. "Oh, fine. I like it here."

He smiled, as if it were a mutual tease. "How did your . . . blind meeting go?"

Her smile turned shy, and she gave a little aw-shucks in the tilt of her head. "Fine. We found we have a lot in common."

That's bad.

Colin puckered his chin and nodded, keeping it casual. "And this guy . . ."

"Brad," Emily said, volunteering what might have been touchy to extract—though a last name would have been helpful.

"Right. Brad," Colin continued. "Who is he? Just a listener?"

"He works nights as a roving security guard, so he listens while he works. He calls me on his cell phone." Her eyes widened in horror. "But we talk for only a few minutes. I'm not neglecting my show, Colin."

"I know that," he told her. "This is not the place to advance your social life, but I know how boring it can get in there at night. Use your judgment."

And drop this guy like a hot rock.

"Thanks," she said.

"I think I've seen him," Colin lied. "Or at least his company. Is it the one with those black Blazers? Lots of chrome, and a white emblem on the side, I think."

That sounded believable.

She shook her head. "I don't know, and I didn't catch the name. The only thing I've seen him drive is a red pick-up."

Colin grinned—*Give me more than that*—and said, "No black Blazer, huh?"

"No," Emily replied, teasing now. "Only an old red truck. No chrome."

Old. Red. No chrome. Could be a Chevy or Dodge. Could be a Ford. Could be a stinking International Harvester, but a truck was a truck to her.

He held in a sigh of frustration and let the silence unfold between them. "How about lunch?" he asked.

"I can't today," she replied, rolling the answer off her tongue as if it were easy.

"Another 'meeting'?" he asked.

"No. Laundry."

He breathed, more relieved than she should know. "Life goes on. Perhaps another time. Why don't you come in next Tuesday for another talk?"

"Okay. What about production?"

"Thursday and Friday are the busiest days." If she came in Friday, she might already have a date for Saturday. "Make it Thursday," he said. "You can get us a little ahead of the rush—but, of course, you can stop in any time to say hello. Let us know you're more than a disembodied voice flying on one-hundred-thousand watts of Diamond dust."

She laughed. Stopped his heart. Started it again when she thanked him. Then she took it with her . . . to the Laundromat.

It was a light flickering in the lobby that caught Emily's eye, calling her attention to the studio's side window.

Colin.

Good heavens, it was nearly ten o'clock, almost twelve hours after his own air shift had ended, but he was strolling this way, leafing through a little stack of pink While-You-Were-Out slips. He looked up and grinned in greeting. Emily watched his progress from the view of one window, then the other, until he disappeared along the wall and stepped in the doorway.

"Don't get nervous," he said. "It's just me."

And just in time. The same old songs and a silent phone had driven her to find paper towels and window spray; the control board and counter were cleaner than they'd ever been.

"What are you doing here?" she asked.

"Catching up. I do that sometimes." He shrugged. "It's quiet; no phones."

The smile couldn't be held—and neither could the opportunity. "You mean, you don't have a date tonight."

Colin's eyes narrowed. "Below the belt, Emily." He paused, eyes smiling. "That may be true, but you see, *I* don't date groupies."

"Ooh, boy, that was a straight shot." She stretched, hands locked and arms reaching high, and singsonged, "That's not what I hear."

He leaned against the jamb, hands in the pockets of his sheepskin coat. "I'd be nice to me if I were you."

"You can't do that," she said with a defiant lift of her chin. "That's harassment. I'll own this station for it."

"Who said anything about harassment? And you can have the station. You'll be begging Sterling to take it back within a week." He nudged his chin toward the window. "I meant, I'm parked behind you."

She gasped. "You wouldn't." Then she whirled around. He was laughing by the time she yanked the curtain open and peered through her pesky reflection to the dimly lit parking lot. His car was parked . . . beside hers—the stink. She turned around to tell him so, but the doorway was empty. So she called it out.

"You're a stink, Colin."

"You loo-ooked," he crooned back.

Emily laughed—for probably three minutes, off and on. Impossible man. Erin should have been a brother, to prepare her a little.

Quietly she worked through the next song and a stopset, occasionally glancing at the light falling on the carpet in front of his door. He was probably working on play lists—adding new releases, removing stale songs, sprinkling in a fresh round of oldies.

It took a moment of planning, but she finally worked through the next stopset, fired her jingle and a song, then rounded the counter and strolled across the corner of the hall to his door, a bank of three more songs already cued up behind her. Sure enough, Colin was at his computer. He looked up, watching her over his shoulder as she leaned against the woodwork. Another hunch proven right—his stereo speakers were on, and the volume up.

"Don't listen to me," Emily said.

He broke into a grin as he sat back and swiveled his chair, his head resting against the blue weave of fabric. "I always listen."

"Every night?"

"Every one," he said. "Not all the time, but for a while."

Oh, gracious. He should have fired her long ago.

"Do you listen to everybody, or is it just because I'm new?" she asked.

For a moment he didn't answer. "It's work, but I also

like your voice," he said finally, quietly and matter-of-fact.

That, coming from him. Well . . .

Well, he sure was easy to take direction from—or as easy as could be, since she didn't normally read instruction books or operating manuals. Whatever the contraption was, just give her a few minutes with the darn thing. She'd figure it out on her own.

"What are you doing?" she asked, seeking a distraction from the spotlight he'd put her in, and the attraction he was.

He glanced at the CDs fanned on his desk. "The playlists."

Just as she'd thought.

Then all thought departed, chased by the picture Colin made. He lifted weights. Had to, to have a physique like that, and it was a crime to conceal it in the collars and long sleeves he wore during the official work day. A T-shirt broke no such laws. This one was black. A good color on him, as it repeated the darkness of his hair, but showed it for the rich brown it was. Neither did ebony beg competition with the navy of his eyes, as blue would have.

He stepped right out of the stereotype; this piece of brawn had brains. The way he strode about the station— calm, shoulders back, stride unhurried—gave the impression he knew exactly what was being addressed on every desk, be it production, engineering, promotion, sales, marketing, budgeting, billing, traffic, FCC compliance, personnel, or on-air. The keen depth in his eyes confirmed it. Perhaps when she grew up, she'd be just like him.

He was staring, though it was an easy thing to wear. More of a comfortable gaze. She'd been staring, herself. Maybe this was how it felt to grow a friendship, to be given the opportunity—and take it—to learn someone else.

"I'm about out of song," Emily said into the silence

between them, as Billy Dean ran through chords, approaching the final few.

"That you are," Colin said.

"Aren't you worried about it?"

He shook his head. "It's not my name in the liner you just played."

Neither did Billy Dean have any grace for interests not his own, but Emily was quick. She made it back to the board with ten seconds to spare.

Later she'd just closed the mike, ending all except the final half hour of her work week, when Colin stepped into the doorway. "I'm nearly finished, but I'll hang around until you sign off," he said. "How about a piece of pie and some decaf?"

Her heart leaped. "I'd love to. I'm not tired for at least an hour after I get off the air, anyway."

He nodded; he understood.

He also knew she'd need a few minutes to switch over to the satellite, take transmitter readings, and pull the songs for the first hour of the next shift. Because of the satellite, that shift didn't begin until 6:00 A.M., but it was still a courtesy among announcers.

"Don't hurry. I'll wait," Colin reiterated on a grin. Every other of her nights on the air, it was he who benefited from her care, since his was the next mouth at the mike.

Twelve

*C*olin turned from locking the front door and gave Emily a brows-raised, are-we-going-to-argue-about-this-again stare. She glanced from him to the cars, hers then his, side-by-side.

"Okay, we'll go in your car," she said on a sigh. That didn't make it a date. It was simply a matter of practicality.

Judging by his grin, she'd made the right choice. He followed her to the passenger side of his BMW and held the door for her, as Daddy had always done for Mother, but it still felt strange. The door closed gently behind her, and he disappeared, though the compartment around her told about him; it was meticulously clean and smelled of leather and the musky scent of his cologne. She was buckling her belt when he slid into the seat beside her.

"Aren't you exhausted?" she asked as he fitted the key into the ignition and started the engine.

Colin was looking over his shoulder to back up. He gave her a glance. "No. Actually, I just woke up."

"Crashing on the couch again?"

"I must do half my sleeping there," he told her as they entered Broadway. "It's a nice couch."

He wouldn't like the short and narrow excuse for furniture that came with the price of her rent, she suspected. But give her as many years in the business, and she'd have a long comfy sofa herself. Shoot, might even be driving a BMW—though it was the sales executives, not the air staff, who drove the pricey cars.

The radio was on and tuned to Diamond Country. As if he knew she'd listened to all the radio she cared to hear today, he turned it off. The nighttime quiet was accented by their splashing through rain puddles and passing under arcs of light from business signs and street lamps.

"How long did it take you to get used to your schedule?" she asked.

That made him laugh. "I'm not sure I am, yet. I'm actually a night person." He cast her a gentle glance. "But I sure would miss watching the sun rise."

The studio windows faced northeast. Emily imagined Colin standing in their light, his old beige coffee cup hooked in his finger, while the sky over the Mission Range of the Rocky Mountains caught the embers of another day firing to life. The station—seemingly the whole world— would be sleeping around him, save for the delivery truck drivers and shift workers passing on Broadway, and the country singers he'd cued up to entertain them. A person had to be lively himself to wake the world.

Emily swiveled her attention from the window on her right to the man on her left. Colin was two people—the witty and clever disc jockey he became at 6:00 A.M. and the pensive observer he settled back to four hours later. It had to be handy to be able to choose who you could be. Much of the time, she'd benefit from being a little less talk and a lot more listen.

He drove the way he danced—relaxed and practiced and fluid, right hand resting on the gearshift, left hand

ANTARCTICA

steering from a reach that started with his elbow propped on the door. The seat—the whole car—wrapped around him like an extension of himself, and he glided through the gears with flawless precision, bending his left leg between shifts so his knee stood up beside the steering wheel. He had fun driving this plush little rocket with the European car purr, though anyone would. If a piece of automotive machinery could be cute and elegant and sexy all at the same time, Colin's BMW was.

His head swiveled, his gaze crashing into hers. She'd been staring—and he was absolutely too good-looking. She grinned and looked away. How he'd managed to sidestep having a wife and three kids by now, she couldn't figure.

"How old are you?" Emily asked, turning back.

That got her another glance. "Twenty-seven."

Could have had six kids by now, if he'd gotten right on it like everyone else seemed to do after—or during—high school.

"Aren't you going to ask me how old I am?" she asked.

"I already know."

"You do not."

"Yes, I do. At your interview, you told Sterling you were twenty-one."

Meaning he either had a good memory, was more composed than she that day, or had made a note of it.

"Smarty."

He laughed and downshifted, rocking the car through the driveway of Cottage House Pancakes, though the wrap-around leather held her firmly in place. The parking lot was shiny from another day of rain and nearly vacant; those who'd wanted dinner had already left, and the bar crowd hadn't yet arrived.

He parked the car and shot her another low-eyebrow warning.

"I won't move," she promised.

"Thank you," he said, and that was his parting before he came around to open her door.

Had to be Southern manners. Or older men. None of the boys at college had been so particular. 'Course, none of them had treated her like anything more than one of the gang.

"Where's your Oklahoma accent?" Emily asked once they settled into a booth overlooking the street. When his brows lifted over the question, she added, "You have to have had one."

"Still do," Colin replied, slipping into its gentle rhythm as if it were a mere half step behind him. Then in an Irish brogue, he said, "But you know there be no way of tellin' what sort of talk you might be gettin' with a Kavanaugh lad." When Emily laughed, he shrugged, his smile dimpled but shy. "The acceptable broadcasting accent is what they call West Coast," he said. "Essentially that's no accent at all. So I practiced. But there's still a hint of Oklahoma there if you listen for it."

Yes, she heard it, just barely. She watched him peruse the menu. So clever. And a man of habit. He ordered apple pie à la mode.

"Make mine coconut cream," she told the waitress, who returned with mugs and a pot of decaffeinated coffee.

"So what got you started in radio?" Emily asked as she poured cream into her cup.

Colin didn't answer. Just poured their coffee.

"Do you have to think about that?" she asked.

"Not at all," he replied. "Let me answer with a question of my own." He took a cautious sip and reclined in the low-backed booth. All the right muscles stood up along his shoulder as he stretched his arm along the back. "If I were to place you in a setting of beautiful scenery—say a beach, the ocean, that sort of thing—what would you notice first? What would you notice most? Would it be the smell, the sound, the sight, the taste, or the feel?"

"Where are you going with this?" she asked, then had to wait while the waitress served their pie. He took a moment to spread his napkin on his lap, while Emily sneaked in a silent prayer over her food.

"Just answer the question," Colin replied. "Close your eyes and think about it."

The only time Emily needed was the two seconds it took to stare into her coffee. "The sound," she said, looking up. "The waves. That would be my favorite part."

"I could have predicted that," he told her, cutting off a bite of pie and ice cream. "Everyone has a sense that's dominant over the other four. For you, it's sound. That's why you work in radio—the music, the voices."

"That's why you're in radio."

His reply was a smile.

"So a visual artist would probably be sight-dominant," she said, smoothing her whipped cream in an even layer.

"I would think so."

She gave a sudden laugh. "It's my sister, Erin," she explained. "You should see her . . . always touching things. When her hair was really long, she used to comb her fingers through it, and she was forever running her hands along the racks of clothes when we went shopping. It used to drive me crazy, because I was so sure she was getting them dirty. I mean, what if everyone did that?"

Colin chuckled. "What does she do for a living?"

"She's an anthropologist."

"Handles little artifacts?" He nodded, verdict reached. "Touch."

His gaze narrowed, turned speculative. Something serious was coming.

"Want to see a movie tomorrow night?" he asked.

"What does that have to do with the station?" she asked.

"Nothing."

Something in the word—or in the way he said it so quietly—made Emily look up from her plate.

"It wouldn't be business," Colin said calmly. "This would be a date."

In an instant, it swept past her, threatened to knock her over. Threatened to hurt her by taking her with it . . . or leaving her behind.

The room was far too noisy for the sweet Swiss atmosphere Cottage House Pancakes tried to fake. Too many forks. Too many conversations, too close together.

"I can't," she told him gently, poking at her piecrust with the tines of her fork.

"You already have a date?"

"Well, sort of . . . but it's not that."

"You're not my employee right now, Emily," he said, "and I'm not your program director. We're simply two people enjoying each other's company. So what's wrong with that?"

Darn him, he needs to shut up—QUIT TALKING—before he ruins it.

"Emmy?"

"Don't," she said, looking to his face . . . that beautiful face . . . the eyes that were so deep and gentle and intelligent. Those impossible dimples.

It was hopeless. She'd left home and was still staring out the window at things she couldn't have. As before, she'd been telling herself it didn't matter, that she didn't really want what was out there.

She stared across the table at what was out there. "Let's not change it. If we leave it alone . . . it will be okay. Please don't ruin it."

For a long moment he said nothing, while puzzlement furrowed his brow and made his gaze probe deep. "What are you talking about?"

She smoothed the napkin in her lap. Shook her head. "I can't explain. Let's just let it go."

"Okay," Colin said, ever so quietly. "Why is it you'll go out with that guy, that groupie you met on the phone, but you won't go out with me?"

"Is that a rhetorical question?" Ouch. Did she have to sound so snotty?

"No. I'd like an answer."

Emily drew a deep breath. Faced him. "He's not my boss . . . and he's a Christian."

Now it was she who watched, waited for his reaction, of which there wasn't much. He might have not heard or understood, except for the slight tensing of his jaw.

They finished their pie in fork-clattering, coffee-sipping silence.

Then he raised the question with a lift of his brows—*Ready to go?*—and she flashed a phony grin in reply. He held doors for her in silence, backed out of the parking space in silence, and drove them in silence down puddled streets whose light climbed over legs that didn't move and faces that stared mutely out windows. On the way over he'd driven with his shoulders relaxed, his right hand splitting its time between the gearshift and the steering wheel. Now the posture wasn't as easy, and he choked the shift knob. Just held on.

It didn't matter. Let it go. It would have come to this anyway. They would have dated a few times, made promises that had a short shelf life, fought for one reason or another, then shared the same space—a production room, the hall, the whole blasted station—in chin-jerking silence. She would have added another *unforgivable* to her list, and it wouldn't have worked anyway.

What was cute and elegant and sexy passed under the station's blue sign, pulling to a stop beside Emily's Rabbit. Somebody had to say something, and it sure wasn't going to be the pensive Mr. Kavanaugh who leaped in with a tension reliever.

"Thanks for the pie and conversation," Emily said, finally cautioning a glance at him.

"You're welcome."

She was tempted to say *I'll write,* or *Don't make a stranger of yourself.* He just stared, a stony expression on his stunning features. Better that she'd never seen them, never had the chance to wonder about the opportunity she pushed away.

"What time do you want me to come in on Tuesday?" she asked. Business as usual; she still had a show to polish.

"About the same time," he replied. Then he seemed to remember. "I'll get your door."

"Don't bother. I can get it." She flicked the easy little handle, making them both blink against the shock of overhead light. Then she realized she was still buckled in, and her cheeks flamed and her fingers shook while she fought with the lock to get free. It finally released and retracted; she was right behind it, calling "See you later" as she closed the door.

Colin and his BMW stayed in the parking space beside her while she unlocked her door, started the engine, backed out, and pulled onto Broadway. All the way home, he followed.

This meant war.

Colin stayed right where he was, waiting in the middle

of the street until the porch light died. Another at the top of the inside stairs replaced it, then a light on the right side of the second story flashed on, illuminating the network of branches in a tall tree beside it; Miss Emily was safely deposited in her apartment for the night.

Colin's was just beginning—and she didn't know the half of it. Tomorrow was his Saturday to be on the air from six to noon.

He slipped the shift into first gear and wheeled to the corner, glancing at the digital clock display while he waited for a pair of headlights to pass; 12:23. If it became necessary to cash in some favors, he'd have to do it before the bar rush started at two. He signaled a right turn and followed the blink of the light. A phone book would tell much, and home was only seven blocks away.

Emily pushed him off balance tonight—for about as long as it took to reach the car. Then he had time to retrace the conversation—and was so absorbed, it startled him when she spoke. He'd already concluded she could overlook the boss/employee thing eventually. She showed that by the way she said good-bye . . . and didn't want to. And the Christian thing? A temporary distraction. Brad, the groupie in the old red pickup truck, was the thing in her line of sight right now—and he needed to be eliminated. *That* was the first volley.

Thirteen

*T*here were two vehicles—an old Bronco and a Taurus—nosed up to the little metal cube that was Missoula Security Systems. There was no old red pickup truck. Since the other two of the three guard and patrol services in Missoula were out of town—one in Great Falls and the other in Portland, of all places—this could mean one of two things. Either Brad The Groupie wasn't working tonight, or Brad The Groupie worked for one of the others.

Colin turned carefully on the muddy road, heading back to civilization from the industrial area by the river. A few moments later he found what he was looking for, three Missoula city squad cars in the lot of the Thunderbird Cafe—'cause Floyd don't never charge for the coffee drunk by soldiers in uniform, be they foreign or domestic.

Bob Betancourt followed Colin's approach from the door. The other two had their backs turned, though one of them looked to be Stan DeBarba.

"Hi, Bob," Colin said as he strode past red pseudo-marble tops and chrome trim and slid into the booth beside the officer. "Hey, Stan, Dennis."

The men broke into smiles. Good. With any luck at all, he wouldn't have to pay too much time socializing before he'd earned what he needed.

It was Stan who spoke. "Hey, Colin. What brings you in here?" He cast a meaningful look at the other diners. "Can't be the women. Must be the food."

Dennis cast a glum look at the finger-paints of catsup on his plate. "It's not the food."

Stan flicked his cigarette over the ashtray in front of him. He was the only one smoking, but there was enough haze in the air to give everyone a dose.

Colin sat back and nodded to the waitress, who'd caught his attention and motioned with the coffee carafe. "Actually, I need a favor," he said.

The men groaned.

"Should have known." This from Stan. "You media people. Always a favor. You either want information, or—"

"You want information," Dennis repeated, playing the follow-up to Stan's crack.

Stan flicked his ashes again and gave a wet laugh that spoke of the garbage coating his pipes. Colin watched him suck a drag of smoke. He could tease about it, but of the three of them, he'd be the one to help. The reflection in his eyes had never been that of a disc jockey; when he looked at Colin, he saw just a guy.

Colin gave the waitress a thank-you glance. "I need some information," he said. The table broke into laughter, Colin chuckling no less than the others. "Hey, how many of those Police Association fund raisers have I emceed—without a dime?" he reminded them.

"That's all we made," Bob said.

More laughter.

"Too bad," Colin told him. "My talents don't come for free."

"Evidently not." This from Dennis. "I'm not the one driving a Bimmer."

Colin nodded his head good-naturedly, letting the laughter wind down. "What do you know about Missoula Security Systems?" he asked finally.

Three of Missoula's Finest exchanged glances.

"What do you want to know?" Stan asked.

"Who works there?" Colin asked. "I'm looking for a guy named Brad. He's supposed to be a roving security guard somewhere."

More exchanged glances. They shook their heads.

"You got a last name?" Bob, the most serious of the three, wanted to know.

"No." Colin shifted in his seat. "He's been calling my new female announcer, who works the night shift, but he's pretty cagey. I thought I'd try to find out what he's about."

Stan pulled a final drag of his cigarette, blew the smoke over his head, and tamped the butt out. "Has he made any threats? Followed her, that sort of thing?"

"No. Nothing concrete."

Bob shifted, the leather-on-leather around his waist creaking. The waitress carried three frosty malt cans to the teens quietly yukking it up across the aisle, and Tears for Fears sang a chart topper—ten years ago—from the juke-box in the next booth.

"There isn't anybody named Brad that I know of at Missoula Security," Bob said, "and I know Jensen, the guy who owns it, pretty well." He set his forearms on the edge of the table, glancing from Dennis to Stan.

"Not a name I know either," Stan added. "They're about all that's left. Cascade Security, that outfit from Oregon, shut down a long time ago."

Dennis agreed. "First of the year, I think."

"Yeah, and that other one, Rocky Mountain, had to

close the books because of a lawsuit," Bob added. He grinned. "Jensen was real heartbroke over that."

Colin sipped his coffee. A no was still an answer, pointing to the strong possibility that Brad The Groupie didn't work as a roving security guard at all.

Later, in the parking lot, Colin lifted his chin in farewell to Bob and Dennis as they drove off in their patrol cars. Stan's idled beside him, warming up.

"Guess I'll have to stop by the station on Monday evening to see who's got you so worked up," Stan said, forearms set on the top of the open car door.

For a long moment, Colin stared at him. "You're scary, you know that?" he said finally.

Stan chuckled. "Naw, just good at my job. Are you really spooked, or just trying to eliminate the competition?"

Colin shrugged. Shook his head. "I don't know. I can't explain it. Something just doesn't feel right." What kind of guy picked up women on the telephone? The unease chewed a little deeper.

Stan's smile disappeared. "That's called gut instinct. I'd pay attention. It's usually right on. What's her name?"

"Emily. Emily Erickson."

"What's she drive?"

"A blue Rabbit . . . four-door . . . about '84, with 'K' county, Idaho, tags."

Stan nodded. "I'll keep an eye out for her. In the meantime, check out this guy. Satisfy yourself. But Colin? Don't do my job. It ticks me off when I have to put my friends in jail."

Colin gave him a long stare. Stan was all right.

Emily shook her head at the grocery bagger and hooked the handles of the plastic bags herself. She sighed as they swung at her side. The world was a sad place when forty dollars' worth of groceries fit in three sacks. She dropped the bags on the passenger seat and fit the key into the ignition switch of her Rabbit. Should have half as much spare money as she seemed to have time. Still three hours until Brad—

The car didn't start.

It always started. Emily pumped the gas and turned the key again . . . held it . . . then let go; with Daddy on the road all week, she knew enough not to wear out the starter or run down the battery. She waited a few seconds and tried again.

Doggonit. What's the matter with this thing?

She jumped when someone rapped on the side window.

He watched Emily's features melt with relief when she saw his face. She rolled down the window, sweeping up the drizzle drops on the glass.

"What's the matter with it?" he asked.

"I don't know," she replied. "It was running fine. Now it won't start."

"Do you have a hood lock?"

She nodded.

"Release it," he said and stepped to the front of the car as the latch thunked and the hood popped up half an inch.

"What do you think the matter is?" Emily asked, closing the door behind her and stepping to his side.

Colin cast her a glance as he set the hood on its brace.

Casually domestic, she looked today, with her hair in a short ponytail, a gray heather sweatshirt under her parka and bagging just above her denim knees. She could be ready to scrub the tub . . . or brush the pebbles from the spot where she intended to roll out her sleeping bag. Except she'd probably never been camping. Not with her mom so sick. She'd try it though, judging by the way she peered at the engine as if she might spot the problem and fix it herself. She looked up, expecting an answer—and those eyes were incredible in the bright light, the facets meeting the day's brilliance spark for spark.

"I don't know," he said and returned to business.

Good for Gordon Erickson. The engine compartment was clean, the battery looked fairly new, the hoses were in good shape and—

The end of the coil wire wasn't connected to the distributor cap. It was dangling beside it.

"Here's your problem," Colin said, pushing the plug back in place.

"What's that?" Emily asked.

"The coil wire. It came off the distributor cap."

"Oh." She stared up at him, the picture of feminine trust and reliance. "How did that happen?"

"They vibrate loose sometimes."

"Should I try it?" she asked.

"It'll start," he said, except she was listening with only one ear. He followed her gaze to the other end of the car, and the vehicle rumbling past.

A pickup truck. A red pickup truck. An old red pickup truck. A GMC, to be exact, with a blue tailgate and a foiled hero inside. Rage rose in Colin's chest—very clever, the *slime.*

Emily swiveled back, her gaze crashing with his; hers held guilt.

Colin pretended not to notice, dropped the hood closed, and motioned toward the interior of the car. "Go ahead. Start it," he said, brushing the dust from his fingers.

As if profoundly relieved to keep his attention on her car, Emily nodded vigorously and dived for the driver's seat. When she turned the key, the car started, just like magic. Just as it would have if Brad The Groupie hadn't happened along and taken an opportunity to *make* an opportunity.

Covertly, without moving his head, Colin watched the truck join the line at the intersection beyond the parking lot. "Guess you're on your way," he told her, giving her a smile to match her own, though hers wielded more power than she'd ever know. He'd never be safe if she did.

"Thanks," she said, adding, "See you Tuesday."

"I'll be there. Oh, and Emily?"

She swiveled back.

"Lock your doors. Even when you're just going in the store."

Her brows furrowed in puzzlement, but he turned away, heading for the grocery store. Behind him, the Rabbit whined in its backing up and, a little more distant, a V8 rumbled away. Colin smiled to himself. He hadn't seen the guy's face, but he would. That was a promise, because coil wires didn't vibrate loose. Ever. They had to be pulled free.

Someone's hands fingered the ski parka, then the tag dangling from its sleeve. Though the price raised an eyebrow, the colors were classy. Tasteful. The shopper glanced around the store. The number of ads played had put a spendable sum on the station's trade account, and the parka was worth the price. And deserved; the shopper lifted the coat from the rack and carried it to the counter.

Colin heard the truck before he saw the headlights in the rearview mirror. Obviously the date began at seven, and Brad The Groupie felt as if he were late. Either that, or he always drove with his foot in the carburetor, probably so he could listen to those burned-out glass packs roar.

Colin curled his lip. So . . . high school.

He leaned over, pretending to reach for the glove box as the GMC splashed by, though the man behind the wheel had no reason to recognize a CJ5 that was almost never parked in the station lot. Few knew Colin even had a Jeep. Just in case Mr. Social Zero had the smarts to check it out, the Bimmer was stationed conspicuously under its carport.

With the truck parked down the street now, Colin sat up and reached for his coffee, watching over the rim as he sipped. As well as he could see by the porch light, Brad The Groupie dressed simply—jeans, denim jacket, dark cowboy hat. And Emily didn't keep him waiting; they emerged a few minutes later. When she glanced his direction, Colin automatically hunched between his cowboy hat and collar, though she wouldn't likely recognize him—not in this dark, in this vehicle, or in this purple-and-blue ski parka she'd never seen.

Colin shook his head when the mannerless cretin let Emily fend for herself with that big old door. Then he waited until the GMC got into the next block before he pulled in behind them, far enough away to blend with traffic and close enough to notice that Emily sat on her side of the bench seat. He stayed with them as far as Brooks, then watched as they sped through a light that should have been orange—and held him back. They faded into the distance, into traffic. He slid the shift back and forth in neutral. Stupid light. Followed the cars whizzing past from the left and right. Out of gear. Back into first.

Come on.

The light changed. He mashed on the gas and dumped the clutch. It didn't catch. Threatened to kill. Caught and lurched forward. He shot through first, and grabbed second. Third.

They were gone.

No wonder. The guy drove like his fuel economy was measured in minutes rather than miles.

"Do you want to ride to church together tomorrow, or shall I meet you there?" Emily asked once they'd settled at a table.

Brad frowned. "That reminds me. I'm not going to be able to make it this time."

The lilt of Emily's heart slipped a little. "Oh. That's too bad."

"I have to work," Brad continued. "One of the guys' wives just had a baby, and she's coming home from the hospital tomorrow. I promised I'd work for him."

She stared at her orange soda. Watched her thumb trace a path through the condensation on the glass. "You usually work Sundays? I wouldn't have thought there'd be much need for security then."

"That's what the thieves would like you to think," he told her. He reached across the table and patted her hand. "I'm sorry. I'll go next week. I promise."

Emily found a smile and offered it to him. Helping your neighbor was one thing, but missing church to do it? On the one hand, charity; on the other, letting the world take care of itself. It was a good question, and she had no answer. Couldn't even be trusted with steadier discernment, much less lines this fuzzy.

Fourteen

Colin peered left and right along the line of businesses. Fast food, car dealerships, banks, department stores, the bowling alley. Your Center for the World's Finest Sewing Machines and Live Bait, for heaven's sake, but no old red GMC pickup truck with a blue tailgate. He pulled into a fast food place and stared out the windshield, mentally tracing the streets and their businesses on this end of town. The parking lot smelled of tacos.

Of course. Food. Brad The Groupie would take Emily to dinner.

Colin wheeled into traffic to drive the circuit again—and found an old red GMC pickup truck at Little Italy Pizza. He parked in the row behind it, but only long enough to jot down some information.

"Aren't we going to pray?" Emily asked, then laughed when Brad jumped and dropped his pizza as if it were on fire.

"Sorry," he said. "I'm so hungry, I forgot." He smiled. "Why don't you say it? I'm kind of shy."

Back home, with the Jeep stashed safely in the garage and the stereo's CD changer loaded with a selection of Moody Blues, the Doobie Brothers, Dan Fogelberg, Pink Floyd, and Fleetwood Mac—no country music tonight—Colin gripped the edges of the padded bench beneath him and lifted his left leg, hefting the weight that taxed his quadriceps. They were probably finished eating by now. Probably on the way to a movie.

Three.

Or dancing, maybe—and Stan was no help; he had the next few days off.

Four.

What had Emily said? Nothing that made sense.

Five.

Colin ran through several deep breath cycles and changed position, lifting with his right leg.

"Don't ruin it," that's what she'd said. And something about leaving it alone. That they could have fun if they "left it alone."

Four.

Ruin what?

Five.

Colin wiped his face with the hand towel heaped on the floor, tugged at the wrists of his fingerless gloves, and sat at another bench. He aligned his forearms with the pads and clapped them together in front of him, arms and elbows each at ninety degrees.

One.

Women. Made no sense, always talking in circles it took a program to follow—"Don't ruin it."

Two.

Okay, he'd be sure to avoid that, whatever it was. Except, if he asked Emily what it was—just to clarify . . .

Three.

. . . she'd probably blink those lovely little eyelashes and say, "If you can't figure it out, there's no sense in telling you."

Four.

Colin blew several breaths and focused on the last lift. If he had a father to consult, the man would be just as lost as he was—or rolling in dough from the sale of his book *How to Understand Women.*

Five.

Colin let his arms fall to his sides, staring at his reflection in the mirror on the opposite wall. Face it. He'd hand over the title to the Jeep, what he owned of the house and the Bimmer, and his weight machine for one, just one, page.

Even before she opened the door, even before she smiled a greeting at Marilyn, even before she tossed a wave into Sterling's office, Emily's stomach tingled with anticipation . . . and dread. She strode straight for Betty's office.

"There you are," Betty said as Emily collapsed in the guest chair. "Where's your coffee?"

Emily leaped to her feet again. "Good idea." A moment later she was back, mug in hand. She slid out of her coat and draped it over her lap.

"You're sighing today," Betty said, glancing over her

reading glasses as she sorted a fan of billing on her desk. "What's up?"

Emily shot her a glance—*If you only knew.*

"Is it Colin?" Betty asked, showing herself to be marvelously astute—and willing to listen.

"We kind of had a fight Friday night," Emily said finally. "He wanted to take me out."

Betty's hands stopped their activity. "Oh dear. What did you tell him?"

"No."

"He got angry?"

"You could have tread the air like water," Emily told her.

Betty's head tipped to the side, her gaze shedding compassion. "What's worse, you like him," she said softly, sadly.

Emily's gaze fell to the floor between her ankle boots. She nodded. "I think I could like him a lot," she admitted, as much to herself as to Betty. With the confession came pain. Then indignation. "It seems like I never get to do what I want."

Just as quickly, the anger faded . . . and the sadness that welled in its place was as lonely as the tick of that old grandfather clock in the entry back home.

"I know," Betty said gently.

Emily looked up. Now would come the sermon, the Bible verses, the bits of wisdom.

But Betty only stared; if eyes could embrace, these did. "I haven't always been fifty-seven and safely married," she said. "I've been where you are."

The stereo speakers played a Brooks & Dunn ballad, Marilyn's phone rang, and Vicky's laugh crawled down the hall.

"What did you do?" Emily asked.

Betty's stare shifted to an obscure spot near the door. A ghost drifted past in her eyes. "Walked away. It was the hardest thing I've ever done," she said.

"You're not sorry?" Emily asked gently, hopefully.

Betty snapped back to Diamond Country. She sighed deeply. "Not anymore. I still see him occasionally." She paused. "Let's just say, his life hasn't been a very happy one."

"You might have changed that," Emily said. It wasn't impossible. Wasn't unheard of.

"It wasn't God's will," Betty replied. "He's pretty direct on His opinion about Christians dating non-Christians, Emily. He simply forbids it."

Emily's gaze fell to the desk, to the hands that had curled around Betty's mug. They were a mother's hands, the fingers slightly wrinkled, the backs definitely so and beginning to thin. The skin would be as frail as parchment in less time than had passed since it had been smooth and creamy.

"You'll find your way through this," Betty said. "You've been prudent this far. You're very levelheaded, you know. Far beyond your years."

Emily swallowed hard. She didn't feel strong. She felt like crying. If she were truly prudent, she'd give Colin her two-week notice. Go on a mission to Argentina. Or refuse to come to the station when she knew he was working—for what good it would do. His presence clung to every place he'd ever stood, strode, or spoken. That was his FM studio, his board in the production room, his lobby where he filled his mug and sprinkled the day with his wit, and his parking lot where a midnight blue BMW waited with such sass.

"Be his friend," Betty said. "That's what he needs most. But be careful and tread lightly. Meanwhile, I'll be praying for your protection—and wisdom."

"Thanks," Emily replied, though the offer seemed a feeble shield.

A moment later, she stepped to the threshold of the room that smelled of Colin's cologne, vibrated with his music—even though it was Starvin' Marvin playing it—and every third fixture and adornment gave back blue. It was his favorite color, that was plain.

"What color is your couch?" Emily asked over the irregular clacking and pause of computer keys.

Colin's head swiveled around. His eyes were just as quick in their pouring her into her shoes. "Oh, hi," he said, finishing the job with a dimpled smile, that mischievous tooth dancing just off center.

Her heart leaped with excitement, then contracted in pain, missing already what it had only dared look at. So what else was new? She was practiced at being a spectator.

"What color is your couch?" she asked again, stepping into his office. She set her coffee on his desk, her purse on the floor, and draped her coat over the back of one of the two guest chairs.

For just a second, his brow bunched in puzzlement. "Blue. Why?"

"What color blue?"

He chuckled. "Navy. Why?"

She sat and stared. How would it be, to be God, to look at such a creature, knowing you'd fashioned it? It had to hurt, had to stab His heart more fiercely than it stabbed her own. So beautiful, Colin, but lost . . . seemingly not even aware there was a God Who longed for his adoration, his fellowship.

Therein lay the problem.

If not the mission field in Argentina, perhaps she'd go to Africa. May as well. She didn't know Swahili, but neither did she speak Spanish.

"What are you up to?" Colin asked, setting folded arms on the desk—and that blue dress shirt could try all it wanted to. She still had a pretty good idea about what it concealed.

Emily shrugged. "Nothing. Just a theory. I figure navy blue is your favorite color. Am I right?"

His eyes smiled. Peered deep. He nodded slowly. "Very perceptive. I told you mine. Tell me yours."

The whisper of his voice made heat crawl up her collar. "Green."

"Green," he said, shaking his head. "Most women prefer blue."

She gave him a smug smile. "Most men prefer red."

"Touché. Have you eaten yet? I'm starved, and we can talk about your show over food as well as we can here. Better, in fact. I refuse to carry a cell phone."

A corner of her heart clapped its hands. "Yes. I mean, no, I haven't eaten."

It wasn't Cottage House Pancakes this time, but Hungry Doug's that Colin drove to. There were already three cars in the lot, a testimony to either the food or the prices, since the building looked as though it had begun life as a neighborhood market—which it had. The air smelled faintly of barbecue smoke, and the six tables and chairs on the right two-thirds of the room had plenty of space between them. For a good reason—the man behind the low work counter to the left rolled along a bank of cylindrical ovens in a wheelchair. He turned his chair around and broke into a happy smile.

"Hey, Colin," he called. "When did they let you out of jail?"

"When I offered to check up on you," Colin replied promptly.

Emily chuckled, and Doug laughed, a warm and hearty sound. He looked to be in his midforties, wore a green T-shirt and sauce-smudged apron, and had a thick mustache and graying hair cut tidy but long. "Well, I hope you're hungry," he said. "I been cooking all morning."

Colin smiled in reply and led Emily to a vacant table. A fortyish woman in a blouse and jeans brought them a menu and water, her smile as familiar as Doug's. Emily ordered a barbecued pork sandwich and an orange soda, which came in a can from the wall coolers left over from when they'd displayed cartons of milk and packs of beer. Colin ordered ribs.

"Thanks for helping me with my car," Emily said when they were alone again.

Colin set folded forearms on the table. "Any more trouble?" he asked.

"No. That was it."

He nodded. "Let me know. I don't mind helping."

It was a generous offer. His cheeks colored slightly when she told him so. Then the waitress set a brimming plate of saucy ribs and fries in front of him, and a plastic basket holding a plump barbecued sandwich and fries in front of her. It smelled delicious.

And it was time to pray.

Emily cast a glance at Colin, gathered a breath, and bowed her head. *Thank You for this food, Lord. Bless it to my body. And thank You for this job.* She looked up to find Colin watching her.

"Don't ask me to lead, but I'd join you," he said. "I mean, I wouldn't be offended, and I wouldn't mind."

Another polite offer—though it wouldn't work if its only purpose was to get her to go out with him. Still, she smiled. "Okay." She took a bite of her sandwich, then said, "You'd do well to buy stock in this place."

He nodded and went to work on his ribs. She watched his hands. Beautiful—if a man's hands could be so. Nimble but not overly long fingers, tidy nails, and a network of blue veins that gave relief to the flesh on the backs.

"Do you play a musical instrument?" she asked.

He looked over a ravaged rib at her. "Guitar . . . and vocal cords."

"Maybe I'll get a chance to hear you someday," she said, pausing long enough for another bite of sandwich. "You were going to tell me about my show," she said, returning to business.

"So I was," Colin said. He finished chewing the bite in his mouth, wiped his lips and fingers on his napkin, and took a big drink of water. "It's improving. You were tense; now you're limbering up, getting warm. But you're a little loose where you should be tight." The puzzlement must have shown on her face, for he added, "Your show will improve when you learn the value of outcues, Emily."

"Outcues?"

"Outcues. When you tell a story or add a funny quip, always have an outcue to wrap it up. Think of it as the punch line, then say it, and go right into the stopset."

"What have I been doing?"

"Banging around, hanging on to the mike as if you think you should say more," he replied. "At its worst, you'll hear announcers launch into this great story—they've got you, you're hanging onto the steering wheel, they get to the punch line . . . and keep on rambling. Explaining it. Beating the thing to death. Then, how do they wrap it up and get out of there?"

She waited.

"They say, 'Anyway,' mumble more garbage to try to save themselves, and finally disappear in a stopset or a song."

Yes. She'd heard that.

Colin scowled deeply. "It sounds so bad. The announcer feels like trash because this great story fell flat, and the listeners aren't happy either—not as delighted as they were when they heard the punch line. They aren't sure why it flopped, but they know it did."

"Am I that bad?" Emily dared to ask.

"Not even close, but you're loose enough that you could tighten up." He glanced up over another rib. "Just plan, Emily. Ten, fifteen minutes ahead. Know where you're going—write it down, if you have to—and don't open the mike until you're certain you can pull it off."

So simple . . . for Colin, who'd logged . . . what . . . fifteen . . . twenty thousand hours at a microphone in nine or ten years of broadcasting?

"Who taught you all this?" she asked.

The left corner of his mouth lifted, as if pulled by a memory. "Trevor Evans," he said, taking aim on another bite of rib.

He chewed; she waited.

He finally wiped his mouth and fingers. "Trevor was the PD at Rockin' 100 in Escondido."

"The station with the bathroom?"

He chuckled. "That's right. And I thought I was the next Wolfman Jack or something. So cocky. So sure. And so bad."

"You?"

Now his smile grew shy, before he caught the handle of his last thought and carried it forward. "Trevor was so subtle. He'd pop his head in the studio and say something like, 'Think outcue, Kavanaugh' or 'Rearrange what you say. That lady peeling potatoes in her kitchen can't go back and reread it.' Then he'd close the door and leave it to me to figure out what was wrong and how to fix it. He made me refine my approach my way."

"So you'd sound like you, not who you thought you should sound like."

"Very astute."

"No Wolfman Jack."

"No," he said softly, his stare growing steady, going deep.

It was no loss. This voice could assume any personality, from cartoon character to politician. Could throw itself to the furthest corner of the largest room or make itself private, as it was now, as if there was no urgency to memorize his face. As if he would forever share his insights and intelligence with her. As if he'd lifted every weight, built every muscle, for her pleasure. He cared about faithful dogs and nervous interviewees who spilled their hot coffee on tender flesh. Truly everything, he was . . .

Except.

Emily looked back at her sandwich. "This is really good."

"So you've told me."

Couldn't help but return her gaze to his face—where the sapphire depths of his eyes harbored something she hadn't seen there before. Just as quickly, it was gone. The air between them seemed to sigh.

"Pretty good for pack rat, isn't it?" he said, motioning to her sandwich. "You just thought it was pork."

"So Doug is not only a good trapper, but a master of disguise?"

Colin laughed. "You're quick, Emmy. Very quick."

❦

Someone's hands clacked the computer keys, conjuring letters that made words that made money. "Ski Marshall," the ad commanded; the typist would, and with the grand welcome of royalty— or the next best thing, as a "celebrity." Could even dress like one.

Fifteen

Stan's coffee was still steaming, waiting for him, when he strode into the Thunderbird Cafe Thursday evening, the leather on his belt creaking and a sidearm jutting from his left hip. Predictably, it was his left hand that lit his cigarette, held it, and hooked the mug.

"Did you get your elk?" Colin asked.

"Yes, sir," Stan replied. "A nice spike. Want some steaks?"

"Sure. I haven't eaten any wild meat in years." Not since . . . no, before that. That one was an unsuccessful hunt.

Stan swallowed a mouthful of bitter brew and hissed about it. "I thought you were a hunter," he said.

Colin had been mistaken for a gun man before. Couldn't be the BMW and Reeboks. Had to be the country music and Montana.

Or maybe others heard the shot too. Still.

"No," Colin replied, torn between saying the word as if he were perfectly willing to talk about hunting in Oklahoma, and the need to kill the conversation now. He'd driven fifteen hundred miles to bury that part of his life—and the man who'd lived it.

If the lawman heard anything unusual, he let it go, asking instead, "Did you get a last name for that Brad guy?"

"No," Colin said again, leaning back and stretching his right leg to pull his silver-on-navy business card from the front pocket of his jeans. He tossed it on the table. "I was hoping you could help me with that."

"What's this?" Stan asked, though he was already picking it up. His eyes scanned the license plate number penned on the back. "I'm not supposed to do this," he said, looking over the top of the card.

Colin just stared at him. *So what? Who would know?*

He still had some goodies in his bag of tricks. He could connect a voice-actuated recorder to the voice coupler on the phone system, trunked into the engineering room, to tape Emily's conversations with Brad The Groupie, except he had no taste for hearing her give the soft inflections of her voice to another guy. Especially since he could listen for hours and never hear even as much as the man's last name. He could tell Stan about the coil wire that Brad The Groupie had deliberately disabled so he could be a hero when he "happened along" and repaired it—a piece of work, this guy. But Stan would have an answer for that and any other "evidence" Colin raised. No, Colin wouldn't beg, wouldn't attempt to build a case. Stan either trusted him or he didn't.

The policeman tapped the edge of the card on the table, his stare speculative. He sighed. "Okay, but don't get stupid on me, Michaels. Don't let this information get you into trouble."

Colin used the Jeep to cruise by the address Stan had rooted out with his investigative smarts. Gladys Ann Stapleton's old red GMC pickup truck was parked in the driveway, as if it belonged there. As Colin passed, a skinny woman in a housecoat and curly gray hair stepped under the porch light, as if she lived there. A cat leaped the steps and ran between her legs to the inside, as if it ruled there.

❦

"I like your apartment," Gordon Erickson said, pausing over his breakfast sausage.

Emily scanned his face for any sign of sarcasm, but he looked sincere enough. "Thanks," she finally replied. "I pay more because it's near the university, but it was also the cleanest place I looked at."

She waited for him to suggest she return to Coeur d'Alene, where her room was vacant and free and pretty, but he only worked on his eggs. Give them another couple dozen breakfasts passed as amiably as this, and they might even like the same music.

Well, maybe that was a stretch.

"Why don't you stay overnight?" Emily suggested on a warm impulse. "I work tonight, but we could do something tomorrow. It's Saturday."

Daddy should have jumped on it, except he hesitated, pausing to wipe his mouth on his napkin. "I can't, honey. I'm sorry."

"Oh," she replied, not sure which was more profound—the disappointment or the surprise. "What's up? Do you have to work or something?"

He chuckled. Fixed great detail on returning his napkin to his lap. "No, I have a date," he finally said.

"A date?"

He looked serious—and grinned sheepishly. "That's right. Me . . . dating."

It was pretty absurd.

"Who?" Emily asked.

"June Gilson."

"Our neighbor? June Gilson from down the street?"

"Don't look so surprised. The four of us were always good friends. You knew Darrell left her a widow eighteen months ago."

Eighteen months. Not "a while back," but eighteen months, as if it had been discussed and counted out to be sure it was a respectable period. Perhaps, but it was June Gilson's mourning time, not Daddy's. Mother had been dead only six months, and June Gilson had been her friend. All those things forgiven, there was one fact about the woman that was paramount, and not to be cast aside with an easy chuckle.

Emily stared at her pancakes, at the syrup seeping into the golden cake. It was a double standard. All through her teen years, her social life had been limited by the nights she could get away, then cut further by whom she could go with: no unsaved boys. No non-Christians.

"What?" Gordon Erickson asked.

Emily set down her fork. Smoothed her own napkin.

"Emily, if you think—"

"It's probably none of my business," she finally began, reining the anger—the indignation and insult—while she tried to grant a privacy she never received, "but June Gilson isn't a Christian, Daddy."

The driver of the red GMC pickup cut the engine before the truck even lurched to a stop in front of the furniture store. He peered through the passenger window to the lot next door, cast in the white light of the KDMD sign towering over it. Just one car, a Volkswagen Rabbit. The studio window was the only one lit, its light seeping around the edges and down the split in the drapes.

He snugged his cowboy hat over his brow and tracked through the narrow bush bed that separated the one parking lot from its neighbor. Pebbles crunched under his boots—so many little helpers to choose from—as he looked to the curtains concealing her. They would conceal him too, because she wouldn't look. No rain, no snow, no reason to. So he strode to the solitary car and dropped to a crouch beside the front driver's-side wheel.

Colin checked his reflection in the bathroom mirror a final time—clean T-shirt, freshly showered hair, freshly shaven face—and eyed the bottle of cologne; naw, too obvious. She'd have to settle for Irish Spring. A few moments later, Bavarian Motor Work's transmission whined softly as he backed from the driveway, and Emily told him, ever so brightly, what to expect of the weekend's weather.

Hesitation created tingles in his stomach as he signaled the turn onto Broadway. He was going to a darkened office when there wasn't enough work to warrant it. Not on a Friday night.

Aw, so what if he looked obvious? Or maybe she'd never know his late night hours hadn't started until she had.

No, she'd see right through him. He should go back home and lift weights. Go to Barney's. Go sit on the couch with a bottle of Maker's Mark.

A date? with June Gilson? Mother's clothes were still hanging in the closet. Her perfume was still on the bath-room counter.

Emily pushed the green button, releasing the Charlie Daniels Band to fiddle its story into the Friday night that wasn't as bright as it might have been.

It was stupid to feel this way, but Daddy was wrong. Wrong to be so easily distracted—as if Mother's death were a . . . a relief. Wrong to be making eyes at June Gilson—she wasn't even attractive. And wrong to be flitting about with a non-Christian. *She* couldn't.

The deadbolt slid into its channel, Colin stepped into the darkness, turned to lock the door behind him—

And heard it in her voice the second she opened her mouth. Something was wrong. The untrained wouldn't notice, but Colin heard it. So it was alarm that seized his heart as he strode toward the FM studio, not even pausing to flick on the lights or pocket his keys. He looked in the studio window. Emily wasn't at the mike she'd just closed—

She rounded the door and walked right into him—and yelped.

Heart failure; the woman did dreadful things to his cardiac system.

"Oh, it's you," she said, slapping a hand over her chest.

Sure enough, she'd been crying. Even now, she wiped her cheeks and lowered her gaze to an obscure spot on his shirt.

"What's wrong?" he asked, gently gripping her arms.

She sniffled wetly, then had the audacity to say, "Nothing."

Emmy, Emmy, Emmy.

"I know," he told her. "Charlie Daniels always breaks me up."

She burst into a laugh, which died quickly. "I'm sorry. It's nothing serious. Just a . . . bad breakfast date."

Him again. And breakfast, now?

Colin dropped his hands and jammed his keys into the pocket of his jeans. No way he'd hold her, comfort her, when it was some other guy making her cry. As her boss, he could insist Emily cut the personal calls. He could demand she pay more attention to the job she was in that studio to do. Except he'd set aside that kind of objectivity and authority over her long ago. If either of them had any power, it was she.

She sniffed again, wiped the jaw line that would fit so nicely in the crook of his lips—and made him curse himself for still wanting to bury them there, even while she wept over some creep who'd never be good enough for her.

"Can you work?" he asked, as Charlie was about finished. When she nodded, his heart swelled with pride. He'd chosen so well . . . and so poorly. She was going to wad him up and leave him in a heap.

"I'm fine," she said.

And a liar, despite what she claimed. He caught that little tremble in her chin.

He motioned toward the rest room on the back hall. "Go on. Get yourself together. I'll cover you."

She looked up, hesitation in her eyes.

"Go on," he told her, starting past her to the FM studio.

"Thanks, Colin," she said, calling as she scurried away. "Just go into another song. I already played a stopset."

"Okay," he called back, though he already knew that. He'd been listening since he woke up from his little snooze on the couch.

She kept a tidy studio, unlike John Vaughn, who scattered every CD he used, or might possibly need in the next week, around him, or Starvin' Marvin, who papered the counters with a collection of the computer magazines he always brought along. Emily's only indulgence seemed to be an open and dog-eared edition of *Radio and Records* from the stash under the counter.

He segued seamlessly into Lorrie Morgan and slid the CD containing Charlie Daniels into the rack. He'd checked the playlist and was cueing up a Mark Chesnutt cut when the phone light blinked on and off. He glanced down the hall; still no Emily. He turned to the phone, his hand suspended over the receiver.

Could be him. Let's see.

Colin snapped it from its cradle. "KDMD," he said into the receiver.

Whoever it was, the caller didn't like what he said—or the octave he said it in. The caller hung up.

The old red GMC pickup truck rolled past the parking lot. The driver peered through the window at the cars parked side-by-side. That big shot—him and his pretty face and his fancy car—was getting annoying. Always stepping in the way. Would have to be dealt with.

The driver raised his arm to hurl the cell phone at the foot well, but mashed on the gas and shot down Broadway instead.

Colin might have come along behind her like a gentleman, turning off lights and now unlocking the door, but he hadn't asked her to pie. Hadn't said much of anything since that humiliating incident in the hall.

"I'm sorry," Emily said again. "That was pretty unprofessional, but I really was okay. I was just going to the bathroom for some tissue."

Colin merely nodded. No praise for how well she'd kept her show going, with tears streaming down her face. No reprimand for letting her personal life interfere with her work. Only a nod.

When he did open his mouth, it was to say, "There's usually a box of tissues under the counter." Then, "Betty has to keep the supply closet locked so people don't walk off with the toilet paper."

Colin held the door open for Emily to pass before him, but left her standing between the inner and outer doors, hanging in the silence cut only by his key fitting in the lock and the deadbolt arcing into place. He smelled fresh. Like soap and the leather of his coat. He looked as if his day had just begun.

"Well, thanks for everything," she said, pushing through the outer door. "See you next week."

Colin watched Emily step to her car, her chin ducked

against the cold. If she thought he was going to ask her to pie, she was crazy. Let Brad The Groupie take her. That's what she wanted. Whom she wanted.

Emily just happened to glance. Should have made it a habit long ago, as Daddy always reminded her, but she hadn't. This time she did, and it was so very obvious.

That tire was as flat as the proverbial pancake.

Emily watched Colin head for his car, thumb pressing the button pad on his key ring, disarming his car alarm and unlocking doors. Their gazes collided. She grinned and looked away. She couldn't ask him. Not tonight. She'd already been enough trouble, and he wasn't in the best of moods. She stared at the tire. The only alternative was to change it herself. She scanned the parking lot. Night. Lonely. Not even a moon to keep her company.

Nonsense. This was America, where the barter system was alive and well. In fact, this was the West, where a man came to the rescue of a lady.

"Colin?" she called, turning around.

He was bending sideways to open his door. He lifted his chin in question.

"Can I trade you a piece of pie for a favor?"

His dimples blinked in the dim light; his mood might be salvageable. "What's the favor?"

"I have a wounded hippity-hop."

"A what?"

"A wounded hippity-hop," she told him again. "My tire is flat. Will you change it for me?"

His expression slid away. "You're joking."

"Would I joke about an injury?"

Sixteen

*T*hat slime. That no good sneak, Bradley Earl Stapleton—twenty-five, five feet eleven inches, one hundred seventy pounds, blond hair, green eyes, still living with his mommy, Gladys Ann, and driving a pickup truck registered in her name—probably because he couldn't get insurance in his own. Look up "Driving under the influence," and he'd be listed as a reference.

Colin fought not to peer up and down Broadway. The cheat was out there, parked somewhere, watching his revenge on Emily for the fight they'd had. What more did he want? He'd already made her cry.

She stared at him, waiting.

"Sure," Colin said. "Tell me you have a jack and a spare that has air in it."

"I have a jack and a spare that has air in it."

He nodded and climbed inside the car long enough to start the engine and back it around so the headlights shone on her Rabbit. He pulled the pocket flashlight from its recharger plug in the glove box and motioned to the car. "Show me where the jack is, then sit in the Bimmer. The front seats are heated."

Emily didn't sit in the BMW. She huddled in her parka beside him, chatting amiably. He gave her custody of the flashlight—and frowned as he loosened the lugs. They weren't nuts, they were bolts, and Emily's little hippity-hop was going to be a nuisance to mend. She helped as she could, holding out her tender palm to assume charge of the lug bolts he spun off the wheel. He'd handed her the last of the four when a V8 roared in the distance. She heard it too, for her conversation tripped, and she looked toward the source of the noise as if she expected to see the truck glide down the street.

Colin lifted the little tire from the hub and set it aside. "No date tonight?" he asked, then thought about casting out a line to reel the question back. He didn't really want to know.

"No. Tomorrow," she said.

Definitely hadn't wanted that answer.

And that jerk wouldn't have flattened the tire if he'd known how miserable it was to change. No bolts on the hub to slip into the holes in the wheel, no bolts to hang the wheel on, and no guide to lining up the slots. Colin sighed—pain in the neck automotive engineers—and dropped to sit on the freezing pavement, straddling the wheel between his knees. After a moment of leaning over, peering into places Emily lit with the pocket light, he had the holes lined up.

She held out her palm of lug bolts. He selected one—warm now—and glanced up at her. The date with Brad The Groupie was still on, despite her tears. Not like any woman he'd ever dated. Waterworks meant a cold telephone receiver, or a campaign of begging that made a man think of taking the next flight out of town.

"Don't you have a date?" she asked, teasing in her voice.

He pushed the first of the lug bolts through the hole in

the wheel, then engaged the hole in the hub. Believe it or not, this was it, but he said only, "Not tonight," and let her wonder about tomorrow and all the nights after.

"I wasn't crying over Brad," she said suddenly.

The second lug bolt would have fallen to the pavement, had the thread not already caught. She was either startlingly perceptive, or he'd been way too transparent.

"Oh?" Colin said with artificial calm, extracting a third bolt from her hand.

"No," Emily replied. "It was my father I had breakfast with. It's complicated, but he's . . . well, he's dating again, and I'm not sure I'm ready for that."

Meaning, the tears were over Gordon Erickson, not Brad The Groupie, and the flat tire wasn't revenge, but rather another opportunity for the coward to play hero. In that case, if there were any justice at all, Bradley Earl Stapleton had gotten an eyeful of the two of them—his opponent and the target of his attentions—working side-by-side in the intimacy of night.

"Can you understand my being upset?" Emily asked, rising from where she'd hunched beside him.

Colin drove home the fourth and last lug bolt, then fingered them snug. "Yes and no," he said, stepping to the jack and lowering the Rabbit to its . . . paws. "Your father is lonely. It doesn't mean he didn't love your mother. Doesn't still love her. He just doesn't see the sense in being alone when there's a perfectly good woman across town who would make pleasant company for the evening."

"She's a neighbor," Emily said. "It's just so soon."

He returned to the wheel, lug wrench in hand. The lug bolts squeaked as he tightened them. He grunted with the effort, then shrugged. "To you. May be an eternity to him. It doesn't mean there's anything serious. Just dinner and a movie once in a while."

"Is it that simple?" she asked.

"I think it could be," he said as he rolled the flat tire into the beam of the headlights and took the pocket light from her to add its illumination.

The tire had good tread and no nails. In fact, there was no apparent reason for its empty chamber.

"Is it okay?" Emily asked, staring at the tire, arms tight against her sides, hands in the pockets of her parka.

"I'm not sure," Colin replied. Stapleton had done something to it, he knew.

He unscrewed the valve stem cap and felt around the base of the stem, where it was attached to the wall of the tire. No cracks, no leaks. He brushed his thumb over the cap—of course. Very handy, the snake, for if one wanted a tire to go flat, seemingly on its own and at molasses speed, a tiny rock in the valve stem cap would accomplish it nicely. Colin's jaw tensed. No telling how many flats Emily would have suffered—how many times she might have been stranded somewhere dark and vulnerable—before someone would have discovered that.

"What is it?" she asked.

"A little rock got jammed in the valve stem cap and held the valve open, but it's fine now." He put the jack and lug wrench in their storage places and began walking the perimeter of the car, unscrewing all the valve stem caps.

"How could a rock get jammed in there? I thought the cap was there for protection."

Quick and not easily fooled, she was, but so innocent of the truth that someone could deliberately set out to cause another harm.

Neither would she hear such a revelation from him. "I don't know," Colin lied, "but it won't happen again." He poured the caps into her hand. "Here. Your hippity-hop will . . . hop now, I believe."

"Thanks," she said, dropping the caps in her pocket.

He brushed his hands together, then wiped them on his jeans. He looked up. She was watching him, her head tilted to the side as if she were pondering something.

"What?" he asked.

"I was wondering how impulsive you are."

"Impulsive. Why?" He peered down at her through narrowed eyes. "What are you up to, Emmy?"

A smile leaped to her lips, her eyes widening as if she'd landed on a great idea. "Let's go to Boots," she said. "I know you're not tired. You just woke up. And I'm sure you have a clean pair of jeans."

Correct on all points, but he said, rather, "No pie? I don't get my pie, just because you want to go dancing?"

Her laugh lit the parking lot. "We can have pie too, afterward. And it's your fault," she said as if it really were. "I haven't had so much fun since the last time we went."

Mmm, she'd never know all she told him when she said that. Maybe it was time to see how impulsive she was.

"Actually, I was meanin' to talk to you about the pie and all," Colin said, awakening his Oklahoma accent. "You see, there's somethin' you need to understand about Southern gentlemen, Miss Emily. They buy their own pie, and that of the ladies in their company. We'll just have to come up with some other trade in this barter."

Her expression melted into dumbfoundedness. He almost burst into a laughter that would have ruined everything.

"I said I'd take you to Boots," she said in her defense.

"See? You're doing it again," he said, staring into her upturned face.

"Then, what?" she asked, so very serious. "You want money?"

He snorted. "That's worse. You keep insultin' me." He

paused. "I could forget the whole thing for a kiss."

Such a thief, the night, for she surely blushed. As it was, the colorless shadow outside the headlights' beam could do nothing to hide the embarrassed smile she tried to bury in the collar of her coat.

"A kiss?" she asked.

He puckered his chin, pretended to consider it, and finally nodded. "Yes. I imagine that would be just fine with me—if it's all right with you."

"Whatever happened to chivalry?" she asked, a playful challenge.

"It's still here," he told her. "My granddaddy would ask the very same thing."

"He would?"

"Purty girl like you? Yes, ma'am."

Now the smile owned her, propelled by the chuckle she let go, though she gave that to the limo parked over yonder.

"You should have told me sooner," she said.

"And give you the chance to change your own tire? Beggin' your pardon, Miss Emily—I may be foolish, but I ain't stupid."

She should have laughed, except her gaiety mellowed into a tremulous smile. "Okay," she finally said. "I'll give you a kiss."

"Don't move," he told her, holding up a finger and striding to the driver's side of the Bimmer. He turned off the headlights, plunging the lot into soft night . . . and Colin took his time. It wouldn't do to appear too eager, though his heartbeat stepped to a tempo that said what approached was anything but casual, anything but simply a payment to exact. He'd entertained this moment ever since he'd watched her sip from a cup of coffee in Sterling's office, a fresh stain on her jeans.

With large eyes, Emily followed his return. Stared up at him. Licked her lips nervously. Expectantly.

Don't be nervous; it's just a kiss, he wanted to tell her, except it would be a lie. *You sure are pretty* might have been more appropriate, though not for a parking lot. *You've been making me crazy for weeks* would have been more truthful, but a man could tell too much. There were times it was better to act first and talk later.

Colin looked into her eyes—those lovely, lovely eyes—gazed at her mouth—soft—and descended.

She was hesitant, nervous. Didn't even lift her chin to receive him. So he set careful fingertips at her jaw and gently tipped her face up—then fought the impulse to groan with satisfaction. No telling when he'd get this chance again, so he made good while he had it, pressing tenderly and moving his head slightly, to keep the kiss chaste, though more than a pucker-lipped peck. So it was even more an act of willpower to keep it as short as it should be—unless Emily wanted a longer engagement. Colin hesitated . . . and Miss Emily gave him no invitation to stay. He lifted his head—and grinned, for even in the darkness, his fingerprints clearly marked her jaw. He brushed at them with the back of his hand.

"What?" she asked, touching them herself. Her fingertips came back dirty. She rubbed, and laughed. "Did you get me dirty?"

"Just a little," he replied. Branded for life, he wished.

"Okay, you got your kiss and smudged my face," she said. "Are we even?"

Never, as his predicament was even more precarious than it had been before, but he only smiled and said, "Even." Then, in his accent, which seemed to delight her, "Come on, Miss Emily. I'll take you dancin'."

The old red GMC pickup truck was parked in the lot, and its driver was inside the building—not in bed, as he should have been at ten-thirty on a Sunday morning. He mumbled through the songs everyone else caroled out, obviously from memory, though the young woman on his left didn't appear to notice. She smiled up at him, so happy he'd taken her to a movie last night, so delighted he'd kissed her at her door—there'd be so much more of that later—and so very thrilled one of her simple little church's chairs was pressed to the back of his knees. He held a bark of laughter and returned her smile instead; if she only knew what an event it was.

Someone leafed through the yellow pages of the Missoula phone book. Time to branch out. Time to pick up some accounts not already on Betty's books. In fact, it would simplify the paperwork, create fewer questions, since there wouldn't be any regular station account to keep separate from the trade handled so personally and so very carefully.

Colin stood in the shadow to the side of his office window, coffee steaming in his mug, traffic passing on Broadway, and Doug Stone crooning from the stereo speakers.

There she was.

Colin jumped back, then eased forward as the Rabbit

hippity-hopped through the pull-out and claimed a parking spot. Emily didn't even look toward the windows. Too busy stashing her car keys in her purse and grabbing . . . what? Oh yes, a can of orange soda. Not one of the cola contestants; Emily never did anything the typical way.

As if it were a happy Friday, rather than a trudging Tuesday, she ran to the front door, her step light. She'd be calling hellos and heading down the hall in a minute.

Colin had stepped across the window to round the front of his desk when an engine outside roared loudly enough for its thunder to penetrate the glass. He swiveled back and looked out as the red pickup truck nearly lurched to a stop, it slowed so quickly and so drastically—then passed as slowly as if it were in a funeral procession. The driver peered out the passenger side window. The slime tipped his cowboy hat.

Colin's jaw tensed. He glanced at Emily's Rabbit, then his Bimmer. He'd adjust the BMW's alarm system, make it sensitive enough to scream at the drop of a snowflake, and the ashtray would be a safer place for its valve stem caps. He'd changed all the flat tires he cared to.

Seventeen

Emily assembled her cheeseburger and asked the question she'd been dying to ask since they sat down. "How's June Gilson?"

Gordon Erickson's eyes lit with a new fire. He smiled. "Fine. Just fine."

"So, do you go out much?"

Her father shrugged. "Well, only a few times—I'm not home except on the weekends."

Yes, she knew. Remembered too well all the nights he hadn't been there to take his turn.

"We have another date tonight," he added.

Friday night? So much for a leisurely afternoon. He'd have to hurry to get home in time. Emily held back a huff. Probably tomorrow night too. And don't forget lunch after church.

"We have so much in common," Daddy said after he'd sipped his coffee. "Did I tell you she used to live in Illinois?"

"No, you didn't," Emily replied, clutching for a polite tone.

"She did. Just down the road from where your mother

and I spent the first years of our marriage." He shook his head. "It's uncanny how the four of us moved to the same state, the same town, and the same block."

Perhaps the coincidence wasn't for his good, wasn't God's maneuvering.

"Only two of you now."

That brought her father's head up from his patty melt. "Does this bother you?"

She swallowed hard and set down her burger. Rearranged her silverware. "Mother's hardly dead, Daddy." Her heart constricted. She'd done this to him, made him lonely and looking. "Can you just forget that easily?" she asked, wishing she could.

"You're being unfair, Emily," he said softly, though no less urgently. "I haven't forgotten anything. I especially haven't forgotten how your mother died to me two years before her body finally gave up. She was sick for years before that."

It doesn't mean he didn't love your mother, Colin had said. *Doesn't still love her* . . . Advice from a man about another man—for what that was worth.

"Okay," she tried to concede. "All that aside, she's still not Christian."

That landed in a tender spot, judging by the way her father's gaze darted away, his features collapsing.

"Or doesn't that guideline apply to you?" she asked, driving another nail.

"You're being disrespectful, Emily."

"I'm sorry, but I think you're wrong."

For a long moment they stared at each other. Then he sighed, his shoulders falling hard. He set the wad of his napkin on the table. "I know," he said softly, "but I can't seem to help it."

Tears rose and pressed stubbornly in Emily's throat, for

he looked so sad, so utterly defeated. It would have been kind to reach out, to pat his hand and say how she understood. Except there'd been no kindness for her all the times she'd been torn between what she wanted and what she had to do. She'd set her life on hold too. And it wasn't kindness that pushed the tears back to the place where they'd always had to reside. It was reality, seldom kind and always patient in its waiting. Now or later, it would be faced.

I'm sorry, Emily. There's nothing I can do. Your mother can't be alone. Though he'd never said it, the knowledge had always been there, making her life less important than anything else. Everything else.

Anger rose in her chest, taking the place the unshed tears had vacated. If she had to admit it, Brad wasn't exactly her first choice when it came to dates, but sometimes the choices were made for you. At forty-seven, Daddy should know that.

"We don't always get what we want," she told him. "And 'wanna' is a feeble excuse."

Colin downed the last of his Maker's Mark, set the empty tumbler on the bar with a tinkling of ice, and waved a farewell to George. He checked the clock behind the bar; Emily was just closing her shift. No pie tonight, no dancing, and no easy laughter, for he couldn't be so obvious anymore. The bourbon on his breath would guarantee he didn't weaken that resolve and see her anyway. However, he could drive by the station, maybe even follow her home at a safe distance, just to be sure there were no flat tires.

Emily glanced through the studio's side window into the lobby; the room was dark. She stepped to the front window and pulled back the drape; the parking lot was empty, save for her Rabbit and the rain. All those cars passing on Broadway kept right on doing just that. She glanced at the clock. Ten thirty-seven. He wasn't coming. He probably had a date tonight—with a girl who would go to Barney's with him. It served her right. She'd turned him down flat, so he was with some other girl. Right now. Maybe even dancing . . . bending her backward—so cavalier—over one knee then the other, teaching her to "dip."

Emily stared at the phone. Sighed. Let the curtains fall closed behind her.

The next afternoon, Colin smiled to himself as he slid his wallet and business cards into the back pocket of his jeans and joined the walking traffic of the mall's midway. Vicky Millian was losing her touch, or the piranha in her would have recognized she needed to send a male sales exec to land The Fast Lane clothing store account. Store manager Stephanie Lee responded quite warmly to masculine attention. If what he wore in her store hadn't proved the point, what he'd bought—black jeans and two dress shirts, one blue and the other the color of Emily's eyes— had. Not all country listeners wore boots. Some wore Reeboks.

As he left, three more people entered. High volume, The Fast Lane. Definitely worth whatever the station's sales manager had to do to rope it into the Diamond Country stable.

Colin's gaze scanned ahead and landed on Stan

DeBarba, obviously off duty. He smiled and extended his hand.

"How you doing?" Stan asked, shaking it. He was dressed in a sweater and jeans and held a toddler on one arm. He turned to the woman beside him. "Gayle, this is Colin Michaels. You know, from Diamond Country."

Mrs. DeBarba smiled shyly from delicate features. "I know. Pleased to meet you," she said, adding, "I listen all the time."

Colin smiled his greeting and started to thank her, but was preempted by the preschooler at her hip. "Mommy, can we go look at the puppies?"

She followed the little boy's pencil arm pointing across the midway to a line of display windows brimming with tumbling white fluff balls. "Sure, honey," she told him, giving Colin an apologetic widening of her brown eyes. "I'm defeated already," she said, then to Stan, "You talk. We'll go look at puppies."

Colin watched her from the corner of his eye. A brood of two, she'd given her husband, and though she was hidden under a coat, the weight and rock of her stride said there was another little DeBarba on the way. Judging by the tender way she held that little hand, she was okay with the idea. Lucky man, Stan, who pulled away a tiny finger that was poking at his mouth and said, "I visited with a friend of yours last night."

"Oh?"

Stan nodded. "Bradley Earl Stapleton. DUI."

"Another one?"

"It gets better. I had occasion to pull up his record and got some new information from Hamilton. He has an assault charge pending."

That wasn't all; Colin waited.

Stan pulled at that miniature hand again; his touch was

gentle, but his eyes were hard. "It seems Mr. Stapleton likes to get physical."

The weight that landed in Colin's stomach was as cold and heavy as an anvil in January. "Women?"

"This one was a rodeo queen." Stan looked disgusted. "I've booked dozens of these guys. Perfectionist alcoholics who can't control themselves, so they control everyone else. Is he still harassing Emily?"

"Yes. Twice he's sabotaged her car—first the coil wire, then a rock in the valve stem cap. I just happened along both times. I think he was planning on rescuing her himself."

Stan shook his head, rousing Colin's sympathy. At least at the end of his shift, he knew he'd done some good, made someone laugh or the silence more melodious. There wasn't a string of creeps determined to stall and even retard his progress.

"Well, he won't be flattening any tires tonight," Stan said, finally kissing the pudgy palm that had discovered his right eyebrow and was happily pulling on the hairs. "He's in jail. We would have had to let him walk—we're so crowded, we're releasing all but the index crime offenders—but Hamilton wanted us to detain him. His arraignment for the DUI is Monday."

Which offered more benefits than Stan realized. Himself, he had to kick off the "Boot Scoot for Granny" dance at Boots at seven, but John Vaughn would take possession of the mike at eight-thirty or so . . . and if Emily had had a date on this Halloween night, she didn't now.

It was about time. He was ninety-nine minutes late, and

he'd better have a good reason. Emily marched into the hall to the front door, tossing contemplations back and forth—let Brad have a piece of her mind, or give him the benefit of the doubt?

She'd decide when she saw the expression on his face.

The wind blew her bangs as she opened the door, carrying a puff of scent—leather and cologne. Navy eyes, rich brown hair, and far too much muscle stopped the breath in her throat. "Colin!"

"Hi," he said, peeking past her. "Am I disturbing anything?" He motioned with the hands in the pockets of his sheepskin coat. "I was driving by and noticed your light was on."

"No—uh, no," Emily managed to say. "Aren't you supposed to be at 'Boot Scoot for Granny'?"

Brad hadn't wanted to go. If she'd known he'd stand her up anyway, she'd have gone without him.

"I handed off to John," Colin said. "Now I'm on my way to the Paramount. There's a movie I need to see so I can talk about it on my show next week." His dimples leaped, full-force. "How impulsive are you?"

Smart aleck. She lifted her chin saucily. "I don't know. Depends on which movie."

"Mel Gibson?"

"Ooh, Mel," she replied.

He rolled his eyes. "I don't know what's so special about that guy."

"You shouldn't," she said. "Let me get my coat."

Colin obviously never paid real money for anything; the high school kid at the ticket window called him by name and motioned him right through. Colin's privileges didn't include goodies from the snack bar, but he'd told her there wouldn't be a discussion about it before they even stepped up to the counter.

Emily watched his bantering—shy but playful—with the young woman bagging popcorn. He spoke quietly, though his voice still carried; anything polished and practiced got attention, like a Bimmer among Beetles. Those who didn't hear him, saw him. A woman heading toward one of the theaters nudged her friend, their attention zeroed in, and Emily's heart swelled with pride—even though it shouldn't have, had no right to. He wasn't with her, didn't belong to her, was just accompanying her. But he was standing beside her, and he was absolutely the most beautiful man in the room. Probably on this side of Missoula. Maybe the state. Perhaps in the English-speaking world.

There was more. Those other women could look, but they'd never know how well he imitated Donald Duck, Rastro the Dog, or Barney Fife. How gentle and hypnotic his Oklahoma accent, when he freed it. How efficiently he scanned the engine of a broken car, then how expertly he thrust his beautiful hands inside to fix it. How swiftly he sat on a cold slab of pavement to wrestle a stubborn tire. How smoothly his body swayed to music that seemed born in him. How he led her so masterfully that she felt as though the melody welled from within her as well.

He looked down at her, eyebrows twitching ever so slightly. She'd been staring. She grinned back—*Nothing*—except he made her heart ache with joy . . . and with need. It was sweet, this forbidden fruit, and so painful.

She isn't a Christian, Daddy. That's what she'd said.

Neither was Colin Kavanaugh, so it was only a matter of time.

Colin held the popcorn between them and smiled to himself each time Emily dug so indelicately for some, pressing the bucket into his hand. Miss Emily liked popcorn, orange soda, and, of course, Mel Gibson.

The popcorn was okay. Mel was better, though not by much. But the company was prime. She smelled soft, and laughed so delightfully, the show should have been a comedy. Too bad it wasn't a horror flick. The scary parts might have had her diving for a hiding place in his chest. No good movies like that anymore. Not like the ones Dad had reminisced about.

No Dad, either, so the circle was complete.

Colin glanced surreptitiously to his right, and for the umpteenth time. It would be so easy to slip his arm around her—except she'd surely send him a stern look he might never forget. Too soon. If she allowed him anything at all, it would be her hand—except it was busy carrying popcorn to that pretty mouth. Might be too soon for even that. Better to hang back, see what signals she transmitted as the night progressed. And she would. He'd make sure.

Eighteen

Emily craned her neck to see the door as she led Colin up the stairs to her apartment . . . and released a breath. No note from Brad that Colin would ask about, meaning all the explaining now belonged to Brad.

That worry alleviated, Emily shifted her attention to the next one—how to conclude this evening with Colin, who watched, silent, as she unlocked the door.

"Do you want to come in for a while?" she asked, while the door—the moment—hung there, not closed and not quite open. "I have some orange soda."

What was she thinking? He didn't even drink Coke. . . . The movies made this look so easy.

"I couldn't hold another bite," he said, motioning with the hands in his pockets. "Thanks anyway."

He'd saved her, though the stair landing they stood on slid into another silence as the conversation dangled awkwardly. Emily cast about for something to say. Looked up at him. Looked away. Looked again—oh, well, here goes—and followed the impulse. Setting a stabilizing hand on his coat buttons, she leaned up and kissed his cheek. He was just as quick, bending slightly to receive it.

"Thanks for everything," she said. "I had a wonderful time."

Now his lips widened, digging deeper indentations in his cheeks. "You're welcome," he said softly.

When she peeked through the last little crack of the door, he winked at her, setting a current of tingles to dart and dance through her like a charged electrical cable.

He wasn't any Prince Charming, but Emily was about the closest thing to Snow White he'd ever seen—and she'd kissed his cheek. Voluntarily. Her own idea. A signal.

Colin managed—just barely—to wait until he got outside to begin whistling.

I'm sorry about Saturday night, the note said. *A security issue called me out of town at the last moment, then my mother fell ill. Please find it in your heart to forgive me. I'll call you Monday night. Love, Brad*

Emily folded the sheet of green steno paper, closed the front door with her foot, and carried the cardboard box that served as laundry basket into the bedroom to the left of the hall. She set the paper on the aged chest of drawers as she passed. If it had been work that had made Brad stand her up, she could hardly stay mad at him. In fact it seemed unpatriotic to grant no grace to one so very conscientious of his civilian corner of crime prevention.

"Hi," Emily said to the man on the other end of the phone line on Monday night. "How's your mother?"

"Better, thanks," Brad replied. "So you got my note?"

"Yes," she said, sliding a CD into a player and nodding a farewell to John Vaughn as he passed the hall window on his way home.

"I'm sorry. It couldn't be helped," Brad said.

"That's okay," Emily told him, though the night had turned out far better than just okay. "What took you away?" she asked, as much to keep him from asking what she'd wound up doing that night as out of curiosity. "Something with work?"

"Yes, but I'm not at liberty to talk about it," Brad replied. "Just something we were helping the cops with."

"Sounds important," she said, cueing up a Tim McGraw song.

"It was," he replied, matter-of-fact. "Sometimes they're lucky to have us. I have more law enforcement experience than most of the boys on the force."

Emily's smile faded. That sounded like a bit of an over-estimation.

The studio light blinked on and off.

"Brad, I have another call. Let me put you on hold," she said and answered the second of the four lines.

"Emily?" the voice on the other end asked.

Emily gasped. "Stacy? Where are you? Just a minute, I've got a call on the other line. I'll be right back." She checked the clock—still two minutes left in the song—and pushed phone buttons. "Brad, it's a girlfriend of mine from Coeur d'Alene. Can I talk to you later?"

"Sure," he said, though he sounded more disappointed than willing.

"Stacy! Tell me you're in town," Emily said when she got back to her friend.

"Sorry, I'm at the good ol' student union building," Stacy replied. "A bunch of us are studying. Our first chemistry exam is tomorrow, and it's going to be a killer."

A year behind Emily throughout high school, Stacy was just getting started on her second and last year at North Idaho College. It had been Emily who'd cut the trail.

"You have Dr. Bayer, don't you?" Emily asked.

"Who else?"

"Study hard, Stace. If he talked about reduction reactions in review, he'll put oxidation reactions on the exam. He turns everything around." She'd studied at the kitchen table until she was cross-eyed and never scored higher than a C on any of the tests. "The good news is, he grades on the curve—which starts in the single digits."

"That's what I hear, but let's not talk about school. How's your job? Did you ever find out if that guy with the really long hair is married?"

"John Vaughn?" Emily asked, starting the second song and making sure the third was cued up. "No, he's not married, but Daddy would flip anyway. Even if John were a Christian, his hair is longer than yours and mine put together."

"Too bad. He sounded cute in your letters," Stacy said. "Speaking of church, any guys there?"

"Not that I've really had a chance to meet. I mean, there hasn't been time."

Mostly because she hadn't made it to Sunday School, where the real getting-to-know-you happened, though Stacy didn't need to hear that. Emily would tell her everything when there was something to report.

"Did I tell you there's a girl in my psych class who's been out with one of your DJs?" Stacy asked.

"Which one?" Emily asked, though dread built in her stomach; John Vaughn had already been mentioned, and

Starvin' Marvin Matthews was married.

"Michael something," Stacy replied.

"Colin Michaels," Emily corrected, "and he's not just one of the DJs. He's the program director—my boss."

"Really," Stacy said as if the news might melt in her mouth. "She said he's a user. A real jerk."

"He's not a jerk. He's a nice guy. And I've heard all that. I think it's a bum rap."

Silence. Then, "Oh, no. He's already moved in on you."

"He hasn't moved in on me. We've just had pie and lunch a few times. He's been training me."

"You should have heard how he treated Laura," Stacy continued. "It was all romance one night, and the next day he acted like he hardly knew who she was. He was doing one of those live broadcast things in the mall in Missoula, and you would have thought—"

"He was working."

"He was rude."

Emily straightened her shoulders and lifted her chin. "Well, that's not the man I know. He's nothing but a gentleman to me."

"You've got something he wants—and you're his employee. How else is he going to treat you?" Stacy wanted to know. When Emily made no reply, she sighed. "Just be careful, Em. From what I hear, he's pretty smooth."

And you're so inexperienced, that's what Stacy was really saying.

Emily might have told her friend, *Don't remind me of how few dates I've actually had,* or *I'm alive for the first time in my life.* Instead she said, "It's okay, Stace. I know what I'm doing."

Emily caught the motion out of the left corner of her eye on Tuesday. Proudly, she kept right on reading until she'd said the last words of the commercial—"The Fast Lane clothing store in the Mountain Valley Mall, Missoula"—and closed the mike. Then she looked to the hall window.

Colin, leaning against the frame, arms folded thickly over his chest, raised his eyebrows in question. She smiled and waved him inside.

"Hi," she said as he closed the door behind him, a motion that puffed a wave of musky cologne her direction.

She dropped her pen on the counter and lifted the headset from her ears. With any luck at all, that spot would sound good enough on the playback to keep, which would leave her only one more to cut.

"You weren't here when I came in this morning," she told him—and she'd definitely looked.

"I've been running all morning," he said, "and I'm not finished yet. I have to go to Piano Bench Music to get a copy of the 'William Tell Overture.'"

"For what?"

"Little Italy Pizza just added a delivery service, and I'm creating an ad to announce it."

"The theme from *The Lone Ranger* and pizza delivery?"

Colin shrugged. Grinned sheepishly.

Emily couldn't help but laugh. "Very clever."

"Thanks," he said. "I thought we had a copy around here somewhere, but I can't find it, and it's probably on vinyl anyway."

"Do we even have a turntable to play records on?"

"Back in a corner of the transmitter room. I'd have to wire it in."

No doubt he knew how. He could do anything—including dance. "I had fun Saturday night," she told him.

Colin motioned toward the board behind her. "Is your mike open?"

Emily turned to the controls over her right shoulder. "No," she said, but pressed buttons anyway.

He leaned against the door, hands in the front pockets of his jeans. Today's shirt was purple, deep and rich and seeming to have navy accents, except it was only the color of his eyes.

"Good. I had fun too," he said. "Which brings me to my next question. What are you doing after work on Friday? Would you like to go dancing? Probably some pie afterward?"

"Sure."

"This wouldn't be business, Emmy," he said quietly.

The seat beneath her seemed to fall away, then suck her into place. "We've already talked about this," she told him, turning to the stack of production copy, gathering it.

"We've already been dating," he said. "For weeks, though we've called it by other names."

Don't say that. Take it back.

"Is that what you meant when you said, 'Don't ruin it?'" he continued, as if privy to her thoughts. "So long as we pretend it's business, it's okay? If we always drive away from the station, that keeps it from being a date . . . officially?"

"No," she said, tapping the papers on the counter, evening the edges. "It's not like that."

"Then how is it?" he asked, still so quietly.

She shouldn't have kissed him. Shouldn't have let this go so far, though it felt as though the merry dance to here, the place where she would have to give it up, had barely begun. At least, she wasn't nearly ready . . . or satisfied.

"We left from my apartment on Saturday," she said, looking up, building a case.

He shook his head. "Spur of the moment, just like last

time and all the times before that, and I'm not doing it any-more, Emmy. I won't be here at the station when you get off the air Friday night. Shall I pick you up at your apartment? Say, about eleven-thirty?"

Nineteen

*I*t was a cruel question Colin asked. An ultimatum, really—asking her to date her boss. Asking her to act as if the reminder she'd given Daddy didn't apply to her. Asking her to tell Betty to stop praying for a prudence and protection she didn't want.

As if summoned by a legion of angels, Betty strode by the hall window and waved.

Emily sent her a grin she didn't feel and turned back to Colin. "I can't do it," she said softly.

"And I won't do it the other way. Not anymore."

Across the short stretch of floor, over the end of the counter, they stared at each other, the room in silence . . . but not silent. Not like the vacuum in a house where no conversation resounded, where the only other inhabitant lay dying upstairs. Where the phone never rang, no one knocked on the door, and a fork poked at a plate at a table set for one. Though the expansion and contraction of Colin's lungs couldn't be heard, he breathed into the space around him, making the silence inhabited.

He's a user, Stacy had said. *He's pretty smooth.*

God is pretty direct on His opinion about Christians dating non-Christians, Betty had said. *He simply forbids it.*

Tell Colin no, and he wouldn't ask again, making Friday night emptier than it had ever been—maybe more so, for the knowing of what it used to be, could be. No different from the Thursday night before it, it wouldn't be a celebration of a work week survived, but the prelude to the solitary weekend to follow—except for Brad, of course.

Brad. Very Christian, and very . . . not Colin.

"Tell me you'd rather spend the evening with Jay Leno, and I'll have to seek counseling," Colin said suddenly.

Breaking Emily into laughter. Which died as quickly as it leaped to life. "How . . . do we . . . handle this? How do we act . . . here?" she asked—hypothetically, of course.

"As we always have. We seldom see each other, so it's hardly an issue." He shrugged. "Vicky Millian and John Vaughn see each other on the side."

"They date?"

"It's ludicrous that they pay two rents."

Oh.

Colin grinned, dimples peeking, and pushed forward as if the decision were already made. "While you're at it, why don't you set aside Saturday night too? I have a special place I'd like to take you to dinner—that is, if you aren't busy." He lifted his brows in question, drawing a grin from her.

"Why should I give you both nights?" Emily challenged. "Maybe I won't have fun on Friday."

You're joking, of course, his expression said.

It was a little farfetched, and the decision was made—by default; she hadn't said no. However, when the door closed behind him, he took all the assurance with him. Emily stared out the hall window he'd glided by. Stared at the floor where he'd stood. Stared at the production in hand.

Foolish. Trouble. Could cost her her job, not to mention her heart. She should step across the hall to his office and tell him she'd changed her mind.

In a sudden flurry of activity, she separated out the copy for This-Is-the-Life Hot Tub and Spa and turned back to the board. A knot balled in her stomach. She told it this was no big deal, little different from the other times they'd gone out dancing or chatted over decaf and pie. Vicky Millian and John Vaughn were going out, and Sterling hadn't fired them. Gordon Erickson and June Gilson were going out, and no lightning had pounced on them. It was no big deal—just this once.

Betty passed the window again, heading the other direction. Emily waved, though she slipped from the station that afternoon without stopping by her office to say hello.

"Hi," said the masculine voice on the other end of the line, so slowly, so intimately, and as if Emily should know exactly who it was. She did, but it was still irritating.

"Hi," she replied, then wished she could rerecord the tone of her voice.

Brad heard it too. "Are you all right? Are you mad at me or something?"

Emily sighed, dreading what was probably coming up. "No, I'm a little tired tonight. That's all." It was no falsehood; a Thursday was a Thursday.

"Well, I'll let you go, but first, how about a movie Saturday night?"

Emily's heart fell to a cold puddle in her stomach. She nearly groaned. Did so silently. It wasn't as if she was practiced at turning down dates. "I'm sorry. I can't," she said, and winced.

Let it go, Brad. Please, let it go.

He didn't. "Why not? You have to work or something?"

She couldn't lie. Wouldn't lie. "No . . . I'm already busy."

Busy with a non-Christian, because she hadn't wanted to spend Saturday night alone. And here was a Christian offering to remedy that. If she'd stood strong, she would have had another choice. God had provided.

Just this once, anyway. Please, just once.

"Oh," Brad said after an eternity of silence. "With one of your girlfriends?"

Emily bit her lower lip. Of course he wouldn't make this easy. "With a friend," she said, adding, "I need to go for now." Then, as a consolation, "Maybe I'll talk to you later."

"Okay," Brad said, except the tight tone of his voice said it wasn't.

Someone scrolled through the assortment of ads, stopping the cursor at the new thirty-second spot Emily had recorded for The Fast Lane clothing store. It was paying off, this little exercise—not because the trade items were especially costly, but because they could trickle in for years. No one would catch on, and the advertisers were only too glad to barter in trade—even Stephanie Lee, who'd been an elusive catch. Emily's voice, those wonderful pipes, had lassoed Stephanie in; she liked men, but supported women. Soon she'd see the whole new market KDMD could bring her, that not all country music fans wore cowboy boots.

The someone slipped the spot into the 7:00 A.M. hour on Friday.

Emily leafed through the paper copy—the official copy—of the program log, turning pages that were also hours of the day. Colin had played her spot for The Fast Lane clothing store this morning. It was silly, but she wanted to see where he'd checked it off. With such a graphic reminder, he'd probably thought about her—the way she'd been listening and thinking about him.

Fridays were busy; it took two pages to represent each of the crowded hours between 6:00 A.M. and 6:00 P.M. She ran her finger over the signature at the bottom of the page for the seven o'clock hour. *N. M. Kavanaugh*—black ink and artistic, with large sweeping capitals, and tidy script trailing behind. It looked as beautiful as if it belonged on a million-dollar contract, and it was readable. Nothing more presumptuous than a signature that couldn't be read—as if the signer should be recognized simply by the shape of his name.

She turned to scanning the list of commercials, and they were many. Fifteen minutes' worth, the total at the bottom of the page reported.

She must have missed it.

She started at the top of the list again . . . and it wasn't there. She picked up the log and peered more closely. It had to be. She'd heard him play it.

There was a vehicle parked beside Emily's Volkswagen when she stepped from the lobby to the parking lot, but it wasn't a BMW. It was a truck.

Emily turned to lock the door behind her. This hadn't

better take long. It was already 11:17. She pasted a smile on her face and trotted around the front of the pickup to the driver's side window. "What are you doing here? I thought you had the night off."

Brad turned down the radio—KDMD—and propped his arm on the window. "Just thought I'd stop by and see if you'd changed your mind about doing something tomorrow night."

Emily bit her lower lip. "I'm sorry. My plans haven't changed."

"Well, how about tonight? We could get something to eat."

"I'm sorry. Not tonight."

He nodded slowly—*I see.*

It was probably already 11:20. Colin could be backing out of his driveway. If she was very late, he would think she'd changed her mind and stood him up.

Emily resisted the urge to bob up and down impatiently. "I'm sorry, Brad. I need to go."

He stared through the windshield. Chewed the inside of his lip. "Okay. I'll give you a call next week, if I don't see you sooner."

No telling what he meant by that, but she smiled—anything to get away. "Thanks for stopping by." Then she waved and trotted to her car as he lit his headlights.

❦

The wooden steps groaned painfully under his boots, and its mashed-down runner smelled musty. Her door was ajar as Colin lifted his knuckle to knock. He tapped anyway, a light disturbance that pushed it open.

"Emmy?" he asked, peering down a darkened hall.

There were rooms on either side, lit by table lamps—a miniature living room under the right dormer, and . . . ah, yes, a bedroom under the left. The bed was made, though the jail-cell iron foot board was decorated with a collection of castoff clothes, and two tall stacks of library books seemed to make the night stand a three-tiered affair. Clean—no dirty dishes or remnant fast food trays—but cluttery, and Emily liked to read.

Colin might have stepped inside for a peek at her literary preferences, except a mumble caught his attention. She stood in a wedge of light from a room at the end of the hall, off what looked to be the kitchen. She was brushing her teeth. She held up a finger—*Just a minute*—and darted out of sight.

He held the chuckle and leaned a shoulder against the jamb of the living room arch, which gave him another study of her bedroom. Her pillows—it was a double bed—were strewn with stuffed animals, all of them Disney characters. Donald Duck held the paramount position. No wonder she laughed so whenever he used his Donald voice—

"I'm sorry I'm late," she said, stepping into the hall from the dark abyss at the end of it. "Everything ganged up on me at the station. I had a nasty time getting away."

Nasty—that's as raw as it gets. Too refined for anything else, Mama would say.

"No problem, I presume," he said, smelling hand lotion and toothpaste as she approached. Maybe she hoped to get kissed.

She smoothed her sweater over her jeans as she stepped past him to the living room. "No. The Teletype just ran out of paper and someone called to get a football score and—oh, it was just a hectic time, that's all."

Then she turned in the center of the living room, in

the center of its soft lamplight, giving him a brilliant smile. Her sweater was one he'd never seen before; the palest, most delicate of greens; it did things to her eyes that were anything but genteel, anything but polite.

She'd get that kiss. Curse him, if she didn't.

With an effort—it wouldn't do to stare—he looked past her to the room, to the brown shag carpeting, the contraption that was too short to be called a couch, and the matching chair and side table set before the wide window. The upholstery was an orange and brown plaid he might have had in his first apartment, and the piping on the cushions held the corners, but crawled over the edge in the centers, remembering the pull of a thousand . . . backsides. The table appeared as if it had served a few keggers, and the window was covered by pull-down shades and white sheers whose ornate pattern looked horribly out of place.

"Do you like it?" she asked suddenly, snapping Colin's attention to where she stood near the floor lamp lighting the room, coat in hand.

"Your apartment?" he asked.

She nodded.

"It's nice," he said. Not expensive, not of this decade—or even the one before it—but clean and in good repair.

"Next time you come, I'll play some Bee Gees music, you know, to complete the mood," she said.

He laughed. There'd be a next time. She'd said so herself.

Twenty

Colin was wrong; this time was different. Different in the way Emily combed her hair so carefully, freshened her mascara, and changed into a dressy sweater. It was different in the way Colin helped her into her coat and walked beside her with his hand riding the small of her back. In the way he seemed to command her attention, her pleasure, and her entire existence. They weren't colleagues having a good time in the same place. Rather, she gave herself into his hands for the full night, until he returned her to her doorstep and saw her safely inside.

Emily watched him turn the ignition key and slide the shifter into first gear. Beautiful hands. Large. Capable and trustworthy.

The good thing about hitting Boots this late at night was the crowds had thinned of those who had to rescue a baby-sitter; the dance floor had maneuvering room.

"Tell me about your family," Emily said suddenly.

Colin scanned her face as they danced.

She didn't look as though it had been a malicious question. Of course it wouldn't be, in intent . . . except it still cut. He shrugged. "What's to tell?"

"You have any sisters?" she asked.

He nodded and changed their direction, two-stepping her backward. Maybe she'd lose the interrogation in the need to concentrate on her steps.

"What are their names?"

Okay. Maybe he could feed her enough to curb the hunger. "Holly is the youngest," he said. "She's twenty-two."

And he'd missed everything. Her graduation from high school. Her first date with some pimple-faced Casanova with bony shoulders. She could be dancing on the same floor, and he wouldn't know her. It was a sure bet, she wouldn't know him.

"Karen is the older one," he continued. "She's twenty-four."

And probably married with a couple of kids. A lot could happen in nine years. The last time he'd seen her, she'd been changing from an awkward, gangly adolescent to a little beauty his buddies eyed when they came to the house. Boy howdy, he'd thrown some punches over that little girl, though she would have been mad as a wet cat if she'd known he'd ruined her chances with them. She probably wouldn't recognize him either.

Emily was getting that inquisitive glint in her eyes again. "Admit it, you're beginning to like this music," he said.

"I'm beginning to like this music," she conceded, then leaped right back on the track. "Any brothers?"

He leveled his expression and gave her what she wanted. "Younger. Bryan. Between me and Karen."

"Were you and your brother close when you were growing up?"

"We spent most of our time fighting. We were too different. He liked school, and I liked cars."

That broke her into a smile. "Don't you know? Opposites attract."

He answered that by lifting her hand, twirling her clockwise, and leading her in a ballroom dip over his left knee. She came up laughing too hard to ask any more questions, so he dipped her over his right, just as the song ended . . . and segued into a slow tune, a two-step gentle enough to pull her close. She hesitated—sort of an uncertain glance—before letting him draw her into his arms. She never did quite settle in, though she did give him a shy grin when he pulled back and looked down at her.

Neither did he get his kiss later, at her apartment, for she unlocked the door and slipped inside before he had the chance to try for it. She peeked at him through a crack in the door. Silly girl, thinking he'd be so easily thwarted. It wasn't a question of what, only a matter of when.

"I'll pick you up at 6:15 tomorrow night," he told her.

She nodded. He was halfway down the steps when she called to him. He swiveled, peering over the banister at her.

"You're on the air in the morning, aren't you?" she asked.

Inwardly, he groaned. Didn't need that reminder. He nodded, adding, "Don't stop by. I don't intend to do much more than crawl out of bed, throw on some sweats, and brush my teeth."

She laughed—a sweet-dreams sound for a man on his way to bed. Her smile relaxed. "Sorry I kept you out so late."

She'd have his undivided attention until fifteen minutes before he was on the air, if she only said the word, but he simply replied, "My pleasure."

"Where are we going? What shall I wear tomorrow

night?" she asked in a rush, as if anxious to keep him.

"Some place I think you'll like." Some place he'd always wanted to try, but had never had anyone he felt inclined to take; it wasn't the sort of place a man went alone. "What you wore tonight is fine," he added.

She nodded. Smiled. But opened that door no further.

He resumed his descent down the stairs. "See you tomorrow, Emmy."

Colin took a mischievous delight in keeping their destination a secret, as if it were more than a surprise, but rather a gift he offered. Emily finally gave up asking and sat back in the leather seat, watching dim meadows, lit by a full moon, alternate with groves of conifers that crept down the steep slopes. Once they turned onto the road that wound into the canyon, and eventually over Lolo Pass, dense woods swept from one side of the windshield to the other and back again before they sped from the arc of headlights like a picket fence. Sensation wrapped about her, the stereo's gentle rock and roll—Peter Cetera, Celine Dion, and Jon Secada—and Colin's fragrances—musky cologne and leather coat. She sighed happily. Rich, it was, and far too real to be taken in at once. It was tempting to slice it off, feel it a bit at a time—and save some for later.

"It's beautiful, isn't it?" Colin asked, adding another sensation to the swirl, this one more intimate.

Emily rolled her head on the headrest, staring across the console at the man whose voice could be charming the Rolexes off advertisers in L.A. rather than straining to climb out of a Montana valley. "Do you miss Oklahoma?" she asked.

He shrugged. "Sometimes."

She shifted in her seat, turning toward him as far as her seat belt would allow. "What ever brought you to Missoula? How did you wind up on the Diamond?"

He chuckled once. "You don't want to hear that."

"Yes I do."

He slanted her a glance. Stared ahead. "Nothing to tell, really," he finally began. "I started at KIMA, that daylight-only AM, in high school, then I went to Rockin' 100 in Escondido—where I learned so much from Trevor Evans. I was there a year and just got tired of California. I didn't want to go back to Oklahoma, so I gave notice, pulled my FCC license from the wall, filled the gas tank, and headed north."

"You're kidding," Emily said, though the mental picture of it was anything but comical. Boxes of possessions stacked in the back seat—as Betty had said—the entire contents of the bank account in his wallet, and no address. "You just got in your car? With no place to go?"

"That's about the size of it."

"Where did you go? Where did you sleep?"

"First I followed the coast," he told her, "except nothing really appealed to me, so I hung a right at Washington."

"And stopped in Missoula, because you loved it on sight."

He chuckled. "Not exactly. I didn't dare go any further. I was nearly broke, and my car was dying. The suspension was shot."

Emily took a side road, asking, "What kind of car?"

That made Colin smile. "A '72 Camaro. Blue, and so sweet." He shook his head. "I should have never sold it, except it was getting to be a hassle to fix. I mean, I did the work myself, and parts weren't expensive, but what was I supposed to drive while it was up on blocks?" He shook his head again and stared out the windshield as if seeing a tender, homesick memory drift by.

The conversation fell away. He seemed content to let it; Emily wasn't. "Okay, so you were in Missoula, and your car wouldn't go any further. What did you do next?"

"If we ever start a talk show, I know who can host it," he said quietly.

She smiled and waited for him to continue.

"So I went to all the stations in town, looking for a job," he said finally.

"And Sterling hired you."

"No. There weren't any openings. You know how that goes. There aren't any shifts available until somebody dies."

Emily laughed. The music on the stereo shifted to the Moody Blues, melodies that used to spill from Erin's room.

"Man, that guy's got a voice," Colin said suddenly. "Justin Hayward. Pipes."

He joined the Moody Blues' lead singer in the next line of lyrics. Betty was right, Colin had pipes—what he let Emily hear of them. He shot her a self-conscious glance, telling her how much he preferred serenading her to telling his tale.

"We're all agreed on that," Emily told him of Justin Hayward's smooth voice. "Don't change the subject. How did you talk Sterling into giving you air time? What did you do, kill somebody?"

"No, but I thought about it. I was getting tired of sleeping in my car. I didn't have much, but everything I owned was in the back. I couldn't afford a motel."

"So?" she asked, urging him to continue.

"So . . . I'd already figured Sterling was the guy I wanted to work for. I liked him. We both liked bourbon." He smiled at that, then shrugged again, as if the telling were getting harder. "I offered to work a week for free if he didn't like how I did a show."

"You said that?"

"I know now, he couldn't do that. Labor law, and all, but it must have impressed him." He laughed outright. "Then the guy on the night shift got sick—then got busted for drugs. He was in jail, and I was down to my last dollars." He paused; Justin sang. "That was eight years ago. I've been at the station ever since."

The rest was history, as they said—except for his coffee mug, the one with those awful orange and gold block letters on the beige background. "Where is KMLA?" she asked.

That got her a glance.

"Your mug. It has KMLA on the side," she explained.

"Those are the old call letters," he said, turning back to the road. "When we built the new image, we changed the call letters from KMLA—an abbreviation of K-Missoula—to KDMD . . . the Diamond."

So, it wasn't only an old mug, but a testimony to the chicken coop image Missoula's country station exuded—willingly or not—before it claimed title to Diamond Country. A trophy, reminding Colin of where he'd been and what he'd built since then.

"You're so bright," she said.

He gave her an embarrassed snort. "Sterling's a born promoter. I just know what sounds good on the air."

A good team. Emily opened her mouth to add that, but the comment died as Colin slowed the car, peering at the wedge of road in the headlights.

"Should be along here somewhere," he said.

Emily wasn't so talkative once they stepped inside the log home tucked into a clearing off the road, but she was just as inquisitive, strolling about the first floor that served as restaurant. A handwritten sign stretched across the staircase climbing into a beamed ceiling declared that the second floor was living quarters.

The dining room might have been spacious, save for the four round tables and the display of sports memorabilia separating them. Set on oversized wooden cubes that might have been borrowed from a photographer's studio, the collection included Johnny Unitas' football cleats, a Bobby Riggs tennis racket, a hockey stick and puck from a guy Colin had never heard of, the same for the polo helmet, and a pair of scuffed figure skates with Scott Hamilton's name on them. There were more, many more, and from seemingly every competitive recreation imaginable; a lifetime of sports coverage treasured carefully. The face of the man who'd answered the door, their host Guy York, showed up in a younger, thinner version in the patchwork of photographs on the walls. His byline sat boldly above the words Associated Press on the yellowed clippings framed among them.

Colin smiled to himself as he took a chair beside Emily at one of the tables. Something for everyone—linen, candlelight, soft guitar and piano music, and a collection of sports souvenirs. The Yorks deserved to be rich.

The petite woman who darted back and forth across the kitchen doorway had to be Mrs. York. Accompanied by courses of delicious fruits and vegetables, the luau pig she and her husband cooked made the best fare from the finest restaurant downtown taste like something from the high school cafeteria. Between courses, which were served to all three inhabited tables at the same time, family style, Guy tantalized them with exotic concoctions of fruit juices and left them to stroll among the artifacts or sit before a blazing fire.

Predictably, Emily preferred the fire. Reclining on a huge red leather ottoman, she leaned back on braced arms, feet stretched toward the flames. Lazily she rotated her ankles, her cheek resting against the ball of her shoulder. If she were a cat, her tail would be swaying above pinched eyes.

"This is so nice," she told him for the third time in five courses. "I'm having a wonderful time."

Colin smiled. He'd gone to much more trouble for much less.

Colin turned off the stereo before he even started the engine; the soft night and soft dark of the car's interior—disturbed only by the red-orange dash lights—seemed too seamless, too much an extension of candlelight and firelight, to jar with the vibration of electric guitars and drums. Emily stared out the side window as the headlights illuminated canyon and trees. She could be so vivacious; now she was the smaller, pensive side of herself.

Her hand lay on her thigh, fingers curled loosely. She jumped when he reached for it, then sent a gentle smile across the console. When he gathered it tightly in his own, she squeezed back.

"How about a walk?" he asked as they approached the outskirts of Missoula.

"A walk?"

"Bonner Park is close, and it's a nice night."

Too early to take her home, and he was too full of culinary brilliance to go dancing, or drop pie on top of it.

Her smile was warm. "That sounds like fun."

And if it sounded like fun, Miss Emily wanted to try it.

"Good," he told her. "We'll take my housemate along."

That furrowed Miss Emily's brow, but she bent right over and scratched Sophie behind the ears as soon as Colin got the front door open wide enough for the dog to squirm through.

"What is she?" Emily called from the living room.

Colin was in the bedroom, culling stocking caps from the shelf in the closet. "Alaskan malamute," he called back.

This would work—a knit scarf Emily could tie around her head, rather than a cap she'd have to pull over her hair. Women never went for that sort of thing, even ones who seemed less fussy about it.

"She's beautiful," Emily said as he strolled into the living room. She was kneeling, kneading the rich fur around Sophie's face, and Soph was taking all she cared to dole out.

"She's demanding," he told her. "Worse than a four-year-old. She'll make a nuisance of herself now."

Emily laughed and smoothed the dog's fur from her face. "Is that right, Soph? Well, I won't mind, girl. No I won't. You're so pretty."

Colin chuckled to himself; never failed. Then he handed Emily the scarf he'd acquired somewhere—his own ears never got cold—and lifted Sophie's choke chain and leash from the bentwood coat rack.

Twenty-one

*T*hey strolled the half block from Colin's front door, as
well as the perimeter of the neighborhood park,
under a partly cloudy sky that held little heat and a
full moon that gave great light. Sophie walked obediently at
Colin's left knee while Emily strode at his right, her shoulder bobbing below his—about three quick steps to his two.
He reached for her hand. It was soft and warm.

"We used to have a dog," she said. "An Irish setter
named Sean—for the Jim Kjelgaard book. Erin picked his
name, but I don't think I would have come up with anything more clever."

Colin asked, "What happened to him?"

"He was Erin's dog, so she took him with her when she
left home."

Though Emily said the words lightly enough, a note of
sadness was there.

"Why didn't you get another?" he asked. Couldn't imagine a house without a dog padding about in it. Preferably a
big dog. The little ones were as annoying as flies.

She shrugged. "Too busy. Too many other things to
worry about."

Such as a sick mother . . . Oh, the ceaseless swimming against a current of mere survival.

"Do you see Erin much?" he asked.

"She comes home at Christmas or Thanksgiving—whichever she isn't spending with her in-laws."

Moscow, Idaho was only a hundred miles from Coeur d'Alene, give or take. If Karen or Holly were no more than a few hours away, he'd see them more than just once a year . . . in a perfect world, of course. The world wasn't perfect. As it was, it had been nine years. One third of his life.

"Kids?" he asked of Erin.

"One. Jessica."

"Did your mother get to see her before she died?"

Now Emily smiled. "Yes. She adored her."

"How did your mother die?" Colin asked quietly, adding, "If you don't mind talking about it."

"Diabetes," she said simply, as if she'd grown comfortable with it ages ago.

"Did she have it long?"

"Since she was a teenager."

Sophie pulled on her leash to sniff at a tree as they passed it. Colin jerked on her choke chain, reminded her to heel, and kept his pace.

"I guess she got through her pregnancies okay," Emily said matter-of-factly. "It didn't get bad until I was in grade school. By the time Erin left home, Mother was totally blind. Then her kidneys failed, and she had to have dialysis twice a week. I thought that would take her, but it was finally her heart that did it."

"I'm sorry," Colin said.

"Thanks. It's okay."

"You were thirteen when Erin left home?"

She nodded.

Thirteen, and assuming the full load of running a

house and caring for a blind and ailing mother.

"Then your mother never saw you . . . later? Never saw you as a woman?" Colin asked.

Sophie lowered her head, peering at something in the shadows. An animal about the size of a cat darted through the playground equipment. Sophie barked.

"Sophie. Sit," Colin told her, snapping her choke chain for the noise she'd been trained to avoid. Her attention was still in the swing set, so she moved as if in a trance, backing slowly onto her haunches.

"No, she never saw me," Emily said, stopping beside him.

Pity. Mrs. Erickson would have been pleased with the face peeking out of his knit scarf. If the night had colors, the scarf would be red, her eyes green, and her cheeks the faintest of downy pinks.

"I'll bet you look like your mother," she said suddenly.

He held a bark of laughter—where had that come from? "Is that supposed to threaten my masculinity?"

She giggled. "No. Not at all." She paused. "I look like my father."

He let his eyes have her, from the poking out bangs to the button of her chin. He shook his head. "I'll bet you don't."

The old red GMC pickup sat backward in the driveway, where its blue tailgate wouldn't show to anything but the garage door it faced, and deep enough that it looked as though the strangers who owned the driveway wanted the truck there—except they were asleep. Even the neighbors hadn't noticed him pushing the pickup into place.

The driver sat up straighter when headlights arced into University Avenue. The car slowed and parked in front of the two-story house across the street. No mistaking that car, even in the dark—though the ski rack was a new addition. He snorted. Cushy jobs afforded the time and money for elitist nonsense like playing in the snow. The fancy man's lights turned off with the engine, then the interior light came on as the driver's door opened. To the porch and inside, the big shot escorted her, his hand stationed at the small of her back as if he thought it his right to put it there.

The driver nodded his head. This had gone far enough.

Emily turned at the top of the stairs, putting her apartment door behind her. "I had such a good time tonight, Colin. Thanks."

"So did I. Thanks for going with me," he said.

She could ask him in. Should ask him in. She'd tossed a box of brownie mix in the shopping cart, intending to bake for him tonight. Hadn't counted on being so full from dinner.

He held out his palm. "Your keys, please."

Emily fumbled in her purse—stupid black hole—and finally handed him the ring. He separated out the one she pointed to, unlocked her door, and handed them back.

Now. Ask him in—

The intense study in his eyes stopped all thought and lit sparklers in her stomach. He reached for her hands and pulled her close. Then it was happening before she could gasp for breath.

Gentle, his kiss. Tender, and as chaste in the privacy of the upstairs landing as it had been over a changed tire in a

Broadway parking lot—though it wasn't as hesitant. This was the second time they'd moved to this music . . . and, goodness, but the man knew how to dance.

"Brad!"

The word was more an exclamation than a name, but it was the calmest Emily could manage with him sweeping into the chair beside her.

"I stopped by your house on the way," he whispered, plucking the hymnal from an empty chair in the row ahead. "That's why I'm late. I thought I was supposed to pick you up."

"Oh. No," Emily said, shaking her head.

"I thought I was," he said again. "How about lunch after church?"

He rose with the rest of the congregation to sing the first song of praise and worship and opened the hymnal, though the tune the piano was playing wasn't in it; everyone just sang it from memory.

"Lunch?" Emily asked. It wasn't the attraction it used to be. Except she should go—to balance out her dating Colin. "Sure," she said. Brad had been pleasant company a week ago. He still was that.

But he wasn't Colin.

It wasn't fair to make comparisons—except they were so obvious, later, when he sat across from her in the restaurant. Brad wasn't witty, like Colin. Wasn't easy in his intelligence, like Colin. Wasn't breathtakingly handsome, like Colin. Didn't even understand what she did for a living, how radio harbored no room for mistakes, no allowing for a bad day or a poor night's sleep. No allowance for a headache or hormones. No pity for a troubled heart. Leave all those things on the other side of the On Air sign and be up, up, always up, and cheerful and spontaneous and quick on your feet. Think fast, think fast, think ever so fast. Or die.

Not stress, exactly. Not in the way people normally think of stress, of pacing or wringing their hands or pinching the bridge of their nose and sighing deep. Speaking into a microphone took little more thought than sucking from a straw—yet the hour-after-hour of putting forth a performance, of listening to two things at once, of counting time down to the second . . . it was busy.

Brad couldn't know the absurdity of it, how she closed herself in a room and talked to no one . . . but everyone . . . and everywhere . . . in their cars, living rooms, bedrooms . . . and that she couldn't imagine doing anything else. Brad didn't . . . couldn't know.

He glanced up. She'd been staring. The waitress saved her from explaining.

"I'll have a cheeseburger with fries," Emily told her. "Oh, and add bacon, please."

"Are you sure?" Brad asked.

"Why? What are you having?" Emily asked. Maybe it was beyond his budget.

"The bacon adds a lot of fat," he replied.

The breath stopped in Emily's throat. She glanced at the waitress, who waited patiently, and back to Brad. "I know, but I like it."

"I just care about you," he said over the top of his menu.

She smiled, trying to sled through this. She already had a father—and had been wearing his shoes, in his absence, for years. "I appreciate that," she said, and turned back to the waitress. "I'll have the bacon."

"Howdy, Bob. How was your weekend?" Colin asked, his voice a liquid rumble in the stereo speakers.

Emily's heart leaped. It was a joy all its own, having dated—having kissed—the mouth whose smooth inflections poured into her living room.

"Well, it was okay, I guess," Bob replied to Colin's question over the telephone line. His inflections conjured an image of faded blue bib overalls, laugh lines etched into a sunburn that just never seemed to fade, a grizzle of graying stubble that needed mowing, and a straw cowboy hat that wasn't so new—or clean—anymore. "How was yours?"

"Mine was great, Bob," Colin replied. "I'll tell you, the tractor pulls were on, so I nearly starved in front of the television for fear I'd miss something."

Bob laughed. Emily laughed harder. Sure he did.

"How's Wanda the Weather Chicken?" Colin asked.

"Well, no eggs, and she's looking a little sleepy," Bob admitted.

"I know how she feels," Colin said. "Mondays are like that. . . . That means precip, but the weather guy says to expect clear skies."

"Yeah, but his record ain't near as good as Wanda's," Bob said, playing the perfect straight man.

Colin laughed, a rich sound for something as light as an airwave. "I'm with you. Since it's already raining, my money's on the chicken, Bob."

"Mine, too," Bob said, with a chuckle of his own.

Emily joined them. Where did Colin come up with this stuff?

"Thanks, Bob. We'll talk to you tomorrow, same time, same station," Colin said, then jumped into the weather bed and a full weather forecast, complete with Wanda's conflicting prediction. Then there was a neighing of horses, he said, "Giddyap," a whip cracked, and an Alan Jackson tune galloped into play.

Emily wrapped her arms around her legs and set her cheek on her knees, where she sat on the floor in front of the stereo. There was something secret about knowing exactly where Colin was at that moment. He was listening to the same song. The Fast Lane clothing store spot started because his finger pressed the green button on pot number eight. He was listening to her voice and maybe thinking about her listening to his.

Colin Michaels was his name, except she knew it was really Kavanaugh, and Michael was only a middle name. Knew the interior of his car was gray leather, that he wore a musky cologne, that his dog was an Alaskan malamute named Sophie, and that his couch was navy leather and long enough to accommodate all seventy-three inches of him—and got to prove it every afternoon.

Emily lost track of Colin after he signed off at ten. He could be anywhere in the station, doing anything from meeting with Sterling to typing at his computer.

At 11:40, he was in his sheepskin coat and on her threshold.

"Good. You're not in your pajamas," he said. "Now show me how spontaneous you can be by grabbing your parka. I'll take you to lunch."

He took her to Cottage House Pancakes, where he ordered bacon on his cheeseburger and reached for her hand when she didn't expect it. In the middle of the table, in full view, he held her fingers in his own, his thumb stroking slowly over sensitive flesh, his eyes seeming to draw her into himself. Far away from scraping forks and the aroma of french fries and coffee, it was warm and gentle and strong and oh, so safe, inside the blue depths of his eyes. This was how it felt to fall in love, to match her breathing to his own, to feel the agony of even the tiniest separation and the glee of each reunion.

Back on University Avenue, he pulled his BMW up to the curb in front of her house.

"Don't bother," she said when he reached for his door handle. "You're probably in a hurry." His lunch hour had already stretched by nearly one hundred percent.

He gave her dimples. "That's all right," he said softly.

The secret tone of his voice said something was up. Her lungs knew it. Her stomach knew it. He knew it, shoulders thrown back confidently while he stepped from the car, came around to her side, then held her hand as he escorted her up the walk, the porch, and the stairs.

On the landing, Colin held out his hand, palm up; Emily gave him her key ring—that much she knew from memory—and watched while he unlocked the door and handed back the key. Then, of all things, he stepped inside, pulling her in after him. Quickly he closed the door, as if they were being chased, backed her gently against the wall, and reached for the tab of her jacket's zipper.

"Sshhh," he said when she started to protest.

He unzipped her coat, slid his hands inside . . . then he was tentative, looking long into her eyes . . . so close . . . hanging back, unsure.

She stared into the bottomless blue of his eyes. Watched his mouth . . . full lips . . . and the tip of that silly tooth as they parted.

Was he going to ask? He was actually going to ask. He didn't have to ask. For heaven's sake, get it over with, before the suspense—

Twenty-two

Finally Colin moved, pulling Emily into an embrace that was all cozy with coats and strong arms and a large and gentle hand at the back of her head. Slowly it started, slow and tender and like a whisper that made her lean forward to get more. Then it built. Swept her in. Washed over her. No chaste kiss, this; it involved everything—her whole mouth, her breath against his cheek, the faint scent of his shave, her hair that he dug with his fingers.

She was nearly senseless by the time he finally kissed her mouth closed—just as he'd kissed it open—and lifted his head. He swallowed hard. Couldn't breathe any better than she.

"Lunch tomorrow?" he asked, his voice a husky whisper.

Emily nodded. Couldn't speak.

Colin gave her a soft smile, a final stroke of his finger on her cheek, then was gone.

She leaned against the closed door. Match her breathing to his own? As if she controlled it? He owned her every breath. Took them all with him.

On Tuesday, Emily got her kiss before lunch. And so generous, Colin; she got one after lunch as well.

Colin played another of Emily's spots on Wednesday morning, this one for This-Is-the-Life Hot Tub and Spa. She smiled as she listened. He was listening to her, had to be thinking about her. However, there was no lunch date later. Colin was in meetings all afternoon with Sterling and Bryce Wiley, the station's owner.

On Wednesday evening, Emily checked the log for her This-Is-the-Life Hot Tub and Spa ad, but it wasn't listed with the others in the eight o'clock hour, when Colin had played it.

"Good evening. KDMD," Emily said in that soft, warm voice that trailed, like playful fingernails, clear to his toes.

"Hi," Colin said, low and soft.

If a smile could be heard, he heard that one. "Hi," Emily replied, sounding as if she'd just leaned into a cloud.

He sat in the corner of the couch, ankle set on the opposite knee. The stereo speakers played quietly, the same Lonestar tune Emily had introduced with the liner he'd recorded for her.

"Don't you know you aren't supposed to accept personal calls while you're on the air?" he asked, teasing. He'd deliberately called on the public line, rather than the number known only to station personnel, just to catch her off guard.

"No, I don't recall anything being said about that when I was hired," she replied smartly. "Besides, I thought this was a business call."

He chuckled softly.

"Don't you have business with me?" she asked, so innocently.

"As a matter of fact, I do," he said. "If anyone should ask, you're busy this weekend. Got that?"

"Mmm. This is only Wednesday. You're kind of taking charge, aren't you?" she asked, sounding as if she liked it. "What am I doing?"

"Whatever I'm doing," he replied. "I'll let you know when I decide."

Actually he already had, but a man couldn't be rushed on these things. There were enticements to buy, not to mention he would build a stronger case with a little more wooing.

What a pleasure it would be.

"What shall I wear?" she asked.

Silently he groaned. "Nothing special. We'll probably go dancing."

Any excuse to hold her. It was a cheap shot, but the best he could do for the moment.

He reached to the coffee table for the tumbler of Maker's Mark and held it up, taking a bead on the red and blue lights of the stereo through the amber liquid. Maybe one of these days he'd teach her to enjoy piña coladas. Coconut, pineapple, and rum—like soda pop in a grass skirt. She'd become all soft and languid, and her eyes would dilate to black pools he could fall into.

Emmy, girl.

"I'll be by your apartment about 11:30 on Friday," he said.

"I'll be ready," she told him.

He'd see.

Emily had hardly hung up when the phone rang again.

"What do you want now?" she asked into the receiver.

"Uh . . . Emily?" the voice on the other end of the line asked uncertainly.

Oops.

"Oh, sorry, Brad," Emily said. "I thought you were someone else."

"Obviously," he replied. "Anyone I know?"

She glanced at the countdown clock at the top of the board, checking it against the time listed for the Wynonna tune playing; fifty seconds left.

"I don't think so," she said. "Just someone I work with."

Just someone whose intelligence demanded respect. Just someone whose face should have its own page on the Internet. Just someone who made her heart dance a new rhythm.

"Oh? Who?" Brad asked.

As if it had anything to do with him. "Just a sec," she said and set down the phone. Maybe he'd select a new topic while she was gone. She donned her headset and picked up her pen. Colin was listening. She needed to make it good.

She set her mouth to the mike, pressed the "on" button, and watched the clock, waiting. Then she smiled. "Diamond Country, Diamond One-O-One . . . taking a little step into the past with Wynonna. We'll hear her latest coming up later in the hour." She grabbed the playlist, holding it up so she could see it without pinching her throat. "Also, some LeAnn Rimes, Ricochet, and a favorite from Garth Brooks. . . . Stay with us."

Press.

The green button depressed under her finger, starting the first commercial in the stopset. Not the best outro she'd ever done—*latest* and *later* in the same breath. Bad. Should have planned better, not been distracted.

Emily closed the mike, sending John Vaughn's voicing of a spot for R & R Sports through the studio speakers, then she returned to the phone. "Okay, I'm back."

"That sounded nice," Brad told her.

It was an amateur opinion, but she said, "Thanks," and began cueing up CDs.

Brad got right to the point. "What are you doing Friday night?"

Dread dropped its weight into her stomach. She'd have to turn him down again, and it was getting ridiculous— except she'd do it every time she could see Colin instead. She glanced at the clock.

Fifteen seconds!

She tapped the key on the computer keyboard, select-ing her liner . . . watched the clock . . . then the last spot in the stopset emptied into Colin's magical voice telling the whole wide world—or at least their corner of Montana— that Emily Brooks was the best little cowgirl in Diamond Country. Funny, since she didn't even own a bandanna, much less boots or ruffled panties. Before the liner faded into silence, she started the next song, a lively tune by Restless Heart—almost rock and roll.

"I'm sorry, Brad," she answered as gently as possible, without sounding as if she pitied him. Men hated that—or so Stacy said. "I'm already busy this whole weekend."

"The whole weekend, and this is only Wednesday. That was quick. Are you going out of town or something?" he asked, as if he'd just assumed legal guardianship.

"No, I'm just busy," she told him, adding, "I'm sorry, but I can't stay long. Somehow I got behind, and I need to catch up. My boss is listening tonight."

"Okay," he sang, as if it were *You'll be sorry*. "You're sure about this weekend?"

"I don't expect anything to change," she said, adding, "I'll see you at church on Sunday."

"I'll be there," he said.

Thankfully, he didn't ask about lunch—for that day or the three in between.

"Hi, Emily," Betty said on Friday from behind the stacks of papers burying her desk. Log books.

Perfect, Emily thought.

"You haven't been in for a while," Betty said. "How are things going?"

Emily dropped into the guest chair, setting her purse and coat in a bundle on the floor. No telling how long she might have put this off. Up to now, the dread had been bigger than the curiosity; it wasn't anymore. "Colin and I are dating," Emily told her, getting the worst over with.

Betty didn't flinch. "You are," she said. She looked like a high school English teacher, with her white blouse collar peeking over the top of a red sweater.

Emily nodded. Her gaze slid to the edge of the desk. "It'll be okay. It's not serious."

Betty's gaze suddenly lifted over Emily's head. Emily

swiveled. Vicky Millian leaned in the doorway.

"Hello, Emily," Vicky said. "How's everyone treating you here at the Diamond? Settling in okay?" The vicious glint in her eyes hinted she didn't need to ask.

"Fine, thanks," Emily replied. Except that the carpeting in the hall should be taken up so the woman's cat walk would be heard approaching.

"Glad to hear it," Vicky said, and turned to Betty.

"I put the folder on your desk," Betty told her, obviously anticipating a question, her smile unbelievably genuine. But then, Vicky didn't talk to Betty as if Betty had just poured sand in her hand lotion.

"Thanks," Vicky said and slid away without a farewell, because work was more important.

She couldn't have chosen a worse time to bring her silent accusations. Emily turned back to Betty, ready to make a defense, except it wasn't a scolding lying on Betty's features. It was pity.

"No one ever marries someone they didn't first date," Betty said softly.

"It's not serious," Emily said again. "We're barely going out."

For a long moment Betty only stared, though it was a gentle, sorrowful attention. "This is going to hurt you very much," she said finally.

The words shot straight into Emily's heart. She was right. Little corners of herself saw it coming, watched her dancing in a space that would get smaller and smaller as the hard differences closed in. Very soon, she'd have to give it up.

"I'll be here," Betty added, then shifted on her squeaky chair and gathered a breath that seemed to sweep her into a new countenance. "Do you have time for coffee?" she asked brightly.

"Actually, no," Emily replied, seizing on the change of subject. "I was wondering when that ad campaign for The Fast Lane clothing store started."

Betty's brow furrowed. "Hmm. Last Thursday or Friday, I think." She wheeled her chair to one of the half dozen file cabinets behind her. "That's a new one, isn't it?" She began fingering through the third drawer down.

"I think so. At least, I've never heard a spot for them before," Emily said, eyeing the stacks of logs, stapled thick, with curled corners, hasty check marks, and lavish signatures. These were legal documents, avowing that each and every commercial had been played during that hour. If the ad was played, it was billed, and for each mark, someone wrote a bigger check.

"Yep, it's new," Betty said, rolling back to her desk, file folder in hand. "One sales exec or another has been trying to snag that account ever since the store opened in the mall." She peeked over the top of her half-glasses. "Did you voice the spot?"

"Yes," Emily replied. Pride wasn't driving her investigation anymore, but she didn't volunteer that.

Betty opened the folder. "It started last Thursday, a week ago today, but if you're hoping to hear your spot on the air, I'll have to check the traffic computer for the time. It's a conservative campaign."

"Can I see?" Emily asked, attention fixed on the paperwork.

"Sure," Betty replied, handing it over.

Emily scanned the yellow broadcast order, which resembled a blank calendar with dates and times penned in. The spot was scheduled for three times a day for two weeks, on Wednesdays, Thursdays, and Fridays, but rather than being placed in specific high-profile segments of the day, the ads were purchased at the cheaper BTA—best times available—rate. They could run literally any time between 9:00 A.M. and 7:00 P.M. Since it was a small order, the 6:00 to 9:00 A.M. prime time slot wasn't even a possibility.

Emily closed the folder. "Do you have last Friday's log?"

"I think it's here," Betty said.

The mess she shuffled through wasn't as disorganized as it looked. Almost immediately she pulled a log from the middle of one of the piles and gave it to her.

"Thanks," Emily said, sitting back to study. Carefully she leafed through the pages and found the three ads scheduled in the 10:00 A.M., 2:00 P.M., and 4:00 P.M. hours. None was slated for seven o'clock in the morning . . . unless it was a make-good. That was it. Colin had played it on Friday to make up for one missed on Thursday and had forgotten to write it in.

When Emily looked up, ready to ask, Betty already had the Thursday log in hand, saying, "You looked perplexed."

Emily smiled her thanks and repeated the careful study. There were three spots scheduled for that day . . . and all of them had been played. Something ugly crept into her stomach. There was no need for a make-good. No need for a commercial for The Fast Lane clothing store during Colin's show on Friday. No need, and no explanation.

❦

Emily peered past the wipers sweeping the windshield, caught between the need to speed—to get home and ready for her date with Colin—and the need to keep her hippity-hop's skin wrinkle free. Her hands held the wheel with a grip equal to her concentration. It was finally snowing like it meant it, as it should in Montana, but it had been drizzling all day. Beneath the fat wet flakes stacking up so quickly lay a fine, unbroken sheet of ice.

A car tried to stop at the light ahead, but slid right through and into her lane. She pumped the brakes, giving the driver time to back up, out of her way. He shook his head as she passed—*Isn't this something?* It was something, all right. It was crazy, for no one except a lunatic would be out here if they didn't have to be. Might be a good night to stay home, leave the roads to the Friday night bar crowd and those with no sense. Tonight they were one and the same.

The intersection at University Avenue was already shiny where tires had skated through it, then there was only one set of tracks through virgin snow. Emily turned around in her driveway and parked at the curb, stepping cautiously around the front of the car and up the walk.

"Emily."

She stopped and turned—

Panic clenched her stomach, her fingers tightened around the shoulder strap of her purse, and she threw out her hand to catch herself.

Colin exhaled a word Emily wouldn't appreciate, one of the many he kept on a leash in her presence, but he couldn't stop it. He meant it and more, for she landed with a sickening thud that sounded like a cobble rock landing in a bed of more just like it. She'd be lucky if she hadn't broken something.

His steps faltered. She wasn't moving. *She wasn't moving.*

Twenty-three

*C*olin's foot slid out from under him, and he nearly fell into Emily before he caught himself and dropped to his knees. She was lying on her left side, her arm under her and her neck crooked at an awkward angle to reach over the bunched-up collar of her parka. Her head rested on the pavement.

He reached—and stopped. Wait. Don't move her. Could be a neck injury. Or back. All those little bones. Could hurt her worse. He settled for setting his fingers against her cheek. It was snowing on her, wetting her skin and hair.

"Emmy? Emmy, can you hear me?"

Her eyelids fluttered and opened, though her stare held all the comprehension of marbles.

"Em," he said softly. "Can you hear me?"

She blinked. Searched. Found him.

"Are you all right?" he asked.

Stupid question. She wasn't all right. She'd been knocked cold.

She peeled her lips apart. "Colin." The word was a little slurred, maybe sounding more dazed than anything.

"Are you all right?" he asked again.

She blinked slowly. "I'm fine."

He stroked the snow from her temple. "Do you hurt anywhere?"

More blinks. "I'm fine."

She squinted, furrowing her brow as if she might have just awakened from a night's sleep. When she struggled to sit up, he helped her, until she was propped on her left arm—which she lifted just as quickly, staring at her palm as if she'd never seen it before.

"It's snowing," she said, as if that were a puzzle. "It's wet," she added—another revelation.

His stomach fell to the sidewalk between them. She wasn't all right.

"Emmy, where do you hurt?" Colin asked, holding her by the shoulders. She wasn't even standing yet, and still looked as though she might fall like a tree.

"I'm fine," she said again, staring at him with a gaze that wasn't quite tuned in. Suddenly her eyes opened wide. "Sick," she groaned and barely rolled up on her hands and knees in time to hit the lawn.

Dry heaves mostly, for she didn't bring up enough to warrant all the effort. Still, this would win her a ride to the emergency room. She wobbled like a rubber-band toy, prompting him to put a steadying grip on her shoulders.

"Come on," he said once she'd stopped retching. "Let's see if you can stand up, and we'll go to the hospital."

"I'm fine," she insisted, spitting into what she'd splattered on the snow. "I'm just hungry."

Sure. He always puked when he was hungry.

"Okay. We'll get something to eat," he said, humoring her, and began lifting her to her feet.

"My bum's wet," she informed him with a pout.

This was serious. She'd never refer to that particular

portion of her anatomy if she were in her right mind, and she'd never call it that.

He had her braced against his side when she took a step, squealed, and collapsed against him.

"My ankle," she moaned.

Great.

Her porch light was on, but the dark windows on the first floor testified that her landlady had slept through the whole thing. He eyed the Jeep and the mile of ice between it and them—and him in cowboy boots. No choice. He scooped her into his arms, treading on the lawn where he could for better traction.

"This is stupid," she informed him as he bent to open the door of the Jeep with the hand under her knees. "I'm fine."

That sounded more like her, except her head fell against the seat and stayed there once he set her inside. He buckled her in and headed for Community Medical Center.

The emergency room was filled with misery. Two guys in snowmobile suits talked quietly, though energetically, as if doing so over beers, while a third leaned his elbows on his knees and watched the double doors leading to the examination rooms. A skinny woman in stringy hair and jeans someone two sizes larger had thrown away looked too young to mother the infant she carried. A pretty blond teenager in ski pants rocked back and forth as if she were trying to ratchet herself from the leg propped on a chair.

All eyes watched their progress through the door, making Emily bury her face in Colin's ear in uncharacteristic bashfulness. They were a little conspicuous, him carrying her this way. He strode past the stares to the sign-in desk and set Emily in an empty chair.

Though the woman behind the desk had a kind smile,

she started right off with bad news. "I'm sorry, but we just received two car accidents. It could be an hour or two."

Filling in the hospital's computer screen took fifteen minutes, since Emily couldn't seem to process the woman's questions. Colin was little help—ignorant of Emily's mailing address, social security number, blood type, and the address of her next of kin. However, he was able to promise the woman a check when she learned Emily had no health insurance.

"You can pay me back," he told Emily, who shot him a defeated glance.

All that finished, he took her to a short row of empty seats under the window and propped her leg on a stool purloined from the other side of the room.

Then began the waiting.

She'd lost her fight. Now she cuddled under his arm— as best she could with the chrome loop separating the seats poking up between them. He smoothed the bangs from her forehead. Her eyes were closed.

"Did you buy a Jeep?" she asked suddenly, though she sounded sleepy.

"No. I already had it," he replied softly.

"Oh . . . It's nice."

How did she know? She'd ridden with her eyes closed the entire way.

"Some date, huh?" she asked.

"Kind of racy stuff," he told her. "Mind if we do something less lively next time?"

Her laugh was little more than a puff of air.

"Do you hurt?" he asked.

She nodded. "My head . . . a little. And my ankle . . . a little. But I think I'm fine."

Right.

"I'm sorry," she said. "If you want to go dancing without

me, you don't need to stay on my account."

Another fine idea. She could take a cab home.

Colin accompanied Emily to the examination room, though he left while the attending nurse helped her into a gown. Even from the hall, he heard her retching again, though she was curled up on her right side and tucked under a white blanket when he stepped around the curtain. The bulk at her feet said there was a pillow between her ankles, propping the injured one on top. Again, her eyes were closed, though she reached for his hand. He held her pretty little fingers and smoothed the hair from her face while she drifted in and out of sleep.

Emily had done the same thing to both ends, her ankle and her brain—she'd bruised them. As for the ankle, she'd be walking in a few days. The concussion? It looked to be a mild one, though she needed to be watched lest any bleeding in her brain go unnoticed. The doctor's orders included bed rest and checks on her condition every few hours for the next twenty-four, with continued quiet and caution the twenty-four after that.

The only one available to do all this checking was Colin.

The Jeep stopped, but Emily's head kept going. She opened her eyes to bring it back. It didn't help. She closed them again. Not fun, this. She'd give anything to be someone else. Anything at all. Anyone else.

"Give me a minute to unlock the door, and I'll come back for you," Colin said as he shut off the engine.

Emily groaned and opened her eyes, though her head was still too heavy to lift. "I can't stay at your house."

Colin sighed, glancing around the interior of the Jeep as if he might find an answer there. He had every right to be impatient with her. She'd presented him the epitome of memorable dates.

"Emmy, I don't know what else to do," he finally said. "Even if the roads weren't bad—and I'll bet the Pass is closed—it's a three-hour drive to your dad's house. You're too sick for that, and I'm too tired. I'm willing to sleep on the floor at your apartment, but you don't have a phone, so how am I supposed to call a paramedic if I need to? And you don't know anyone else well enough to call them at 2:30. The only other alternative is to check you into the hospital."

She shook her head. "Take me home. I'll be fine."

"That's not even in the running. You heard what that doctor said, and I'm not going to simply deposit you on your doorstep and drive away." He paused. Stroked her cheek with the backs of his fingers. "It'll be okay. You'll see," he said more gently.

She closed her eyes. Absolutely impossible, this situation, and such a stupid way to wind up in it.

The Jeep jiggled as Colin stepped out of it. Emily expected to wince when he closed the door behind him, but the noise didn't even matter. Her head ached, except not like the usual headache. More fuzzy. Swirling, if that made any sense.

He might have been gone two minutes, it might have been twenty, when he opened her door, letting in a rush of cold air that crawled along her right side. She sat up and tried to release her seat belt, except she must have been bungling the job, for he reached across her and freed it with one deft stroke.

She was no good for anything.

"It's stopped snowing, but it's still slick," he said. "Why don't we wait until you get in the house before you try out the crutches?"

It was more a directive than a question. So she wrapped her arms around his neck and let him carry her one more time, out of a garage whose door closed with a mechanical hum behind them, under a carport edging the side of his house, up the front steps to a wooden porch, and through the front door. The floor lamp beside the couch was already lit.

"Move, girl," Colin scolded Sophie softly as he closed the door with his foot. Then he kept right on marching, past the couch she'd seen the night they'd taken the dog for a walk, through the dining room's wide arch, into a hallway to his right, and left to the room in the right rear corner of the house.

Colin's bedroom.

The scent made it his before Emily could even see his bed against the far wall, and the nightstand and lamp between it and the closet. He set her gently in the lamp's light and helped her out of her coat, which he draped at the end of the bed. He'd already taken his off. She'd missed that somehow. He stole the pillow from the space beside her, stacking it with the other behind her. When he strode from the room with her coat, he came back with another pillow for her foot—which was wrapped to huge proportions in an elastic bandage.

"Where's my shoe?" she asked. And when had she taken it off?

"In the living room," he replied. "Your purse is out there too. I'll bring it in a minute. Let's get you settled first."

Settled. In Colin's bedroom. A man's bedroom. Her

boss's bed. Daddy would never understand, and no one would ever believe it was something other than what it looked and sounded like. Above all, God wouldn't be happy about this. She wasn't on His gold star list as it was.

Colin was rooting around in his chest of drawers.

"These should work," he said, closing the drawer and handing her a pile of knit garments. "You're going to swim in them, but it's the best I can do."

Colin's clothes.

Emily tried not to cry, but she didn't even have the energy to cover her face or turn away, much less stop the tears.

"Aw, Emmy," Colin groaned. "Don't cry, sweetheart. It's all right." Effortlessly, as if she were a doll, he scooted her over, making room to sit. He pulled her into his arms, pressing her cheek against his chest. "You've been holding up so well," he said softly, his voice a solid rumble beneath her ear. "Don't fall apart on me now."

"I can't help it," she cried.

Even to herself she sounded like a toddler.

He stroked her hair. "I know," he said, as if he were just then admitting it to himself. Then he said nothing at all, merely held her tight and rubbed her back while she soaked his red-and-gray western shirt with tears, which he dabbed at with a tissue pulled from the drawer of the nightstand.

Long after her crying had wound down to the occasional sniffle, he held her. She should be ashamed for keeping him awake, for needing him so, for being so juvenile about a simple fall on the sidewalk. She was helpless, a baby . . . and didn't care.

She sighed, content. No place she'd rather be than in his arms, held this way. God help her, she loved him. Loved him so very much. She was helpless in that too.

Twenty-four

A cozy place, Colin's bed.

He'd left her in privacy to change into his gray sweatpants and navy sweatshirt. It was like being ballooned in a blanket, even though she'd folded back the sleeves and cinched the waist. When he tapped softly on the door to see if she was ready, he brought her a glass of ginger ale on ice, a pain pill from the prescription he'd filled on their way home, an ice bag that smelled suspiciously new for her ankle, and two mugs of warm tomato soup, one for each of them.

Now, half the soup in her stomach, topped by enough ginger ale to quench a thirst she hadn't known she'd had, Emily cuddled between the green comforter tucked over her and the navy one under her. Her ankle was propped beneath the ice pack, the codeine was taking the aches away, and her cheek lay in the cloud of Colin's pillow. It smelled of his cologne, and maybe his shampoo. She didn't know. Hadn't ever smelled his hair . . . such lush hair. So soft looking. She focused on his face. . . . He lay on his side across the corner of the bed, cheek in one hand, the other hooking a mug of soup.

"How's your tummy?" he asked.

She nodded—all she could give.

Thankfully he was too intelligent to need a diagram. "Good," he said. He drained his mug, sitting up to set it on the floor at the foot of the bed. Sophie seized the opportunity to investigate. "No," he told her quietly. The malamute nuzzled his hand, which got her a fluffing of her head and ears.

Colin reclined again and dug under the comforter for Emily's hand. "Do you mind if I stay here?" he asked, stroking her fingers with his thumb.

She shook her head. Closed her eyes. Told him she didn't care about much of anything at the moment. . . . No, she hadn't said it. Hadn't dragged her mouth open to tell him. Too hard. Tell him in a minute.

"Sleep, Emmy," he told her from the other side of the swirl.

. . . His hand was strong and so sure.

This little girl was sick. No way Emily could take care of herself this weekend. So afraid of imposing, she wouldn't even open his bed, but insisted on lying on top of the comforter with another one over her. So careful of the boundaries—hers and everyone else's.

She didn't share herself with just anyone; her price was high.

Colin scanned her pale face. She slept, though it was scary how she barely moved, even when she was full awake—"full" being a loose term.

He pushed back the comforter and studied the hand he'd been holding. So delicate, compared to his own. So pretty, with slender fingers and white-tipped nails gently shaped just beyond the pads of her fingers. So precious the skin, as tender as if it were brand new.

He let his gaze trail the bumps she raised in his comforter. Soft. Small. Woman.

Emmy.

No amount of fluff could steal the shape of her. At every opportunity he watched her most feminine curves—whether on the move or at rest. She dressed so carefully, in her high collars and long sleeves, as if they were any ammunition against an imagination. That made him grin. No one had ever accused him of lacking that.

He left her long enough to take the dishes to the kitchen and change in the bathroom, tossing the shirt she'd cried on into the clothes hamper. Then he washed up, locked up, shut off, and lay down under his last blanket and pillow on as small a portion of the mattress as he could comfortably inhabit. Emily had turned on her "good" side, cuddling toward the center of the bed. Toward him. He reached for her hand and held it. She gave him the faintest squeeze in reply.

At 6:30 Colin slapped frantic fingers on the snooze button of the alarm clock screaming from the floor at the foot of the bed. Reaching across Emily, he turned on the lamp and shook her awake. As if she were most perturbed at the insult, she blinked to shield her light-shocked eyes. But her pupils were equal in size, she knew where she was and the day of the week, and none of her symptoms—dizziness, nausea, headache—had worsened appreciably. It appeared she might live, despite her probable but unspoken desire to die.

Colin repeated the check at 9:30 to the same satisfaction.

It was stiff muscles that woke him just shy of 11:40; sleeping discreetly bore no kinship to sleeping comfortably. Again, Emily knew where she worked and her father's name, but she was terrifying—wobbly, uncertain, and slow—on the crutches when she needed to go to the bathroom. He watched her disappear inside, gave her a few minutes, then tapped on the door.

"What?" she growled, sounding profoundly hungover.

"I bought you a toothbrush," he told her through the wood.

"Oh, bless you," she groaned, opening the door almost immediately.

She looked steady enough.

"My mouth tastes like a litter box," she said through the crack.

He smiled; she'd also regained her sense of humor. "That's scary," he replied. "How do you know?"

"Don't ask," she grumbled, grabbed the brush, and closed the door in his face.

He cooked her scrambled eggs and toast, though she did little more than pick at them—so he pushed more ginger ale and a pain pill on her.

"Do you want me to go get a video?" he asked once he'd returned from taking the dishes to the kitchen.

Settled against a bank of pillows, she set her mug of coffee on the nightstand and shook her head. "It drives me crazy to have my eyes open. Everything moves."

He'd brought a resin chair from the patio. Now he sat, a second cup of coffee in hand. "You didn't tell me that, about your vision. Is it something new?"

"Yes, but don't worry about it. Maybe I'm just noticing it because I've been up, and it's daylight."

It better be that simple.

"Really," she said, giving him a stern look through the slit of her eyes. "I know I'm getting better. I'm beginning to care what I look like."

He grinned; that was a sign. Unlike twelve hours ago, she was moving around on her own and could hold a conversation, though she talked softly, slowly, and there were long pauses sometimes, as if she swung between on and off.

She'd cried off the black stuff on her eyelashes last night, and she looked frightfully frail . . . though deliciously soft against the pillows. Sweetness in his bed. Should wear it—his bed—more often.

"You look fine," he told her.

"Shows what you know," she replied, closing her eyes again. "I have a terminal case of bed-head."

"You can take a bath when you feel up to it," he said and sipped his coffee.

That got him another scolding slit-of-the-eye glance.

"Pretend this is the YMCA," he added.

"The YMCA? That's worse."

"Oh—the YWCA," he corrected.

"Then you're in trouble," she said.

Yes, he was beginning to see that.

She closed her eyes. "Don't miss out on my account—the video, I mean. I'd listen with you, if you want."

"I can live without it. Shall I read to you?"

She grinned weakly. "You'd do that?"

Not his favorite thing, but, "Yes. This is a professional voice."

Eyes still closed, her grin widened. "Lucky me, having it all to myself." She paused. "I love your voice. I could listen to you all day."

She'd never said as much. It warmed forgotten places.

For a long time she didn't move. Only lay against the

pillows, the delicate arc under her eyes matching the blue of the case, and her face nearly as pale as the cloth was pastel. She cuddled under the comforter as if she were cold—and stirred suddenly, the way she always did with this concussion thing. She sighed deeply and opened her eyes, giving him a little wisp of a grin in greeting.

"Are you cold?" he asked.

She shook her head. "It just feels good to be cozy."

"Do you want me to go into the other room so you can sleep?"

Her eyes opened wider, a note of desperation in them—about the most emotion he'd seen in her since she fell. "Do you mind staying? I don't want to be alone. I'll go in the living room if you want—"

"This is fine."

She exhaled and gave him another weak grin. Then she pulled her arms from beneath the blanket and reached for her coffee, wrapping both hands around it as if drawing on the warmth. The cuffs of her—his—sleeves were folded back. "Have I thanked you for all this?" she asked.

"Not in so many words, but you don't need to." He wasn't doing it for her gratitude. For no reason, except he couldn't not be here for her. It wasn't the weekend he'd planned for them—he'd hoped to take her cross-country skiing—but it could work as well. Maybe better, such forced proximity.

"Thank you," she said, green gaze locked on his.

"You're welcome."

She winced ever so slightly and closed her eyes, sipping her coffee by feel. "Tell me about Oklahoma."

Oklahoma? "What about it?"

"Everything," she said, drawing the word out as if it were music. "What it looks like. The games you played as a boy. About grade school and junior high and high school.

Your junior prom, and that '72 Camaro that was so blue and so sweet."

He grinned, though she wasn't watching to receive it. This wasn't an invasion of privacy, a treading over graves. He wanted to tell her. Wanted to fill in a history—minus the holes.

See me. Where I'm from. I'm solid. Capable.

He shifted, setting ankle on knee. "Well, Miss Emily," he said, picking up the accent of the first word he ever spoke, "it's warm and flat where I come from."

Comfort won over propriety, driving Emily to Colin's ancient and generous bathtub after she woke from a lengthy afternoon nap. Hair wet around her shoulders—and smelling like his shampoo—she crutched across the hall and into the dining room, the aluminum braces clicking both her location and progress.

"Feel better?" Colin asked over the back of the couch.

"Much. Thanks," she replied, feeling the gratitude more than he could know. Anything was an improvement, even if she was reduced to stuffing yesterday's underwear in her purse and going without. He'd offered to drive to her apartment for "a few things," but she'd declined—couldn't imagining him rooting around in her clothes.

He watched her hobble around the end of the couch separating the living room from the dining room and cross to the front window. She pulled back the curtains. It was dark outside and snowing lightly. Had to be after six.

"What time is it?" she asked.

"About 6:15," he replied.

She glanced over her shoulder. He hadn't even looked

to a clock anywhere, and he didn't wear a watch. She turned back to the window. Time. He knew it too. Innately. Born of hour-after-hour of measuring it, filling it, and living under its rule. She almost chuckled to herself. Few would even understand that it was something to notice.

"How do you feel?" Colin asked behind her.

Emily turned around, putting the window at her back. He sat in the corner of that navy leather couch in a set of heather gray sweats that made his eyes look positively midnight. His ankles were crossed on the oval coffee table, which was made of a dark wood in a simple but thick and heavy design. Beside his stockinged feet a glass of something cold and clear—water, knowing his appreciation for it—sweat onto a *National Geographic*. His finger held the place in the middle of a library book, and sometime during the day, though she didn't remember when, he'd showered and shaved. His hair lay in enticing layers, and his face looked new and begged to be touched.

"I have a blow dryer, if you want to dry your hair," he said.

A blow dryer? Somehow it seemed the contraption of vanity, a good pairing with hair spray or bobby pins. Maybe growing up without a brother had been a handicap.

"No. Thanks, anyway," she said. Not enough energy to stand in front of the mirror. Not enough wanna. Clean would have to suffice. "Do you mind if I look at your house?"

"Please."

Permission given, Emily began where she was, taking in the shelves recessed into the wall behind the floor lamp beside him. They were filled with books, most of them hard-covers, and spaced with hand-sized . . . rocks?

He chuckled. "Every family camp-out turned into a geology field trip when I was a kid," he said. He shrugged.

"Habit, I guess."

That was an image. Colin with a stripe of sunburn across his nose, the pockets of his dusty jeans bulging with rocks, and more fine specimens stacked in his hands. Mother had said little boys never really grew up. Perhaps she was right.

Emily grinned and looked more closely at the pile of magazines on the floor. *Sports Illustrated* on top. An over-stuffed chair in navy leather sat beneath the bookcase, making an L-shaped conversation area with the couch and coffee table. His coat closet was a bentwood coat tree beside the front door, and the only things on it were her parka and Sophie's leash—but then his sheepskin would topple the spindly thing.

She turned to her left. The television was fairly good-sized and new enough to include one of those stereo sound systems. The rest of the nook was vacant except for the oak entertainment center housing his stereo system. Not a CD, cassette, or LP in sight; probably behind the cupboard doors on the bottom. They weren't the only things conspicuously missing.

"Where are the speakers?" she asked. At the least, she'd expected massive things with six-foot woofers.

His dimples flickered into his cheeks. "All over the house. The basement ceiling looks like spaghetti—very thick spaghetti, so the wire won't lose any of the signal." He paused. "Would you like to listen to something?"

The glint in his eyes said he knew she'd appreciate what he was obviously proud of—except she had to disappoint him.

"Maybe later. The quiet feels good."

He accepted that and continued to watch as she head-ed toward the dining room, where a computer sat on a small desk that looked to be something he might have brought home in a box and assembled with a tube of glue and a screwdriver.

The kitchen came next, with the dining area against the wall to the right. If he ate here, he seldom entertained, for the table was pushed against the wall and one of the four chairs had been called to service at the desk. The business end of things was to the left—and it was spotless, except for the pizza box rising out of the garbage, and the keys, mail, newspaper, and empty ice pack box on the counter.

"Why is your house so clean?" she asked. Maybe he never cooked. Maybe he actually lived in the garage.

He grinned. "Because I'm every woman's dream?"

Right.

"Okay," he said. "Heston Hall's daughter mucks the place out every Friday."

That sounded more like it—and at least he cared.

Emily steered to her right, past Colin to the hall. The bathroom where she'd bathed separated the front and back bedrooms and included an old claw-foot bathtub— probably an original, judging by the width of the house's woodwork—a new pedestal sink, and the colors blue and brown.

She peered down the hall to the front bedroom, where a glint in the dark pulled her to the threshold. She flipped on the light and gasped. If the rest of the house was spare of decoration or expense—save for the electronics and leather—this was where Colin lavished his time and money. The complicated assemblage of high-tech bars, captive stacks of rectangular weights, and three benches fanning out like spokes was as massive as would fit. The space would have looked crowded, except the machine was designed to fit against a wall—which Colin had mirrored, creating an illusion and tossing the overhead light into every corner.

No wonder he filled a T-shirt the way he did, had carried her so effortlessly—

"What do you think?" he asked suddenly.

Emily turned. He'd been standing behind her long enough to get a shoulder familiar with the wall, arms crossed over his chest.

"You appear to be rather serious about this," she replied.

He simply stared back. "Have you ever lifted weights?" he asked finally.

"No. Never had the opportunity." She looked at the equipment more closely. "I think I'm curious about it."

"I'd be glad to show you."

That sounded like fun—for some crazy reason. Erin would say it was just like her to try something so unusual, but maybe it wasn't so much the course of study . . . as the teacher.

Her gaze climbed his chest, settling on his face. He stood nearby, for the hallway was narrow. He was comfortable and exciting and intelligent and witty and talented and tender and—

"I probably love you," she said quietly.

Twenty-five

*O*h brother, that was a mistake, except the words had been there, had needed to be shared with someone, for so long; Colin was the logical choice. Emily watched his face for the inevitable reaction, whatever it might be. He didn't look particularly startled—if her opinions were to be trusted at the moment and in her present state. In fact, his expression hadn't changed in the least. He just stared. Watched her.

"Think so?" he asked simply.

"Probably," she replied.

Those dimples threatened, and the expression in his eyes was one of amusement. He'd better not laugh at her.

"Is that okay?" Emily asked, then groaned inside. Wanted to duck into the generous collar of the sweatshirt she wore. Stupid pills. She was only making it worse.

Colin grinned. "Probably."

Her heart stopped. She waited for more—which he didn't volunteer.

She took as deep a breath as her paralyzed lungs would allow. "So, do you love me back?"

He might. He'd taken care of her—had never left her

side—as if he did. He sure kissed her like he did.

The grin relaxed, the expression in his eyes growing warm. "Probably."

From top to bottom his gaze strolled her face, but her reactions were slower than his. She'd hardly absorbed what he'd said before he lowered his head for a kiss. Gently, he pulled her close . . . and kissed her long and leisurely . . . holding her strong in the circle of his arms, an embrace that let one crutch fall against the door jamb and felled the other to the floor. When he did release her, it was only so far as her cheek to his chest. He held her tight, one hand at the small of her back, the other stroking up and down.

For a long time they clung to each other, her thoughts drifting between wondering what it all meant and how she might never feel quick and clear-headed again.

As if he sensed the latter, he leaned back, lifting her chin with the bend of his finger. "You're looking a little peaked, Emmy. You should be lying down."

That's right, they were still standing in the hall. "You've been so nice to me," she told him.

He stared, then chuckled suddenly, as if she'd said something a little out of synch.

The old red GMC pickup truck slowed as it passed that particular house on University Avenue. It was Sunday, and the Volkswagen was still parked at the curb, the snow on the windshield undisturbed. The car hadn't moved. She didn't answer the door, and she hadn't gone to church. She was with him, that big shot with the fancy car. Had been all weekend.

She shared herself with everyone; her price was cheap.

Emily pulled the comforter up to her chest while Colin straightened it over her propped foot. She'd just awakened from a nap and returned from a trip to the bathroom. He'd come from the living room, where he'd been watching the Sunday afternoon football game. The stadium crowd cheered over another exciting play. The announcers gave commentary.

"How do you feel?" Colin asked, stretching out on the bed, cheek in hand.

"Better," she replied. "Still weak and . . . fuzzy, except things aren't moving the way they were."

"Still dizzy?"

She nodded sadly. "Some, but the seas have calmed a little."

He reached for her hand on top of the comforter, rubbing his thumb back and forth over her fingers. He'd held her hand most of the night, where he lay beside her in his sweats and under a separate comforter. She couldn't bear to be alone; he'd been a gentleman.

"I'll get someone to take your shift tomorrow night," he said.

She groaned softly. "I don't have much sick time built up."

"You can't stand at that board for five hours, Emmy," he said more firmly. "Give yourself another day."

She sighed. Sank more deeply into the pillows. What a mess. And expense. She owed him nearly two hundred dollars for the emergency room visit. Who knew how much for the prescription and crutch rental?

"When do I get to go home?" she asked.

He raised the eyebrows over those eyes and sent those dimples her way. "Get to go? You hurt my feelings."

"It's been fun, but even the greatest of slumber parties must end," she told him gently.

He'd need to go to bed early to be up at four and on the air at six.

Colin only stroked her fingers, his grin relaxing as if he were considering something. Suddenly he rose from the bed, strode to his chest of drawers, and drew an object from the top drawer. Returning to his spot, he turned her hand over, palm up, and set a key ring in the middle of it. With the tip of his finger, he put a space between each of the three keys—the head of one of them was encased in black plastic windowing a BMW symbol—drawing her attention to the brass oval with her name engraved on it in flourishing script.

Emily's stomach tingled. Knotted into a ball that rolled over and over. This was no casual thing. Colin hadn't left the house all weekend. Hadn't had these keys and the nameplate delivered like a pizza, or even plucked them from the mint rack beside some cash register. This was planned. Important.

"Don't go," he said to her hand. "Stay."

Stay?

As if he'd heard her confusion, he finally looked up. "We'll go to your apartment, get enough clothes to see you through a few days. Then when you feel up to it—next week or so—we'll move you out of there." He set the key ring on her stomach and lifted her hand to his mouth. Slowly, gently, he began to kiss her fingers. "I'll come home early tomorrow . . . just because you're here and waiting," he said in a low voice.

Hypnotic to watch, heart-stopping to feel, the pressing of his lips to the sensitive skin at her wrist, his own eyes closed as if she were delicious. They opened slowly— stepped right inside her, those navy eyes and dark lashes.

Such dimples. Lush hair. Thick and virile physique built a lift at a time. Velvet voice, and kisses that sparked connections to insides of her that had never been traced before.

"You want us to live together?" she asked.

He shifted, scooting up beside her, right arm over her. Solid. Strong. Male. "What I want is to make love to you," he said softly, "tonight . . . and every morning."

Gently, tenderly, he set his mouth on hers . . . until his kiss deepened, making her head spin . . . while he coaxed and demanded at the same time, making her breaths shallow and heating her blood. This was how it felt to be alive, so very alive. . . . She was floating at a dreamy speed of light to the top of a roller coaster . . . so high . . . and so easy to go for one who was unforgiven . . . unforgivable.

Think. Think.

Emily felt torn into several people. One of them hungered for more of this passion, leaned toward the dangerous, irresistible places he was taking her. Another heard the declaration of love—no probably about it. He'd considered this long and hard before he'd presented it to her. This was the proposal of the unenlightened, the carnal man's version of bended knee. It was also a miracle—only by the grace of God—that she saw deep inside him to know he meant all this as a compliment, wished her to feel chosen.

Another of her selves cringed; it was all about sex. At the root of it, just sex. No promises. No future that was any more solid than the next disagreement or change in mood that could sever it. Trade what you could give only once, for a set of keys . . . and only a portion of himself. It was temporary. A trial run. If it didn't work out, well, no hard feelings, you understand.

Emily backed into the pillow, dragged her mouth away, and pushed at his shoulder. "No, Colin," she breathed, desperate to get away from where she might let herself go.

He stopped and lifted his head. His eyes, dilated to black above her, stared intently, as if she held his future as surely as they held her reflection. "No, to which?" he asked, his voice low and intimate. "This," he said with a nudge of his chin at what they'd been doing, "or to moving in?"

It had never been a secret. She'd always known he would hurt her. It had just been so darned tempting to try to beat it, to try to be the one exception who would dance around the pit and not tumble in. They would dabble in . . . attraction, then merely walk away when they reached the impasse. Or they would skirt all the issues, all the soul-dividing differences, by his simply coming to the Lord at the crucial moment. But it would never be an agony, never rip her heart from her chest until she thought she'd despair of even breathing. That sorrow, that severance, stood at the end of this decision, and it was here now. Time now. No more "just maybe." No more hope. Break every rule, or break her heart. Either way, she lost.

She managed to speak calmly over the anger and crushing hurt. "Both," she replied. She paused. Found the courage to finish it. "I'm saving myself . . . for marriage."

Twenty-six

Almost imperceptibly, Colin's brow furrowed. He tilted his head—*Say what?* Then suddenly, and still so slightly, his eyes widened, and he jumped as if he'd awakened in his sister's arms. He hadn't known of her innocence. Had simply assumed she was *that* kind of girl. If his reaction didn't tell, the key ring between them shouted it.

Emily split again, stretched between pride in her commitment to a husband she hadn't met and shame for the oddity she must seem. Colin held himself away as if she might break—or get something on him.

"I'm sorry," he said, though his features were stiff, void of remorse.

He rolled away, scooted off the foot of the bed, taking the key ring with him . . . and walked out the bedroom door. Simply walked away, leaving her with the ache to call him back and the fury to hurl whatever was within reach.

Instead she cried. Silently, while John Madden talked about that iron-wall Steelers defense, Emily released just enough stomach-trembling sobs to relieve the pressure, just enough to ensure she wouldn't break down in front of

Colin. Then she made a tidy stack of the extra comforter and pillow and hurried to the bathroom, where she changed into her Friday night clothes—minus the left shoe—and dropped Colin's sweats into the bathroom hamper. She checked her appearance in the mirror—her eyes only looked tired, not heartbroken—then crutched across the hall, purse swinging on her arm.

Colin had been watching the game. He followed her progress into the dining room.

"I'm ready to go," she said.

He nodded, though the movement was too animated, as if she'd caught him snooping in her purse. "Do you want to eat first? I could go for chicken."

"Thanks anyway, but I've imposed enough."

He nodded. Looked away. Then he drove her home.

"You sure you're going to be all right?" he asked once they were in her apartment.

She turned, surprised his voice came from so far away. He hadn't even stepped beyond the front door. It hung open behind him.

Emily swung back to the doorway. "I'll be fine."

It was a half-truth. Her head and ankle would heal; it was the tender portion in her chest that would get another kick every time she stopped by the coffeemaker and watched Colin tease Betty or attended an announcers' meeting he presided over, legs crossed so casually, so confidently. Every time she heard his voice . . .

It was a Kodak moment, the way she would always remember him—standing rich in stature and beauty, hands stuffed in the pockets of his sheepskin coat, lush brown hair falling over the collar.

"Thanks for everything," she told him.

"You're welcome."

"I'll see you Tuesday," she said, then, "Well, I probably

won't see you, but I'll be in. You're sure it's no trouble to find someone to work my shift tomorrow night?"

"No. Get well."

She nodded. He nodded. He was the first to move.

"I'll see you later," he said, taking the two steps required to put him where he could lean the rest of the way for a kiss. A kiss that was quick. A kiss that was set only near her mouth. A kiss that was good-bye, because neither of them could go any further than they already had.

Sunday nights were the best; the police force was at its leanest, and all expectations were set on recovering from the revelry of Saturday night. Even so, he took his precautions, parking the old red GMC pickup truck behind the lawn and garden store early in the afternoon, then walking home. Anyone who drove around back would assume the truck belonged to the owner or an employee. Anyone looking for more overt activity would watch the snowblowers displayed in front.

Unless things had changed drastically—and Chintzy Bill, the owner, had loosened his grip on the green—there would be no one patrolling the strip mall tonight, and the key to the padlock was . . . right there, hanging on a chain inside the left side pipe bracing the gate, just as it had been when Chintzy Bill did retain a roving security guard.

On a singsong squeak, Missoula Lawn and Garden's gate swung wide.

"Hello?"

"Colin? This is Sterling," the voice on the other end of the line announced.

Colin squinted at the red numerals on the digital alarm clock. He'd dived for the phone—stupid. It wouldn't be Emily, even if she had a phone. "Did you know it's 1:47?"

"I know that," Sterling replied. "I just received a call from a listener who said the transmitter's cutting in and out."

"Cutting in and out?" Colin turned on the lamp and rubbed his eyes with the heel of his hand. "You mean we're off the air?"

Not good. Could be a problem that crept into the day parts. And Betty would have to scramble to reschedule the missed spots; the time was gone, the Diamond could never make it back.

"Not right now—I've listened," Sterling replied. "The caller said it's been sporadic."

"How did he know to call you?"

"He didn't say and didn't give me time to ask."

It wasn't so farfetched. Nearly everyone who owned or managed a business knew Sterling. He was a regular at the chamber of commerce meetings and somewhat involved with local politics, whereas Colin was hidden; his telephone bills were mailed to Nicholas Kavanaugh, and his number was unlisted.

"Did you call Ernest?" Colin asked. The quick little man who ruled over the miles of wires, thousands of buttons, tons of machinery, transmitters, broadcast tower—everything that needed a screwdriver to make it go—was the one who could help. That's what the man was paid for, to engineer and be on call, which meant he got to answer the phone at one forty-. . . nine on a Monday morning.

"Tried to," Sterling said. "No answer. Can't raise him on his pager either."

That wasn't like Ernest, who kept nearly every station in town—TV and radio—on the air. Regardless, it left only one candidate to take his place.

"Okay. I'll take care of it," Colin said.

"Thanks. Let me know what you find out."

Colin started by dialing the transmitter at its location on TV Mountain. Sitting at the side of the bed, he pushed buttons, asking the computer specific questions. Oddly, the automated voice on the other end answered with reasonable numbers.

His plan could have backfired. There could have been an engineer Barclay called when there was trouble at the station, but apparently the big shot got to handle it. The driver of the old red GMC pickup truck laughed out loud, watching from his position down the street. Oh, and wasn't Mr. Radio devoted and Johnny-on-the-spot, trotting down his steps and backing out of the driveway in his fancy car? He laughed harder.

Too bad the big shot didn't take his dog with him though. It barked at a back window, probably a bedroom, the whole time it took to park the pickup beside the backyard gate, push a specimen of Chintzy Bill's inventory down the ramp, and nestle it behind the detached garage, where the big shot wouldn't see it when he put his dog outside. However, anyone driving down the wide, paved alley would. The dog served its purpose, after all. Thanks to it, the snow was already chewed up; it would show no new tracks.

Hands on hips, Colin stared at the control board in the FM studio. The satellite was receiving the signal from Dallas. The STL—studio-to-transmitter link—was sending the microwave signal from the station to the transmitter on TV Mountain. The computer was switching back and forth from the satellite feed to local broadcast for local commercials. And the modulation meter was bouncing in time with the intensity of the Deana Carter tune playing. There was no problem. The station was on the air.

Colin lifted the clipboard from its nail on the wall and scanned. The station had been on the bird since 6:00 P.M., but everything looked normal. Cal Braithwaite, noon to six, had been the last announcer to stand at the board, and though he was prone to writing down numbers within a few digits of the last transmitter readings, rather than take new ones, he would have noted it on the log if he'd been knocked off the air. There was no such comment.

Colin sighed and replaced the clipboard. If there was a problem, he couldn't see it. There was nothing to do but go home, assume it would make itself plain during the waking hours, and call Ernest tomorrow—and pay next month's bill on the man's pager himself, if necessary.

Emily listened to Colin's show Monday morning; she was awake anyway and needed to hear his voice. She also listed the ads he played; she needed some answers—and a distraction.

A knock echoed down the hall. She froze where she sat up in bed, a library book in her lap. She glanced at the clock; 11:45. Could be Colin. *Would* be Colin. He knocked again.

"Emily?"

A woman's voice.

"Just a minute," Emily called, throwing back the covers. A moment later she opened the door and peeked around the edge. "Betty."

"I hope you like rice," Betty said, holding up a white paper box from the takeout. "I brought Chinese."

It smelled delicious, heaped on the plate she handed Emily a few minutes later. Her own portion balanced on her lap as she blessed the food from the occasional chair she'd scooted from the living room. A pan of water heated on the stove for tea.

"How did you know I was hurt?" Emily asked.

Betty looked as though she'd just come from the station, in her brown slacks and pink blouse, her graying hair teased into a cotton candy puff.

Sure enough. "I overheard Colin making arrangements for Dave Sommer to fill in for you tonight," Betty replied, taking a bite of lunch. "Dave is still in high school, so it's not as easy as just calling his home."

"Was Colin able to reach him okay?"

"I didn't hear any more about it, so I think so. Dave is pretty good about filling in."

That was a relief. Emily had been enough trouble.

Wait a minute. "I thought you were supposed to have today off."

"I was," Betty sighed. "I even worked Saturday to make up for it, but Vicky Millian needed some account information right away."

So demanding, Vicky. So conscientious, Betty.

"So does everyone know I'm hurt?" Emily asked, treading closer to what she really wanted to know.

"Everyone's concerned," Betty replied.

Nice to know, but Emily took a bite of her fried rice, working up the courage to hear a more important answer. "Does everyone know I was with Colin when I fell?" she asked quietly.

The room settled into silence. A siren whined outside, conspicuous for its rarity. Emily waited. Finally looked up.

"I don't know," Betty told her. "I assumed it, since you're dating, but I didn't hear anyone talking about it. Colin's been a bear all morning," she added, as if it told more than the words said.

It did; Colin's mood hadn't improved. He hadn't said a thing, not a syllable, as he'd driven her home yesterday. By the time she saw him tomorrow, he'd be ready to fire her— or stab her to death with a phonograph needle.

Emily let her head fall against the pillows. Only twenty-some-odd hours since she'd had to give it up—give him up—and she had no tears or energy left to cry them. Served her right. She'd hoped to cheat, and hadn't gotten away with it. That was that.

The fried rice lay on her plate. Betty's gaze stirred trust.

"We . . . had a fight," Emily admitted—if fight was the word for it.

"I'm sorry," Betty said gently.

That's what he'd said, but he hadn't explained what for. Either her values were not his values, or he wished he'd never met her. Pick one.

"He asked me to move in with him," Emily continued, so calm, so flat . . . so hollow.

"Oh dear," Betty said, her tone as kind as if she knew the shock of reality the question had prompted. "What did you say?"

"I told him no. That I'm saving myself for marriage. He got angry."

"And it's over."

Emily nodded. Held back a bitter laugh. It hadn't ever really begun—another situation that had pressed her nose to the glass. Times before, she'd wanted out; this time she'd wanted in. She hadn't been able to go then; she couldn't go now.

"It seems I've always been so . . . lonely," Emily said.

That was the word—lonely. Desperate to get out, or at least connect with someone who knew . . . alienation. Who'd had to face death too soon, who'd had to put their own life on hold to assume someone else's. Stacy had been a dear friend, but she hadn't understood. Not really. Her biggest worry had been how to convince Rachel Rutledge she wasn't panting after Jason Garvey, and whom to go to homecoming with. Emily had been juggling a freshman year of college—clutching for some semblance of normality—and cooking through a menu of foods to find one Mother could tolerate on her diabetic diet and still keep in her stomach for more than twenty minutes. Stacy had been living high school; Emily had been living survival. Hadn't even gone to her own graduation dance.

"You'd said that about Colin, hadn't you?" Emily asked. "You said he was lonely."

Betty nodded.

Emily combed her memory. It wasn't anything he'd said, wasn't anything she'd noticed in his daily life, but she'd seen it. Early on. Maybe as soon as that first breakfast when he'd told her about landing in Missoula because his Camaro just wouldn't go one more mile.

"He seems to have no family," Betty continued, "no one who cares about him. He works every Christmas so the other announcers can spend the day with their families."

So sad—Colin standing in an empty studio, playing a rotation of Christmas carols, six an hour, while snow fell gently outside, and Missoula windows all across town fogged over with the steam from boiling potatoes, bubbling gravy, and glazed hams in need of slicing.

Oh, so what? He was a loner. He was happy that way, or he'd change it. She'd been a distraction, a possibility to explore . . . and let go when she'd dented his pride.

"I admire your resolve," Betty said suddenly. "Colin may never come to the Lord, but you stood up for what was right, and that may have more impact than you'll ever know."

"I'm no witness to anyone," Emily replied. "Mine is the last life that will ever stand as an example."

"Why do you say that?" Betty asked. "Look at the way you took care of your mother—loved and nursed her—during her final days."

Emily jabbed at the rice getting cold on her plate. "I wasn't as selfless as you think."

Betty made no reply and no argument. She set her plate on the end of the bed and rose, saying, "I'll bet that water is hot." Her loafers padded softly down the hall.

Betty hadn't wanted to hear any more, that's why she'd escaped. Fine enough. Emily had said all she was going to say anyway. The memories were humiliating enough without adding the stab of Betty's censure.

Emily closed her eyes and sighed. Her head hurt. Not as bad as Saturday. Nothing was as bad as that—

"Here you are," Betty said brightly, strolling into the room and handing Emily a mug. She sat again, crossed her legs, and set her forearms on the deeply pillowed arms of the chair, cup in hand. "Jim died of cancer," she said suddenly. She picked at something on her slacks. Checked her manicure, a finger at a time. "I don't know if I ever told you that, but it was awful. In his brain, you know. He was like a toddler toward the end."

Emily winced, just imagining.

"Wandering out of his bed and down the street in the middle of the night, leaving faucets running. He made a pot of coffee one time and forgot to put the carafe under the spout. The coffee poured all over the counter and onto the floor by the time I found it. It's a miracle he didn't burn himself. Before the disease was through with him, he'd forgotten how to feed—" Her voice broke. She cleared her throat and swallowed. "He even started soiling himself." She stared at her mug, her lips working—purse, release, purse, release. Then she peeled them apart and said, so quietly, "Sometimes I hated him."

Twenty-seven

$\mathcal{E}$ mily's heart stopped. Of all the things this gentle woman might have said, that was the most unexpected. What it must have taken to admit it—and then voice it.

Betty gazed at her mug, seeming to see beyond it. "We were going to retire in a year. We were making plans, putting everything in order. Then he got sick . . . and everything died. I hated him for doing that to me, for making me change my life when I was getting excited about the next phase."

Yes. The next new beginning . . . on the other side of the glass now. Out of reach. A tease.

Emily stared at her blanket, at the way the yellow fluff was beginning to pill into little balls. There'd been that time Mother called from the bedroom, her voice so feeble. A whine, really, that scraped up Emily's back like the dry and yellow fingernails she cleaned and clipped every other week. Emily didn't answer. Just stood at the back door, book bag slung over her shoulder. Mother called again . . . and Emily moved so silently, turning the knob, then closing the door behind her.

What kind of daughter did that to her mother? Her dying mother?

What kind of daughter cried no tears admitting it?

It was for Emily that Betty made her confession . . . so Emily confessed. "I hated her," she told the little ball of blanket she rolled between her fingers. "Every time I had to clean where she'd vomited, or leave my friends to go home to her, I hated her. But I loved her so," she heard herself say, just before the warmth flooded and filled in the place where the words had sprung from. "I love her. She's my mama. And she's gone. I miss her so, and God will never forgive me."

"Forgive you for what, Emily?" Betty asked. "For losing patience? For wishing she'd die and get it over with so you could get on with your life?"

Emily's stare darted across the bed.

"I felt the very same things, you see," Betty said, as if her heart heard.

"I thought it would be better, but it only left Daddy more alone than he'd been before . . . " Emily paused. "She suffered so."

"It's so hard to watch them die," Betty said. "It's so hard for those who dare to be healthy around them. They die too. Everything normal, everything that came before, stops. The dinners, the social functions. No one knocks on the door, no one calls."

Betty must have been standing in an obscure corner, watching.

"They don't mean to be inconsiderate," she continued. "They just don't know what to do with it. Maybe they're afraid to intrude—and maybe a little afraid of death."

"Our culture doesn't 'do' death," Emily replied. She gritted her teeth. "If one more person said one more time that I 'lost' my mother, I would have screamed. I didn't lose her. I know exactly where she is. I could take you to her grave."

"You're angry about it."

"I'm angry with them," Emily spat, hearing it for the first time herself. "They let us down. They abandoned us." She waited. Held her breath.

"Yes, they did," Betty said gently.

Relief washed over her. Real. The feelings were real.

"But not maliciously," Betty added. "They didn't know, Emily. Please don't be hard on them. They did the best they could . . . just as you did the best you could." She paused. The world was silent. "If you're hard on them, you're harder on yourself."

The words fell into the room slowly, but no less softly. Then the tears came, rising to the surface without drama . . . just rising and welling and rolling over Emily's cheeks.

"Stop punishing yourself. The answer to your anger—and your loneliness—is forgiveness," Betty said.

Colin slammed the refrigerator door and ambled into the living room, unscrewing the bottle cap and tossing it onto the counter as he passed. It twirled and rattled to rest while he was already tipping his head for a draw of cold brew. Leather stretched softly beneath his weight as he claimed his favorite corner of the couch, nudged his shoes off, and dropped them on the floor. He slouched down, took another long swallow, and stared at his stockinged feet.

A virgin, of all things.

She shared herself with no one; her price was all a man had to give.

Colin shook his head. Began picking at the label on the bottle. There couldn't be more than a dozen such innocents old enough to wear a bra in all of Missoula. He snorted. Would have thought she'd had at least one boyfriend she'd been intimate with along the way. Couldn't even imagine such a thing as she hoped for, marrying someone without trying them out first—though Gimpa and Gram probably had. He chuckled, the sound jarring the room. Gram would have slapped Gimpa's hand and told him to behave himself. Colin's smile relaxed. No, Gimpa wouldn't have even tried. Too much the gentleman. Too much the Christian. Too committed to saving himself for marriage.

Emily wanted God? Colin was born in the Bible Belt. Could tell her about prayer meetings where the building throbbed with the sound of song and clapping hands.

He shifted and recrossed his ankles. Something poked his leg. He dug in the front pocket of his jeans and pulled out the key ring . . . fingered the brass name tag—*Emily*. Engraved for her.

For all the good it did him. He separated out the keys for the house, the Bimmer, and the Jeep. All he had. All he'd built of his new life since rolling to a stop in Missoula. He scanned the living room. It was a pretty good life. The best radio job in town, with the salary to go with it. A good house, dependable cars with low miles and good paint, furniture, a savings account. The Jeep was paid for, and he'd cut the mortgage on the house by adding extra to the payments. He even had a washer and dryer and a retirement account. Now that was solid. He wasn't bad looking. Some women said he was cute. He worked out, kept a tight tummy behind his belt.

And she'd turned him down flat. No discussion. That fresh little thing with the pretty green eyes, tender mouth, talent, a sense of humor, an admirable measure of smarts, and an honest heart, was saving herself for marriage.

And, therefore, saving herself for someone else.

Emily propped her elbows on Marilyn's desk and stared at the patchwork of notes the receptionist had written to herself on neon-colored stickies. The radio station was empty around her, save for the voice of Dave Sommer, on the air in her place. The phone rang in her ear.

Please let him be home. He shouldn't be, but make it so anyway.

The connection clicked. Gordon Erickson said, "Hello?"

That was enough to start Emily crying.

Thank you, Jesus to One, then "Daddy?" to the other.

"Emily? What is it? Are you all right?" There was alarm in his voice.

He'd lost so much, that was why he panicked.

"I'm fine," she said, her voice clogged with tears, her heart full of sorrow for taking out on him what hadn't been his fault, for hanging on him an anger he hadn't earned. "I need to talk to you," she said, a sob tearing loose and bursting into the phone. "I'm sorry, Daddy. I'm so sorry."

Someone's hands scrolled through the ads, selecting the one for Hog Heaven Harley-Davidson when it rolled into view. It was a strange time of the year to be advertising motorcycles, except the deal had been a sweet one, both ways. It was an aggressive ad campaign, an expensive one, and the waiting list for new Harleys was long—unless you knew someone. This little baby made four spots

each hour—the most ever played was three—but it would be worth it. That Hog with the charcoal paint and throaty roar looked like a panther preparing to spring.

Emily listened to Colin's show Tuesday morning; she was awake anyway and needed to hear his voice. She also listed the ads he played; she needed more answers—and more distraction.

Emily started the first of a two-song set and stared at the logs on the counter. Monday's and Tuesday's. Yesterday's and today's. She wiped her sweaty hands on her jeans . . . and stared. Then she shook her head at herself; she wanted to know, so find out for heaven's sake.

Make it okay, Lord. Make everything all right.

She pulled Monday's log close, opened it to the six o'clock hour, and set her list of Monday morning's spots beside it to compare. . . . Then what was left of the world began to slowly complete its crumbling.

The old red GMC pickup truck pulled into a parking spot in front of the convenience store. The driver left it running, just as the woman with the pretty legs and the Saturn had, except he wasn't there for the mocha mint coffee that was Wednesday's special. He was there for anonymity. He pulled a quarter from his jeans, dropped it in the slot, and dialed the number. It rang only once.

"Missoula Police Department," a woman's voice said.

The driver cleared his throat, visualizing a nervous citizen, and added a little warble to his voice. "I'd like to report a— Is this where I call to report a crime?" he asked. "See, I think I know someone who stole something."

Colin started another set and turned to the computer keyboard, scrolling through the spots to cue up the next stopset. He glanced up as Heston Hall—sounded like a building on a college campus—plodded his mustached bulk past the window, studying folds of paper he'd torn from the Associated Press Teletype. Colin glanced at the clock. The station newsman had one more newscast at nine before he was free until noon. He'd have brunch with his wife. Always did. Always seemed to have somewhere else to go, someone waiting for him. Lucky man, Heston.

There'd be no lunch with Emily today. No pie tonight. No kisses. She was saving those—her whole self—for someone else.

Fury rose in Colin's chest—another man kissing her, handling her? Let him at 'em. The snake would be breathing out a hole in the back of his head in the space of five minutes. And who was it Emily was saving herself for? Some puke like Bradley Earl Stapleton—who'd knock her around just because he could? Or someone else who wouldn't listen long enough to learn she wished she had another Irish setter like the one her sister took with her when she left home? Wouldn't have any idea how many foolish teenage antics she'd missed out on, how modest she was, how much she liked music—sound—and the peculiar pressures of her job. Only he knew those things.

No probably about it; he loved her.

Colin combed his fingers through his hair and blew a long and heavy breath. Maybe that would be enough. Maybe he could convince her. Maybe, just maybe, she'd have a guy like him.

The driver of the old red GMC pickup truck stared through the windshield at the parking lot across the street, where a Missoula city squad car parked in front of Missoula Lawn and Garden Supply. The store was closed, wouldn't open for another hour, but the officer in blue strode to the front door and knocked. Stupid idiot, Chintzy Bill. Didn't even know he'd been burgled, and only opened the door a crack now. No, he finally let the cop inside. The scrooge should be thankful it had been brought to someone's attention that he was missing some merchandise.

Colin was still on the air. That was the only thing that even made it possible for Emily to walk in the front door, the knowing that he wouldn't stroll around a corner and glue her to the spot with his eyes. She glanced at the FM studio window, where Colin stood at the board. Too busy; he didn't even glance her way.

Put on the whole armor of God . . . the breastplate of righteousness—yes, a forgiven heart—*the shield of faith*—could use more of that—*and the sword of the Spirit . . .* I can't remember the rest, Lord. *Just help me—help Sterling—get to the truth.*

Vicky strode into the lobby from outside, briefcase in hand, and offered a cat smile as she took her phone slips from Marilyn's desk.

"Hi, Vicky," Emily said.

"Hi," Vicky replied, though she was already engrossed in her messages and heading for her office at the opposite corner of the building.

Emily turned to the receptionist, who hadn't gotten even a glance from Vicky. "Hi, Marilyn. Is Sterling in?"

Marilyn looked up from her word processor and nodded. "Better hurry. He has to leave for a nine-thirty appointment."

It was amazing how Marilyn not only kept it all straight, but kept it all going, all at once. Emily gave her a smile, promised herself she'd buy the woman a plant for her desk or something sometime soon, and rushed toward Sterling's office.

Now, Lord. Now would be a good time for a little boost.

"Emily," Sterling called when she tapped on his open door. He waved her inside. "What has you out of bed at this hour?"

The old red GMC pickup truck rumbled slowly down Hilda Street, while the driver peered down the alley between Hastings and Beverly Avenues. He smiled to himself. A squad car was parked in about the middle of the block, about even with the chain-link fence whose alley gate opened into the backyard with the paw-pressed snow, detached garage, and tall structure under the blue tarp behind it. It wouldn't be long now.

All the small talk talked, Emily gathered a deep breath. "I think something is wrong here at the station," she said, speaking quietly even though the door was closed.

Sterling's overzealous growth of silvery brows lowered. "What do you mean?"

She gathered another breath, to tell it all before she lost momentum. "About a week ago I noticed one of my ads played on the air," she began, "but when I looked for it on the log, it wasn't there. I thought it might have been a make-good or something, but I heard it about the same time the next day. When I checked the play schedule in Betty's files, the times didn't match up. So Monday and Tuesday, I made a list of the spots I heard on the air. Last night I compared them to the logs."

Emily paused, her stare descending to the point of reflected light on the gold base of Sterling's executive pen set. His chair ceased rocking.

"I'm not sure what it all means, but every hour there are three or four spots being played that aren't on the log," her voice said. "They aren't being billed."

Colin fired the five-second legal station ID—*KDMD, Missoula*—which ended at the exact moment the network popped on the air with its introductory music to the news. Heston's three-minute cast would follow, then one more hour, and the Wednesday morning shift would be shot through the air and signed off. Speaking of that, Colin checked off the last stopset of commercials and scripted his signature in blue ink at the bottom of the log for the eight o'clock hour. Then he began pulling his final hour of music.

"This is a pretty serious charge," Sterling told Emily, his voice quiet and calm. "If I'm hearing you correctly, you're telling me one of my employees is stealing from me, taking money—or trade—under the table."

Emily winced. "That's the way it looks."

"Who?"

She clutched her purse a little tighter on her lap; the lists were inside. She should have never come to this place, to this station, to this town.

It couldn't be true. Must be another explanation. Please, make it not so. Make Sterling know something I don't.

The room was anything but quiet. Randy Travis twanged from the stereo speakers, the phone at Marilyn's desk rang, and Betty drew nearer in the hall, bringing her gentle laugh and a snippet of conversation with her—as if there were parts of the station where there was reason to carry on so carefree this Wednesday morning.

The name dropped in the center of it all, as if it were a rock in a glassy pool. As if it should echo in rings that rocked the shore. "Colin," she said.

The old red GMC pickup truck was already parked at the feed supply store down the street, out of the line of sight, though the driver still had a good view of the squad car wheeling under the silver-on-blue sign. When the officer stopped to look closer at the BMW parked in the next spot—and shook his head—the driver laughed out loud. That's right, the big shot drove a pretty fancy car for no harder than he worked. Someone should knock him down to size.

Colin looked up as Marilyn led a police officer past the hall window. He'd made no appointment for the locals to cut a PSA or to catch some publicity for one of their fund-raisers. Must be an emergency announcement, an accident blocking the highway or something, though the police usually just phoned.

"Hi. What can I do for you?" Colin asked after Marilyn closed the door behind her.

"You're Nicholas Kavanaugh?" the officer asked, his thumbs hooked ever so officially around his belt buckle.

Something dark crept into Colin's chest. This wasn't an invitation to emcee the next oldies concert for the cause of battered women—

Emily. No, the police would contact her next of kin, her father. But whatever it was, it still wasn't good news.

"Yes," Colin said finally.

"Nicholas Kavanaugh, you're under arrest," the officer said, "for the burglary of Missoula Lawn and Garden Supply."

Twenty-eight

*W*hat?" The room faded out of focus—taking everything except this figure of authority and his grave expression with it. "This is a joke," Colin said.

The man didn't smile. "This is no joke, Mr. Kavanaugh, and before you say anything more, let me inform you, you have the right—"

"I know my rights," Colin snapped. A laugh tumbled from his throat. "This is ludicrous." He turned to the board. He was on the air. *On the air.* "Look, I'm trying to run a radio show here," he said, scanning all the buttons and lights and displays, but not really seeing.

"You have the right to remain silent," the man continued, oblivious to the havoc he was wreaking on this moment or the threat he posed to all others to follow.

Colin stared at him. Glanced at the board and back again.

"Anything you say can and will be used against you . . ." the man droned.

Colin clenched his jaw. Thousands—tens of thousands—of hours on the air; it would take more than this to make him lose his rhythm. Colin scanned the board again, seeing this time. He was in the last of a two-song set. Another minute to go. The next stopset—two minutes' worth—was cued up, ready to fire. He turned to the officer, who was finally winding down.

"Look, I'm sure I can get this cleared up," Colin said. "Do I need to talk to you right now? Can I finish my show first? I'm off at ten."

"I'm sorry, sir," the officer said. "I have to take you in."

"To the station?"

The man nodded.

Colin ran his fingers through his hair. This was nuts. He peered at the man's name tag. "Officer . . . Nelson, can you give me five minutes—" Colin checked the playlist and the clock. "Actually, exactly two minutes and forty-five seconds, then I can walk out of here."

Officer Nelson nodded.

Colin turned back to the board.

Unbelievable.

"What did you say this place was? The place I supposedly robbed?" he asked.

"Burglary," the man replied. "Missoula Lawn and Garden Supply."

"Right," Colin said, picking up his headset. "Two-and-a-half minutes, then I'll find someone to take this mike, and we'll get this cleared up." Though he said the last part mostly to himself.

The quick tap on the door made Emily jump. Sterling looked up, and she swiveled.

"Sterling—" Colin was already saying as he opened the door. He stopped, his stare darting to Emily and hanging there.

The blood drained to her feet. He probably hadn't heard the conversation, but his face looked as stricken as if he'd witnessed every word, knew every question in her heart.

The muscle in his jaw tensed, and his stare shifted to Sterling—then he didn't seem to know quite where to set his attention. "I'm glad you're here, Emily," he said. "I have a problem."

"What's that?" Sterling asked.

"I have to leave right now—I mean right now—so somebody has to finish my shift." He looked to Emily. "You're the only one in the building besides Sterling with an FCC license."

Emily's hand flew to the base of her throat. "Me? Where's Starvin' Marvin or John or Heston—"

"Out to lunch or breakfast or whatever. They're not here," Colin replied quickly. "You can handle this, Emily. You're ready, but come on. You're going to have a whole lot of dead air in a minute if you don't get back there."

Then he just vacated the doorway. Emily stared from the opening to Sterling.

"Go on," he said. "We'll finish this later."

She nodded, grabbed her purse and coat, and limped out the door. There was a policeman in the lobby, walking in a small circle in the conversation area as if he were standing guard and trying to be very casual about it. She gave him a little smile and scuttled down the hall.

Colin was in the middle of the workstation. She stepped up beside him.

"How are you feeling?" he asked, though he wouldn't look her in the eye.

He knew. He'd been angry Sunday; he'd hate her now.

"Better," she said. "Almost back to normal."

"Good," he said, then plunged ahead. "You're in the

first song of a two-song set, and I've checked off the spots I've played and signed the log. Sign your name under mine; you're responsible for the last forty minutes."

She followed the motion of his head to the log and scanned the board and clock. Everything looked as if she'd never seen it before. Like stepping into the middle of a choreographed dance. There were no reference points. It wasn't her show. Not her studio.

"What's this all about?" Emily asked. "Are you okay?"

"Just a misunderstanding," Colin replied, then continued, "The spot load's a killer this time of day. Just put as many ads in each stopset as you can—up to three-and-a-half minutes—and still get some music in."

Now he looked at her, and though his gaze was hesitant, it still had the power to stop her heart . . and break it into pieces.

"Well, thanks," he said. "I'll talk to you later."

Then he turned, stepped around the counter, and strode from the room. A moment later he passed the hall window, straightening the collar on his coat. He didn't look up. He never looked back. He left with the policeman.

❦

The interrogation room wasn't ten feet long and eight feet across—little more than a closet—but it had a one-way mirror on one of the long walls, a scratched-up table pushed against the other, and three full-sized men in it. One of them, Officer Nelson, leaned against the door, while the other, Detective Shumaker, sat at the table with Colin.

"If you didn't take it, how did it get in your backyard?" Detective Shumaker asked, peering over the book of

Holiday Inn matches he was playing with.

Colin set his elbows on the table and balled one hand in the cup of the other. What a mess. And ludicrous. As if he'd want a fiberglass fountain for his backyard—for Sophie to make a mess in—badly enough to steal it. Not a Harley-Davidson with charcoal paint. Not a hot tub for two. A rock fountain—a phony rock fountain, and he, the son of a geologist.

"How did it get in your backyard?" Shumaker asked again.

Colin shook his head. "I haven't the faintest idea."

"It was under a blue tarp," the detective continued. "Like you meant it to go through the winter in good shape."

"Or you were trying to hide it," Nelson added from his position at the door.

"If I'd wanted to hide it, I would have put it in my garage," Colin told him.

This was getting old.

"Why would I steal something like that?" Colin asked, opening his hands in entreaty. "If I'd wanted some stupid decoration for my backyard, I would have gone out and bought it."

Shumaker shrugged. "We pick up people every day who don't need the stuff they take. Most of the time they have enough money on them to pay for it."

Colin leaned his mouth against his knot of hands and closed his eyes. All too familiar, this.

Are you sure that gun discharged accidentally? An experienced hunter like you? I wouldn't think you could be so careless.

Colin held the temptation to sigh—the air in the room was months old and clung to the stale and sour stench of a thousand mouths and twice as many armpits. Jail wouldn't be much better—ticked-off men, cigarette smoke, the occasional fistfight, and someone else at his microphone in the morning.

Sophie.

He groaned silently. She'd need to go outside in the next few hours. She'd never messed in the house, but she'd never last until he'd been arraigned and could make bail— tomorrow at the earliest. He hammered his fists against his lips. Whom to call? Emily? He'd die in jail first. Starvin' Marvin . . . John Vaughn . . . Sterling?

"I didn't steal that fountain," Colin said again.

Shumaker was the one to sigh. He'd been plowing dirt from under his fingernails with the corner of the matchbook. Now he tossed it at the corner where the table met the wall, as if he were shooting craps. "Well, I don't have an exact time for the crime, but I will, so I suggest you make a detailed list of your whereabouts for the past week or so. You'll be hearing from us."

Colin's stare darted to Shumaker's face. "I can go?"

"I don't have an empty cell to put you in, or you'd be spending the night, believe me," Shumaker said.

Uncanny, how disaster reduced a person to rejoicing over the smallest privileges; he could put his dog outside to piddle, and go to work in the morning. The bad news was, regardless of what night they decided on for the burglary, he'd never come up with an alibi—he lived alone, had no roommate, no wife . . . and no girlfriend.

Emmy. She'd never have him now. Not a guy whom the police took away in the middle of his shift.

Shumaker slapped his palms on the table and hefted his desk-job paunch out of the chair. "Don't leave town, Kavanaugh."

"What are you doing here?" Starvin' Marvin wanted to know as he ambled into the FM studio at a 9:59. Today's baggy T-shirt was green and Tweety Bird yellow. "Where's Colin?"

"Well, no one's certain," Emily replied, watching the clock to time into the station ID and the network news. "Something pretty important came up. He left with a policeman. I had to finish his shift."

Marv's head jerked back on its lengthy neck. "Police. Whoa, wonder what that was all about." He stroked the right point of his mustache, as if he could pull the answer from it.

Emily pushed buttons. From the speaker over Marv's head, the intro music for the news began. "It's all yours," she said. And not a moment too soon. Her first forty minutes of prime time had singed all her wires.

Marv grinned. "A little hectic, was it?"

"Let's just say the night shift is a silent movie compared to this." She rounded the counter, letting Marv have the board. "How do you guys get all those spots in and still make it sound like we're here to play music?"

He shrugged. "You get used to it." He bent over the log for a look at what was ahead of him.

"If you're set, I've had enough," she told him and waved on her way out the door.

Sterling had apparently given up on attending his 9:30 appointment. He met her in the hall and led her to his office.

"Is Colin back yet?" she asked as soon as he closed the door behind her.

"Not yet."

"Oh, well, he's been gone only forty minutes," she said, sitting down and swallowing the obvious question—Why did the police take him away?

"I'd appreciate it if you'd keep our conversation this morning to yourself," Sterling said as he reclaimed his throne. "Don't share your suspicions with anyone. That sort of thing."

"Of course," Emily said—as if she wanted to tell such a thing about the man who made her heart stop with a glance. "Do you mind if I ask what you intend to do?"

"Well, I'm not ready to call the police until I know a little more about what's going on around here, and how he figures into it."

"He didn't do this, did he?" she asked softly.

"I don't know," he said as quietly. He, who'd known Colin as many years as the number of weeks Emily had known him, could be no more certain than that. "But I'll find out."

They stared at each other, a program log's worth of questions, confusions, and disappointments passing between them. She might have discovered the crime, but she wasn't a hero. There would be no rejoicing. Nobody won.

She clutched her purse and coat. "I'd better go. I'm on the air again in eight hours."

Sterling's bushy brows shot up. "You did a fine job pinch-hitting."

"Thanks," she said, though the praise was small consolation.

"Thanks," Colin said as he closed the passenger door behind him, though it was as much a humiliation as a consideration, Officer Nelson giving him a ride back to the station. Emily's Volkswagen was gone, so he was spared that much. His stomach growled. There'd been no regard for a man who ate breakfast at 4:45.

Marilyn's curious stare met him when he stepped into the lobby.

"How's it going?" he asked as if the day, up to now, had been just like the one before it.

"Fine," she replied, though her tone tacked the words *for me* on the end. Then she watched, telephone receiver seemingly forgotten in hand, while he lifted his telephone message slips from the slot bearing his name.

"I'm going to order a pizza. Buzz me when it comes," he told her.

She would. He always ordered a large—and shared.

He leaned to get a view into Sterling's office, and stepped inside the threshold. "Sorry about this morning," he said to the man at the desk.

Sterling had been writing on a yellow legal pad. Now he dropped his pen and sat back in his high-backed chair, wrists draped over the arms. He nodded. "Anything I can help with?"

A good friend, Sterling. An eight-years friend.

"Not at this point, but thanks." Colin paused to practice phrasing. "I'm tangled in a misunderstanding, but I'll get it cleared up. How did Emily do?"

Sterling grinned. "Oh, she wasn't smooth, and she sounded gruesomely nervous, but I don't think the casual listener would have noticed. She's quite a lady."

That was an understatement—and an interesting choice of words. A lady, the sort of woman a man hoped—but wasn't quite sure—he had enough of what it would take to win.

All gone, probably. It would take a miracle now.

Colin turned in the doorway, tapping the woodwork in farewell. "I have work to do."

The only light breaking the night—the sun set early this far north—came from the studio, all the chairs were vacant and pushed against the desks, and Emily's shoes whispered on the carpeting as she crossed the lobby. John Vaughn and Reba McEntire made their presence known, one in the flesh, the other in digital sound.

She scanned the room. It told nothing about why the police wanted to talk to Colin. His car wasn't where it had been, so he'd at least come to get it, but there was no one to ask and she couldn't call him to relieve her worry. She'd no-thank-youed herself from his life.

Would that she could so easily extricate him from her heart.

She barely got out of her coat before the curiosity—and the hope—were too much. "Have you seen Colin today?" she asked John Vaughn.

"No. Why?"

"Just wondered," Emily replied, hanging her coat on the hook.

The afternoon prime-time Mr. Vaughn had shaved his goatee, and today his hair was hanging in a wall of golden highlights down his back, undulating with each bob of his head as he kept time to the music. The ends were as thick and healthy as the beginnings. Any woman would kill to have his mane.

"Guess he's in some kind of trouble, huh?" he said suddenly.

Should have known he'd know more than he let on. The transmitting equipment from studio to studio, station to station, rivaled the mountains of machinery sending the signals to the public.

Emily shrugged and leaned against the counter. "I don't know what to think," she said, trying to at least discount the severity of the occurrence. "I doubt he was under arrest. The policeman didn't handcuff him or anything. Could it have been station business?"

John gave her an incredulous look out the corner of his eye and slowly shook his head. "No way. That sort of thing comes here, and it doesn't take an announcer out of his studio in the middle of his show."

She'd rather not hear that.

A few minutes later, John had hardly locked the front door behind him when the phone rang.

"I heard you on the air this morning," Brad told her. "You sounded great, but what happened to Colin Michaels?"

"He got called away from the station—kind of an emergency," she replied.

"Oh? What was the problem?"

Emily started her liner, then the first song in the set. "I'm not sure," she told him. "Just something came up." She sought to change the subject. "How's work?"

"The job's fine," Brad replied. "What are you doing Saturday night? How about pizza and a movie?"

Not again. Should have left the topic where it was.

"You're feeling all right, aren't you?" Brad added.

He'd phoned last night, Tuesday night, though she'd told him only that she'd been too sick to work Monday night. He—or anyone else, for that matter—didn't need to know she'd fallen, knocked herself unconscious, then spent the weekend an invalid in the bed of Colin Michaels, Diamond Country's notorious program director.

"I'm fine," Emily replied. Just a little remnant of a limp and an exhaustion that overtook her at times. Except there were her cry-burned eyes and that ache in her chest. "I hate to be vague, but I don't want to commit to anything yet," she added.

Not to be brushed off, Brad jumped right on that, saying, "Why don't you plan on it for now, and I'll check with you later in the week?"

"Why don't you just check with me later in the week," she said more firmly. She wasn't up to a fight, but he'd get it if he insisted.

She checked the playlist against the clock; another minute to go in the first song. She glanced at the computer monitor and the first stopset John Vaughn had lined up for her. Hog Heaven Harley-Davidson, the leading spot in the trio. She'd heard it for the first time this morning when she'd played it on Colin's show—and in Colin's voice. She *hmmmed* to herself. Twice or more in one day seemed an aggressive schedule for advertising a toy that couldn't be played with until spring, but more experienced advertising minds than her own had come up with it.

"I might have to go to Helena in a week or two to help with some law enforcement issues they're having over there," Brad was saying. "Would you like to go along? It could be fun."

"To Helena? With you?"

Didn't exactly make her heart race. In fact, it didn't sound fun. Might even prefer being bruised and concussed at Colin's.

"Separate accommodations, of course," Brad added.

As if there were ever any question of it being otherwise.

"I have to work," she told Brad, watching the clock and listening to the music. She started the second song in the set. "I couldn't take time off," she added, leafing through the log in search of the nine o'clock hour.

"I know that. I can't either," he said, a little tersely. "I'd be going on a weekend."

There it was, the nine o'clock hour, and her signature beneath Colin's.

"Oh," Emily said. "Well, maybe. I don't know. I'd have to think about it. What would I do while you work?"

"I wouldn't have to work but only two or three hours," Brad said. "We'd have Saturday evening and all of Sunday to spend together."

Oh joy.

She scanned the list of spots, searching for the Hog Heaven ad.

"We wouldn't have to start back until Monday, don't you think?" he asked.

Emily stared at the log. The ad wasn't there.

Twenty-nine

*T*he ad had to be on the log—unless she'd missed it. Emily started at the top and read again, more carefully.

"Emily?"

"What?"

"I said, we wouldn't have to start back until Monday, would we?" Brad asked, his tone tight. "Not since you don't have to work until six that evening."

"Five forty-five," she said, absently. "I have to be here fifteen minutes before my shift."

That spot wasn't there. Something wasn't right.

"Okay—"

"I'm sorry, Brad," Emily said, interrupting him. "Something's come up. I need to go."

"What's wrong? Is someone there?"

"No, it's just something I need to do. I'll talk to you later," she replied while George Strait began singing his final chorus.

The phone in its cradle, Emily hurried to look again. That ad had been on this log, and she'd played it that morning in the . . . what was it? The 9:40 stopset? Yes . . .

and . . . it wasn't listed.

Something was screwy. Really, really screwy.

Coffee cup in hand, Colin stepped inside the general manager's office.

"Close the door, will you?" Sterling asked from his executive chair.

This was important—important enough for privacy, and important enough that Sterling hadn't even given him time to hit the bathroom after he got off the air.

Colin closed the door and sat down, ankle on knee. "What's up?" If it was about that business with the police yesterday, well, he'd have that taken care of in a few days.

For a long moment Sterling made no reply. "Something's recently come to my attention," he finally said. "Do you know anything about spots being played that aren't passing through Betty's bookkeeping?"

Not the bit about that stupid yard fountain. This was serious, and he, the station PD, should have known about it. Should have known one of his employees had figured out a way to make money under the table.

"No," Colin replied. "Who's doing it?"

Couldn't begin to guess. Heston Hall was too honest. Starvin' Marvin was too lazy. And John Vaughn had been with the station too long. As the newest member of the air staff, Emily was the likely candidate, except she'd search up and down the sidewalk for the rightful owner before she'd pocket a fallen dollar bill.

Sterling leaned forward. Set his arms on the desk, fingers linked as if this were a commercial for funeral homes. "Did you have any make-goods this morning that weren't listed on the log? Some that Betty wrote in, by chance?"

Colin's stomach tightened. This conversation wasn't shifting in favorable directions. "Make-goods? No."

"Then I'm afraid all suspicion points to you," Sterling said quietly.

Colin's stomach plummeted to his feet for the second time in as many days. "What?"

"I checked the log against your show this morning," Sterling continued evenly. "Each hour, you played four spots that weren't on it."

"Sterling—" Colin started, then stopped. He tried again, saying, "I don't know where you're getting your information, but I'm not on the take."

As if he hadn't even heard him, Sterling said, "I'm afraid I'm going to have to ask for your resignation."

Colin's insides died.

Resignation? Fired, he meant. How could he do that? He couldn't do that.

"I'm fired?" Colin asked, because he'd heard wrong, or this was a sick joke.

"I'll accept your resignation," Sterling clarified.

As if there were any difference. Fired. Final. Disaster. Panic.

Then dignity came to the rescue. "Okay," Colin replied, just as gently. "If you don't trust me any better than that, there's no future in our working together."

Sterling didn't argue. Because it was true. So Colin rose, dug into the front pocket of his jeans, rounded three keys—to the front door, the limo, and the transmitter building on TV Mountain—from the ring, and set them with a calm metallic clatter on Sterling's desk. Pulling his wallet from his back pocket, he began following them with discount identifications—free car washes at Big Sudsy, five gallons of gas per week at Tidrick Texaco, free membership to the YMCA, a 10 percent discount at Little Italy Pizza, free admission to the Paramount, half off at Video-to-Go, 10 percent off at Piano Bench Music, a media pass to the University of Montana sporting events, and a free consultation and adjustment at Browning Chiropractic, of all things. He'd never used the last, but the little pile in itself was worth thousands of dollars a year; the position he was about to walk away from would be difficult to replace.

"Betty will cut your check tomorrow," Sterling said.

"Just mail it," Colin told him and hooked his coffee mug. "See you later."

He strolled through a hallway of activity that was no longer his responsibility. The quality of Starvin' Marvin's show wasn't his problem. All the production copy in his bin, not his to do. That thing with the transmitter last Monday morning, not his concern. He rounded the hall to the transmitter room, lifted his FCC license from the cork-board, then rounded the hall again to the back of the building. Taking three empty coffee boxes from the utility room, he headed back to his office, closed the door, and rang Marilyn's desk.

"Yes?" she asked.

"Hold my calls, will you please?" he asked her. Let Sterling tell her it was forever. Not a time to answer questions. Not a time to do anything but what he had to do, as quickly as possible.

"Sure," she said.

Obviously she didn't know yet. She would. Very soon, all of Missoula would know. That was the one thing about radio—it was ever so public.

He began filling boxes. He needed a vacation anyway. It could start in thirty minutes.

A knot of dread balled in Emily's stomach as she pulled into the station parking lot. Colin's BMW was parked in its usual spot in front of the door, even though it was his habit to get something to eat soon after he got off the air. So much for hunger and habit. She parked her Volkswagen on the far right side of the parking lot, far from Colin's window, and hurried into the lobby as fast as her tender ankle would let her. She aimed for Sterling's office; he was on the phone.

Now what?

Go see Colin, a quiet and steady voice replied.

She paused to consider it. Could be a good idea. Could solve a mystery. Could feed hungry eyes. She headed down the hall.

Colin's door was closed.

Emily braced herself with a deep breath and tapped lightly.

"Yes?" he asked from the other side.

"It's me," she replied. "May I come in?" She glanced behind her to the studio window, where Starvin' Marvin watched. Thankfully, he closed his eyes and began to speak into the microphone. She turned back to the door.

Silence. Then, "This isn't a good time."

It can't wait—the small voice said.

"It can't wait," Emily said, then got to focus on the door for several seconds before it opened.

Her stare climbed the deep green of Colin's dress shirt, and in less time than it took to draw her next breath, she knew—he didn't do it, and she had to help him prove it.

"What's up?" he asked, though he didn't invite her in. It was difficult to read his expression. If anything, he looked a little harried, as if she'd interrupted something important. She glanced past him. There wasn't anyone else in his office.

"Can I talk to you for a minute?" she asked.

He actually hesitated before finally nodding and stepping aside. On leaden feet, she walked to a chair while she stared at his desk, at the box in the center of it, the papers and file folders, and the absolutely nothing on the bookshelves.

"You're leaving," she said, sinking into a seat as he stepped behind the desk.

"That's right." He was filling the box, choosing to keep or discard from the stack of papers beside it.

"Why?"

"I resigned," he said simply, as if they were discussing dog food.

"Because of the fraud?"

Colin glanced up. The glance became a stare. "So it was you who figured it out," he said finally. His blue eyes grazed. He grinned softly. "I should have known. You're a smart lady, Emily," he said, returning to the papers.

He didn't want the next group that were stapled together. It landed with a slide and thud into the wastebasket he'd obviously pulled close behind his desk.

"But you didn't do it," she said.

Another glance. "Are you sure?" he asked, as if she shouldn't be.

It wasn't until she clutched more tightly to her chest— to her parka—the pages photocopied from yesterday's log, that she realized she'd been gripping them at all. "Yes," she said.

He just kept looking at her, fingering her face with his eyes as if he were sketching her with their path. He gave his attention back to the box, opting to add the next folder to its contents. "How do you know?"

Someone who knew had told her, was how, but Emily said only, "I thought about it all night, and I'm not sure I have it figured out yet, but whoever's doing it is actually changing the log. They're actually adding spots to the computer, then printing another copy of the log for the studio. Later, after the extra spots have been played, they replace the phony pages with the real ones and change the computer log back."

"How do you know that?" he asked again, though he kept right on loading that box. He was nearly through the stack of papers that had been so tall when she'd walked in.

"When I worked your shift yesterday, I played an ad for Hog Heaven Harley-Davidson. When I looked at the log last night, it wasn't there."

That swung his attention from the box to her face.

"It was a different log last night, Colin," she added, more vehemently. "Sometime between ten in the morning, when I handed it over to Starvin' Marvin, and six last night, when I came on for my own show, the paper log had been changed—back to the real one."

No response, no reply. Rather, he picked up the remaining papers in the stack, leafed through them, and dropped the whole thing in the wastebasket. The thud was growing less hollow. "That's pretty thready, Emily," he said, bending to open another drawer that he drew a shorter stack of papers from. "What about the signatures? They'd have to be forged."

"I know," she told the edge of his desk. She hadn't figured that part out yet.

"Are they close?" he asked.

Begrudgingly she nodded. "Mine looks the same."

He lifted his brows, indicating he wanted to see, which lifted her heart. Maybe he'd find something she hadn't. Wind curled the corner of the top page as Emily sent the photocopy to arm's length, where Colin could lean over the desk for a look. He peered at the paper as if it were nothing more grave than an ad for a movie he wanted to see.

"That's my signature," he said simply, and added the papers in hand to those in the box.

Emily returned the log to her lap and evened the edges. "Well, you still couldn't have done it."

"How so?" Colin asked, closing a drawer and opening another.

"Because I figure it would take at least fifteen minutes to add the spots to the electronic log and print it. You don't have that kind of time during your shift, and there are too many people around after that. The only time the thief wouldn't get caught would be after I leave at night."

Now he was moving a bottle of aspirin, a pair of sunglasses, and the foam basketball for his toy hoop from a bottom drawer. "I could do it first thing in the morning, before I'm on the air."

"I thought of that," she admitted, "but Heston Hall comes in just as early as you do, to do the news, and there was one time you couldn't have come in to change the computer."

He gave her a glance.

"Friday night," she said.

His hand stopped in the box.

"See, the paper log gets changed, from the phony one back to the real one, sometime between your shift and mine. But the electronic log has to remain the same—it has to have all the extra spots on it—until after I leave, because there are too many people around during the day. You couldn't have gotten to the computer to take the extra spots out, because you were with me all Friday night, all day Saturday, and until Sunday evening."

"I could have changed it Sunday night after I took you home."

"Too late," she told him triumphantly. "Betty told me she came in for an hour or so on Saturday so she could take Monday and Tuesday off. One of the things she worked on was the logs—including Friday's. It must have already been changed by the time she came in, or she would have noticed. That means it was changed Friday night after I left."

Across the desk Colin stared at her, hands over the box, a gold-on-white Will Walker BMW mug in one hand and a granola bar in the other. His eyes narrowed—he was thinking serious thoughts.

"I'm going to Sterling," Emily said. "I'll tell him you have an alibi."

Colin's stare focused sharply—intense, piercing.

"I can tell him I was with you all weekend," Emily continued, "that you never had the opportunity to change things back before Betty came in on Saturday."

He resumed his packing. "I don't need your help."

"How else will you clear yourself?" she asked. "Whoever's doing this has covered himself, thought of every angle—"

"Look, Emily," he said patiently, "I appreciate the offer, and you've done some clever detective work, but I'm a big boy. I can take care of myself."

He was crazy, and his pride would lose him his job—at the least.

"Big boys go to jail," she said.

He glanced up, eyebrow cocked sardonically, and began picking up the rest of whatever was in that drawer— paper clips, pennies, cough drops. "Looks like I hired a fool on top of everything else," he said, throwing the items away, one at a time, and getting more angry with each toss.

"If you insist on telling Sterling you were in my bed all weekend, go right ahead."

"I wasn't in your bed—at least, not the way you make it sound," Emily retorted.

Colin laughed. "Like anyone's going to believe that."

"You'll tell Sterling—you'll tell everyone—we slept in our clothes. That we just . . . slept."

"People believe what they want to believe, what's fun to believe." He chucked the last item—a button—in the bin. "Look, it's been a bad day, and—" He stopped and shook his head. "Aw, so what? I'm out of here anyway." He glanced around the room as if the conversation had grown tedious. "This is where we go our separate ways, I think, Miss Erickson. We had some laughs, but you're not really my kind of woman."

The world began to wobble.

"See, I watch football on Sundays, not go to church," he continued, "and I'm definitely not interested in celibacy. You're a little . . . sweet for me."

Her heart stopped. "What?" she asked weakly.

"Go to Sterling if your Bible-thumping ideals drive you to do so. It's just too bad I didn't get the pleasure of the conquest I'll be credited for. It would have been fun to teach you why sex sells everything from baseball to back-hoes."

She might have gasped, but wasn't sure. Wasn't sure of anything, except the world fell into a pit, and her stomach roiled. It was all a lie. The pie and dancing and kissing in the parking lot—all of it—was nothing more than a drama to get her into bed. Everything, to get sex out of her.

No. He'd been genuine. He'd called her Miss Emily in his Oklahoma accent and held her hand at the hospital. She'd misunderstood him.

"You don't mean this," Emily said. "You'd defend me if

I went to Sterling. You'd explain the way it really was."

Colin set his palms flat on the desk and leaned forward, over the box—and she may as well have been looking down the barrel of his gun, so cold was his stare. "You obviously have me confused with someone else—at least someone in a better mood," he said calmly. "If I can't have the victory, at least I'll have the points, and only your . . . husband will know I didn't really score."

The room darkened. She might throw up. He had to stop.

"No—"

"Now, go," he growled, jerking his chin at the door. "And don't lose any more sleep over this. I may not be worth it. Did it ever occur to you I just might be guilty?"

The chair teetered and fell behind her, she rose so fast. He was someone else, someone cruel. Hot and angry tears of humiliation overwhelmed her, and she spun and nearly tripped over the chair. Get out, get out, she had to get out. Had to crumple in a heap and cry before she exploded. Had to crawl beneath the covering of her hands and bury what had been murdered. Had to forget he'd ever said "Probably."

Thirty

*B*oxes in his arms, Burger King sack locked in his teeth, and Sophie pressing excitedly at his legs, Colin kicked the front door closed with his foot and dropped the load onto the kitchen table.

"Come on, girl," he said. He let the dog out the back door, then made two more stops—at the fridge and the table—before collapsing on the couch. He drank of the barley pop before he opened the burger sack. Cold and carbonated, the grainy alcohol slid down his throat and into his empty stomach.

He'd made her cry. As sure as he was out of work, he'd made his Emmy cry.

Colin's eyes fell closed. The woman didn't give halfway, didn't hold back, if she thought she could step on the tracks and stop a runaway train—and that's what the inevitable rumors would turn into, for no one would believe she'd left his house with her virtue intact. Had to stop her from ruining herself. He winced; those lovely eyes had widened, looked stricken, and the color had drained from her cheeks—like he'd punched her in the face. Her hands had already been shaking—she'd been barely hanging on—when she'd whirled away and run from the room, slamming the door with a crack behind her. She'd never understand he'd had to get vicious, had to draw out every threat at his disposal to keep her from going to Sterling. She'd simply despise him—and that was how it had to be. Whatever it took to put her at a safe distance, to get her as far away from him as possible. If her God had any mercy at all, those who'd suspected anything about the two of them would be stricken with amnesia, and her name would never be associated with his again. Especially now.

Colin groaned. Emily should have come to him with her suspicions. He shook his head and downed another third of his brew. She would have, if she'd trusted him. He unwrapped his double cheeseburger; it didn't look as appetizing as it had sounded at the drive-through.

Sterling had given him a job when no one else would. Had dreamed with him, brainstormed with him, then talked the station's owner into investing the money to build a radio station that would shake the old-established. And they'd done it. With each annual Willhight rating, Diamond Country owned every time slot for every age group—except the teens, whom the Contemporary Hit Rock stations could have. The real money lay with the adults, who bought cars, trucks, boats, RVs, snowmobiles, snow throwers, and furniture. And Sterling thought he, Colin, would undermine that—what he loved more than anything—at its very foundation? Colin heaved a breath. He'd always thought Sterling a pretty good judge of character. So much for thinking for himself.

Colin bit off a chunk of burger and chased it with the rest of the beer. Then he gave up on the burger for another brew, strode to the bedroom for the pillow Emmy had lain on, stretched out on his stomach, and stared at the carpeting. Had to devise a plan, map out a new direction for his life, which was ticking off at a faster and faster pace. Good thing, since he spent more and more of it alone.

Emily had barely stepped inside the lobby when Sterling called to her. He was sitting in his executive chair, the station quiet around him, except for the stereo speakers playing softly. Outside it was full dark. He should be home.

"If I give you a raise, will you get a phone?" he asked. "It's pretty inconvenient that you don't have one."

"A raise?" It was nearly all she'd heard of what he'd said. "For what?"

He leaned forward, setting folded hands on the desk. "The morning drive shift has opened up."

"Yes. I know." And had been crying about it all afternoon. Even from across the room, Sterling could probably see that.

"I've moved John Vaughn into the morning slot, and Marv will take afternoon drive, so I need an announcer for middays. Are you interested?"

Middays. Prime time. Granted, the third in a ranking of three, but in the top three just the same.

Thank You, Jesus!

"Yes," Emily rushed to say, except the excitement was chased by doubt. "Are you sure I'm ready?"

"I think so," he said. "Nothing is etched in stone, you understand. This is radio. It could all change, but let's try it tomorrow, and we'll have a meeting—you, me, John, and Marv—at one on Monday. I'll get someone in here to cover you for that hour."

Emily nodded. "Thanks, Sterling," she said with genuine gratitude . . . though the promotion was bittersweet.

Colin pressed the remote control button that displayed the time of day on the television screen: 5:59. Buttons on a second remote brought up lights on the stereo, then John Vaughn slid from Patty Loveless to a five-second ID to the news. On the television, the Channel Six news team gave a tease of what he was about to learn of the day's tragedies that weren't his own. He turned down the volume on the TV, making it less than equal to that of the stereo—listening to two things at once was no challenge—drained the last of his second beer since waking, and treaded to the kitchen for another. He stared into the refrigerator for only a moment before he slammed it closed and swiveled to the cupboard. Forget the beer. With no work tomorrow, this was a Friday night—one day early. He filled a glass tumbler with ice and immersed the cubes in Maker's Mark. The bottle of bourbon returned to the living room with him, taking a position among the empty beer bottles and Burger King sack.

Emily used the liner he'd recorded for her to segue from the news to the first song of her shift, a kicking Chris LeDoux tune. Colin chuckled as he lifted the bourbon to his lips. She'd been so tickled with that liner. Like it was the greatest thing anyone had ever done for her. She'd never know it, but it made him want to do more—hence the others he'd recorded; *Diamond One-O-One and Emily Brooks . . . hired because she has the goods on the boss. Emily Brooks . . . the softer side of Diamond One-O-One . . . and I had to say that, or she'd hit me. You're listening to Emily Brooks on Diamond One-O-One . . . because she can't find a real job.* Colin chuckled again and leaned forward to refill his glass. She'd liked that last one. Had laughed out loud with a sound sweeter than the music surrounding her, her green eyes twinkling with delight. She'd owned him and hadn't known it.

The video clip on the television walked around the wreckage of a Blazer that had center punched a utility pole in East Missoula, and Tracy Lawrence was winding down on the FM frequency. . . . Then there they were, the best pipes in the world.

"Diamond Country, Diamond One-O-One . . . more than 100 percent country, if you think about it. Hi, I'm Emily Brooks, and boy, do I have a great evening planned for you. . . ."

Colin smiled to himself and closed his eyes in satisfaction. The warmth—the delight—bubbled from her like the best day a man could ever come home to. Like the best night he could ever hope to wrap around himself.

". . . We'll hear the latest from Tracy Byrd, Little Texas, and Pam Tillis," she continued, "and some boot stompers you haven't stomped to in a while. Stay with us . . . Diamond Country . . . Diamond One-O-One."

Kevin Sharp started singing, and Colin made a careful study of the amber liquid limning the ice cubes in his glass. She didn't sound as if he'd verbally decked her today, and he'd never know if she'd gotten over it—or seen through it. He drained the glass and filled it again.

Sterling would put her on middays, with John Vaughn on morning drive and Starvin' Marvin bringing up the rear, because it was the old fogey thing for an old fogey to do. That's not what he, Colin, would do. Marv was too sleepy for afternoon drive. It was Emily who had the energy to push the work-weary through a maze of red lights, lane changes, and what-will-we-have-for-dinner. So what if she was a female? Timbre didn't matter anymore, so long as it was full and rich; she was both.

He sipped his bourbon. Drank it all. Then ditched the glass to swallow forgetfulness directly from the long neck of the square bottle.

Even if he weren't arrested on fraud charges tomorrow, he'd never work in a Missoula studio again. Maybe nowhere. Ever. Suspicions such as these didn't die, they followed. From state to state. Because there were only so many microphones and so many voices, and the latter of the two traveled and remembered and talked, creating a network for the rumors to cross state lines on.

He'd have to put the house up for sale, sell the Bimmer, and load what was important in the Jeep. Oregon, maybe. It was pretty there. Or Idaho. Not quite the Montana attitude, but close enough for a fugitive from life.

Should punch Brad The Slime some new breathe-holes on his way out of town.

Bottle in one hand and remote control in the other, Colin sank into navy leather and rifled through television channels. Should go into TV. It needed help—satellite dishes and cable feed, and there was still nothing on.

He blew out through pursed lips. Phew, he was drunk.

"And will probably get drunker," he told Sophie, with a toast, before he set the bottle at his mouth for another drizzle. He smacked his lips. Too good. The stuff drank like the best iced tea on the hottest day. Better enjoy it—and the rest of the case in the basement. Wouldn't be able to afford it in a very soon while. In a very while. In a short very. Soon.

He pointed the remote control at the TV and fired. Nothing happened. He tried again, harder. The channel flipped once. Pressed again. Nothing. Harder. Nothing. He swore and let his arm drop to the couch.

"I ain't walking over there, Soph, so you'll just have to watch what's on this channel," Colin told the dog, who only stared at him through pretty eyes from where she lay on the other side of the coffee table. "Fall on my . . . backside, then I'd have to sleep on the floor. Bad enough I have to sleep alone."

He turned to the malamute and shook his head. As if waiting for her cue to reply, the dog lifted hers.

"Everybody's right. I'm no good for her, Soph," he said. "She's a nice girl. You understand? A niiiice girl. The kind mamas like. No playing nasty. No bad words. Backside. That's what she'd say. And no puking on her shoes." He motioned with the bottle. "Wouldn't be in this condition, I'll tell you that."

He closed his eyes and let the room spin around him. Let the weight, like molten metal, club his limbs and slosh in his head. Let Emily's voice slide into his ears and animate an undulating ribbon of memories. So brand new.

"And smart, Soph," he added, with a wobbly gaze at the dog, who'd given up, setting her chin on her paws again. "She's the one who figured it out, this whole thing," Colin continued. "I never saw it. Nobody saw it. She just did. She'll figure out who did it too." He closed his eyes. Sighed. "But it'll be too late. Already too late."

"Right now, even as I speak," the man on the television said, "someone's getting drunk."

Thirty-one

Some TV preacher, it was.

"And a very perceptive so-and-so you are," Colin said in his best imitation of a drunk Irishman. He lifted his head and added, "Emmy don't take to bad words, you understand, so you'll have to be fillin' in the blanks for yourself there, lad." His head fell back, and he stared at the ceiling.

"Even now," the man on the television continued, "a twelve-year-old is smoking his first marijuana cigarette."

"Don't bogart that joint, son. Pass it on over here." This from Colin.

"Even now a fifteen-year-old girl is giving away her innocence . . . because she's bought into the lie that this is her only worth."

Colin lifted the bottle and drank.

"Even now a housewife is getting raped by her husband's friend. Her husband thought—she thought—this was a good friend."

Colin swished another drizzle in his mouth and swallowed hard, while the ceiling moved as though it was on a conveyer belt.

"Even now a husband of twenty-three years is meeting a woman at a high-priced hotel room only twenty-three years of life-building could buy. This is not the woman who helped him build it."

Colin was silent. Didn't move.

"Even now a father is teaching his adolescent daughter about sex . . . by illustration. Even now a woman is selling her integrity for the twenty-dollar bill she's sliding from the cash drawer to her pocket. Even now a woman is signing the clinic paperwork, giving the facility permission to reverse a moment of passion, to vacuum from her life the body of evidence that proves she just couldn't stop herself. Even now a hand is raising a loaded gun and pointing it at the face of another. Anger will pull the trigger."

Colin raised his head and focused on the man behind the pulpit. "That's close enough. . . . So what's your point?"

"This is a hideous place, where we live," the man replied as if he'd heard the question. "You think it's sin that separates us from God? The murder? The fornication? The theft?" He nodded. "It is. I'll give you that. But I pro-pose . . . there's more." He surveyed his audience, the expression in his eyes sad. "Listen carefully, and you'll hear the voice . . . of guilt," he said, dropping the word with a resounding thud.

Colin pulled in another slug of Maker's Mark.

"The drunk and the pot smoker will feel guilty for their lack of self control," the man said, hands gripping the edge of the pulpit. "The young girl will feel guilty for giving a piece of herself away—because sex isn't the same for women as it is for men, folks, despite what the get-liberat-ed books will try to sell you. The housewife will feel guilty for being assaulted, and her husband will feel guilty for not protecting her. The man at the hotel will feel guilty for cheating on his wife, the father will feel guilty for molesting his daughter, and his daughter will feel guilty for letting it happen—as if she had any choice. The employee will feel guilty for stealing. The unwed mother will feel guilty for aborting her baby. And the killer will feel guilty for letting emotion stop a beating heart."

The preacher paused to let the words find their mark; Colin waited for the next shot.

"This is a hideous place, where we live," the man said again. "This is where sin wins—and it wins more than once. It wins in that moment when the act is inked into history . . . and it wins again and again, when its memory, its reminder, its vicious nagging, return to pour its filth over a human heart that's already broken."

Colin swallowed hard.

"It will beat you down," the man said. "Unforgiven? Unforgivable. Therefore, hopeless. Destitute. And ever, ever so lonely."

Colin leaned forward, banging the bottle on the coffee table when he overestimated the distance. He set his elbows on his knees and rubbed the heels of his hands into his eyes. He shot his fingers through his hair—needed to get sober . . . or drunker.

"Your guilt is a chasm, you know," the man said. "It's a pit that calls you to fall in, every day. Sometimes moment to moment. It wants your life. It will have it, too. It will have all you are and all you could have become. It will have your happiness . . . and your peace."

"Peace?" Colin spit, turning to the television. "What's that? You got a box of that, Brother Bob or whatever your name is, and I'll write you an open check right now."

"You want freedom?" the man asked.

"Oh boy, here it comes," Colin replied, though he was careful to make the statement short, lest he miss the preacher's next words.

"Freedom is found in a Man."

Jesus, of course. Gimpa and Gram had taught him that much.

"But more than a man," the preacher added. "God in the flesh. God Who was tempted in every enticement we suffer, but Who remained sinless. A prisoner can't free a prisoner, you know. It takes someone from outside the fence . . . and He's the only one Who's there—free, peaceful, able to forgive the unforgivable."

The man held up a finger. "This is the one time when too-good-to-be-true doesn't apply. It's too good for any and all of us, but it's true. Jesus has all the answers. The only question remaining is, how miserable are you? How miserable are you going to have to get before you do something about it? Before you trust one more time, with a faith that will be well-placed?"

The crawl—a ribbon of words running along the bottom of the screen—gave a toll-free number to call.

"Only you can decide," the man said.

Colin glanced over his right shoulder at the telephone on the computer desk in the nook of the dining room. Stared at the number. He could call. Should call.

Naw. He shook his head and reached for his favorite bourbon. Raised it to his lips. And didn't drink. Just stared over the bottle at the phone number marching again and again across the bottom of the screen.

"Diamond Country, Diamond One-O-One . . . the kicking country you love," Emily said from the speakers, that warmth in her voice. "I'm Emily Brooks, and if there's something you want to hear, let me know about it. I'll do my best to make you smile."

Something he wanted to hear? Something *he* wanted to hear? From her? Got no reason to smile. He glanced at the phone again.

Do it. Do it. Do it.

Might be his only chance. God knew, he was miserable enough—or at least, didn't care to get any more so. Maybe it could work for him. Maybe not, but maybe he'd just check it out.

He slammed the bottle on the table, shuffled on heavy feet to the desk, and brought the phone back to the couch. The extension rang twice.

"Pure Beginnings Ministries. This is Chris," the voice on the other end said. "How can I help you?"

"You're a man," Colin said, then, "wait. I'm sorry. I didn't mean it like that. I mean—"

Chris laughed. "That's okay. I understand." He paused. "Who's this?"

"Colin," Colin croaked. He cleared his throat and tried again, "My name is Colin. I was just watching this TV show, and I— The crawl said I should call."

"Okay," Chris said, his voice slow and calm, implying there was more Colin wasn't telling him. "Have you been drinking tonight, Colin?" he asked.

Colin groaned. "Man, I'm drunk. Pretty bad—but don't hang up. I'm serious about this. I'm . . . fairly sick of things. You know?"

"I know," Chris said quietly. "I'm glad you called. Why don't you tell me about it?"

Silence stretched between them. Spanned the connection that crackled softly in Colin's ear. He swallowed. "Everything's falling apart. I'm under suspicion for a burglary I didn't commit, and I lost my job today. I got fired."

And Emmy . . .

"What happened?"

"Somebody's defrauding the station," Colin said sadly, "and all the evidence points to me."

"Did you do it?"

"No," he growled. "I may be a lot of things, but I'm no thief. I didn't take that stupid yard fountain, either."

"Okay," Chris said, as if he really did believe someone could have that many fingers pointing to him and still be innocent.

Then silence.

Colin's mouth was dry. He eyed the bourbon. He shook his head and stumbled to the kitchen, taking the phone and its over-long cord with him. He crooked the receiver between his ear and shoulder and splashed water into—and out of—a glass. He turned down the stream and poured more gently.

"I used to have a girlfriend," Colin said. "I mean, I almost had one, but I'm not good enough for her. I'd ruin her. I'd take her down. So I got her ticked at me—I made her hate me—so she'd stay away."

"Wow," Chris said. "That's tough. You really love her, huh?"

"More than anything," Colin replied. "I used to think I loved radio—that's my job; I'm a DJ—but I lost that today, and I survived. It's Emmy who's killing me."

He trudged back to the living room and slumped into the couch. When he set the dripping glass on the table, he nearly fell into the space between the furniture, reaching for a magazine coaster.

"What else?" Chris asked quietly, after a moment.

"How do you know there's more?"

"I can hear it. I'll wait."

Colin swallowed hard, so hard, pushing at what tried to surface, while he focused on the window across the room . . . at the far edge of the coffee table . . . at the puff of couch cushion between his thighs.

"I killed my little brother," he said without preamble, and heard the blast like a cannon . . . felt the recoil of the

rifle against the bench seat of the pickup . . . saw Bryan's
head jerk back in a spray of red anatomy . . . watched his
body fall in slow motion against the open door of the truck
. . . watched him slide down and his elbow catch where the
bend of the door met the window . . . heard the bone-by-
bone thud of his body hitting the concrete driveway. . . .

Deep and long, Colin gathered the breath, while the
misery knotted and rose from every crevice. The next
breath was sucked in with great and noisy effort before it
exploded from his mouth in torment.

"I shot him," he cried. "My little brother. I loved him,
and I shot him. As sure as if I'd been holding the gun
myself, I shot him. And I wish it'd been me."

With sobs that tore loose from deep places, shook 220-
some pounds of disciplined flesh, and flung anguish
against the walls in their need to be free, Colin sobbed,
head bent, eyes buried deep in his right hand, and left
hand holding the telephone in a grip that should have
snapped it in two.

"My mother," he wailed. "She heard the shot . . . and
Dad . . . they came out the door . . . I tried to stop her, to
turn her around, to block her view, but she saw. Her son.
He was only sixteen . . . She was so proud of him, and she
saw him . . . like that. Oh, I wish I could die. The horror on
her face. Why wasn't it me? Mama, Mama, I'm sorry. I'm so
sorry."

With an occasional sound of acknowledgment—*I'm still
here*—Chris let him cry, simply let Colin ramble and babble
and weep, until the words came no more and exhaustion
took over. Then Colin, who talked for a living, couldn't
think of a single thing to say.

"This was a hunting accident," Chris said finally.

"Yes. We'd just come back. We hadn't gotten anything,
so I left the rifle loaded—in case we saw something on the

way out. We never did, and I forgot about it. I was on the driver's side, gathering up the binoculars and food and all that stuff. Bryan reached in to take the guns from the rack on the back window and . . . I don't know . . . mine must have caught on something. It discharged. He was dead before he landed." He sighed, a shaky inhalation.

"You think it should have been you?"

Colin stared at his jeans, preparing to complete the confession. This was harder to admit. Was more deliberate. "I had a little business going," he began. "I wrote excuse slips in high school, so kids could cut class, and when they started asking questions, Bryan told them the truth. I got suspended from school and thrown off the football team, just when there were rumors about a scholarship." He paused. "I got back in school, but the football thing was history." The next part was the worst. Loved ones, these, the people who believed in you when no one else could. "And they thought . . . When the gun . . . They thought I did it on purpose."

The despair of it shook stomach muscles well trained to stand solid and drew a silent stream of tears from eyes that would trade every sight to come if they could be free of just one they had seen before.

"I don't know you, but I know you didn't do that," Chris said. "I bet they didn't believe it either. You just thought they did. A guilty conscience will play tricks that way. How old were you, Colin?"

"Eighteen. I graduated from high school and couldn't stand to see my mother's grief anymore. I left. That was nine years ago."

"Can't run far enough, can you? And can't find enough distractions."

Colin heaved a feeble, bitter laugh. "I've given it a noble effort."

The conversation settled to a simple but expectant quiet, while Colin stared at the couch cushion, wishing he could bring it into focus. The television relayed the broadcast of a gospel quartet of men singing about a love that never fails, and Emily promised a weather forecast.

"You don't have to carry this anymore, Colin," Chris said. "I know Someone Who'll take it from you. He'll put it as far as the east is from the west."

"Jesus."

"Jesus. You know a Christian, or you have one in your family?"

"My grandparents. My parents, I think. At least, we were in a church, but I don't know. I was never listening. I wasn't the most obedient member of the family, you understand. That was my brother . . . the one I killed."

"I understand," Chris said. "Jesus can fix that too."

"He's just a fixer of everything," Colin said.

To which Chris replied matter-of-factly, "He is." Then, "You have a Bible there, Colin?"

"Somewhere—the one I had when I was a kid—but I couldn't find my backside with a bloodhound, so it's—"

"Never mind. Just listen," Chris said. "I'll send you some material that outlines all this so you can check it out for yourself, but basically you're a study in the plan of salvation, all by yourself."

Colin nodded.

"I don't think I need to tell you you're a sinner," Chris continued, "that your disobedience is part of your human makeup—you're helpless to it—and that it's enough to separate you from a holy, sinless God. He wants fellowship with you, Colin, but you don't know Him, and His throne room is restricted to all but those who are worthy."

Now came the hard part, the getting worthy part. This time Colin verbalized his nod. "Okay."

"Would you like to be worthy?" Chris asked. "Would you like to know Him? Be forgiven?"

Time to decide.

Emmy told him how pretty the new round of snow showers would be this weekend, the TV camera panned a smiling crowd of hand-clappers, and the tears that had dried up a moment ago found a new well of provision, rolling silently down Colin's cheeks. He dug with awkward fingers through the Burger King sack, found the little stack of napkins, and used them to wipe his face. "Yes," he managed to say around the saliva pooled in his mouth. "What do I do?"

"Just ask," Chris said. "I know it sounds too simple, but He gets to decide how it will be done, and in His Word He said things like this: 'For God so loved the world that He gave His only begotten Son, that whoever believes in Him should not perish but have everlasting life.' 'For all have sinned and fall short of the glory of God.' 'The gift of God'—a gift you don't deserve, Colin—'is eternal life in Christ Jesus our Lord.' And this: 'But when the kindness and the love of God our Savior toward man appeared, not by works of righteousness which we have done, but according to His mercy He saved us.'"

"This sounds familiar," Colin said.

"Ah, see? You were listening," Chris said. "I would guess you tried to measure up, that you tried to be a good person on your own, but when it wasn't getting you anywhere, you simply gave up."

"Am I that typical?"

"Yes and no. I've been where you are. Different circumstances, same misery. God doesn't grade on the curve, Colin. You'll never atone, you'll never be good enough on your own. Jesus did it all. He doesn't need your help; you need His."

That stroked against the grain, considering all he'd built by sheer determination . . . and enjoyed alone.

"Okay," he said.

"Let's pray, Colin," Chris said, words that had the opposite effect of what he probably desired. "There is no special prayer, no special incantation. I'm just going to act as the witness to your approaching God and asking His forgiveness."

Colin heaved a frustrated breath. "I'm not sure I can do that. I don't know what to say . . . and I drank a lot."

"You're bleary, but you're getting this. You've come this far. Don't stop now," Chris said. "Pray like a child. It's okay. In fact, it's the best kind of faith. Just tell Him what you want."

Colin sat back in the couch and stared up at the ceiling, left elbow high as he held the phone, the fingers of his right hand digging in his hair. This was embarrassing—except the only one who seemed to feel that way was him. Chris acted as if it were an ordinary thing. Well bet him, if he couldn't just step right into it too. Talking in front of people was no big deal, he'd already made a fool of himself, being so drunk, and he had enough premium bourbon in him to put a bash into bashful.

He closed his eyes. "God, I don't know You." The tears started again, rolling toward his ears. "I don't know if You know me—"

"He knows everything about you," Chris said softly.

"Oh," Colin said, then, "You know everything I've done—and that's humiliating, because I've done some pretty raunchy stuff—not just writing those excuse slips . . . and my brother, but . . . other things." He sniffed. Barely controlled a sob. "I . . . I don't want to do it anymore. I don't want to be like that . . . and I'm tired of running." Another sob. "If you'll forgive me, I'll—"

"No bargains," Chris said softly.

"Then what?" Colin asked in earnest, opening his eyes.

"Please forgive me. Make me a new person and help me live for You," Chris said.

"Oh." Colin sniffed again. Closed his eyes. "Like Chris said . . . and just . . . just help me, God. I'm sorry. So sorry. And I want to change."

He opened his eyes and stared at the ceiling. Waited. Not much else to say.

"I couldn't have said that any better," Chris said.

Colin's shoulders settled in relief.

"Do you feel any different?" Chris asked. "Not that faith is based on feelings, but you might not feel the same."

Thirty-two

C olin sniffed and wiped at tears and tear-trails with the pad of his thumb. The room still wobbled, that was for sure, but there was a warmth—inside and out—no quantity of Maker's Mark could take credit for. More than relieved . . . grateful. Happy. Loved. And not alone.

The tears started again, though a smile sprang to his lips. "I feel good," Colin said. "I can't describe it. I just feel good."

"That's great," Chris said. "You're going to need some fellowship now, Colin, a church where you can learn about God and about what just happened to you. Tell me where you are, and I'll check our lists to see what's nearby."

"I think I've got that covered," Colin said. "Emmy is a Christian. I'll just go where she's going—if I can face her."

"The plot thickens; you didn't tell me she was a Christian. This is the woman you're in love with?"

"Yes."

"She love you?"

That hurt.

"Probably. But probably not anymore," Colin said.

"You love her that much—enough to send her away—and she loves you, then ask God for her," Chris said. "He'll let you know whether or not it would be a good thing."

The fingers combing through Colin's hair stopped. "I can just ask like that? For a woman? For her?"

Chris laughed. "Absolutely. Talk to Him. All day—He never sleeps. Besides, who knows? That might have been what the Lord had in mind all the time."

Colin grinned; an air shift that never ends, a frequency that never switches to an impersonal feed, and Emmy—maybe. Miracles.

He pulled in a deep breath. His stomach was beginning to flop around like a beached fish.

"Go to church on Sunday, Colin," Chris said. "Tell the pastor what happened tonight, and get yourself some friends who will help you get stronger. It's an ugly world out there. It's looking to trip you up."

Colin nodded, then remembered Chris couldn't see that. "I will."

"Okay, give me your address so I can send you some material."

Colin sat up, forearms to thighs, and sipped water while he gave Chris the information. His stomach rolled over and over. He blew out harshly, eyeing the bottle of bourbon dubiously.

"What's the name of this church you're thinking of attending, by the way?" Chris asked.

No good. Colin began to pant, while a wave of heat raised a bead of sweat on his forehead. "Valley Bible or something," he replied, then, "I have to go, Chris. I'm going to be sick."

Of all things, the man laughed. "You asked for that."

Later Colin would smile, but not now. "I know."

"I'll be praying for you."

"I'll be counting on it," Colin replied, slammed the phone down, and barely made it to the bathroom in time. He deserved every bit of his misery. What nagged him was, he'd never thanked Chris.

Colin opened his eyes—and dived for the nightstand, arm arcing high and landing hard on the silent alarm clock.

Work. He'd slept in. It was daylight already.

Sophie scratched her neck, rattling the tags on her collar in her signal to go outside.

"Just a minute, Soph," Colin mumbled, squinting at the digital display. He glanced around the room, trying to get familiar with whatever was different. His clothes lay in a puddle beside the bed. The lamp was still on, the TV and radio played in the living room . . . and there was no work today. No work ever—in Diamond Country, anyway. Ooohhhh, and he'd drunk too much—drunk being the operative word. He rolled onto his back, rubbed his face with both hands, and threaded his fingers through his hair. He'd called some guy on the phone and prayed with him. And cried—like he hadn't cried since he was in diapers. Maybe he had never let go like that.

Colin stared at an obscure spot above him . . . and breathed free. It was gone, that torment that had been his only companion for nine years. Bryan's death had been an accident—not an unconscious retaliation, not an act of malice, but an accident . . . now laid to rest, granting peace to the one left behind. Starting today, he could stop punishing himself.

It wasn't the only thing different. For sure, he felt as if

he'd just crawled from a dumpster, but something was better than it had ever been. Here he was, hung over, out of work, and in love with a woman who was absolutely unattainable, and . . . it didn't matter. Couldn't explain it, just couldn't muster up any panic, for Someone else was taking care of it. It had all been real, and Someone loved him.

He pushed back the covers and moved, albeit a little gingerly, through a Saturday ritual played out on a Friday. Coffee, a shower, a shave, jeans and a T-shirt, buttered toast. Then he cleaned the war zone, while his head pounded from abuse and whirled with questions.

Did Christians sleep in the buff? There were things he'd done that he'd stop doing, and things he hadn't done that he'd start doing, but he'd rather quit radio than wear pajamas.

Did Christians enjoy sex? Had to be married, of course, but could making love be . . . play? On the couch? In the shower? Could it be for more than filling the high chair every couple of years, and a once-a-month duty? Exactly what . . . games were allowed?

Did Christians drink? Emmy didn't. Gimpa and Gram didn't. Mama and Dad didn't. Colin eyed the bottle of Maker's Mark. The odor clinging to it made him gag, and that was enough to convince him. Since it had been so much a part of that other life, the one that other Colin lived, this Christian didn't drink either. So the remaining third of the bottle fell, a casualty to the kitchen drain . . . because it didn't matter. The rest of the case in the basement might have been sold for something near the $130 the bottles were worth, but in a bloom of victory he lugged it up the stairs and glugged it all through that hole in the sink. Smiled about it, because it didn't matter. He didn't need Maker's Mark; he had The Maker's Mark; was The Maker's Mark. Then, because he wasn't alone, because he was free, because One Who loved him had come—and paid—he closed his eyes and cried . . . for gratitude, for joy, for peace . . . because nothing else mattered.

It didn't even matter, the outcome, when Colin dialed the Missoula Police Department.

"I'm in some trouble," he told Stan, who just happened to be working the day shift—though it didn't feel like a coincidence.

"That's what I hear," Stan replied, "except I'm having a hard time understanding why you'd steal a birdbath."

Colin chuckled. "It's not a birdbath, it's a yard fountain. Get that straight. It could be an important distinction."

Stan laughed, then his mirth slid into silence. "You didn't do this. What's going on, buddy?"

"I don't know, but give this thought a chance, will you?" Colin said. "I think I was framed."

The wheels turned speedily. "Bradley Earl Stapleton."

"That's what I think. You said it yourself, I didn't do this. Even if I'd just had to have the thing, I don't have anything to haul it in. I'm not the one with the truck."

"Right," Stan said. "Have you hired an attorney?"

"Not yet. Haven't had the time—or the concentration. I've been a little distracted."

Good friend that he was, Stan didn't ask for details. "Well," he said, "let me turn over some rocks, see what I can find. Give me that telephone number you guard so carefully, and I'll get back to you."

"Thanks, Stan," Colin said, the word richer in its meaning than it had ever been.

And it didn't even matter, the outcome, when the next telephone number Colin dialed was the one he knew best.

"Good morning, KDMD," Marilyn said on the second ring.

"Hi, Marilyn. This is Colin," he said into the mouthpiece. "Is Sterling in?"

"You just missed him," the receptionist replied, sounding sincere enough to one who'd been banished. "He's on his way to a meeting for the Missoula Uptown committee. You could probably get him on his cell phone."

"That's okay. Could you check something for me?"

"I guess so," she said weakly, as if she didn't really want to.

"Look at yesterday's log and tell me what color ink I signed it with."

"What color ink?"

It was just a hunch—he'd seen only a photocopy himself—but it was worth a shot. It was also a cryptic question, but anything more was none of Marilyn's business.

"If you don't mind," Colin replied.

"Okay," Marilyn sang as if he were sending her on a fruitless search.

"Thanks," he said, then listened to Clint Black while he was on hold and Marilyn checked on the availability of his future. If this didn't work, Sterling would have to go to the advertisers whose spots were receiving extra air play. Someone at the station was ordering the stolen time. Those on the other side of the agreement could tell who— if they would. If Sterling would ask, for no matter how he phrased the questions, the Diamond was going to look bad.

The line clicked off hold, and Colin arced the mouthpiece to his lips again.

"It's your day," Marilyn told him. "Thursday's log just happened to be on Betty's desk."

Another convenient coincidence.

"And?" he asked.

"You signed in black ink," Marilyn replied.

Colin nearly yahoo-ed, except he'd need his energy for a long night.

That settled, now what mattered was that Colin paused, wanting to ask Marilyn to page Emily to the phone. It mattered that he wanted to be in the station to encourage her before she stepped up to the first prime-time microphone that was her own. It mattered that it wasn't him, as it should have been, to walk her through the midday log that held a schedule of programming she'd never seen before. It mattered that she believed he'd deliberately ruin her reputation, cheapen her, hurt her in any way.

"Is that all?" Marilyn asked.

"That's it. Thanks," Colin replied, adding, "Have a nice weekend, Marilyn."

Then something else mattered a great deal. It was easy to call the information operator in Oklahoma, just to make sure the number he remembered still rang the telephone on the little alcove shelf plastered into the wall beside the kitchen. What was difficult was working up the courage. As it was, Colin stared at the phone for several minutes. Passed the time fetching a refill on his coffee. Then filled it again, even though he hadn't drunk it down by half. This mattered.

Help me. I won't know what to say.

His prayer was simple, and the choice was no-choice. Had to call, because he had to know, and had to say . . .

Colin picked up the receiver, punching the eleven numbers. The connection clicked . . . the phone rang . . . four times . . .

"Hello?" The voice was high pitched and genderless.

All thought, all plans and anticipations, froze.

"Who's this?" Colin asked, then didn't breathe.

"Bryan."

There were any number of reasons why a child would answer this phone. The most likely one—and the child's name—raised a lump in Colin's throat.

"What's your mother's name?" he asked.

"Mama's not here," Bryan replied.

Colin chuckled. "No. What's her name, Bryan? What's your mama's name?"

"Hahwy."

Holly. The smile brought a wind of relief, blowing away questions that had been too tender to ask, but now pressed in with urgent hunger. His baby sister had a baby son, and she'd named the child after their brother who'd died. She'd lost two brothers that day; their mother had lost two sons. One of them was back.

"Hi, Bryan," Colin said softly. He swallowed and cleared his throat. "How old are you?"

"I'm this many," the little Bryan replied proudly.

Colin laughed. "I think those fingers are too far away to see, little guy. Is Gimpa there?"

There was a confused silence, then, "Gimpa's outside."

"Go get him, Bryan. Tell him to come to the phone."

"Just a min—" the little voice said, then the phone thunked on a hard surface, short feet scurried away, and the chipmunk voice called at the top of its lungs, "Gimpa! Phone, Gimpa!"

The door gaped open and the interior was shadowed as Emily stepped to the threshold of Colin's office. It looked moved-out-of, stacks of *Radio & Records* and *Billboard* magazines on the shelves, spots of clean desk in the dust, the curtains closed.

She stepped inside and leaned against the wall, away from curious eyes. She stared at his empty chair. He was really gone, and he'd really said those mean things.

It hurt. Sometimes. Sometimes indignation made her glad he'd lost his job over a crime he didn't commit. If she were a man, she'd beat him up. Sometimes humiliation made Coeur d'Alene more attractive than it had ever been.

He'd left those posters of country singers behind. They were mounted in dime store plastic frames, anyway. The carpeting in the traffic pattern around his desk needed a shampoo. The whole room needed to be cleaned. Beyond these walls, the studio windows were painted with finger-prints, the counter in the production room was chipped, there was a kick-hole in the men's bathroom door, the paint on the limo was scratched, its upholstery was faded, and one too many chairs teetered on one-too-few casters—or was missing its backrest. The factory wasn't as polished as its product. She could admit that now.

Handsome packaging, all, for Diamond Country was only an advertising business struggling to keep its hold in a highly competitive market, and Colin Michaels was only a man who capitalized on his assets, though someone so opportunistic would be disappointed at how quickly he was forgotten. Little more than a half-dozen or so listeners had even been curious enough to call during John Vaughn's debut in Colin's old time slot. Cool head that she was, Marilyn had simply explained, "Colin doesn't work here anymore," and "No, I'm not sure where he's gone." Those who didn't call probably figured he was sick, or didn't care. So fickle, so fleeting, this fame.

So fickle and fleeting, love. Surely he couldn't have been lying all along, all those weeks. Surely he'd meant some of what he'd said.

No, he'd been playing her, just as Stacy said he would.

"I miss you, Mama," Emily whispered aloud.

The grief pressed on her chest, choked her heart. There were times when a girl needed her mother, though

Daddy had done his best, becoming as much a brother in the Lord as a father on the phone the other night. Once she'd unburdened her repentant heart, she'd poured out her story of the womanizing non-Christian she'd fallen in love with, the man whose greatest promise was to make a space in his closet for her clothes. It had been easy to be honest, to seek Daddy's sympathy—and advice, imagine that. Maybe because he fought the same battles with himself over June Gilson. Courageous, he'd called her. Said he admired her conviction, that Mom would be proud.

That was Monday, before Emily received her crash course in *They-were-right.* Nothing admirable about being duped, as everyone from Stacy to Marilyn said she would be, and the only courage she needed now was what it would take to hold her head up as one of Colin's many leave-behinds.

Maybe she'd go home Saturday for a quick visit, tell Daddy about her new air shift and hug the chest she knew by heart.

If she had any real courage, real integrity, she'd go to Sterling with Colin's alibi anyway. Instead, she was Herod, who'd been humiliated by the man he had the power to save, had cowered under Herodias' intimidation, then made his decision by default when he was too afraid of being embarrassed in front of his party guests. Herod knew Herodias was wrong, knew it was a mistake to let her sway him, but that hadn't kept John the Baptist's head on his shoulders.

Emily's jaw tensed and she stood away from the wall. She was stronger than that. Colin could do what he would—defend her or smile triumphantly. He would anyway. For her part, she would tell the truth . . . just tell the truth . . . trusting that Sterling would be discreet and God would see her through the outcome.

Trust in the Lord with all your heart, and lean not on your own understanding; In all your ways acknowledge Him, and He shall direct your paths.

Colin had read her well. She couldn't do anything less.

Courage worked up to the pressure of a shaken soda pop, Emily approached Sterling's office after she got off the air at two and peeked inside.

Not there?

"Where's Sterling?" she asked Marilyn.

"He's been out all day, working on that Missoula Uptown promotion," the receptionist replied from where she stood at the postage machine. It thunked as an envelope sped through it. "I think by now he's not coming back. He and Joyce were going out of town for the weekend."

Emily's shoulders fell in disappointment. "Out of town? Where?"

"I don't know," Marilyn replied. "Can I help with something?"

Emily gave her a grateful smile. "No. Thanks anyway."

Emily looked back to Sterling's desk—in case he might have materialized while she'd been talking. She heaved a frustrated breath. Now she'd have to wait until Monday to talk to him.

"Is Betty back yet?" she asked; maybe she could help.

"I'm sorry," Marilyn said. "Since she ended up coming in on Monday, she took the rest of the afternoon off."

Thirty-three

*T*he door hadn't even closed behind him before Colin noticed the store smelled of candles—or some kind of stink-pretty—and was brimming with music.

"Who is that?" he asked, pointing to the ceiling.

"The music?" the woman behind the counter asked.

He nodded.

"Michael W. Smith," she replied on a warm smile, stepping around the counter. "It's his newest. Would you like to see it?"

"Yes, please," Colin replied, following her to the far side of the store.

A whole wall of shelves with CDs and cassettes under headings like Gospel, Contemporary, and Alternative.

Alternative Christian music? Tell him there was Christian rap, and he'd eat the ribbon of analog tape it was recorded on.

"These are all Christian artists?" he asked, incredulous.

She nodded happily, then peered at him, head tilted. "You haven't ever heard any Christian music?"

"I'm a little new at this," he replied.

"You just got saved?"

"I think so—I don't know the terminology. I just became a Christian last night."

It must be so obvious, though it wasn't embarrassing. Rather, it was a joy to share, like galloping down the street ahead of Dad's truck with the new boat on the back and wanting to shout to the lawn-mowers and car-washers— *Look everyone. Look, look, LOOK.*

Her eyes widened. "Last night! Praise the Lord." Then she beamed as if she might actually hug him. She poured her excitement into a wide flourish toward the display instead. "What kind of music do you like? We even have Christian rap."

It was ridiculous that a man who had a fairly large car payment, a house payment, a few expensive tastes—and no job—would drop $203 on items that weren't food, shelter, or medical care. Colin left The Mustard Seed with a leather-bound study Bible, five CDs, a T-shirt, and three paperbacks—a Christian novel, a book about being a Christian man, and a comparison of creationism and evolution; with a geologist for a father, he couldn't leave that one behind. Even though it didn't make any sense. Could even be ridiculous. But it didn't matter . . . because Someone wise carried his future, his past, his present, his whole existence, in steady hands.

Later that afternoon, Colin turned on the porch light and opened the door—and lost his heart, heartbeat and all, to his socks.

"Hey, Stan," he said, automatically opening the storm door in invitation.

"Thanks," Stan replied, striding past him to the living room, the leather on his belt creaking with each step. Fresh snow melted on his shoulders.

Colin closed the door and turned. The officer was alone; that was a good sign. He was working late; that was bad. So he'd either let Colin return to his couch and the book he'd been reading, or suggest he fetch his shoes. Colin waited for the verdict.

Stan broke into a smile. "Don't look so nervous. This is good news."

Colin got his heart back, though it was beating in his stomach. "Really?"

"Really," Stan replied. "You were right. We just arrested Bradley Earl Stapleton for burglary."

Colin's shoulders collapsed. "Are you sure?"

"You want us to change our minds?"

"No." Then, "How did you catch him?"

Stan folded his arms and rocked back in a stance of confident authority. "I took a look at that fountain. It had been dragged on something, and there were tiny red flecks embedded in the scrapes. Paint."

"Stapleton's truck."

Stan nodded, then shrugged. "Not good enough in itself, but when I examined the truck, I found a piece of the fountain in the bed. Apparently the edges of the fiberglass were so uneven, no one had noticed a chunk had broken off. Looks like you're clear. The charges have been dropped." He grinned sheepishly. "I'm supposed to apologize for the inconvenience."

Colin broke into a smile, and the words *Praise the Lord* sprang to mind.

Colin hid in plain sight, parking the CJ5 at the end of the front row of motor homes at the RV dealership. Across the street, Dave Sommer, the high school kid filling Emily's old shift, backed out of his spot, crossed the parking lot, and glided into the sparse Friday night traffic.

Emily was at home; he'd already checked. Maybe, once he took care of business, she'd date him again.

He pulled a long swallow of convenience store coffee. The mug was a tall one, since taking care of business could take all night. He hunched his neck into his sheepskin coat and eyed the blanket on the seat beside him.

Make it happen fast, though, Lord—or make it warm up. I can't be inconspicuous with exhaust billowing out of the tailpipe.

God answered his prayer in the affirmative, for Dave wasn't gone but fifteen minutes when a familiar car rolled down Broadway and into the station parking lot. With the mystery solved—with the "who" unlocking the door and stepping into the darkened building for no legitimate, no honest reason—Colin's heart fell. Disappointing, this. You thought you knew someone, then . . .

He shook his head, started the Jeep, and entered Broadway, headlights off. He dropped a quarter in the pay phone at the Gas-N-Go down the street.

"Hello?" the voice on the other end replied, sounding a little dazed.

"Sterling? How fast can you get into some pants and get down to the station?"

"To the station—What's this about, Colin?"

"I'd give you the thirty-second audio version," Colin replied, "but I think you'll want to see the video."

"Do you know it's nearly midnight?"

"Sorry. I didn't pick the time. And hurry, or you'll miss it."

Someone's hands pulled the last page from the printer, added it to the stack, and rolled the mouse around on its pad, returning the computer to the window that had been on the screen in the first place. The someone crossed the lobby to use the big stapler on Marilyn's desk, then strode to the FM studio and set the new and improved edition of Saturday's log on the counter for tomorrow. Curling the legitimate log pages, Betty's pages, into a scroll, one of KDMD's own turned off the lights and hummed a tune on the way out the door.

The engine ticked as it cooled, snow tires whined over the pavement of Broadway, a floodlight across the street buzzed, the deadbolt on the front door slid and clicked as the key swiveled in the lock, and blood pounded in Colin's ears. He clenched his jaw. If this were before his miraculous conversion, he'd be balling his fists. As it was, crying seemed more appropriate.

"You stopped surprising me a long time ago," Colin told Vicky Millian as she stepped from the station, "but I thought I knew you better than this," he said to John Vaughn.

The pair froze midstride, Vicky's full-length leather coat rocking around her ankles. An arctic sigh of a breeze blew the words back in Colin's face where he leaned, fists in the pockets of his sheepskin, against the right front wheel well of the Jeep.

"Hanging around empty parking lots now, Colin?" Vicky said. "What's the matter? Did your little protégé finally face up to your colorful history, or did she give in after all, and wasn't as thrilling as you thought she'd be?"

Colin's heart had been aching with disappointment. Now it seized, shocked by the ice it was suddenly forced to circulate.

Make her a man, Lord. Just this once. For just five seconds. Half of Missoula would praise You for it, believe me.

"You know why I'm here," Colin replied. "Stand by for this important announcement—you're caught, Ms. Millian."

She tsked. "You know nothing. You're—"

"Shut up, Vicky," John interrupted impatiently.

Her mouth snapped closed—a man of a thousand talents, John—though she tried to kill Colin with her eyes.

It was John who exercised more intelligent thought, studying Colin. His stare shifted to his car.

"You're not a runner," Colin told him. "In fact, you're not really dishonest, John."

John's attention snapped to Colin.

John had barely been out of high school when Colin had first heard him on the rock station across town. Pretty bad, he'd been then. A lot better two or three years later, when he'd approached Colin about a job.

Sterling's Riviera roared into the lot, rocked to a jerky stop, and he stepped out, the door alarm dinging like an elevator bell. Vicky gave this addition a haughty lift of her chin; John's gaze slid slowly to an obscure spot near Colin's feet.

"My guess is, that's a portion of the real log, the one Betty prepares every day," Colin said, nodding toward the paper in John's hand.

Vicky folded her arms and pursed her lips; John glanced at Sterling, who approached as if he would see what the meeting was about before making any commitments. He glanced at Colin: *Is this what I think it is?*

John's shoulders slumped. "Don't blame the advertis-ers," he finally said.

"What are you doing?" Vicky screeched, turning on him.

"It's over, Vicky," he told her.

"Not for me, buddy," she snapped. "This was all your idea."

"Sure, Vicky," he replied tiredly. "And I'm not stupid twice."

Apparently he had a gift for shutting her up, for she rolled her eyes and checked her manicure.

He drew a shaky breath. "The advertisers thought it was all legit. We sold them two campaigns of ads—one Vicky turned in to Betty for billing, the other we kept secret. I came in at night, after Emily went home, to add spots to the electronic log and print new pages for the paper copy. I was always worried that Betty might notice the extra spots if she had to check the log for something, so I replaced the dummied up pages with the real ones, and forged yours and Marv's signatures as soon as I could get to them . . . when I started my shift at two." He motioned with the paper. "I couldn't get to the computer until after Emily left, so that's when I changed the electronic log back to what it was and doctored the next day's log again."

"You as good at signing Marv's name as you are at sign-ing mine?" Colin asked.

John shrugged and asked a question of his own. "How did you figure it out? I was careful about how many spots I added, so no one would get suspicious."

"It worked, until Emily looked for one of her ads that I'd played on my show. You'd already stripped the evi-dence, so it wasn't listed. That prompted her to do some more checking."

Vicky laughed. "Now we know the story. She thought you did it—and turned you in. That's rich."

It also prompted Sterling to swivel back to his car, where he got inside and punched some numbers on his cell phone.

"Besides," Colin continued, giving Vicky the disregard she deserved, "I always sign in blue ink, so an original stands apart from a photocopy. You forged my name in black."

"You idiot," Vicky groaned, turning on John. "How could you be so stupid?"

John gave her an assessing stare. "I don't know," he replied, his tone saying it wasn't his choice of ink pens he was beginning to question.

Sterling stepped out of the Riv, joining them. "Did you limit yourself to Vicky's accounts?" he asked.

"At first," John replied. "We were just starting to branch out."

"That would have gotten you caught," Sterling said. "All it would have taken was one comment from an advertiser to their regular account executive."

John nodded. "Eventually, I suppose. I don't know. We felt pretty invincible."

Colin nodded, though what they'd gleaned from the operation couldn't have been much more than the standard trade-account sorts of things—restaurant meals, car washes, store discounts. Astounding, the trinkets people would steal just to get them for free.

"I'm sorry," John said, looking from Colin to Sterling and back again. His attention darted to the street when a police siren sounded in the distance. He watched with weary resignation.

"Wonderful," Vicky told her fingernails.

Sterling stared into the street long after the last squad car had rolled onto Broadway, his silence, his disappointment, begging to be undisturbed. So Colin waited. It was cold, and getting colder, since the skies were clearing.

Sterling suddenly chuckled, his attention swiveling to where Colin leaned against the Jeep. "You handled this with your usual style," he said. "I was still trying to figure out how to approach our advertisers and not look like fools, when I got tied up with that Missoula Uptown promotion all day. If nothing else, I hoped your innocence would surface when the stealing continued in your absence." He shook his head. "You never gave me a chance to do anything."

"I figured you'd already done enough," Colin replied wryly.

Sterling chuckled. Coins jangled in his pocket as he fingered them. "I'm sorry this came out so bad for you," he said. "I couldn't do anything but come down hard on even the rumor of this sort of thing. Our advertisers have to be able to trust us; they can't listen to be sure we're playing the ads they ordered at the times they ordered them. I'd like to have you back, and not just because I'm in a pinch. You helped build this station . . . made it the powerhouse it is today. You're an exceptional talent. Don't take it to one of our competitors."

Our competitors. The KDMD sign cast its brilliance onto the patchwork of pavement and snow. The limousine reigned over the lot, introducing Diamond Country and looking even larger for the emptiness around it. When it came right down to it, Sterling couldn't put Colin outside any of it. Sure, he'd cut a swift swath, but that was Sterling—ruthless in the cutoff, but just as urgent in splicing it together.

"I accept," Colin told him.

Sterling nodded.

That done, it was on to the next thing. "Did Emily come to you any more about this—about my innocence?" Colin asked, though he already knew she would.

"I was out all day," Sterling replied. "Was there something else she knew?"

A lie—to protect her—sprang to mind. Colin cast it aside, opting instead to admit, "Yes, but I'm going to ask you to let it go."

Sterling did. He smiled, as if over a new thought. "Did you hear her on the air?"

Only the entire show, though Colin simply said, "Yes. She did a fine job."

Sterling laughed as if she were his own little girl. "She sure did."

"I'm moving her to afternoon drive."

That gave Sterling pause. "I assume you have a reason."

"I do," Colin replied. "It'll be better. You'll see."

Sterling nodded. He glanced at his car as if preparing to leave. "Well, I better get back before Joyce steals my pillow. I'm already in the doghouse because we were supposed to go out of town." He held out his hand to shake, the contact first energetic, then warm. "Welcome back," he said, then he jumped. "Oh, and here. You can have all this junk back, get it out of my coat pockets."

From them he drew three keys and a stack of discount cards.

Thirty-four

*D*addy would be in the kitchen laying a plate with a homemade deli sandwich and a handful of chips, then heading for the Saturday documentaries and news programs he loved so well. Emily passed the turn she would have taken to reach him. She'd travel that street, surprise him with her brief Saturday visit, in a moment. For now she parked at a different curb under a less familiar line of barren trees. They'd been budding the last time she'd seen them.

Old and undisturbed, the snow crunched around her shoes; not much foot traffic here. For a crazy, dizzying moment she had to search—she hadn't been at her best the last time—then she found it.

Margaret Elizabeth Erickson, Beloved wife and mother, Gone home to her Lord on a joyous spring day.

The marker gave no dates and no age for the topic of its discussion, just as Margaret Elizabeth Erickson had requested. Mother was quirky that way. Not because she kept such things as her age and weight secret—she told anyone who asked—but because, as she had said, "There is no time, to the Lord—or where I'm going."

Emily pushed her fists deeper into the warmth of her parka pockets and smiled to herself. Strangers would think the marker's inscription vague and outside propriety. They didn't know Mother; she was propriety—but her own person. Who else could have raised the daughters of a man who traveled all week? Mother hadn't survived the solitude, she'd marched through it, serene and face-forward, staring ahead through sightless eyes.

Emily's smile faded as the invalid of memory seemed to rise from her bed and turn a new face. Faded and pushed aside, these things—that Mother had been strong, had been brave and determined not to impose any more than she already had, by her surviving as long as she did.

. . . Meaning, her feeble call from the bedroom that day hadn't been over a frivolous need. Hadn't been one of a stream of nagging complaints. Hadn't been selfish.

The tears built.

"I'm sorry, Mama," Emily told the snow at the foot of the marker. "I should have gone to you. Should have seen that you were just so very sick. But I couldn't. I didn't want to see it. I didn't want to feel sorry for you. I wanted to feel angry . . . because it was so much easier than the fear. You were dying, and I didn't want you to go."

The tears flowed quietly.

Images came with them . . . Emily washing Mother's hair, reading the newspaper to her, changing her sheets for no better reason than that fresh ones felt better.

The tears flowed easily.

Mother's final years hadn't been all bad, any more than they'd been all good. Rather, the guilt—so misplaced—was what pushed memory into a grotesque mockery of truth. The unbent version said Mother hadn't been a perfect patient; she'd been a real one—

sometimes tolerant, sometimes irritable. Emily hadn't been a perfect caregiver; she'd been a real one—sometimes gracious, sometimes abrupt. Each—even Erin, who had no stomach for illness—had lived through the dying, moment by moment, one weary and terrified step in front of the other. Each had done the best she could.

"I love you, Mama," Emily whispered, riding on memories of a more youthful parent who oohed and aahed at crayon drawings of stick people and stick dogs, who bit back a wince as she shifted on a metal folding chair in a school auditorium, who smiled from a face as pale as the pillow under her while Emily read off her choices for the fall semester.

"I miss you, Mama," Emily said, torn between the wish to have her back at any cost and the mercy of releasing her to death.

No—death was better for one who'd suffered daily, but whose first sight in nearly a decade would be the face of Jesus. For one who'd died slowly but valiantly. Who'd known her leaving would come early. Who'd prepared her daughters, had raised them to be strong . . . by example.

Emily heaved a little chuckle. "Oh, yeah? Well, Mom, I did something stupid. I fell in love, and he played me for a fool. He really hurt me." She reached for a grin and held it. "But I came out the other side, and I learned some lessons . . . and you should have seen him."

Colin smiled with warm satisfaction before his ring was even answered on Saturday evening.

"I don't talk to you for nine years, then you call two

days in a row," his mother said. "Not that I mind. Call anytime you want." She paused. "Have you booked your flight?"

Colin grinned. "Not yet, Mom. I got my job back, so I'll have to check the schedule."

And find a good time for two of them to be gone, if he could fix what he'd broken.

"Praise God," she said. "You let us know as soon as you know. We're so excited." Her voice broke. She cleared it. "Just a minute, baby. I'll go get your daddy."

The receiver banged softly in Colin's ear, then he heard the sounds of shuffling and conversation before the middle of the Kavanaugh men drawled, "Hey, Nicholas. What's up, son?"

"Well, I need to talk to you about something, Dad," Colin replied quietly while making a careful study of the warp and weft of the denim stretched around his thigh.

Nicholas Michael Kavanaugh II paused, as if the mental gears were grinding. He chuckled. "By chance does this have anythin' to do with women?"

Nicholas Michael Kavanaugh III grinned, himself. His father might be nine years older, but his radar was still state-of-the-art. "Yes," Colin replied, "and one in particular."

The elder Kavanaugh laughed again. "Go ahead, son, but I have a feelin' this is goin' to be a short conversation."

Emily stepped to the bedroom window and pushed back the curtain. Lonely things, Saturday nights. Nothing to do. Nowhere to go.

Pitiful case, she, who shifted between rage, humiliation, heartbreak, and an agony of *If only*.

She'd never fall in love again. Was through with men . . . men who melted hearts with their velvet voices, gorgeous blue eyes, and irresistible dimples . . . who moved the standard for any who might come after—and never measure up.

Colin stepped to the kitchen window and pushed back the curtain. Lonely things, Saturday nights, when there was no one to share them with.

It would be a miracle if she didn't hate him. It would be another if she believed how he'd changed, how even the sunset looked different now that he knew the Artist as a friend.

For a long while Colin stared out the window. Sometimes he prayed. Sometimes he fingered the key ring he couldn't seem to empty from his pocket. Sometimes he sniffled.

. . . Then he put Michael W. Smith on the stereo, sat on the floor with his guitar propped on his leg, and picked out chords for music that had been written with a piano by a man who seemed to know the heart of one who lived in Montana.

Colin glanced at the left section of the congregation, cradled the hymnal in his hand, gave his baritone to the bass staff . . . *Take my life, and let it be, consecrated, Lord, to Thee* . . . Specifically Colin watched the aisle seat, one row ahead, where Emily stood, shiny hair pulled back in pretty sweeps over her pretty ears, pretty emerald dress falling in pretty drapes, and pretty, pretty legs in gray heels—and she was going to come across the aisle and club him with that hymnal when she finally noticed him.

Given the choice, he'd have sat on the back row. "Choice" was the price paid for sneaking in after she took her chair.

Suddenly Emily turned her head, as if listening to something behind her. His voice. She recognized his voice—or noticed the deep harmony. Before he could react, she turned around to chase her curiosity. Their gazes collided in the center of the aisle. Her eyes widened in shock. They narrowed in anger. Then she faced forward.

Through the whole service, that little chin held an unnatural height, supported no doubt by the rigid line of her back. Never once did she look over her right shoulder. Never once did she give herself a chance to notice how Colin followed the sermon with a new Bible, embossed NMK, how his attention drifted her way every ninety seconds, or how his eyes occasionally misted.

When the service was over, the aisle filled with parishioners as if animal pens had been let open, and Emily—never the coward—turned full toward his approach as she pushed her arms into her coat.

"Hi, Emily," Colin said once he finally reached her, and reached again to help her with her coat.

She jerked away, her voice as cold and steady as her stare. "I don't care why you're here, and I don't have anything to say to you, so have a nice day," she said. She bent for her purse and Bible, then turned to leave.

"Wait," he said, grabbing a handful of her arm.

She stopped, but her glare would melt rocks. Such

was the stage for his big chance, his dramatic tale of how a man who'd always run finally admitted he hated himself . . . and was lonely.

"Emily? Are you coming Wednesday evening?" a woman in the far aisle called, obviously her second try.

Emily swiveled and nodded. "I'll be there." Then she turned back, prepared to do battle, judging by the flash in her eyes.

"May I take you to lunch?" Colin asked.

Wrong question. She turned away again. He grabbed her arm again.

"I have a lot to explain," he said, tossing out the barest truth. "I'd appreciate it if you'd at least hear me out."

After an eternal moment she gave a succinct nod and turned, leading the way through conversational clumps of people to the parking lot.

"Over there," he told her, pointing to where the Bimmer was parked in the middle row under a gloomy sky.

All through the ritual of escorting her inside, Emily remained silent, giving him not a glance.

"I'll start the engine, get some heat going," Colin said once he sat beside her, to warn her so she wouldn't bolt. He turned in his seat, assuming a more relaxed position. Maybe she'd get the idea.

"The reason the police came to the station Wednesday was to arrest me for burglary," he began. "Someone had taken a yard fountain from Missoula Lawn and Garden and put it under a tarp behind my garage."

She'd been glaring at the glove box. At his words, her eyebrows furrowed.

"It was Brad," he said.

Her stare swung to him.

"He was taken into custody Friday—and not a moment too soon for me," Colin continued. "He already had charges pending in Hamilton for beating up a rodeo queen. I was worried he'd do the same to you."

For a moment she stared. Then the surprise in her eyes turned flat. "I'm sorry he did that to you. I seem to be a pretty poor judge of character," she said with as much emotion.

He disregarded the comment, clearly meant to refer as well to her choosing him, and continued, "The thieves at the station were John and Vicky."

Almost reluctantly, her eyes widened. "John and Vicky? Are you sure?"

"I waited outside the station on Friday night and caught them. John confessed everything."

Dazed, she turned back to the glove box. "Gosh, I liked John," she said, as if shock wouldn't give her anything more.

So had he, but Colin pushed on, pressing toward the words that would keep her in that seat long enough to convince her. "I talked to my folks for the first time in nine years Friday. I was on the run—from myself—when I landed in Missoula. I'd . . . My brother died. We'd been hunting. I left my rifle loaded when I put it in the truck . . . it discharged. He was my little brother . . . and it was my gun, Emmy."

Though it felt so different now. Such freedom. Such gratitude. He swallowed hard. She looked again, though this time there was a begrudging agony in her eyes.

"I became a Christian on Thursday night," he said.

Now her eyes widened. "You got saved? On Thursday night?"

The stupefied expression on her face was too funny—wait till she heard the rest. "First I got drunk, then I got saved. I thought I'd have a drink before dinner, and . . . kind of forgot the dinner part. Then I couldn't change the channel and wound up with a TV preacher." Colin paused. Remembered. "He seemed to know my life. I poured the rest of my bourbon down the drain and bought myself a Bible—and some CDs. You didn't tell me Christian music was so good."

Emily stared back in . . . what? Puzzlement? Disbelief? Hope? All three? It wasn't clear. What was plain was, those were the prettiest green eyes he'd ever seen, and he'd do anything to win the right to lean over and kiss that soft mouth, about now. She'd go in a few minutes. Get in her car and drive away. Leave him. Sentence him to spending the rest of his life doing whatever, but doing it without her.

And Thursday was Thanksgiving.

Her lips leveled in a disgusted line, she clutched her purse and reached for the door handle. The wall was still up.

"Were you going to tell Sterling about spending the weekend with me?" he asked, stopping her, while taking great care that his tone held no accusation.

She wouldn't lie. She didn't. "I tried on Friday, but he wasn't in," she told the door handle.

Not a surprise. Time to try a few on her.

Please make her believe me.

"I figured I could solve the mystery without your alibi, Em," he said softly. "It would have looked very bad for you if you'd told Sterling. I was prepared to buy a bill-board explaining everything, but I doubt it would have done any good."

Her head swiveled around, tilted sharply. "Look, this isn't necessary," she said. "Your name is cleared, you have your job back, and I'm not going to quit. You're a big boy, and I'm a big girl," she said, throwing his own words back at him. "We can work together like nothing ever happened."

"I'm not trying to placate you," he told her. "I'm trying to tell you I'm sorry—about a lot of things. That offer I made you . . . to move in . . . I had no idea. I knew you were fairly principled, but . . . it was insulting. I apologize."

"You aren't used to being told no, are you?" she asked, though it wasn't a question, and her tone wasn't sympathetic. Then she heaved a breath that made her shoulders sag, and in a gentler tone she said, "I'm sorry. I don't mean to be . . . I really am glad things turned out okay."

He nearly groaned. Not that. Not kindness born of conscience. Not compassion slapped together like a soup kitchen sandwich. "Don't do that, Emmy," he said. "If you're miffed at me, just say so."

"You didn't speak to me after that," she shot back without hesitation. "You took me home on Sunday without a word. Not one word."

"I was . . . I was embarrassed that I'd asked you to move in."

She heaved another breath of frustration. "Look, I don't know what this is all for, but it's very nice. I'm glad you got saved and bought yourself a Bible"—she pulled on the door handle—"but I have to go now."

Like a shot he reached across her, though he set his hand gently over her small one. "I'm sorry about what I said when I was packing on Thursday. I didn't mean any of it. I know you don't believe that, but I had to do whatever I could to stop you from telling anyone you'd spent the weekend at my house. No one would have believed what really happened, Emmy. It would have ruined you—

and for nothing. By the looks of it, I was going down any-way. Can't you see? I said all that to stop you, to make you so mad you'd put a continent between us."

"Congratulations. It worked."

His shoulders collapsed—along with his heart. She didn't believe him. Now what?

All he had left.

Effortlessly, he pulled her hand from the door latch, turned it palm up, and dug into the pocket of his jeans. "I didn't mean any of it," he said, setting the key ring in her hand. "I'd never do anything to hurt you—though I know I already have. I love you, Emmy. More than myself, I think."

He fanned the keys he'd offered her last Sunday, spacing them and separating out something new—a ring on a ring. She gasped and clapped her other hand over her mouth, eyes wide and staring, while the diamond winked back, the circle of emeralds it rested in, matching the green of her eyes—which met his gaze, drowning in . . . shock.

"I know you don't believe me, but you should," he said. "I'm asking you to marry me."

Help me, Lord. She could throw it in my face.

Thirty-five

*A*nd she did, though Emily was kind enough to toss the key ring in Colin's lap.

"How could you do this?" she shrieked. "How could you offer me this ring when three days ago I was nothing to you? Less than nothing. Just a piece of meat," she added with a wide flourish.

Dad had seen that coming, that she'd be at full pressure and wouldn't purr until she let some of it go. Colin set his forearm on the top of the steering wheel, stared at the console between them, and let Emily explode.

"Stacy was right," she continued, shifting her flashing eyes from one spot to the other on the dashboard, her head bobbing as if the car had offended her so. "You're nothing but a womanizing jerk. A user. The kind of man mothers warn their daughters about and fathers think about shooting. Tell me I'm too sweet for you. You wouldn't know sweet if it smacked you in the face. Of course you wouldn't," she decided, "considering the kind of women you take home to meet Sophie. Who knows how many have sat in this very seat?"

That sounded like jealousy. Colin's heart tripped.

"I've had it with men," Emily said. "They're all liars. The only thing they're good for is moving furniture."

Colin risked a glance. She might be finished. Looked as if she were finished, scowling at the glove box, a death-grip on her Bible, its leather worn colorless along the top of the spine. She was everything that book on Christian marriage said he should look for. Odd that he'd seen it in her before he recognized what it was, before he'd even met the Author of such gracious virtue.

"You're right," he said. "I was all those things and worse. No different from Brad, except the damage I inflicted was invisible."

Her scowl softened to a glare and fell to her knees.

"If I could go back and change it, I would," he said. "I hated myself and was completely justified in it."

She swallowed and said so softly, "You broke my heart."

Which broke his. "I know," he said. "I'm sorry, Emmy. I didn't know what else to do. I had to protect you and . . . honesty wasn't in my repertoire."

She swallowed again and rolled her lips inward. A tear rolled down her cheek and dripped on her hand—making his heart constrict in sorrow, and leap in hope. She felt enough to cry. Perhaps she wasn't lost to him yet.

"You didn't mean it?" she asked while another tear dripped from the other side.

"Not even close."

She sniffed. "That stuff must have occurred to you, or it wouldn't have been so handy in your mind."

Doomed. He was doomed to a round of female reasoning—though it bore no resemblance to reason. "I'm very creative," he tossed out in his defense.

She didn't smile. Didn't grin. Didn't even look as if she'd heard him.

"If you don't love me, Emmy, say so," he said.

Silence—unless one counted the idle of the car engine and another sniffle. She fished in her purse for a wad of tissue that looked as if it might have already given its service and wiped her nose.

"Tell me why we shouldn't get married," he said.

No good reason except fear. The responsibility had been too great for too long. There was no relaxing, no letting go, no letting someone else be . . . the parent. Frivolous wishes came true for others, for the lucky ones on the other side of the glass. Emily could watch forever, and the door would never open for her to go outside.

As the Father loved Me, I also have loved you . . . These things I have spoken to you, that My joy may remain in you, and that your joy may be full.

Though not for her—except she was staring a full-fledged miracle in the face. Such a succession of steps to bring her here. Sterling had called her. To give her a job. So she could work with this man. Whom she fell in love with. Who got saved. And who just happened to love her.

The heart that was beginning to listen cautioned a step to the threshold and peeked outside. There were good things, laughing things, out there—for no more profitable reason than to make her light of heart. To simply smile.

"I'm not going to beg you," Colin said suddenly. "I told you I didn't mean any of what I said. I was just trying to protect you—and that, by the way, is what the Bible says I'm supposed to do. Looks like God is not only the Author of the world, but of chivalry, too."

She could only stare at him.

He shrugged. "I've been reading," he said almost in apology. "Husbands are to love their wives as much as Jesus loved the church." He paused. Said softly, "He died for her, Emmy." Then his gaze peered deep, an ocean to fall into. "I figure I love you that much . . . on a bad day."

It is not good for man to be alone . . . For this reason a man shall leave his home and cleave unto his wife . . . And the two shall become one.

It was love—love, not independence; running to, not running away—that kept it all going, made a Man hang on a cross. Made another drive all night to be home with his ailing wife for the weekend. Made this one tell all he was, then hold his breath to hear whether he was good enough—as if there were ever any doubt. As if she shouldn't beg God to take her raw offerings and make of her a worthy wife. As if she shouldn't thank Him for His grace in letting her run from one man who loved her smack dab into the sure hold of another.

Emily's heart sped on wild excitement—like the moment just after the lap bar dropped into place and the roller coaster lurched forward. She could have it, have him; yes was the key. So easy.

As if he heard the race of her heart—he'd always read her—Colin retrieved the key ring and set it in her hand. "I was thinking we could go to Disney World for our honeymoon, see if that life-size duck bears any resemblance to the one on your bed." He tilted his head. "Can Emmy come out and play?"

Couldn't help but smile. She looked from the ring to him—such eyes, such tenderness, such mischief. "Have you talked this over with Sophie?" she asked.

"Sophie? The dog?" he replied, obviously a little shaken, for he was usually quicker than that. Then understanding dawned, for his expression collapsed, just before the dimples darted into his cheeks and a light into his eyes. "She's the one who suggested it," he said. "She got used to having you around last weekend. She also said something about getting her a playmate—an Irish setter, maybe."

Emily laughed, while tears threatened to make a silly ninny of her.

Colin's eyes grazed her face. "Is that a yes?"

"Probably," she said, closing her hand around the key ring.

His eyes fell closed for a second, as if her assent gave him the most profound relief, then he smiled, dimples blazing, that silly tooth winking.

She held up a cautionary finger. "We wait until our wedding night."

"Of course," he said as if he'd already thought of that. "Although I'm not exactly sure how that's accomplished."

"No dating anywhere except in public places," she replied.

His brow furrowed. "Hmm. Guess that means the submarine races are out, huh?"

He knew better than that.

He grinned anyway and scanned the parking lot. "I hope this is public enough, because I'd like a kiss. Don't be shocked, but maybe two."

Emily barely had time to smile before Colin leaned across the console, setting his mouth on hers. It was an exuberant kiss at first, as if he had to convince himself she'd be there for the duration. Then it was warm and possessive . . . and new, for the beginnings it rose from and the promises it sealed. Emily's stomach threatened never to recall the laws of gravity again. For sure her head wouldn't, for this hope was the stuff of novels, movies, and songs. Country songs . . . and Emily's name lifting onto the air, spoken with a velvet voice.

Colin broke away suddenly. "By the way," he whispered. "I'm moving you to afternoon drive, so I'll be working mornings and you'll be working afternoons, but don't worry. I'll have dinner ready when you get home—so we can get to bed at a decent hour."

Emily tried not to. Really tried. She blushed—and laughed anyway.

Dear Reader:

We love to hear from our readers. Your response to the following questions will help us continue publishing the excellent Christian fiction that you enjoy.

1. What most influenced you to buy *Airwaves*?
   - ❑ Cover/title
   - ❑ Subject matter
   - ❑ Back cover copy
   - ❑ Author
   - ❑ Recommendation by friend
   - ❑ Recommendation by bookstore sales person

2. How would you rate this book?
   - ❑ Great
   - ❑ Good
   - ❑ Fair
   - ❑ Poor

Comments:

3. What did you like best about this book?
   - ❑ Characters
   - ❑ Plot
   - ❑ Setting
   - ❑ Inspirational theme
   - ❑ Other_____

4. Will you buy more novels in the **Promises** series?
   - ❑ Yes
   - ❑ No

Why?

5. Which do you prefer?
   - ❑ Historical romance
   - ❑ Contemporary romance
   - ❑ No preference

6. How many Christian novels do you buy per year?
   - ❑ Less than 3
   - ❑ 3-6
   - ❑ 7 or more

7. What is your age?
   - ❑ Under 18
   - ❑ 18-24
   - ❑ 25-34
   - ❑ 35-44
   - ❑ 45-54
   - ❑ Over 55

Please return to
ChariotVictor Publishing
Promises Editor
4050 Lee Vance View
Colorado Springs, CO 80918

**If you liked this book,
check out these great *Promises* titles from
ChariotVICTOR Publishing . . .**

Mr. Francis' Wife
by Sandy Gills
ISBN 1-56476-689-6

*T*he cold air rushed across Frank's bare feet as he opened the door of the trailer. It was dark, but he could see the clear outline of Hannah Petersheim as she stood huddled outside his doorway.

"Mr. Francis," she said haltingly, "I—need for you to marry me." Her eyes were misty from the sting of the cold night air. She shuffled her feet and pulled the shawl closer around her.

"I am losing the ranch," she continued. "I cannot pay you throughout the winter." She peered at him from beneath her shawl and said quietly, "And I am with child."

Frank Allison blinked at her, speechless. It was 2 A.M. and the late October wind was promising an early freeze. He fought the look of incredulous astonishment that threatened to spread across his face.

Frank had worked for the Petersheims for nearly five years now, ever since their move from southern Illinois. He had liked Eli, who was an honest, if a little eccentric, man with a natural gift for working with animals. He had always liked Hannah, too, and their ever growing family. But to take on a widow and her twelve—almost thirteen—children . . . !

"Mrs. Petersheim," he said, opening the door wider, "you'd better come in."

Hannah shook her head. "You know the testimony of my faith," she continued, as though listing her prime asset. "The ranch is without debt and would offer you security. The children know you and are comfortable with you. I—" She paused and glanced hesitantly at him, the crystal blue of her eyes meeting the paler shade of his own. "I . . . respect you, and I . . . I trust you."

She lowered her head, as though ashamed of the rejection her heart was anticipating. Clearly it was a long gamble asking him, but it was the only way she could think of to keep her children together in the home she had worked so hard to build.

Frank scratched at his thermal shirt. He could see what the woman was thinking. Still, friendship went just so far. "Don't you have any relatives back East?" he questioned.

"No, Mr. Francis," she told him. "Eli and I left our homes and families more than fifteen years ago. We have not been welcome there since."

She looked at him again, directly and without emotion. "You needn't answer now," she told him. "But think it over."

Frank nodded his head, then watched as she turned and disappeared into the darkness.

And these titles coming soon . . .

Alone. Without a job or money. This isn't what recently widowed Tabitha bargained for when she left England for a new life in America. Now, in the pioneer village of Waukegan, Illinois with just the clothes on her back and a strong faith in God's provision for her, how will she provide for herself? Handsome, charming Etienne Rousseau offers one solution to her loneliness, while rough-edged Lucas Hayes offers another. Can either of these men be God's provision for her when neither shares her faith?

Freedom's Promise
by Suzanne D. Hellman
ISBN: 1-56476-718-3

September 1998

Best friends—that's what Scott and Beth have been since they were teens. Why is Beth blind to his desire for more than friendship? "You'll make *somebody* a good husband," she says. How can he make her see that she's the *somebody*—especially when Michael, the latest guest at her bed-and-breakfast, is a handsome, debonair Englishman? Scott doesn't trust him or his motives for romancing Beth. Could Michael's presence have more to do with something valuable hidden in the inn than with Beth?

Lord, where are You? Scott was so sure of God's plans for him and Beth, but perhaps he didn't have a clue about perceiving God's will. . . .

January 1999

Best Friends
by Debra White Smith
ISBN 1-56476-721-3